The Bridge Between Love and Lies

Stacey Wilk

The Bridge Between Love and Lies

Heritage River, Book 2

This is a work of fiction. Names, characters, places, and incidents are either the product of the author's imagination or are used fictitiously, and any resemblance to actual persons living or dead, business establishments, events, or locales, is entirely coincidental.

The Bridge Between Love and Lies

Cover Art by *Diana Carlisle*

Publishing History

The Wild Rose Press, Inc.

First Champagne Rose Edition, 2018

Print ISBN 978-1-5092-2337-4

Digital ISBN 978-1-5092-2338-1

Heritage River, Book 2

Published in the United States of America

To my inner circle of women I call friends.

To M. Kate Quinn.

To my editor, Roseann Armstrong, your humor and
guidance make me a better writer every day.

And to Robin Rottner, thank you for reading the Heritage
River stories, giving me your feedback, and making space
for the Savage family in your heart.

Chapter One

Harley Kenyon loved bridges. Bridges connected the old and the new. Bridges signified art, beauty, and romance. The most extraordinary bridges left their marks on the world.

She crossed over the Heritage River Covered Bridge, leaving her art studio—well, it was more of a classroom she rented at the community college—behind her. Her quaint bridge with white clapboard beneath the gabled roof knew her secrets the way an old friend would. She loved standing on the walkway to watch the sun set over the water's edge, dressing the sky in pinks, purples, and gold. Her small bridge with crisscross posts reminded her of a time when life still held possibilities the way a blank canvas always did.

The balmy Tennessee November day swirled its way inside the open windows of her Dodge Durango. With Thanksgiving in the rearview mirror and Christmas on the horizon, how many more days like this would be adding up? The snow and ice were just playing hide-and-seek at the moment.

She pulled up to Maybelline's Bakery, lucky to find a spot, and shoved the truck in park. She wanted one of May's famous cups of coffee this side of the county and one of her best sugary treats. She should head home to her son and make sure he finished his homework, cleaned up the leaves in the yard, and swept out the garage. She had to enforce the rules she'd laid down, but that would mean an argument. Since his recent act of teenage stupidity, she and Knox fought as often as breathing.

Main Street was dressed for the holidays and bustled with afternoon activities. The church on the corner boasted a Christmas craft fair today. A line snaked its way outside Eat at Jake's. Toy's Galore looked as if it might explode with people. The only thing that was quiet was Cream and Sugar. Not much call for ice cream this time of year. Plus, the owner, Rosemary, visited her family in Virginia from Thanksgiving to New Year's.

She hadn't eaten anything since the greasy fast food that morning. She scooped up the waxy wrappers off the passenger seat, tucked the empty coffee cups under her arm, and heaved her purse onto her shoulder before sliding out and locating a garbage can to dump her mess.

She yanked open the door, and the warmth of May's surrounded her like a crocheted afghan. The store smelled sweet and savory. The glass case was filled with cookies, cakes, and doughnuts covered in the colors of sidewalk chalk. A variety of breads lined shelves behind the counter. Their outsides would be crunchy and the inside soft. The checkered floor was spotless. The small, round tables were filled with people talking and laughing. Shopping bags in reds and greens and golds decorated the floor beside their legs.

Ella waved to her from a table in the back. She returned the wave and indicated with a few hand gestures she'd be joining her friend in a minute.

She slid in line and ordered a coffee and a chocolate croissant from the unfamiliar young lady behind the counter. This new face working in Heritage River had hair to her waist. Her brown eyes lit up when she smiled, and her skin glowed. Harley let her gaze drop over this young woman as she took her money. The unmistakable baby bump in the center of her pink sweatshirt was hard to miss. Pregnant women popped up more and more. Now that Knox was a senior in high school, she missed being pregnant in a way she never had. Which was surprising, because being pregnant hadn't been ideal.

"How's my favorite teacher?" Maybelline Lewis stepped around the counter, her gait smooth, her hips swaying gently. She wiped her hands on a towel and tossed it on the counter. She wore a smile worth falling into. Her hair was short and spiky, but her hug long and soft. Her smell of flour and sugar drifted around them. "How you holding up without Hank? The whole town loved him. He was a good man."

Uncle Hank had been gone two months. Besides Knox, he was her last living relative. She hadn't been blessed with a large family who gathered for Sunday dinners and holidays. "I miss him. He was our rock."

3

"I know." May patted her cheek. "How's Knox?"

The death of her uncle Hank might've been the reason for Knox's recent bad decision. She suspected Uncle Hank's passing was also the reason Knox resurrected the one question she could never answer for him. "He's mad at me, mad at the world. Probably mad at Hank for dying."

"You remember what it's like to be that age. Give him time. He'll come around."

May's buttery words and a warm croissant seemed to be the only things that gave her any comfort these days. How is it she could offer advice to others, help them understand their feelings through paint, but she couldn't do that for herself?

Harley took her goodies and scooched into the chair opposite Ella. Ella's dark hair fell straight around her shoulders. She wore a bright blue woolen scarf loosely around her neck. Her coffee cup was half empty, and her book half-read.

"Can you believe how packed this place is? I was lucky to find a seat." Ella tugged at her scarf, loosening it more.

"I'm glad you did. I just want to wrap my hands around my hot coffee and catch my breath before I have to go home to Mr. Grumpy."

Ella chuckled. "Teens—they test our patience. Stephanie is driving me crazy with that family-tree project for history. Did Knox finish his yet? I think it's due before the winter break."

She kept her gaze on her croissant. Half of his tree

was blank. "I hate family-tree projects. Why does it matter how big your family is for a history class? Some kids don't have a big family to fill in all those boxes with."

"Maybe it's time to search for that other half." Ella raised her eyebrows.

"Why can't one parent be enough? He had Hank until recently. He wasn't deprived a male influence in his life." Was he? Hank had been just like a father to him. "It doesn't matter. I didn't even know the man's last name." She held Ella's gaze this time. "We couldn't find him even if we wanted to." She absolutely did not want to search for Knox's father. No matter how easy it might be to find him.

Ella patted her hand. "You know what's best. No judgment from me. Really. Would you excuse me a second? Too much coffee."

Her laughter cracked open the tension forming in Harley's chest and around the subject of paternity. Her mouth watered for her Colombian-roast coffee.

"Hey, Harley."

Her hands hovered over the mug while she turned toward the direction of the deep voice.

Cash Savage, one of her students from the art classes at the college, towered over her. His smile unrolled as he removed the scarf from around his neck. The uncanny resemblance among all the Savage men never ceased to amaze her. They shared the same strong jaw and broad shoulders. Their eyes reminded her of slate flecked with gold.

"Hi, Cash. We missed you at class today." She licked the chocolate off her thumb.

He adjusted the backpack slung over one shoulder. "Yeah, I couldn't make it. I was practicing for a gig coming up. I need to finish up my art project, though. I'm using it for a grade in another class. Can I come to your relaxation class and work on it then? I won't take up much space."

"We can squeeze you in."

"Would it be okay if I brought a friend? He needs some help dealing with stress."

"Sure." Her art classes were meant to assist. Helping people iron the wrinkles out of their lives was what she did and why she was so upset she couldn't stop her son from making mistakes.

"Cool." He gave her a thumbs-up and that signature Savage dimple as he swaggered away.

She turned her attention back to her sweet treat and hot, soothing coffee.

"Harley, is that you?"

She forced her gaze away from her decadent beverage to find Joann Humphreys staring down at her. "Hi, Joann." Couldn't whatever the principal of Heritage River High School was about to say wait until Monday after the first bell rang?

"I can't believe I ran into you." Joann unbuttoned her coat. Her gray hair was tied back in a tight knot at her nape that pulled her Dementor eyes into slits.

"Small town. Small world."

"I wasn't planning on saying anything until next

week, but since I've run into you, now is as good a time as any." She glanced over her shoulders. "We won't get interrupted here the way we would at my office."

"My friend is in the restroom. You might want to hurry." Her coffee was getting cold, and she didn't want to share a second of it with this woman around.

"There's talk of instituting an artists-in-residence program for next fall. Since the school budget didn't pass again, the board is looking to cut costs wherever they can and still allow the students to experience art with a real artist."

In other words, Harley was anything but a real artist. "Are you saying the art program is being cut?" What would she do without a job? How was she going to pay for her life? Joann thought May's was the best time and place to share that bombshell? She tore a piece of the croissant free, almost sending the rest of it and the plate to the ground.

"Nothing is definite yet. Don't panic. They're waiting to see what class registration looks like for next year and what your evaluation says."

"What does my evaluation say, Joann?" She sat straighter. Joann had been gunning for her for a while. Her last performance review came back *below expectations* because she refused to follow a ridiculous rubric. If she received another bad review, her tenure would be revoked.

Joann pulled off her coat and folded it over her arm. "I haven't finished the reviews yet." Of course, she hadn't.

"I thought you should hear the news from me first."

The smile on her face didn't reach her flat, sharklike eyes. "I'll see you next week. Enjoy your coffee."

Harley chomped on a large piece of the croissant. Who did Joann Humphreys think she was, anyway? The sweet taste exploded in her mouth. She tried to stifle a groan.

Ella slid back into her chair. "I saw you speaking with the Wicked Witch of the South. I waited until she walked away so she wouldn't cast her evil spells on me."

"She's casting her spells on me. She's going to give me a bad review. I just know it. Nothing would give Joann more pleasure than to see me lose my job. She thinks I'm the parent with the out-of-control child, and she probably thinks Knox is that way because he doesn't have a father."

"It's easier for her to blame someone else than take responsibility for her own poor parenting choices."

"I know Knox wasn't innocent, he drank too, but he isn't the reason why her son keeps getting into trouble. He's doing that all by himself."

"Don't let her get to you. That's exactly what she wants."

"I could lose my job because I didn't insist my son find a new friend." Harley pushed the now-hard croissant away.

She should have opposed that relationship from the beginning, but Knox didn't have a lot of friends. He was like her, an observer. He waited for others to come to him first, and that personality didn't lead to slews of people hanging on your every word. He could've used a little of his father's overzealous temperament.

She sipped the coffee, but its bitter, cold taste stung her tongue. No regrets. The best choice she ever made was to let Knox's father go after his dreams and not get burdened with her and a child. Their one-night stand hadn't meant anything to him anyway. He probably didn't even remember it.

She didn't—not one stinking detail.

Chapter Two

Colton Savage peeled the drawing of the Heritage River Bridge off the cement wall and tucked it away in the pocket of his duffel for safekeeping. The plastic cover he stored the picture in was the only thing keeping that drawing intact after so many years of it following him around the world.

He heaved the duffel bag and his Gibson onto his shoulder and took one final look around the plain beige room. The single bed was made. The bathroom clean. The curtains open. Just as the powers that be wanted it. For luck, he patted his duffel, knowing he'd packed everything. He wasn't coming back here—ever again.

He hoped to sneak out without anyone seeing. He didn't want any cheering, clapping, and hugs to punctuate his return to his normal life. He had tried to keep to himself as much as possible during his stay, but alone time was frowned upon. Alone with only your thoughts led to trouble. *Don't walk the path by yourself.*

If he heard that one more time, he would shove his guitar down his own throat.

His boots squeaked against the waxed floor of the empty corridor. The smell of disinfectant followed him. All he had to do was turn the corner, and he'd be home free.

Instead of finding a clear path to the outside, he was met by the eight people in his therapy group. They clapped and sang "Let the Sunshine In."

He dropped his duffel and hung his head. "Jesus Christ, people. You're still off key. How many times do I have to tell you that?"

"We've been practicing, Colton." Belinda, the front-desk coordinator and mother hen, shouted over the lyrics. Her red-lipstick smile was wide.

"This song sucks. You couldn't have picked 'Whiskey on My Mind'? That was my number one hit for ten weeks in ninety-five." He laughed. He had to admit this group of misfit addicts had grown on him the past thirty days.

Belinda walked over and handed him a large manila envelope filled with some personal items he couldn't keep until the end of his stay along with instructions on how to steer clear of this place. He didn't need to look inside. It wasn't his first time at the rodeo—unfortunately.

"We wanted to pick a song from your band, but Frank was afraid to play the guitar and mess things up." Laughing, she wrapped her arms around him. She smelled like magnolias. He returned her hug.

Colton opened his guitar case and pulled out extra

strings. He eased the acoustic guitar out of Frank's hand and strung the new string into the sixth spot, then handed it back.

"Don't play my songs, bro. You'll break your fingers." He patted Frank's back.

"I'd say I'll see you all soon, but I don't plan on seeing your sorry asses ever again." He gave a wave over the top of his head as he walked through the automatic glass doors into the sunshine with shouts of goodbyes, good lucks, and one day at a time following him out.

The car service hadn't arrived. Colton checked his watch. "Fuck." He wanted to be as far away from this place as quickly as possible. He wanted a long hot shower to get the stink of failure off him. He needed to blur the memories of the shakes, sweats, and vomiting that occupied his first days here.

Thirty days ago he would've poured himself a stiff drink to accomplish that task, but no drinking this time. No, this time sobriety was for real. It had to be. He wasn't ready to die. That much he knew.

He walked to the edge of the parking lot, and his breath caught in his throat. His instincts said turn and run, but he didn't. He wouldn't. His ride was there after all. "You canceled my service, didn't you?"

Billy Lewis and his nephew Cash leaned against Billy's green pickup that hadn't seen the inside of a car wash in two years. Billy wore a cap pulled low over his eyes, an unbuttoned, thick black-and-red flannel shirt over his long-underwear top, and faded blue jeans. His smile was slow and present.

Colton's insides warmed at the sight of his nephew. He was as tall as his father, Colton's younger brother, Blaise. Cash's dark, wavy hair had grown out, and it was no longer bleached blond. The black eyeliner was gone, and the brightness in his eyes had returned. He'd missed this kid.

He yanked Cash into a hug. The kid was all muscle but lean like his father. He grabbed Cash's shoulders and held him at arm's length. "Did this old man drag you out here?" He pointed to Billy.

"It was my idea. And my idea to cancel your car service. Don't get mad at Billy."

"That's going to cost me, you know."

"You can afford it." Billy pushed away from the truck. "You ready to go?"

"What are you two up to? 'Cause I'm not going to Heritage River with you."

That was the last place on earth he was stepping foot. His big, empty house in Bayton was waiting for him, and he planned on putting his feet up in front of his sixty-five-inch television and watching old footage of Savage shows when his hair was long and he could jump a mile high and not miss a note. He wanted to go back to the time before he had to cut his hair close to hide the receding hairline and his fingers ached in the cold, like now.

"Where you gonna go? Back to that mansion you call a house with no one waiting for you? The lake and some fishing will heal you up." Billy tugged on his cap.

"There's no fishing this time of year." But Billy's lake house had always been an escape place for him. This time going back to Heritage River would mean stepping into a minefield. His brother and sister would be close by.

"Why you always gotta smart-mouth me?" Billy yanked the truck door open. It protested on its hinges.

"I'm just saying there's no fishing right now. If you were planning on fixing what's wrong with me through fishing, you'd be wasting your time, and I know how much you hate to waste your time."

"If that were the case, I wouldn't be here picking you up." Billy grabbed him when he was no more than an arm's length away and pulled him into a bear hug.

The rush of affection for the old guy staggered him. He hesitated, but before he could wrap his arms around Billy's big frame, Billy pushed him away.

"We're going to get you fixed up." Billy patted his shoulder.

"I want you to come to the art show my photos are in. It's tomorrow morning. I figured if you made it all the way home you wouldn't be able to get back in time. This is the last show for the semester. I'm really proud of these shots."

Colton's heart strummed in his chest. A few short months ago, Cash seemed lost, and now his eyes shone. He eased out a long breath. How could he say no to this kid, the kid he wanted to protect like his own? Even though Cash didn't need any protecting. He had a father who loved him something fierce, so fierce he was willing to break up their band.

"Is your old man going to be there too?" Avoiding Blaise had become a mission statement.

14

"He has to miss it. He and Grace have a holiday party back in New Jersey this weekend. I'd really like to have someone from my family there."

He knew better than to ask if Savannah would be there. She was boycotting all the Savage men in the family these days, especially him. "Okay. I'll come. For one night." He held up a finger. "I can't stay in Billy's place more than that. I'm too fucking old for those cold showers."

"You just don't know how to work the plumbing, Mr. Superstar. My place ain't the Ritz Carlton, but it serves me just fine."

"That's fucking for sure." He hoisted his bag onto his shoulder.

"Get in. It's a long ride back." Billy held the door open.

Colton threw his bag and guitar in the back and slid into the passenger's side, with Cash in the middle. "You don't have to worry about me, you know. If that's what you're thinking. I'm fine. Really. I've got it all under control."

"No one said you weren't fine. You just need to pull your act together a little. Make things right with your brother." Billy pulled out into traffic.

He rested his head against the back of the seat. "Don't start."

"Dad misses you, Uncle Colton. Couldn't you just try to talk it out with him? He left the band because of me. Is that so bad?"

He missed Blaise too—like a toothache. "Your father

cut my career off at its knees. The only reason why I didn't break every one of his fingers is because he left for you." He understood the need to be there for Cash, but Cash was practically a man now. Blaise didn't have to ditch the band altogether, leaving him flapping in the wind.

"Why don't you just hire another drummer?" Billy tossed the idea out as if it were that simple.

"I didn't like anyone I interviewed. But that's changed. I pulled a few guys together, and we're hitting the road in three weeks. Right after Christmas. And I can't wait."

"Do you think three weeks is enough time considering what you've been through? You need to focus on getting better." Billy eased onto the highway.

"I am better. It was a stupid slipup. I haven't wanted a drink since." If the tour hadn't been canceled completely, if Blaise hadn't screwed him, he would not have needed a drink in the first place.

"You think thirty days in that place is enough to keep you on the clean-and-straight road? It ain't. And don't you argue with me about it. When you're ready, you're going to go over to your brother's house and talk to him and fix things. You hearing me clear enough?"

"He's right, Uncle Colton."

"Billy, I'm not up for your lectures. Just drive, okay?" He had no intention of speaking with his brother. Blaise made his choice. He pinched his eyes shut. His head throbbed.

The only other person on the planet who spoke to

him the way Billy had was his father. He didn't much like it coming from his old man either, but he had taken it, as he would continue to take it, from Billy Lewis because Billy was like a second father to him. In some ways, he was more like his actual father. Billy understood Colton in ways Jedidiah Savage never could. He hadn't wanted his boys going into music. He never believed they'd make any money.

His father had been wrong. There was plenty of money for the band Savage. Well, there had been. As the years passed, the fans dwindled, but he loved the road. As long as they kept touring, they made money. Nothing in the world meant as much to him as standing on stage, playing his music, and hearing crowds chant his name.

When Blaise had ditched the band, the tour derailed permanently. He had felt betrayed and angry. He'd figured that much out in rehab. And what did he do when he was angry? He drank himself stupid and crashed his car into a fence. He didn't need Blaise. He didn't need anyone.

"We're here." Billy threw the truck in park.

He bolted up in his seat. "Did I fall asleep?"

"Yup." Billy shoved his way out of the truck.

"And you snore." Cash slid out after Billy.

Colton grabbed his duffel and his guitar. The lake house hadn't changed. Much like Billy never seemed to change. The clapboards on the house had aged to a dark gray. The screened-in porch kept the mosquitos away on hot nights. This time of year the dark blue lake was as smooth as the back of his Stratocaster.

Cash stuck out his hand. "I've got to get going. But I'll be back in the morning to pick you up for the art show. Around eleven."

Colton grabbed his arm and pulled him in for another hug. "Thanks for coming out to meet me. Means a lot." Something like warm emotions caught in his throat.

"That's what family is for."

"You hear him? Family. Don't forget who your family is." Billy eased himself up the front steps.

"Be quiet, old man. You're making me need a drink."

"Oh pooh." Billy swatted the air and headed into the house.

Cash laughed and dropped into the driver's seat of his four-door silver sedan parked off to the side.

"You get girls in that car? Shouldn't you be driving something black with chrome wheels and low to the ground at your age?"

"No time for girls. And the insurance is cheaper on this thing."

"Boy, you and I need a heart-to-heart. Where Savage men are concerned, there's always time for girls."

Cash backed down the driveway and honked his goodbye. Colton turned back toward the lake and thought about the one girl he had brought there. Where was Harley Kenyon these days? She was probably married with three kids and had long since forgotten about him. Better that way. Savage men might have time for women, but no time for love. The road called, and she was his first mistress.

He turned away and climbed the creaking front steps and let the screen door slap shut behind him.

The inside of the house was the same too. Dark leather sofas worn and cracked from years of people gathered around the brick fireplace. The tables were made from logs Billy had cut down himself. The water had never run hot enough for a good shower, and the extra room only housed an air mattress. He wasn't into roughing it any longer.

The only thing new was the Christmas tree. It took up the whole corner of the room and left its cedar scent everywhere. Billy had thrown some colored lights around it and a gold star on top. He guessed Billy was going for the minimalist approach.

The kitchen was clean but small. The appliances were the plus side of forty years. But the view from that room was the best. The sun cast its long orange rays across the lake's glass surface. The whole lake could be seen from that window.

"Thanks for picking me up from the...you know." He really wanted to forget about that place, and one night here wouldn't kill him. He wouldn't let Cash down. After the kid's art show, he'd call the car service to take him home. In and out. Easy. He needed easy these days.

Billy grabbed two mugs from the cabinet and dumped instant coffee into each. He put the teakettle on the stove for hot water. "I want you to stay in town for a while. This place is good for you."

"Billy, are you hearing me? I'm not staying past one night."

"Sit down." Billy's voice echoed off the walls.

Colton dragged out the chair and dropped down.

Billy sat opposite him. "You're a screwup, Colton. I say that 'cause you're like a son to me. Thirty days ain't enough to fix what's wrong with you. When you called and told me what you'd done this time, I knew what you needed. If your daddy was still alive, I'd have told him to take care of it, but he's gone and your ma's gone, so that leaves me. Family is everything. You're going to fix things with your siblings. You need some peace and quiet. No bright lights. No ladies throwing panties at you. No drinking. You're staying if I have to hog-tie you to that chair myself, and you know I will."

"There's nothing to fix between me and Blaise. He wanted to leave the band, so he did. End of story."

"Yeah, then why won't you talk to him?"

"I'll talk to him."

"You sent him away from the rehab twice. He told me. And what about Savannah? Why are you avoiding her?"

"She's avoiding me. I've tried to talk to her about what happened last summer, but she won't take my calls. She didn't answer my letters. She wouldn't come for the family day where we're supposed to sit there and let those who love us yell at us."

What Savannah's son did last summer was wrong. He couldn't pretend what his nephew did hadn't happened, even if Savannah could. The rehab counselor said he should try and accept Savannah's decision to protect her son's wrongdoing. The counselor didn't understand his family.

Billy rubbed the back of his neck. "Blaise said as much. You should still talk to her. She was just trying to protect her son."

She was blinded by her son. "Forget it. Please." His head hurt again.

The kettle whistled its steam into the room. Billy pushed away from the table. "You're as stubborn as an old mule. You need this town, Colton." He lowered his voice and stared him down. "You've lost your way. You've forgotten where you're from. You're just like everyone else. I've never been more disappointed in you than I am right now. I don't know you anymore. Where's that young man full of heart and soul? If you find him, let me know. I miss him." Billy turned his back.

Colton shoved out of the chair and stormed through the house. He paced the front porch. He patted his pockets looking for his smokes and remembered they were inside the duffel. "Shit." It would've been better if Billy had yelled at him or threw something. Anger, he could handle. He was always pissing someone off and he didn't care, but to have Billy look at him with disappointment in his eyes was too much.

Billy had been the sounding board he needed when his dad turned a deaf ear to his son's desire to be in a rock band. Billy told him to go for it, follow his heart. He had helped him and Blaise pack the pickup with their gear when they headed to Los Angeles to record their first album. Jedidiah Savage had stayed inside the house and watched from the window. Billy had gripped him in a bear hug, tears in his eyes, telling Colton to go make him proud.

He continued to pace the porch. The sound of his boots echoed off the wood. The cold air nipped at his skin. He hadn't even bothered to put on a coat when he raced out here. His head hurt, and his hands ached from the cold. He shoved them under his armpits for some heat.

Billy pushed the screen door open. "How long you going to stand out there? You'll catch the death of you." He tossed him his coat. "Come back inside and finish your coffee. I'll start supper soon."

That was the closest thing to a peace offering he was going to get. He shrugged into his jacket. "I'll stay out here for a while longer."

"Have it your way."

"Hey, is Harley Kenyon still around?" He hadn't meant to ask about her, but being back here and seeing the lake at dusk and smelling the burning wood in the air drove him right back to being the same age as Cash. He rubbed a hand over his face. When had he gotten so damn old and worn out?

"She's teaching at the high school."

A teacher? He hadn't seen that coming. She was so determined to do something with her art. "How's Hank?"

"Hank passed a few months ago. Harley and her son are alone up there now."

Hank had died? Of course, no one would've told him. He'd distanced himself from Heritage River the minute the band took off, and after last summer he hadn't even spoken to his siblings. Harley and Hank were close. "Did you say her son?"

"Yup. She went off to New York to make something of her art. Instead, she came back two years later with a little boy. Ended up like her ma, but at least Harley didn't ditch that child. Hank took them in with open arms, happy to have her back and one more person to love."

He hadn't seen that coming either. Harley had been hell-bent on not ending up like her mother. Alone in New York with a baby and trying to make a career for herself had to have been tough, but she always was.

"Harley must be pretty upset about losing Hank. Was he sick?"

"Not that he knew of. Came on out of nowhere and took him before he had a chance to get his head around it."

Harley had lost so many people in her life. Maybe he'd stop by to check on her. If she'd let him anywhere near her. "Is she okay?" He'd only ever wanted her to be happy. He couldn't ever give her what she wanted— his undivided attention. She didn't understand his career came first. She complained about his playing in clubs and parties. She really hated how other girls threw themselves all over him. She wouldn't have liked his life on the road. Yeah, it was better he'd never made her any promises.

"She's holding her own. Always does."

"She ever ask about me?"

"Nope." Billy let the door slam shut with a laugh.

No big deal. He was Colton Savage. Plenty of other women wondered about him.

But none like Harley.

Chapter Three

Harley turned off Winding Way and onto the dirt drive leading to her house. The Durango bumped and shook over the uneven ground. What was she going to do if she lost her job? She had Knox to provide for and protect.

The golden light spilled from the house's front windows and called her in. The now-empty guesthouse blended into the darkness. Hank loved to cover the little house in colored lights for Christmas, making it bright enough that the house could be seen from the moon. He'd climb a ten-foot ladder with no one around. Every year she begged him to wait for her to help him so he didn't fall and break his neck. He never listened. He'd put wreaths in every window and an inflatable Santa with all ten reindeer on the lawn. Christmas was his favorite time of the year.

He loved her unconditionally, even when she came home with a baby and she had refused to talk about the father other than to say their time together hadn't meant anything.

She should think about renting the house out. She couldn't bear to see it dark all winter. Not to mention they could use the money if she was about to be jobless. Her career hinged on her review, but what if she found a way to raise more funds for the art program? Would Joann toss her to the curb after that? Probably. Wicked Witch.

Her stomach growled, but she had no plans for dinner, as usual. Why couldn't they just eat cupcakes for dinner? She could order a pizza tonight. It would be better than greasy fast food. At least pizza had three of the food groups in it. Tomorrow night she'd get her act together.

She unlocked the front door. The blast of heat soothed her. The kitchen was exactly the way she had left it earlier. Cereal box still sat on the counter. Dirty dishes were in the sink because the dishwasher needed to be unloaded. Grains of breakfast dusted the table. A pile of mail leaned like a tree with dead roots. The stovetop needed an appointment with a scouring pad. Knox had added the open chip bag and the salsa trail across the counter. Her head pounded. He hadn't cleaned anything in here, as she'd asked.

She marched over to the bottom of the steps and yelled up. "Knox, I'm home." Nothing. "Knox?"

She marched up the steps and knocked on her son's door. She had thought about taking the door off the hinges after he got in trouble, but the truth was sometimes she liked having her space. She'd taken his phone and his gaming system. She'd sold his car and forbade him to go anywhere for the next month.

What she should have done was taken his guitar, but she didn't have the heart. She knocked again. When she didn't get an answer, she opened it slowly, always a little afraid she might find her teenager in the middle of what most teenage boys did when left alone long enough.

Knox lay on his bed. He stared at the ceiling, earbuds shoved in. One lamp spilled light in the corner. His room smelled like sweat. Dirty clothes circled the floor around his hamper. Basketball was not his sport. She'd allowed him to use her old classic iPod to listen to music since she had his phone. He took to that idea the way she took to a stranger following her in a dark parking lot. But he caved. Score for her.

"Hey," she said louder than usual.

Nothing.

She stepped in and shook the corner of the bed. "Hey."

Knox jumped and yanked the earbuds out. "Hello, Mother."

Still on the *mother* term. "How was your day?"

"Sucked."

Of course it did. "You didn't clean the kitchen, like I asked."

"I forgot."

Convenient. "You still have to do it."

"I'll do it after dinner." He shoved the earbuds in and went back to staring at the ceiling.

Hearing aids would be in high demand when his generation's ears were older than dirt. "No. You'll do it now." No response. "Knox." She yanked one earbud out of his ear. He jumped.

"What?" His lips curled in a snarl, a look she knew so well. He wasn't the only one who could sneer like that. Arrogant rock stars could curl their lip with the best of them.

"I'm still speaking to you. You need to clean the kitchen now." She crossed her arms over her chest and hoped she was giving off her best I-mean-business mother look.

"The kitchen is only going to need to be cleaned up after dinner. I don't feel like doing it twice."

"There are plenty of things I do all day long that I don't feel like doing. That's life, pal. Embrace it." She turned to leave. She'd engaged in this conversation longer than she should have. Rookie mistake.

"Hey, Mom."

She stopped. Should she turn around or keep going? "Yes?" She turned. *Sucker.*

"I was thinking. Could I move into Uncle Hank's place? Just to sleep. I could practice late at night like I want to and not disturb you."

"Nice try, but no." She turned to leave again.

His feet hit the floor, and his footsteps followed her into the hall. "Why not?"

"Because there is no reason for you to stay there. We have plenty of space here, and you don't have to practice at midnight."

Back in the kitchen, she grabbed the sponge and handed it to him. He took it with force, but he wiped up the counter.

"I don't see what the big deal is if I sleep there. I might be going to college next year. You have to get used to me not being around. This would be practice." His smile filled his face and lit up his brown eyes. The smallest dimple appeared on his cheek. If she blinked, she'd miss it, but she knew to look. She was constantly in awe of how much she loved that boy. He was her greatest accomplishment, and now her one success had one foot out the door. She wanted to yank him back in.

"I'm going to rent out the guesthouse." It appeared she'd decided.

"Why?"

"The extra money will be helpful." She didn't need to tell him yet just how helpful. If the review came in with glowing marks, she might not lose her job. Joann would have to find another way to get rid of her.

"I don't want a stranger living in Hank's place." He threw the sponge in the sink. "It isn't right."

"The decision is mine. I'm renting it out."

"The decision should be both of ours."

"Wrong. I'm the adult here. The decision is mine. We're renting." She'd need to put an ad in the local paper, or maybe one of the students at the community college needed a place to stay. The rent would ease some of her worries about money.

"You're keeping Hank's place from me to punish me.

When are you going to forgive me? It was one stupid mistake."

"It was a big mistake that could cost you. How do you think colleges are going to view your suspension?"

"Maybe I don't want to go to college. I just want to play my music. I don't need college for that."

Not this conversation again. "You're going to college. You can't get a decent job without a degree." How could she make him understand this? "Even if you do play music as a career, you still need to know how to run a business. Finding people to buy your music is a business. A degree will help with that."

"If I don't hand in my family-tree project, I'm going to fail. How's that going to look on the transcript?"

"Hand in the project, then. I gave you all the information I had." And all the info they found on the ancestry site, which cost her a hundred bucks. She hated this assignment.

"Can we try to find my father?"

She clamped her tongue between her molars and forced air out of her nose. "You don't need that information for the project. Can we please change the subject? What do you want for dinner?"

"I'm not hungry, I'm not handing in that project, and I'm not going to college." He stormed out of the kitchen and pounded up the steps.

She waited with her fists clenched for the slam of the door. The sound of his guitar shook the house's foundation. She held her head.

She wanted to run after him and tell him he could

stay in the guesthouse. She'd make waffles for dinner. He loved waffles. She'd give him back his phone and his privileges. She could buy back his car, which she only sold because he got caught with an open whiskey bottle in the boys' bathroom.

She wanted to forget about everything that happened these past weeks—Hank's dying and Knox's showing up at school drunk. She wanted to be the good guy for once. She wished someone else could carry the burden and the worry of being the parent for just a little while. Tears stung her eyes. She'd made the choice to raise Knox alone. Some days that decision was harder to live with than others.

She lit a fire in the den, then poured herself a bowl of her favorite sugary cereal and plopped down in an oversized chair. There had to be a cheesy Christmas movie on some channel. She couldn't think of a better way to spend a Saturday night.

The doorbell startled her. "What the heck?" She pushed off the chair, padded to the door, and peered through the small window that acted as a peephole. She yanked the door open. "Hey."

"I brought dinner." Ella held up a pizza box and a bottle of white wine.

"Come on in." The pizza smelled savory and cheesy. She held the door wide open. "But I already ate."

Ella wore her knit hat pulled low on her forehead, but the top stuck up like a nightcap. She leaned in and planted a kiss on her cheek. "Please." She rolled her eyes. "You probably forced Knox to eat cereal. The boy needs a real dinner." She plopped the box on the kitchen table and whisked off her coat and hat. She wore a long sweater over leggings, and around her neck was the colorful pendant Harley had made for her last birthday.

"How is our little delinquent?" Ella grabbed plates out of the cabinet and handed one to Harley.

"What he did isn't funny." She forced the beginnings of a smile back down.

"Oh, come on. He's a kid. You did some pretty stupid things at that age too."

"I wasn't stupid enough to get caught, and I didn't do it where Hank and Katherine worked." Harley leaned against the doorframe and picked at a chip in the plate. Her smile made a slight reappearance. "I have to be the adult here. He has to know there's a consequence for his actions."

"The school took care of that. It's just unfortunate you work where he showed up drunk." Ella smiled and shrugged.

"Right. As if running around Macy's drunk instead would've made what he did any better."

"Only if he got a discount." She winked and pulled hot, cheesy pizza from the box.

A week's suspension wasn't enough punishment in Harley's book, but the school had considered that he'd never done anything bad. Kids did make some pretty big mistakes. She might've taken too strong a hand, but she'd been afraid that showing up to school drunk would lead to something bigger.

"Is he home now?" Ella pulled the wineglasses

bought at a discount store from the cabinet and gave them a rinse.

"Knox locked himself in his room." She pointed to the ceiling. The music was more of a thump now.

"We'll save him a slice or two. Let's go in the den. I smell the fire. It's heavenly."

They took the food and the bottle of wine and sat by the fire. Flames danced in the hearth and spread their warmth over them. Spending time with her friend was much better than spending time alone.

"Ben Myer is taking a leave of absence." She pulled on the cheese and twirled it around her finger.

"Wait, the music teacher?" Ella took a big bite of her slice. The sauce and cheese dripped down her chin.

Harley handed her a napkin. "The cancer's back. He can't make it to winter break. The treatments are kicking his backside."

"That's horrible. I saw him at the last football game a few weeks ago. He looked so good."

How a person looked on the outside had nothing to do with what was happening to the inside once cancer got a hold of it. No one knew that better than she did. When Hank had sat her down to tell her the news, she hadn't believed him because he didn't appear sick.

Then in a blink of an eye, he was gone.

"Is the school bringing in a substitute?" Ella asked.

"Just to have a warm body for his classes. They need someone with actual music experience if the holiday concert is going to happen." There wasn't time to interview a new teacher before the show, and no one else had agreed to fill his shoes.

"Do the students know this? Stephanie hasn't mentioned anything to me."

"Ben made his announcement last week. Yesterday was his last day." She finished off her wine and started on her second piece of pizza. Okay, the cereal hadn't been a real dinner.

"Canceling the holiday concert will kill those kids, including yours and mine. Is the wicked witch going to do anything for them?"

"I doubt Joann Humphreys cares about canceling a holiday concert. Music isn't exactly on the standardized tests. Plus, the school budget didn't pass again. The funds are low. Music and art always get hit first. She might push the music program right out the door. Who knows."

"Is there any way to save the concert?" Ella poured more wine.

Harley covered her glass. If she drank anymore, she'd have a headache. "About a million dollars and a new teacher." What could she do to save the arts in her school? Even if she lost her job, those students deserved to have access to the arts.

"There must be a long line of teachers looking for a job. What about you? You're artsy." Ella held out her necklace.

"Art and music aren't exactly the same thing. I don't know the first thing about music. Those kids will sound like a dying rhinoceros if I get my hands on them. Who needs a music program, right?"

"You don't mean that."

"Of course, I don't." Harley grabbed the box and their plates. "It isn't fair that when there isn't enough money, it's always the arts that get cut. The football team will get new uniforms, but the music kids have to suck it up. Where are the imaginations going to go? Music, not just music, but art changes lives." She pointed a finger at Ella. "And I tell you what—she's coming after me. Nothing would give that woman more pleasure than to watch me go." She marched out of the room.

Ella followed her. "The school isn't going to fire you."

"Really? The attendance in my classes has been low, and our reviews will be in any day now. No one wants to take art, especially art they have to use their hands for. Everyone wants to create on a computer. That's fine, but there's more to art then just a swipe and a click. The kids are missing out on the feeling of art between their fingers. Sorry. I didn't mean to have a pity party when you were nice enough to bring me dinner."

"That's what friends are for." Ella took the dishes from her and gave them a rinse. She searched for a spot to place them since the sink was full. "It's okay to be passionate about your art."

"Leave those. I'll clean up later. It doesn't pay to be passionate. Passion doesn't pay the bills." She flopped down on a stool at the center island.

Ella started to unload the dishwasher. "I remember someone who had big dreams about showing in a gallery. Where did that girl go?"

She jumped down from the stool and gently pushed

Ella aside to unload the dishes herself. "We've been over this a thousand times. Artists need to be extraordinary, and I'm not. I failed in New York. The museum in town isn't banging on my door to exhibit my work either. Besides, I had to think about Knox. Teaching gave me a paycheck I could count on."

"Do you keep discouraging Knox from pursuing a music career because he won't have a steady paycheck?" Ella eyed her over the wineglass.

She didn't want Knox making her mistakes or have his heart broken if his dreams didn't work out. She shoved the dirty dishes into the dishwasher. "He needs to a have a practical plan. That's all."

But the paycheck wasn't all. Not even close.

Chapter Four

Colton woke to sun streaming into the room and throwing ribbons of gold across the sofa. The fire had gone out, and a chill had crisped the air. The house smelled of coffee, which he badly needed. He'd only meant to close his eyes for a second and somehow it was full-on morning and his entire body ached from sleeping on the sagging sofa. He should have gone home last night. Did Cash really need him at this art show?

He pushed himself up as his joints played out an old tune. "Billy, you around?"

The kitchen was empty, and the dish drain filled with one plate, one mug, and a small frying pan. He checked the other bedroom, but all he found was a perfectly made bed. The bathroom was designed for one person. Billy must not entertain any lady friends. He didn't know one woman who'd put up with sitting on the toilet and banging her knees on the sink.

He messed with the faucet, hoping for some hot water, before he jumped in the shower and almost jumped back out when the cold water smacked his skin. Well, the shower might be good for one thing and one thing only—curing swollen nuts. Not that he'd ever had that problem. Well, not since Savage first ran up the music charts. Too bad they couldn't even get in the race these days, but he'd have to pump out new tunes for that to happen. He didn't write anymore. That was that.

The icy water shook some of the sleep from his brain. There was a time he might've popped a pill to wake up in the morning. His drug phase didn't last long. Blaise kicked the shit out of him once when he was high enough to drive down train tracks while a train was coming the other way. He couldn't play his guitar for a month. That was the last he took any pills. Whiskey became his drug of choice instead.

The cold water lasted longer than he could. He ran a towel over his body, which still ached. His phone sang out Savage's "Girls in the Rain." A text message. *I'm here.* From Cash.

He dressed quickly and stepped outside. The December sky was bright blue and clear. The air smelled clean and crisp. He always liked Billy's house, which was far enough off the road no one could see it, but right up against the lake. It might be old, but if Billy threw a little elbow grease into it, he could sell it for a fortune. Though Billy would be carried out of this house in a black bag before he sold. He was one stubborn old coot.

"I didn't have my coffee." He slid beside Cash in his silver old-man car.

"We'll pick it up along the way." Cash let the backup camera guide him down the driveway.

"Not at May's. Don't even think about going there."

"Why not?"

Colton shot him a look.

"You are one stubborn old coot."

Harley checked the clock above the classroom door. Class was half over. Fifteen students stood in front of canvases. Some stared at their paintings with arms crossed. Others chewed on the end of their paintbrushes, while others dipped bristles into colors and washed away their tension by expressing themselves on the canvas.

Only one student sat hunched forward on his stool, hands fisted in his lap and brows stitched together. The canvas was still blank.

She slid up beside him, careful not to startle him. "Andy, how's it going?"

Andy Henson was around Knox's age, taking her class because his parents forced him. On paper he looked like the perfect kid. He took all the advance classes, earned his way into the honor society, edited the yearbook, played in the school band, performed countless hours of community service, and held a job.

Andy also had anger issues and suffered from anxiety. When he realized he'd forgotten his calculator for the

SATs, he kicked the stall door in the bathroom. Unfortunately for Andy, a young man was inside that stall. As a result, the boy lost a tooth and suffered a broken nose, and part of Andy's punishment was her class.

"I suck at this." His shoulders slumped further, as if that were even possible.

"No, you don't. Do you have your photo?" Two sessions ago she'd asked everyone to take a picture of something they'd like to paint.

He whipped out his phone, tapped at the screen, and held the phone out for her to see.

She gasped. "You took this from the bridge."

His eyes bulged. "How did you know?"

How didn't she know? "You caught the sunset on the water. The tree line is unique with the combination of blue spruces and Douglas firs. What color do you like best in the picture?"

"I don't know. The blues and greens, maybe."

"Start with those."

"But what if I don't do it the right way and I mess up the whole painting?"

She put a hand on his shoulder. "Here's the good news. You can make as many mistakes as you want. I have plenty of paper for you to practice on if you want to save the canvas. There is no judgement here. My class is a safe place to explore and relax. Okay?"

He nodded, but his furrowed brows said otherwise.

"How about a doughnut?" She'd stopped off at May's on the way. She liked to bring treats for her students—and, okay, for herself too.

Andy shook his head, but at least he picked up the paintbrush. Progress.

She checked the time again. Cash hadn't made it. Strange. He was always so diligent about his work. Hopefully, everything was okay.

~

"Will you hurry up? We're late because you had to drive out of the way for that coffee."

Colton followed Cash down the hall of the art building in the community college. The floor gleamed with wax. Voices traveled to meet them.

"I needed some caffeine. What's the hurry? Don't these shows go on for hours?" He'd wanted a smoke too, but the kid wouldn't let him smoke in the car. The least he could do was let him get some of the coffee down his throat.

What if he ran into a fan or two? He needed to be on his A game. At that hour of the morning, he should be asleep.

Cash turned into a classroom at the end of the hall. An art show in a classroom? Didn't schools like this have little galleries? Colton stopped. The voices had thinned out. He cocked his head. He'd heard the cadence of that voice before. He couldn't place where.

He moved near the door, hesitated, but Cash waved him in. People painted at easels. His mind tried to catch up to his out-of-beat heart. What was going on? He stepped farther into the room. His gaze swept the space.

41

The woman standing at the head of the classroom turned in his direction.

Time's tempo slowed down.

Distortion filled his ears.

His past elbowed him in the jaw.

He needed to be anywhere but there.

Cash grabbed his arm. "Uncle Colton, you remember Harley, don't you?"

Chapter Five

When Colton had crashed his car into the fence, the airbag had deployed and pounded his face. He'd sat there with blood running from his nose and white spots flickering in his eyes, his whole body shaking. When he'd tried to get out of the car, his legs had given way and he'd fallen to the ground. His legs wanted to do the same thing now as he stared at the only woman who honestly loved him.

He turned to Cash. "You told me this was an art show."

"I lied." Cash tried to keep the grip on his arm, but Colton swung his arm away. "Harley teaches an art class on relaxation. I thought you might like to check it out." Cash unraveled his scarf.

What had Cash done to him? "You said you wanted your family here." Was Blaise about to walk in too? Was this some kind of walk-down-memory-lane intervention?

Every person in the room had eyes on him. He didn't wait for Cash to respond. "I'm gone."

He headed for the exit door. His boots smacked against the tile floor. His heart played an unexpected rhythm. What was his nephew thinking?

"Uncle Colton, wait." Cash's words weren't far behind.

He needed fresh air and a smoke. He hit the metal bar on the door and shoved it open. Cold air smacked him in the face, finally waking him up. Of all the classrooms in the world, he walked into Harley's.

"Did you do that on purpose?" he said over his shoulder.

Cash caught up to him. His breath came in short bursts. "Do what? Bring you to a place that might be able to help you? Yeah, I did. So what of it?" He stood his full height. The curl of his top lip and the line of his jaw were all Blaise. The stubborn glare reminded Colton of himself at that age.

"Did you bring me to Harley on purpose? Why Harley?"

"She runs the art club I'm in at school. I like her. I thought she could help you."

"There's more. What else?" Colton patted his pockets for his cigarettes, yanked out the pack, and lit one up.

"Do you have to smoke?"

"Christ, you young people. I smoke. Big fucking deal. Answer my question."

Cash tugged on his ear. "I saw the drawing of the bridge you had up in your room at the rehab."

"So?" He'd forgotten to take it down when Cash came to visit. He never shared with anyone that he had that picture. Too many questions would be asked, and he wasn't going to answer any of them. His time with Harley was his business.

"So Harley has a photo of the exact drawing in her office. I know enough about art to know that picture was used to create that drawing. She gave it to you."

So what if she had? "Are you trying to play match-maker? Because I don't need you stirring up things you don't understand." He took a long drag and let the nicotine burn his lungs. He coughed. He was going to have to give up smoking too. What next—sex?

"I thought you might be willing to take a class she taught because you know her. I know you won't take one with anybody else. If you two hook up again, that's on you. I just want you to stay sober."

"I'm not going to take any art class for relaxation, kid. Forget it. I'm going back to my house in Bayton, and in three weeks I'm hitting the road."

"Please do this for me. I don't want to lose you. When Billy called and told Dad what happened, well, I was upset. Dad and Grace were worried too. Please work with Harley. She'll help you deal with your anger."

"I'm not angry." He smoked the cigarette down to the filter, tossed it on the ground, and smashed it with his foot.

"You won't speak to Dad, and Aunt Savannah has cut

us all off. I want my family fixed. I want things back to the way they were."

"You want to go back to when Jud tried to get you in trouble for something you didn't do?" That's what had started the whole family feud. Colton had stepped in and defended Cash over Jud, and Savannah had written them all off for good.

"I told Dad and I'll tell you—I could've handled Jud. You didn't have to do what you did."

"Too late." And he'd do it again. What was right was right. The truth had to come out whether Savannah wanted to hear it or not.

"Can't you at least try Harley's class? For me, Uncle Colton. I don't want you to drink anymore. Please."

He wiped a hand over his face. "Was Billy in on this too? Of course, he is. Why am I even asking?"

"He wants you to stay in town and get help too. He thought Harley was the only person you might listen to."

Even the old man was trying to play Cupid. They didn't understand what they were getting involved with. "I did get help, damn it. I went to rehab for thirty days. I'm clean, Cash. I swear. It was one slip-up. It's over. I promise. You can check in on me anytime you want. You can even come on tour with me. I love you, kid. You know that. But I'm not going to paint. I've got my music. She's all the therapy I need." He patted Cash's cheek.

"Just try the class a few times before you go back on the road. You'll need something besides music to help you handle the stress of touring. Music is your job. It's not therapy." Cash offered a half smile.

He couldn't give his nephew what he wanted. Cash didn't understand that music wasn't just a job. She was his whole world. "You want to get some lunch? My treat."

"That's it, then? The subject is closed?"

"Closed. For good. What about that lunch before I hit the road?"

"Sure." Cash turned toward the car, his shoulders slouched.

The door to the building swung out, and Harley stepped into the sunshine. Her warm-brown hair was streaked golden. Sunlight sparkled through the pieces falling around her face. Although her coat was buttoned up, he'd caught enough of a look at her inside to notice the curve of her hips in those jeans. Well, maybe some of that knowledge came from memory too.

He shouldn't have run, but seeing her had been a shock. Now that he'd had a chance to swallow the surprise, he wanted to talk with her. Just for a few minutes. That wouldn't hurt anything. "I'll meet you at the car."

Cash saw Harley and waved. "I thought you said the subject of art classes was closed, Uncle Colton?"

"It is. I'm not going to say anything about that. You're the one that brought us together. Can you just give me a minute?"

"Me and my bright ideas. Be quick. I'm hungry."

Colton hurried over to cut her off on the way through the parking lot, and she stopped in her tracks. She yanked her big tote over her shoulder.

"Can I help you carry your books, Teach?" He

pushed back his shoulders and gave her his best stage smile. Her honeysuckle smell drifted toward him.

She shifted the bag again. "If you'll excuse me...I have an appointment." Her dark brown eyes searched for something to rest on. She decided on something off in the distance.

He stepped into her line of vision. "It's been a long time, huh? I'm sorry about what happened in your class-room. Cash told me I was coming to his art show. I didn't know you'd be there. I wouldn't have bothered you if I'd known." He hadn't planned on saying that much. Well, he hadn't planned on saying anything at all, but he didn't want her to dash off like an opening act now that she was standing in front of him.

"Cash meant well."

"It's nice to see you." He meant that. She hadn't changed in all the years they'd been apart. She was still as beautiful as ever.

"Well, then. Take care." She shifted the bag and tried to sidestep him. He blocked her path. "Colton, get out of my way."

"So you're an art teacher?"

She let out a long breath. "Nothing changes with you, does it?"

He stepped aside to let her pass him. "What does that mean?"

"Nothing. I have to go."

He followed her to her truck. He glanced over at Cash, who raised his hands in a questioning gesture. Colton pointed to her back, hoping Cash understood he wasn't done talking. "Do these art relaxation classes help people with stress stuff?"

She fumbled in her big bag. "Yup."

A few people spilled out of the building and shouted goodbyes to her. She waved and called back. Her smile was full and vibrant for them. She used to smile for him like that.

"I'd like to hear more about your work."

Her head snapped around, and her icy gaze locked on him. "Nice try, but we both know that isn't the truth."

He leaned against her truck and crossed his legs. "Harley, please don't be mad at me. What happened between us was a long time ago. I'm sorry." Wasn't that what she wanted to hear? He was sorry for hurting her feelings. He'd never meant to do that. Unfortunately, he'd been successful at hurting her more times than he liked to think about.

"Where have I heard that before?"

"Let me show you how sorry I am. Are you free for dinner tonight?"

She rolled her eyes. "No, I have plans." She jerked open the door and dumped her bag inside.

"Change them. I'm only in town for one night."

She slid in and slammed the door without answering him. The engine came to life and the window hummed down. "Please step away. I don't want to run you over. Your fans would never forgive me."

"Why won't you have dinner with me?" He thought she might be cool toward him. After all, a lot of time had passed between them. Something like twelve years, maybe more, and he hadn't bothered to come to see her last summer when he was staying with Blaise, but she usually warmed to him right away. It was their thing.

"Enjoy your visit with Cash." She raised a hand and backed out. The truck sped away, leaving him staring after her.

"Ouch." Cash stood beside him.

"Shut up." Colton turned to him. "When did you walk up?"

Cash laughed. "In time to witness the great Colton Savage crash and burn with a lady. That ever happen before?"

Never.

Of course, Colton was older than the last time Harley saw him. Yet the lines around his slate eyes had surprised her. Eighteen years had mixed white into his dark hair that he wore shorter but still curled close to his collar. Her fingers longed to tangle in his hair. The scruff on his jaw was speckled with grays and white, like paint splatter. The lazy smile that ended in a dimple was still the same, and it could still make her knees go weak. Damn his wide stance and broad shoulders. Under no circumstances could this man walk back into her life. Under. No. Circumstances.

She turned into her driveway and pulled up to her house. She tugged her bag over the console and dragged herself up the front porch. At least she'd ignored his dinner invitation. Once upon a time, she would've jumped at the chance to have dinner with him, but that time was no more.

The metallic vibration of a guitar solo met her inside the door. Why couldn't that kid play something like the tambourine? If she could've planned it, he wouldn't want to play music at all, but life rarely turned out the way it's planned.

Knox was determined to take on an unforgiving career with little possibilities and a ton of disappointment. He deserved more, but he had dreams, and she wasn't about to shatter those. She just wanted him to have a backup plan.

She dumped her coat and bag on the chair in the kitchen and picked up the take-out menu from the pizza place that delivered. She'd order a salad and a pasta dish for her and Knox to share. That sounded healthy.

She had wanted Colton to think he missed out on something by choosing music over her, but Savage had shot to stardom, and he never looked back for her. Well, once. One time that she misunderstood to mean more. Even though it had killed her to set him free, she couldn't deny him his dreams either. She hadn't wanted to be the reason he turned his back on his music.

She phoned in the dinner order and hoped she had enough cash in her wallet.

The vibrations coming from upstairs stopped, and the house was once again covered in silence. Knox pounded down the steps and into the kitchen. "What's for dinner?"

"I ordered something from Enzo's. The food will be here soon."

"Mom, can I ask you something?"

"Sure." She reached for the chips in the cabinet, grabbed a handful, and left the bag open on the table.

"Have you ever tried to find your father?" He dropped down into the chair and spun the bag around.

She crushed the chips in her hand. Fear dragged a cold hand down her back. This was coming from that stupid history project. "Once, but I couldn't find him."

Hank and Katherine had tried to talk her out of it, but she wouldn't listen. She knew better. Her mother had dumped her on her aunt and uncle and disappeared into a world of drugs and despair. No matter how much they loved her, she still couldn't wipe clean the grime of abandonment layered on her skin. Finding her father would have been a way to scrape away some of those dirty feelings. He might not know she was even born. She'd hoped her mother had never told him and when he met her, he'd be glad she'd searched for him. Maybe she even had some siblings.

When she had knocked on the door of his red brick colonial with white columns and black shutters on sprawling acreage, he opened the door and his face fell. He told her she'd meant nothing to him. She was the result of a drunken night in a bar with a whore. He didn't even remember her mother's name, just that she'd worn a blue dress that showed off too much leg. He had no place for her in his pristine life. She was no more welcome than stepping in dog shit in brand new shoes.

"Aren't you curious?" Knox's words dragged her back to the kitchen and the handful of crumbs dropping onto the floor.

"Uncle Hank and Aunt Katherine were the only parents I needed."

He tilted his head up to her. "Do you ever think about finding my father?"

All the years he never even questioned her about his father. They had been a team, building forts together, walking along the river and skipping stones, his small hand securely in hers, and now this desire to dig up a past that would bring no good crushed her.

"I wouldn't even know where to start."

"You could Google him."

The heat flushed against her cheeks. "I lost track of him the minute he left New York. And without a last name..." She turned and busied herself at the sink.

"Don't you think he had a right to know he was going to be a father? I'd want to know if I got someone pregnant."

She spun around. "Did you?"

"Yeah, Ma, I got some girl pregnant. We did it under the bleachers after a football game while we were both drunk. You're going to be a grandmother. Surprise." His face cracked open into a smile. He threw his head back and laughed. "I got you."

"Not funny."

"Seriously, then, don't you think he had a right to know about a baby?"

"I went to tell him, but he was so excited about his big

opportunity. I didn't have the heart to ruin his chance. We didn't mean anything to each other, and it happened only once. I wouldn't have given him a second thought after that night if I hadn't ended up pregnant. I'm sorry. I'm sitting here telling my teenage son about my bad judgment with a man and how he was the result. Not the best of my mother moments."

The lies had piled pretty high. One of the biggest lies being his father didn't mean that much to her. Back then, he'd been her whole world, and she thought she was the love of his life too. She'd been wrong about them.

His fingers pulled at a loose string on his shirt. "If you knew how to find my father, you'd tell me?"

The words staggered up her throat. The doorbell rang, probably their dinner right on time, but she wasn't saved. "Absolutely."

Chapter Six

The way to Harley's house was etched in Colton's mind. No matter how many years went by, he would never forget how to get there.

Billy's old pickup sputtered and bucked. The thing was likely to die. If he thought Billy would accept it, he'd buy the old man a new truck or give him his truck tucked in the garage in Bayton. He really didn't need as many vehicles as he owned.

He hadn't been able to get Harley out of his mind yesterday after Cash's little stunt. Whenever he saw her, no matter how much time went by, she settled under his skin like an itch, and nothing could scratch her away. A drive over to her place before he hit the road might be the cure.

May's hot rolls and cinnamon buns sweetened the air in the truck. The pastries were Harley's favorites. Well, at least they used to be. What if after all this time she started eating healthy? Not his Harley. He caught himself—she wasn't his Harley anymore and hadn't been since Savage got the word the record label wanted them. They had spent that one week together after his father died, but one week didn't add up to a relationship. It didn't add up to anything. She let him know yesterday with her icy glare and clipped words she hadn't forgotten about his leaving her more than once.

Maybe they could be friends, talk over a cup of coffee and pastries. She could tell him what she'd been up to these last years, and that was it. *Friends.* He liked the sound of that.

He turned onto the dirt drive. Hank called this place his little vacation home right outside of town. He always liked Hank. A waste he passed too soon.

When they were young and first dating, he'd park his car back on the road and sneak down the long drive at night so Hank and Katherine wouldn't hear him coming. He'd climbed up the trellis under her window. Most nights she'd be on the roof waiting for him. They'd watch the stars, hold hands, and make out until his lips were swollen and his nuts aching. He'd tried to charm his way through her window, but she'd sent him packing each time. Eventually, she'd given him her greatest gift, but it was not in her room. A smile tugged at his lips. He hadn't thought about any of that in a long time.

Her house needed a new coat of paint and maybe some new shutters. The guesthouse and a garage sat a ways back. The guesthouse wasn't much more than a square box. Hank used to have chickens, but he didn't see any signs of the coop.

He parked alongside her dusty Durango and grabbed the box of pastries. He'd stay thirty minutes, or maybe an hour, but nothing more. He had to get on the road.

She stuck her head out the front door, rested her squinty gaze on him, then pushed her way onto the porch. Her eyes grew to the size of amps. She held a mug in one hand and waved a finger at him with the other.

"Oh no. Don't even think about coming up this porch, Colton Savage. Turn yourself around and drive back to wherever it is you came from."

"Come on, Harley. Don't be like that. You can't still be mad at me. I just came by to say hi. I brought your favorites from May's." He held up the pink box and flashed his photo-shoot smile.

She pressed her lips together and looked down at the porch before returning her gaze to him. "Well, since you stopped at May's." She glided down the steps and licked her parted lips. Her fingers played with the silver necklace catching the morning sun.

His heart changed rhythm as she approached.

She slid the box from his grip. "Would you like some coffee?" Her voice was soft.

"That'd be great."

She turned her mug upside down and dumped its contents on his head.

He jumped back, but he was too late. Coffee ran down his face, down his neck, and under his shirt.

"Christ, woman, have you lost your mind?"

Harley was in her complete right mind. Coffee mixed with milk ran in streaks down his face. She bit her bottom lip to keep from laughing. She might've overreacted, but he had it coming for showing up at her door eighteen years ago, professing his feelings, and then leaving without so much as a look back. He also had it coming for showing up here with a box of pastries, trying to sweet-talk her.

"What are you doing here?" She didn't want him there or anywhere near her. He'd never wanted her before. Why was he coming around now of all times?

"Can I have a towel?" He shook his head, sending coffee splatter her way.

"I guess." A small laugh snuck out. Okay, she'd over-reacted just a little.

"You're not funny."

"I'm a little funny. Admit it. You didn't answer my question. What are you doing here?"

"Harley, the damn towel, please."

"Oh, all right. Don't even think about coming inside my house." The last thing she needed was Colton anywhere near Knox.

She ran in, swiped a dish towel off the kitchen counter, and turned, only to collide with Colton's solid frame standing in the doorway. Her hands flattened between her and his muscular pecs before she bounced off him.

"I told you to stay put."

"It's too cold out to stand there dripping in coffee."

"Here." She shoved the cloth at him.

He wiped his face and neck. "Thanks. Why did you dump your coffee on me?"

"What do you want?" She fisted her hands on her hips.

He took the kitchen in. "The place looks the same."

"Colton, I don't want to make small talk with you. Did you come here for a reason?" *Dear Lord, please don't let there be a reason this man is standing in her house.*

She cocked her head to listen for Knox. Thankfully, he was still asleep. Hopefully, he'd never be any the wiser of this little encounter.

"I wanted to come by and see how you're doing. Old friends do that kind of thing."

Old friends? Is that what he thought of them? He had to be kidding, right? She might've called them old lovers—maybe. She preferred old boyfriend and girlfriend. At least then, she'd know she'd meant something to him.

"I'm fine. Thanks for asking. Now you can go. You need to change anyway."

"Really? I thought coffee running into my ears was a good new look for me."

Guilt scratched at her throat for the whole coffee thing. "Let me get you a clean shirt. Sorry about your coat."

He peeled off the wet coat and tossed it on the chair. His broad shoulders filled out the thin, black sweater also wet with coffee. His waist narrowed into his faded jeans.

Harley tore her gaze back up to his face before she looked any lower.

"Forget it. I know when I'm not welcome. I only wanted to say I'm sorry about Hank. I liked him."

"Thanks."

Hank wasn't very fond of him, especially after he'd caught Colton in her room that very last time eighteen years ago. They had been lying in her bed after making love, and he'd made her laugh. Colton's gift was making her laugh—well, one of his gifts. He clamped his hand over her mouth, but it was too late, and she was too loud. Hank banged on her door. He suspected Colton was in there. Hank wasn't stupid. When she said she was sleeping, he barged in before Colton could get out the window. She had been mortified, even though she was twenty-seven at the time. Her uncle hadn't said a word. He just glared at her and slammed her door shut behind him. They hadn't spoken for weeks, and then he moved into the guesthouse.

He'd said afterward Colton should be taking her out on his arm, not sneaking into her room like some sloppy teenager. She had assured him Colton came in the front door, but Hank didn't find it funny. Unfortunately, Hank had been right.

"You know, if it's not too much trouble, I think I will take that clean shirt. The coffee is freezing my skin." He stuck his hands under his arms.

Her stupid ideas were going to get her a lot more than trouble. "Stay here this time. I mean it. I've got some old shirts of Hank's in the guesthouse." She certainly wasn't going to give him something of Knox's to wear. Absolutely not.

What happened to "under no circumstances" was she going to let that man in her life? Now here he was, standing in her kitchen. *Her kitchen.* She had lost her mind after all.

"I have some coffee pods on the counter if you want to make yourself a cup and warm up." She handed him a mug. "Do you still take it black?"

"Good memory. I see you still eat kids' cereal." He shook the box.

He remembered. Her memory had been her nemesis. She had waited for the moment she'd forget the sound of his voice or his smell or the way he made her laugh, but that never happened, not even when she prayed.

"I'll be right back." She didn't need a coat, not after standing feet from him in her kitchen.

"Hey, Harley?"

She turned. "Yes?"

"It's great to see you."

Heat filled her cheeks. "Thanks." She hurried outside to the guesthouse.

She threw open the front door and headed to Hank's old room. They'd packed up most of his stuff, but she couldn't part with everything. She yanked an old green-and-blue sweatshirt from the closet.

She tried to catch her breath. What had she been thinking dumping that coffee on him? The sight of him and the sound of his deep voice had dragged her right back to eighteen years ago. He'd stood at her front door with tears in his eyes because his father had been buried that day. Before she'd realized what they were doing, his lips burned trails across her skin. Their hands had been a tangled mess, touching and searching. There had never been anyone like Colton. No one had ever made her feel so alive or feel as if all things were possible. Her sheets had smelled of his cedar-and-oak scent for days.

She needed to get back to the house and tell him to go. She hurried across the lawn and shoved open the kitchen door.

Voices reached out to her. "How did you spill coffee all over yourself?"

"Don't ask."

Small cracks splintered her heart.

Colton held the pink box open. The smell of butter, cinnamon, and sugar danced around the smell of coffee. Knox stood on the other side of the island, shoving a bun in his mouth. His blond hair hung in his face. They were the same height, and they filled up the space with their muscular bodies—Knox's still lanky, and Colton's more filled out.

She bumped into the table and tripped over the chair trying to give Colton the sweatshirt and remove him from her kitchen before her heart stopped all together.

Colton eyed her less-than-graceful performance across the room. "Are you all right?" He took the sweatshirt.

Uh, no.

"Mom, you didn't tell me Colton Savage started taking your Saturday class." Knox's smile lit up his face, threatening to reveal that dimple that hid from sight most times.

She hadn't seen that smile in a while and hated it was because of someone else—and not just anyone else. But it wasn't every day a kid got to meet one of his guitar idols. The irony of Knox's guitar hero being Colton wasn't lost on her.

Knox had even asked Blaise in the grocery store if he could meet Colton. Blaise said he'd try, but Colton didn't come around much. She didn't need his presence threatening all she had held together by herself.

"He's not taking my class. That class is full." The cracks over her heart grew wider. They must be able to hear the creaks and the groans.

He pulled his black sweater over his head as if he were the only one in the room. Colton never suffered from modesty. He'd play shirtless on stage in front of thousands. She stole a glance at his torso. The lines of his muscles bent and curved as he reached for the clean sweatshirt and yanked it over his head. She tried not to think about the feel of his skin under her touch.

"Would you like one?" Colton held out a bun.

Her hand didn't budge. She was too busy thinking about his chest to order her arm to move.

"I was telling your son about running into you yesterday." He turned back to Knox. "So you play guitar and... What was the other thing?"

"Bass in the school orchestra. I can also play the violin."

She wanted him to go before he destroyed everything

she held dear, but she couldn't order him to leave without making a scene and giving herself away. Protecting Knox was the only thing she cared about.

Colton let out a whistle. "Impressive. Who's your big influence?"

Knox shrugged. "Perlman and Menuhin for violin."

"Menuhin has the longest running contract with a music label in history. Not too many kids your age know about him."

"Anyone who cares about music should. More modern influences would be you." A flush climbed up Knox's neck.

"Wouldn't expect anything else. You have a smart kid, Harley."

"Of course he's smart, but that has nothing to do with you." Well, it had a little to do with him, but why split hairs?

"I like R&B and some blues too. That's what Mom listens to. She likes Motown and stuff. I kind of do too."

"Nothing wrong with that. My biggest influence was Clapton. Love his bluesy style."

Thank God Colton didn't say something stupid and arrogant about Knox's musical tastes. She would've hit him with a pot.

"Could I get a picture?"

"Fine by me." The corner of Colton's lip curled up. He puffed up his chest and swaggered those thin hips. Taking pictures with adoring fans never got old for him. "Mom, can I have my phone? Just for this? I'll only post it on Instagram. Please."

If she said no, then she'd be the worst mother in the world, having committed an indiscretion that could never be forgiven. If she said yes, she'd be going against her own rules. These were the moments when she missed Knox at five years old.

She fumbled through her purse looking for his phone. Was she sweating? She tried to take a discreet sniff. "You want me to take it?" She'd snap the photo if she could keep her hands from shaking.

Colton wrapped an arm around Knox's shoulder, and Knox did the same. Knox beamed. Her breath caught and nearly choked her while watching the two of them. Colton held up a thumb and flashed an oversized grin. *Ham.*

"See if you like it." She gave the phone to Knox.

"Great." He tapped at the screen and handed the phone back. "Thanks."

"Well, um, Colton, thanks for the visit, but I was about to run out." She was about to run to the bridge and drown herself in the water.

"You weren't going anywhere. You're wearing your ugly sweater." Knox grabbed another cinnamon bun from the box. "Thanks for the breakfast, Mr. Savage."

"*Colton*, bro. Just *Colton*."

Knox laughed. "Cool. Colton." He meandered out of the kitchen.

"I'm getting the impression you don't want me here." Colton split a roll in two.

"Perceptive. Please go." She pointed toward the door. Her heart still clamored around, but could not be still.

She wanted to sit down and put her head between her legs.

"You aren't eating your roll."

"This isn't a social visit. I'll pay to have your sweater cleaned, but you and I have nothing to say to each other anymore."

"Don't worry about the sweater. I've got plenty."

Of course he does. She couldn't carelessly toss a sweater to the side, especially not with the threat of losing her job looming over her.

"Thank you for the food, but please leave." She didn't want him this close and didn't want the image of him shirtless in her kitchen forever etched in her mind either.

"I want to hear more about your art relaxation class. Cash says it helps people. Is he right?"

Her legs had a mind of their own and dropped her in a chair. She pulled her bulky sweater closed. Why did he have to show up on comfy-clothes Sunday? Maybe if she gave him a little information he would leave.

"Art has been known to help people deal with stress and anxiety. Using the form of painting for relaxation allows adults and kids a way to unwind. Since stress is a major factor in so many problems, art helps lower stress levels and allows people to cope with what's going on in their lives."

"How long have you been at this?" He brought over the bakery box and took the chair opposite her. His long legs stretched out within inches of her own.

She pulled her legs up under her. "I've taught the relaxation classes about ten years now." She picked at another roll. The cereal she had earlier was long since forgotten. Her stomach betrayed her by making gurgling sounds loud enough for the entire town to hear.

"Are you some kind of a therapist?"

She'd never had the time to get her license. Life had been hard enough juggling a toddler and going to school for her teaching certificate, and somehow the years had blended into each other. "I'm just trying to give low-income kids and adults who can't afford private art lessons a chance to feel like they fit in."

"If I had some stress in my life—not much, but maybe some—could your art do something for me?

"What kind of stresses do you have in your life?" She tilted her head toward the ceiling and let out a loud sigh. He had money, fame, albeit fading, and a family who loved him. He'd had women in every corner of the world.

"Like I said, it's no big deal. I have everything under control, but Cash wants me to find an outlet. He worries like an old man. Have you seen the car he drives?" Colton shook his head. "He needs to get laid."

"Colton, that's your nephew you're talking about. You shouldn't be encouraging a young man his age to have sex."

"Why? I was having sex at his age, and aren't uncles good for buying beers and condoms? I always had to buy my own condoms, not that I minded. In my position, I couldn't have women everywhere claiming to have my baby."

Her throat dried up. "You don't think you ever made

a mistake, maybe fathered a baby? You've slept with most of the female population."

He narrowed his eyes. "Maybe we shouldn't talk about my past sex life."

You think, jackass? "Good idea."

"But I know there isn't a child of mine anywhere. I'm too smart to screw up like that."

She willed her face into neutral.

"I'd be a lousy father anyway, because I'd have to be the authority figure, and we both know I challenge authority every chance I get. Blaise can be the boring dad with rules. Fatherhood was never for me."

She'd made the right decision. He never wanted the burden of a family. They were better off without him in their lives.

"You said your class is full, but it didn't look full."

Her class size was a safer topic. Best to stay on it. "I try to keep the attendance down so I can help all the students."

"If I can't join your class, then I want to hire you."

She almost choked on the roll. "Oh no." She stood. "I'm not for hire." Even if the extra money would be nice, she could never handle leaning over his shoulder, smelling his rugged scent, and pretending everything was okay between them.

"Why not? I've got three weeks to kill before I go back on tour. Cash seems to think I need this. It's not like we don't know each other." He leaned forward and offered up a wink.

She put the chair between them. "That's the problem. We do know each other." She couldn't have him this close. It was too dangerous. Too much at stake.

"My nephew really wants me to do this. I hate to let that kid down. He's the only family member I'm getting along with right now."

She wanted to ask more but kept her mouth shut. She would not encourage him. "I could recommend someone else for you."

"No. I don't want to work with a stranger. I can't trust that they won't go bragging to some rag or social media site about my taking a class for stress. It's bad enough I spent thirty days in rehab. That hit the news, and Savage barely makes news these days."

That much was true. Savage became a band of the past when they stopped putting out new music. The fans bored of their old country-rock repertoire and moved on to newer sounds. "Why were you in rehab? Are you really okay?" She wanted him to be fine, even if he had to do it without her. His drinking had always been a problem, though. She wasn't surprised he managed to land in rehab again.

"I'm fine. It was a stupid mistake. Anyway, I'm willing to paint for Cash. He's trying to repair our broken family by fixing me first. I don't think all the painting in the world will do any good, but I can go along with his crazy idea if it makes him happy. It would be nice for you and me to spend some time together. Like old times."

She paced the kitchen. "This would not be like old times. Let's get that straight right away. I'm not that same person holding the door open for you to jump into her bed." She couldn't possibly be considering this, could she? But she wanted to help him find his way.

"Whoa." He threw his hands in the air. "Relax. I wasn't trying to proposition you, though if you were game, I wouldn't mind."

She growled. "Get out of my house. You are the most arrogant human being I've ever met."

He stood, but that lazy smile played games with her. "I'm sorry. Truce. Okay?"

She clamped her lips shut.

"Just friends. Nothing more. Three weeks. Private paint lessons. I'll pay your top price. You tell my nephew I'm doing better."

"I won't lie for you." No, but she'd lie to him, as if there were a difference. She needed to sit again. She might be sick.

"I'm not asking you to lie. That would be unethical, wouldn't it?"

She nodded, her arms crossed over her chest.

"Colton, if you need a therapist, there's no shame in talking to one." Maybe he'd be better served by meeting with a trained professional who could really help him with his demons. Her art classes might not be enough of the kind of help he needed. She didn't trust herself to give him support without hurting herself in the process.

"I don't need a therapist. I saw enough of one in rehab. Do we have a deal?"

"Why me?" She held his gaze and bit her tongue.

"Because I don't trust anyone else. Because you're a

fantastic artist. Because your kid thinks I'm a musical hero. I need more of that in my life at the moment."

"I don't want you influencing Knox. I want him to do something else with his life. Music is already taking him down the wrong road. Music isn't going to give him a reliable income or health benefits." And she wasn't a fantastic artist. She was second rate.

"Music has been good to me."

"Things are different now. Harder."

"I don't believe that. If you want something badly enough, you work your ass off for it. If he wants music, she'll be there with open arms. I can't believe you of all people are discouraging him from a life in music. You had dreams."

She stood again and started cleaning the kitchen. "That's all they were. Dreams. I couldn't make it, and believe me, I tried. I came back here with my tail between my legs, humiliated. Now I'm a mediocre art teacher in a small town, trying to raise my son and make ends meet. Not everything works out the way you dream. At least not for me. Maybe you, but not me."

"It's not too late for you either. Try again."

She threw the sponge in the sink. It bounced out. "It's way too late for me. That ship has sailed."

Why was she sharing so much with him? Her shoulders slumped. Talking with Colton had always been easy. They'd take long walks—he'd have a guitar slung over his back—and they'd end up at the bridge watching the sun set. They'd talk for hours. It was the only time she ever felt as if she were more than the girl abandoned by her mother. The coolest boy in town had liked her. *Her.*

"Enough talk about me. How is your family?" If he was going to stay planted in her kitchen, she could at least steer the conversation.

"Don't ask. Other than Cash, it's been a shit storm."

"You shouldn't keep your stressors bottled up." She reached for the untouched roll because, heck, it was from May's, and he grabbed her wrist. His touch sizzled against her skin.

"Give me art lessons, Harley." His gray eyes turned to ash.

Art lessons were too much to ask for. She made all kinds of mistakes when he was around. Colton had the power to make her lose common sense because her heart was driving. She had Knox to think about too. What kind of an example would she be setting for him?

He kept her wrist between his strong, calloused fingers. "It's only for three weeks, and then I'm out of your life for good. I want to give this to Cash so he can go on thinking I'm a good guy, and if you can shed some light on why I do stupid things, that's fine too, but I don't really need that part. I know who I am, and I don't apologize for that."

"You never did." Her words were a whisper.

"What do you say? Art lessons for an old friend?"

If it were only that simple.

Chapter Seven

Colton drove to the end of the Harley's drive and stopped. Not because cars were coming, but because his hands shook and his head buzzed. That impossibly stubborn and completely beautiful woman could still get under his skin.

He'd thought of her during long nights on the road when their tour bus would travel from town to town and sleep was nowhere in sight. Harley had been the only woman who fascinated him. Every other woman he'd been with hadn't come close to her, but there had never been the right time for a relationship. Savage had toured as much as they could. He owned a house in Bayton, but his home was the road. When she called with her endless highways, he didn't look back.

His sister would say his return to Heritage River was divine intervention. He would say an old man and his nephew needed to stop playing matchmaker. Colton shook his head. Those two together were cooking up trouble, but when he saw Harley in the classroom with wide, bright eyes and a flush across her face, he wanted to spend some time with her. Three weeks wouldn't hurt anything.

He turned onto the road and made his way back to Billy's. Looked like he'd be taking cold showers there for the next three weeks. With Harley nearby, he might need some cold water dumped on his head.

A vehicle took up residence in the driveway. A big dark truck that belonged to only one person he knew. He could back up and disappear, or he could get out and deal with what was waiting for him.

He threw the pickup in reverse, but before he could look over his shoulder, his brother appeared at the top of the porch steps. Blaise had been waiting for him. Colton had missed him in the sun's shadows covering the porch.

Blaise cupped his hands around his mouth and yelled. "You can't keep running away from me. You're going to have to talk to me eventually."

"Bullshit," he said under his breath. He didn't get far, though. Another vehicle pulled in behind him and blocked him. The dark red sedan stopped. Billy and Hoke Carter stared at him before pushing their way out of the car.

"You going someplace?" Billy walked over to him. "Did you put gas in my truck while you were out?"

"I was heading out to do that now." He resisted the urge to hang his head. He was in a damn *Twilight Zone* episode.

Billy patted the door. "You can do that later. We've got ourselves some guests, and we're going to be humble hosts. You remember how to be humble, don't you? Park it over there." He pointed to the empty spot beside Blaise's truck.

Colton gritted his teeth and threw the truck in park. He was almost fifty years old, a recovering alcoholic and a famous rock musician, but when he was around Billy, he felt like a sixteen-year-old kid getting caught in the liquor cabinet. He twisted the keys out of the ignition and shoved the door open.

Blaise stood before him. He stared into his brother's eyes, and it was like staring in a mirror and seeing his own eyes reflected back. Blaise had been his best friend his entire life, and now he couldn't find the words he wanted to say because anger fogged out his brain.

"Hey." Apparently, Blaise didn't know what to say either.

Billy patted Blaise's shoulder. "I've got some apple cider if you'd like. Or I can make some coffee. Need to warm up these old bones. The house is dry, so don't go thinking you're getting any whiskey."

Blaise smiled. "Not me, sir. I gave up drinking a long time ago."

"Wise boy. Maybe you'll rub off on your brother."

"No, sir. Colton is his own man."

"Come on, Hoke. These boys have some talking to do."

"Afternoon, boys." Hoke hiked up his pants.

"Hoke," they said in unison.

75

"Billy, make my coffee strong. Lu's got the coffeepot under lock and key. Says it's bad for my ticker. I have to sneak around my wife like a raccoon in the garbage."

The old men laughed. Colton shook his head. Billy eased himself up the front porch, and Hoke followed. The screen door slapped shut.

"That's going to be us someday." Blaise tipped his chin in the direction the men went.

"Fuck that."

"Cash told me you were here." Blaise looked off in the direction of the lake.

The water's surface gleamed like glass. The afternoon sun shone bright and strong, but the still air had a bite to it. A fire burned somewhere in the distance.

"That boy masterminded a whole plan, didn't he?" Colton's fingers played chords on the side of his leg. He had to hand it to his nephew. Cash was nothing if not determined. But he couldn't fix what was wrong with their family. Nothing was going to fix that anymore. Too many lines had been crossed.

"Why did you turn me away when I came to visit you at the rehab?"

"There was nothing to say, like there's nothing to say now." He had avoided Blaise's visits. His therapist said Colton would be wise to speak with his brother, but ultimately it was up to Colton, and his therapist didn't know dick about your brother ditching their band for some quiet life and acoustic playing.

"I'm sorry about leaving the tour."

"You've said." They'd been down this road a hundred times since the end of the summer.

"Are you going to stay mad at me forever?"

"Maybe."

"Christ, Colton. You knew the day would come when the band would break up. We couldn't keep going on without writing new music. No one wants to hear our old shit. We needed to reinvent ourselves."

"Under Fire didn't."

Blaise raised an eyebrow. "That's the band you're going to compare us to? They suck, but at least they put out new stuff once in a while. We were the best once, and you're still the best damn guitarist on the planet. Come and listen to me and Cash play. You could jam with us."

"No fucking way. You and me, we're through. You walked away, and I can't forgive that. Our band is the most important thing in our lives. If you don't feel that way anymore, then I have no place for you. I've got guys lining up a mile long waiting to play with me. I'm hitting the road again without you. I don't need you."

"You are such a jerk. My son is the most important thing in my life, and I had been too stupid to realize that until Grace stepped into my life. Your problem is you've never loved anyone except yourself."

"I love Cash."

Blaise put his hand up. "I know you do, but it's not the same. You can love him at a distance, where it's safe. You stopped putting your heart into your music a long time ago, and the fans knew it. I knew it. Patrick and Troy knew it too, but they were just too scared to say anything to you, and I was too busy following my big brother around. Find your heart again, man. I'd like to have my brother back. I miss the hell out of him."

"You're throwing bullshit. I've had my heart in my music my entire life. It's because of my heart that we made it as far as we did. I dragged all your sorry asses along. Me." He pounded his chest with his finger.

Blaise shook his head. "That might have been the truth once, but no more. You're stuck, and your last drinking binge showed it. Are you getting the help Cash wants you to?"

"He told you that too?" Colton yanked his cigarettes out of his jacket pocket and lit up.

"When are you going to stop smoking?"

"When you get the fuck out of my face." He blew smoke at Blaise.

Blaise waved the smoke away. "Okay, I'll go. You aren't ready to talk. I'm here when you are. I'll always be here for you. I love you." He took a few steps but stopped. "I hope you change your mind about coming to see us. We're playing in White Oaks at the brewery, if you're interested."

Colton threw the cigarette down and smashed it with his boot. Blaise turned his truck around and drove out of sight.

Family was more trouble than it was worth. He turned to find Billy staring at him from the porch. "What?"

"First, you're going to pick your trash up from my

property, and second, you're going to forgive your brother if I have to beat it into you."

Colton bent down and picked up his butt. "Better put your boxing gloves on, old man, because it will be a cold day in hell before I forgive Blaise."

Billy slammed the door on him.

"Christ." He needed a drink. He searched for the stupid word rehab told him to say when he felt stress. *Calm.* Who's screwed-up idea was it to repeat *calm* over and over?

He marched up the porch steps and shut the screen door behind him. Hoke and Billy were arguing in the kitchen about some football game, but they stopped and turned their stares on him. His hands ached from the cold, and his head hurt from fighting with Blaise. He wanted to go back to his life before Savage tanked. Instead, he looked over and found Billy filling out the doorway to the kitchen.

"You can't keep running away from the stuff that gets under your skin. It follows you."

"No disrespect, but not now." Colton swiped up his duffel and guitar and pushed his way back outside, with Billy fast on his heels.

"Where you headed?"

He swung around in the driveway and faced Billy. "Stop your meddling. What did you think you and Cash were doing bringing me to Harley?"

"I'm trying to save you before you kill yourself. Are you going to take her art classes?"

"No." He couldn't stay in Heritage River, not with

his family around every corner. Cash would have to get over it. He was going to his big, empty house for the next three weeks.

"That girl is good for you. She can set you straight. You need that."

Colton stopped. "You aren't trying to set me and Harley back up, are you? That will never happen." She didn't want him like that anymore. "I'm not sticking around this one-act town. And you know what I really do need? A drink." He marched down the drive.

"Let me drive you wherever you're going," Billy yelled.

If it had been anyone else, he would've given him the finger. But it was Billy, and no matter what, Colton wouldn't hurt him.

"I don't need a ride. I got it under control." He had no idea where he was going. He didn't even have a car.

"You haven't had anything under control in a mighty long time, son. Come back inside and have some supper with us."

He kept going. He didn't need anyone. He'd been proving that his entire life. He was Colton Savage, for Christ's sake. He could do anything. He'd taken the world by storm. He'd do it again.

He marched down the drive. He punched numbers on his phone, but the call didn't go through. The phone showed one bar for cellular service. "I hate this fucking place."

He moved down the tree-lined road and tried again. The phone began to ring, and then the screen went black.

"What the hell?" His finger punched the screen. He tried all the buttons. Nothing. The battery died.

He had two choices. Go back to Billy's and see if his phone was working to call for a car service or keep walking into town and use a phone there. He wasn't going back to Billy's even if his life depended on it. He wasn't mad at Billy. He was mad at Blaise and had taken it out on Billy. He wasn't in the mood to eat crow. That left going into town as his only choice. He didn't want to see anyone he knew, and there would be no way to avoid it in town.

The smallness of Heritage River pressed on his lungs. He reached into his pocket and yanked out his smokes. His last vice. He took a huge drag and let his shoulders drop. The sun dropped below the treetops. The evening air cooled down more, and a breeze picked up. Gray clouds rolled in from the west. Colton zipped his jacket and flipped up the collar. He had a long walk before he saw civilization.

The rev of an engine approached. He wouldn't turn around as he kept his course down the road. *Keep going.* Billy was probably fast on his heels, ready to drag him back and knock some sense into him, but Colton already had sense. He didn't want to fix anything with Blaise. Blaise hurt him in a way that couldn't be undone. Taking the tour away from him was like stealing his girl. Worse.

The vehicle slowed beside him, forcing Colton to turn in its direction. He took another drag of the cigarette.

"Those things are going to kill you." Adam Montgomery looked over at him from his dusty Ford Fusion. His face was thinner than it had been last summer. It might be December and no one was sporting a tan, but his skin looked more like the color of a cadaver. Dark moons hung under his eyes.

Colton saluted his brother-in-law with the cigarette. "Something's going to." He kept walking. There was no easy way to explain why he was walking on the side of the road in Heritage River, and as certain as Colton knew how to play chords, Adam would be on the phone to Savannah spilling his whereabouts.

"I know you're not lost. You having car trouble or something?"

"Considering I don't have a car at the moment, yeah."

"Hop in. I'll take you wherever you're going."

Colton stopped. "I appreciate it, but picking me up might not be in your best interest."

"My wife doesn't have to know everything I do."

"I'm not getting in between you and my sister. She's madder than a pig in a shower about last summer. I've had enough of her wrath. I figured you'd be pissed at me too."

"Get in, Colton. You look like an ass walking on the side of the road."

Colton put out his cigarette on the bottom of his boot and tossed it. He dumped his stuff in the back and slid in beside Adam. A car freshener in the shape of a candle dangled from the rearview mirror and coated the inside of the car with its pumpkin scent. The car was neat and clean.

Adam took off down the road, putting distance between them and Billy's place. "I'm not mad at you. I'm mad at myself for not being a better father and seeing what my son was up to right in his own family. You did the right thing, though Savannah doesn't see it that way. She's a protective mother bear and blinded by her love for her children. She'll come around. There are more important things to worry about in this life than the mistakes our children make."

"Yeah? Like what?" Savannah held family in the highest regard, nothing else compared. When their mother died, she took on the role of mother hen even at her young age. She took care of her brothers and their father. She slid into the role of wife to Adam and mother to her three kids without a hitch and thrived on it. No one was better at family than his sister.

"Where do you want to go?" Adam turned onto Meadow Lane.

"You didn't answer my question. What's more important to Savannah than her kids?"

"Nothing. Where can I drop you?"

"Are you and Savannah having trouble?" Their marriage wasn't any of his business. He should stay out of it, but trouble at home might be the reason why Adam looked as if he'd seen past his best days.

"We're fine."

Adam could tell him or not. He'd protect his sister if she needed him to, but he wouldn't step on a man's pride.

"I was heading to Chester's to pick up some light-bulbs, duct tape, and a new hose."

"You aren't trying to fix things again, are you?"

Adam slid him a sideways glance. "We can't all be Mr. Fixer-Upper like you. You want to come for the ride, and then I'll drop you someplace? Are you staying with Blaise?"

That was a laugh. "I wasn't planning on being in town. Can I use your phone? Mine's dead."

Adam handed over his phone, but Colton couldn't remember the number for his assistant. He only ever punched in his name. "You have a charger?"

"Nope. The kids are always taking it out." Adam turned onto Main Street. The road was bustling with Christmas shoppers. Every store was lit up in white lights, and a big Christmas tree decorated with red ornaments stood tall at the town square.

Colton wanted the car to swallow him up. No way he could blend in or not be noticed with this crowd. He wanted to get away from Billy's, and he landed himself right in the middle of Heritage River's Christmas rush.

Adam found a place to park. "Do you want to wait here?"

"Can I smoke in your car?"

Adam raised his eyebrows. "Have you met your sister?"

Colton shoved his way out of the car. Adam unfolded himself from the driver's seat but stopped halfway to hack up a lung.

"Are you all right?"

Adam waved him away. Tears spilled down his red

84

face. Spit dripped from his lips. The coughing fought its way free. Would he have to call an ambulance?

Adam caught his breath. "Sorry about that. I got a tickle in the back of my throat."

That was more than a tickle. "I'll come with you into Chester's." If anything happened to Adam in there and Savannah found out Colton was present, she'd start talking to him, if only to kill him.

"Have your smoke. I'm fine." He turned away before Colton could say another word.

The man said he was fine. He hoped that was true, but he knew better. He leaned against the Focus and lit up. Christmas music piped through the PA system the town installed along the street. His ears hurt. No music was worse than Christmas music.

How long had Adam been sick? Had he been to a doctor? How much did Blaise know? He had more questions, but if he asked Savannah, she wasn't going to answer them. And if she needed help, she wouldn't ask.

"Oh my God, is that Colton Savage?" a female voice screeched from somewhere behind him.

He swung his head in the direction of the caw. He'd become lost in his thoughts and forgot standing on the street in town was the same as standing on stage. Everyone was a fan.

Dixie Bordeaux, the local realtor, barreled up the street toward him, dressed like a roll of round, hard candy in her red down coat. She planted a big pink lipstick kiss on his cheek. She smelled like funeral flowers. "We haven't seen you since the summer." She leaned in and lowered her voice. "I heard about the trouble with Cash and Jud. A shame, that is. I'm sure they'll work things out. How's your sister?"

He widened his stance and projected his voice. "You know Savannah—kicking ass and taking names." He smirked when Dixie paled under her painted-on face. He would never tell her his family's secrets. She'd spread them like apricot preserves on toast.

He checked over his shoulder for Adam. Where the hell was he? Colton was ready to get off this street and back on the road. Maybe Adam could drop him at the bus station.

"Spending the holidays with your family? Your brother's lady friend is lovely. I never thought she'd fit in like she does, but the town has taken a shine to her. Do you think they'll get married? Wouldn't a spring wedding be nice? Oh, look at me, going on. What brings you back to town?"

He pulled out a cigarette, lit it, and blew a puff of smoke out of the side of his mouth. "I drank myself into a stupor again since my brother left our band permanently and forced me into early retirement. I crashed into a fence on someone's property in a town much like this one, where a pissant judge with a hatred for musicians decided my punishment would be thirty days in a shithole rehab. I was ready to go home and never return to this place, but Billy Lewis saw fit to abduct me. He's holding me prisoner until I agree to marry the child bride he shipped in or until I agree to become a celibate monk who never utters another fucking curse word and gives up whiskey."

Dixie stumbled back as if Colton's words had shoved her. She blinked. He reached out a hand, afraid she might fall over, but she didn't notice. Instead, she unzipped the candy roll of a coat and fanned herself. "You're pulling my leg, Colton Savage. You always were a kidder."

He took another drag. "I can't fool you." He winked. She might've blushed, but he couldn't tell from all that pink paint on her cheeks.

He checked again for Adam's return. Instead, he found something better peering in the window of the empty shop two doors down from Jake's deli. "Hey, Harley," he shouted.

Harley turned in circles in search of the person calling her. She found his gaze and made a small *o* with her lips. She juggled the brown bags she carried.

Dixie turned and waved Harley over. *Thank you, Dixie.* Okay, he shouldn't have teased her so much.

"What are you two up to?" Harley saddled up alongside him. She kept her gaze on Dixie.

Her smell of honeysuckle drifted toward him. Her scent and her closeness made his lower belly strum a favorite tune. He took a drag on his cigarette to settle down the memory of her beneath him. "Dixie is getting me up to speed on the local gossip."

Dixie waved his words away with a big smile. "Not really. We're just having a few laughs. I'll be on my way. I have an open house in an hour. That cute little bungalow on Willow Street is for sale again. It's a perfect house for a bachelor, Colton."

"Oh no, not me. Heritage River doesn't want me moving back in."

Dixie laughed and shoved his arm. "Colton, you are such a kidder, sugar. Merry Christmas." She and her coat waddled away.

Finally, he had Harley to himself.

"Well, I've got to get home." She offered a thin smile.

"Wait." He reached out and took her arm, and she nearly dropped her bag. "Have you thought about giving me those art lessons?"

"I'll call you tomorrow after school. Merry Christmas." She turned to go.

"Why won't you say yes to me?" Sure, they were older, and maybe she was tired of his dropping in and out of her life, but didn't she still have feelings for him? She'd never said no before. He couldn't push his feelings for her aside that easily.

"Hey, Colton."

He nearly hung his head. He'd forgotten about Adam.

"You still need a ride?" Adam held a plastic bag in one hand. The skin around his eyes was darker than before. "Hi, Harley."

"Hi, Adam. It's nice to see you."

Was she glad to see *him*? All she'd been doing was trying to get away from him. "Harley's going to take me."

She squinted at him. "What? Oh, I can't give you a

ride, really. I have to pick up Knox, and we have errands to run."

He tried to ease a bag out of her arm, but she held on tighter. "Adam has to get back home. Savannah is waiting for him. I don't want him to get in trouble because of me. What do you say?"

Adam patted him on the shoulder and laughed. "Nothing changes in this town. I'll be seeing y'all." He opened the back door and handed over Colton's duffel and guitar before easing in behind the wheel and backing into traffic.

"Now he's going to go tell your sister we're hanging together. I don't need that rumor running around this town." Harley leaned in and hissed. "I must be crazy. Let's go." She marched down the street to the Durango. "You're not smoking that thing in my car." She pushed the brown bags into the back of the truck.

He shoved his belongings in beside the bags then dropped the cigarette onto the street and smashed it with his boot.

"Really, Colton?"

"What?"

"The earth isn't your ashtray." She pressed the button for the hatch to drop. "Are you going to pick it up?"

"No."

She opened the hatch again, yanked some paper towels out from a compartment in the side, and shoved them at him. "Pick it up. You're nobody special here. There isn't a fan lurking in the corner, hoping to grab your nasty cigarette off the street as a souvenir." She stormed around the driver's side and slid in.

He stood there, staring at the back of her head. His fist gripped the paper until it was nothing more than a ball in his hand. If he didn't pick up the cigarette, he'd look like an ass, but if he did, she'd think she won. He gritted his teeth and scooped it up. He stomped over to the garbage and dumped his trash.

He met her gaze and sneered.

She threw her head back and laughed.

Chapter Eight

Harley grabbed her purse off the floor of the SUV's passenger side and tossed it in the back with the extra clothes she kept there—in case a crisis ever ensued— and the art supplies she liked to have handy. Letting Colton sit this close to her was probably a mistake, but the words had jumped out of her mouth before she could stop them.

"Do you live out of your truck?" He slid in beside her, smelling of cigarette smoke. His legs filled in the space between the seat and the dash. His jeans pulled tight against his muscular legs.

Stop looking.

"I like to be prepared. You stink." She lowered his window.

"You're still a mess. You have paint on your neck." He laughed with the confidence and ease that fit him like a second skin.

She had never been that sure of herself. Well, except

91

when his arm had been around her and he held her close. His confidence would rub off on her, and she could forget for a minute she had a mother who never loved her. A mother she hadn't seen in over forty years.

She swatted at the paint on her neck. "Where can I take you?" Hopefully, it wasn't far. She didn't want to be this close to him longer than she had to.

"That depends. If you'll give me art lessons, I need a place in town. If you refuse, then drop me at the bus station. I'm going home."

She held the power to keep him in Heritage River. He'd never left that decision up to her when she wanted it. Now that it would be better if he left for good so she could go back to the life she'd created, the safe—well, as safe as an eggshell—life, she could keep him with one word.

"You say you're getting back on the road in three weeks?"

"Right after Christmas. You'll never have to see me again after that."

She could handle three weeks, couldn't she? How many art lessons could he really want? After the first one or two, he'd get bored. She could teach him at the college, where he and Knox wouldn't cross paths. The extra money would be helpful, especially this time of year, and with the threat of losing her job, she could add celebrity client to her resume.

"Is Billy willing to put you up for three more weeks?"

His dimple showed. "So that means yes. Cool. What about your guesthouse? Can I rent that out?"

"Oh no. No way." She turned her gaze back to the road and choked the steering wheel with both hands.

"Why not? It's perfect. Your house is out of the way. I won't run into anyone there, and I won't have to stay in Billy's old place with his cold shower. Don't you have your art studio there?"

"Colton, I'm not renting Hank's house to you. Forget it. You'll have to ask Dixie if that house she's selling is for rent if you don't want to stay with Billy."

"Come on, Harley. I can't stay in town. I'm not getting along with Blaise or Savannah right now. You know how it is here. I'll be running into them every other minute."

"Why are you fighting with your siblings?" She would give anything to even have a sibling to fight with. Growing up, she'd envied the Savage family. They took care of each other. What could've come between them?

He stared out the window into the dark night lit only by the Christmas lights framing the houses. The sun had said goodbye to the short day while she was waiting for Colton to throw out his cigarette. He'd taken her challenge—so unlike him.

"You're not going to tell me what's going on between you, Blaise, and Savannah, are you?" He never did anything he didn't want to.

"It's nothing you have to worry about. So what do you say? Can I rent your guesthouse?"

"I still don't understand this newfound interest in art or me." Why couldn't he have been this persistent years ago? It was probably because she'd practically begged him to stay back then, but he didn't want to be tied down to a relationship when his wildest dreams were waiting to seduce him.

"I'm just trying to keep my nephew and Billy happy. If I do what they ask, they'll stop nagging at me. There's that, and I have some time to kill. Idle time causes problems for us drunks, you know."

"Don't talk about yourself like that." He had a disease, which was nothing to be ashamed of.

He never fooled her with his false bravado. He'd been running from the void his father created in him. This fight between him and his siblings must have bust that hurt open even wider.

"Why, Miss Harley, I do declare you might still care about me."

She couldn't help but laugh. "You're ridiculous." She stole a glance at him. Her fingers remembered the silky touch of his hair. They long to find out if it still felt that way.

"I'm taking that laugh as a yes." He rubbed his hands together and wagged his eyebrows.

She was going to regret this decision. "There's going to be some ground rules if you're renting my guesthouse."

"I wouldn't expect anything less."

"Don't be sarcastic."

He sat up straighter. "I'm not. Ms. Kenyon, what are your rules?"

She shot him a look. His smile filled up his face again. She wouldn't smile back. He'd already gained too much ground with his charm. She had to stay somewhat strong.

"Other than when we're working on art together, you need to stay on your side of the property. In fact, you will take lessons at my classroom at the community college. No coming to the house uninvited. This arrangement isn't a friendship. It's strictly business."

"So I guess a blowjob is out of the question?"

She veered into the shoulder and slammed on the brakes. "Get out of my truck."

His laughter filled the inside of the SUV. "Relax, Harley. I'm joking. I get it. It's all business."

Her heart pounded on her ribs, reminding her she had stepped into dangerous territory. "Don't talk to me like that. It's not like it used to be between us."

The smile dropped off his face, and his eyes clouded over. "Okay. Sorry. Bad joke."

She pulled back into traffic. "There's one more thing. No influencing my son about music."

"I don't think he needs me. He's into music all by himself. And he's got good taste too."

"You would say that."

"Come on, babe. Admit it. Who's better than me?"

"Do not call me 'babe.' I'm not your babe, and another thing—"

He put a hand up to stop her. "Would it be okay if we didn't fight right now?" His long, heavy breath made her look away from the road. The fingers on his left hand tapped on his leg. "I can't argue with one more person today."

"Fine." She turned on the radio to the oldies rock station. A Savage song filled the cab.

Colton reached over and turned it off. "No music. My head hurts."

"You don't want to hear your own songs? Since when?"

"Since my brother abandoned our band and my car made love to a fence. Tell me what you've been up to instead." He leaned his head against the seat rest and closed his eyes.

"You want me to tell you what I've been up to for the past eighteen years or just recently, because we're going to be at the house in about five minutes. We might not have time for the entire recap." She tried to hide the sarcasm from her voice, but it slid in and stole the win.

"Let's start with recent stuff. You can beat me over the head with the past eighteen years another time."

Ouch. "Sorry. I went too far."

"Hey, it's just Colton. He can take it. He's the big bad musician with no feelings except for himself, right?"

"I didn't say that."

"What did you say, then?"

Harley turned into the drive, and the Durango bumped along the dirt. The golden glow from the house spilled into the night, cracking open its opaqueness. The guesthouse would be cold inside. She'd kept the heat low to save on the electric bill. She parked and cleared her throat.

"I'm sorry for being so tough on you. You've been through enough." He didn't need her to remind him of how his behavior affected his decisions. He was a grown man. He could see what he was doing without any help from her. "I'll grab the key and meet you by the guest-house." She shoved open the door to slide out, but Colton grabbed her wrist. His touch sent shivers across her skin.

"Does this art stuff really work?"

"If you let it. If you fight it, you'll say I don't know what I'm talking about." She thought of poor Andy Henson who fought her every step of the way. She needed to find a way to rescue that boy from the pressures he put on himself. Apparently, she was doing a lot of rescuing if giving Colton art lessons was now in her plan.

"I have never said you didn't know what you're talking about. In fact, you might be the only person I know who does." He looked at her with a storm brewing in his eyes. His deep voice was raspy and made her belly flutter.

She fought free of the electricity charging the space between them. "I'll meet you in a few minutes."

She hurried through the front door, afraid to look back. If she saw him watching her, she'd lose all control and run back to him. She forced herself forward through the house.

"Knox, I'm home." She'd forgotten her bags in the car. The sandwiches from Eat at Jake's should be fine for a while. It was cold enough out. She, on the other hand, burned from the inside out.

Knox shuffled out of the kitchen, a piece of bread in his hand. "I'm hungry. What are we going to have for dinner?"

She opened her mouth to tell him to grab the bags but stopped. "I picked something up."

"Good. I thought you were going to try and cook."

"Listen, smarty-pants, I can cook."

He raised an eyebrow at her. The look took her breath away. There was so much of him that wasn't her, but now was not the time to think about it with Colton waiting outside. "Did you do your homework?"

"It's Sunday."

She rummaged through the junk drawer in the kitchen for the extra key to Hank's place. Over her shoulder, she said, "Wouldn't hurt to get ahead of things."

"When are you going to take me off this house arrest? I want to go hang at Tim's house. We're going to jam."

She gripped the key in her hand. "When you're ready for retirement." She pushed past him.

"Is that Uncle Hank's key? Are you letting someone stay in the house? Please tell me it's Colton Savage." Knox ran down the hall after her.

She stopped, one hand on the door. Did she tell him now or later? Hadn't that been the question stuck in her throat all these years? "He's renting the guesthouse for three weeks. I don't want you to bother him. He isn't here to play music. Do you understand?"

"Wait till I tell Tim. I'd text him if you'd give me my phone back."

"Forget it." She pulled open the door. The cold air blasted her.

"Can I go to Tim's?" Knox yelled at her back.

"No." She yelled into the wind.

Was she being unreasonable? He'd served his suspension. It had been a few weeks since he showed up at school stinking of alcohol, but that had scared her in a way nothing else had. He was coming home straight after orchestra practice and staying in his room. She knew he was doing his homework because she was checking. Still, she wasn't ready to return his freedoms.

Colton had climbed the stairs to the porch of the guesthouse and stamped his feet outside the front door.

"I'm freezing my nuts off out here."

Might do him some good. "You're worse than a child. Step aside." In the dark, she fumbled with the key in the lock.

"Let me." His fingers covered hers as he slipped the key from her hand. His rough skin left a sizzling trail against her fingers.

She looked up into his eyes. They stood inches apart. His breath made white steam puffs in the air. Late-day scruff covered his chin. She wanted to reach up and run her fingertips over it, feel the prickly tips scratch her skin.

She took a step back.

He dropped the key.

They both bent to grab it and banged heads.

"Ow."

"Hey."

She rubbed her head and caught his contagious laughter. "Let's try that again."

This time the door swung open wide. He waited for her to enter first. The inside of the guesthouse wasn't much warmer than outside. She switched on a lamp in the living room and made her way to the thermostat. "There's wood by the fireplace if you want to light a fire."

She hurried into the bedroom and the bath. Everything looked in place. "There are clean towels in the linen closet, and the sheets are clean on the bed. Everything is new." The tasks of removing her uncle's belongings and replacing them with new things made the mourning process easier. Her heart ached without him. Knox was her only family now.

She had been grateful for her aunt and uncle taking her in when her mother decided motherhood wasn't in her list of skills and abandoned her before her first birthday. Her aunt and uncle loved her like their own. But now they were both gone, and Knox wasn't far from leaving her for good. And if music got her hooks in him, Harley may never see her son again. She'd already lost Colton to music. How would she handle losing her son to the same temptation?

"I'm afraid the cabinets are bare. If you want food, you'll have to shop for it. Hank had his meals with us, but, but—"

"I know. No fraternizing." He tossed his duffel on the couch and leaned his guitar against the wall. "Thanks. This is great. Better than Billy's."

"You never asked about the rent."

"Doesn't matter. Whatever you want is fine."

That was a loaded statement. "Normally, I'd rent by the month. I'll have to do a little math to figure out three weeks. Math isn't my thing."

"Just charge me for the month, babe."

"Stop calling me that." She didn't mean to yell. Or maybe she did. "I can't work with you if you keep saying that. I have to keep this professional, Colton." Because anything else would unhinge her and the life she'd so carefully stacked. "I can't handle another one of our let's-sleep-together-for-now situations. I won't do that anymore. I'm worth more than that, even if you don't think so."

The hairs on her neck stood up. What had she said? She turned to go and tripped over the corner of the coffee table. Colton's strong hands caught her.

"Careful." He eased her back up. His gaze pinned her to the spot. "Harley, you're worth more than you know, but nothing is going to happen between us. You don't want that, and getting involved with anyone is a bad idea for me right now. You don't have to worry about me coming on to you."

No, she needed to worry about herself. "I teach the art club on Tuesdays until six. Be there by quarter after. We'll start your lessons then."

"Six fifteen. Sure."

"How many times a week?"

"Every day? Might as well make the most of my time."

She clasped her hands together and tried to find a place to settle her gaze. "Okay. Some days will have to be here. I don't have the space at the college every day. Um, I charge for lessons."

"No problem. Just give me the bill on Tuesday. I'll pay you up front."

101

"You can pay at the end."

"Nah, I trust you."

Famous last words. "Good night, Colton."

"Night." He hesitated, and she turned on her heel to leave him. "Harley." She turned back. "Thanks."

"You're welcome." She was on a runaway train she didn't want to get off.

Chapter Nine

Colton lit a fire in the small guesthouse to give himself something to do. He could take one step and be in every room. It wasn't his house in Bayton—that was for sure—but at least the water ran warm here, unlike at Billy's, and he'd have time to himself.

Did he want time to himself? The shrink at rehab didn't want him to spend too much time alone because boredom could lead to drinking. He'd be better off at Billy's and should go there right now to stop himself from doing anything stupid, but he wanted to see Harley again. Being here would let him do that. The art lessons would make Cash happy, a bonus.

What would Hank say about him living in his place? He'd be pissed. He was never one of Hank's favorite people. He had that effect on a lot of people. Screw them. He'd made it big all on his own. He didn't need anyone.

His phone belted out the chords to one of his guitar solos. He hesitated to pick it up, but if he didn't, there'd be hell to pay. He swiped the screen and hit the speaker button.

"Yeah?"

"Where are you? I've been searching this whole town for you. You haven't answered your phone neither. I have a right mind to pummel you."

"Hello, Billy. I'm at Harley's, just like you wanted."

"I didn't say to move into her house. Just take those art-class things Cash told me about. Are you completely batty staying with her?"

"I'm going to rent the guesthouse."

"Hank's place? Dear God, what have you done?"

"I haven't done anything. What's the big deal? We're both adults. If I'm going to take those lessons, I can't drive back and forth from my place. This makes Cash happy."

"Don't cause that girl trouble. She's had enough of it. You hear me?"

"Christ, Billy. What do you think I'm going to do to her? And you and Cash set this whole thing in motion. If you'd just let me go the hell home like I wanted, I wouldn't be here now. Make up your mind."

"Just don't go causing her any trouble, is all." Billy ended the call.

Colton wiped a hand over his face. What did that man want from him? To get healed or to go away?

He kicked off his boots and dropped onto the couch, letting his weight sink into the cushions. He closed his eyes. The smell of wood smoke filled the room. His body ached from the long day, and the joints in his fingers complained. He made fists, hoping to stretch them out. His stomach growled, but he was too damn tired to get up. Harley wasn't going to let him borrow her truck anyway. He'd make arrangements for his car tomorrow. He'd get some food then.

That woman was going to be the end of him. He could still feel her soft skin under his fingers as he tried to take the key from her. His mind turned to the feel of her arms and legs around him. Thinking about the past caused trouble. She was done with him now. She believed he'd made his choice—and he had. He wouldn't have turned his chance down for anyone. She could've come along, but she had wanted to stay in Heritage River and make a go of her art.

He sat up. Her artwork was all around the place. He recognized her style in the art on the walls. Worn wood frames surrounded small pieces in soft, warm colors, like photographs. She always used soft colors. She liked to paint grass blowing in the wind, bare trees, and their bridge.

Her touch was everywhere in the small space. The tin box on the coffee table was filled with glass jars. The dented metal bowl on the white kitchen counter and the distressed stools in front of that counter were all her.

He checked the cabinets. Sure enough, they were empty of food. Only plates and glasses. The stainless steel fridge had been wiped clean. The place might be small, but it was updated and neat. She'd taken care of the house and probably Hank too. How was she holding up without him? How had the last years been for her? Was she struggling for money? How did she end up a single mom?

When he thought about her late at night on long rides on the tour bus, he never imagined her as a mother or even alone. He only thought about what had happened between them, the way she looked at him when he played, or what it might be like to bump into her somewhere. He always wanted her to be happy. He couldn't picture her everyday life.

The television provided no relief. He couldn't stay focused on any one thing. He turned it off. Hank had some books on a shelf tucked into the wall, but none of the mysteries caught his attention. Now what?

He stared at the Gibson. The guitar case was giving him the middle finger. He could take the guitar out and strum some Savage songs, maybe even put down a different solo for one of their better hits, but there would be no new songs. He hadn't wanted to write in over a decade, no matter how hard he tried, and he'd tried.

No one knew this, not even Blaise, but he'd even taken piano lessons again just to see if going back to his classical-music roots would inspire him. Nothing.

He'd written everything he had to say. Whatever inspired him in the beginning was gone. He feared the drinking had been the only inspiration, and he wasn't about to admit that to anyone.

His head pounded. He was Colton Savage. Why the

hell couldn't he write a decent stinking song? He tried counting to ten with deep breaths to stop the need for a drink.

When that didn't work, he grabbed his coat and barreled down the steps and headed across the lawn. The lights were still on downstairs. He knocked on the back door.

Knox yanked it open. "Hey, Mr. Savage. Is there something I can help you with?"

"Seriously, you need to call me 'Colton.' Mr. Savage makes me think of my old man."

"Sure, uh, Colton. Come in. Mom's upstairs." Knox held the door open.

The kid had Harley's light hair and high cheekbones. They shared the same wide-set eyes. He saw her in Knox's smile. Colton stepped in, not entirely sure what he was doing there. It had been impulsive to march across the lawn. Now he'd need to come up with an excuse.

"Hey, Mom, Colton is here." Knox yelled from the bottom of the steps.

And he'd better come up with one fast.

Harley hurried into the room. She'd changed into plaid pajama pants and a big sweatshirt that swallowed her up. Her hair was tied up on the top of her head. Her scrubbed-clean look made his belly tighten.

She scrunched her face up at him. "Did you break something?"

"Why do you think I broke something?"

She crossed her arms over her chest and pressed her lips together. Was she wearing a bra? He needed to stop thinking like that, or it wouldn't just be his stomach feeling tight.

"Knox, don't you have some homework to finish?" She raised her eyebrows at the kid.

"I did it." Knox smirked.

"Double-check it."

"No way. I'm staying."

"Knox." She shot him the stern look that mothers mastered. He'd seen Savannah shoot that same look at her kids.

Knox shoved in his earbuds and marched away. Before she said anything else, his guitar playing drifted down to them.

"He's a good player." Colton tilted his chin up toward the ceiling.

"Thank you. What can I do for you? Is the heat not working?"

"The place is fine."

"What are you doing here? Wasn't I clear earlier?"

The emptiness of the small place had closed in on him. He was hardly ever alone anymore. And the last thirty days in rehab, he had a roommate snoring and farting all night. He thought he couldn't wait to be alone, and the second he was, he wanted to fill the space up with anything to block all the thoughts in his head.

"Can I grab a snack? I'll have my car tomorrow. Then I'll go buy my own food. I didn't think you'd want to lend me the Durango to go get something now."

"You're right about that much." She opened and closed cabinets maybe a little too hard. She pulled out bags and boxes and dumped them on the island. "Take your pick."

He liked seeing her cheeks fill with red splotches he caused. "You're still eating all that junk-food shit."

She growled under her breath. "I like this food. Do you want anything or not?"

"You let your kid eat this stuff? Aren't you supposed to cook him vegetables and have fruit out on the counter or something? Isn't that what moms do?" He tried to bite back the laugh.

Her eyes smoldered. She picked up a bag of chips and threw them at him. "I have to get up early for work tomorrow. Take your snack and go, please. Not all of us have your life and can sleep all day."

"It's nice to be me."

She made tracks around the island and shoved him toward the door. Her hands against his chest surprised him, enough to make him stumble back. When she pulled away, he could still feel her hands on him.

"You want to put your hands on me again?" He'd promised no more teasing, but he couldn't help it. He wanted to turn those cheeks red. He wanted to feel her hands on him. He'd always wanted that, and if he were going to be honest for a minute, he wanted to stay in her guesthouse so he might get the chance again. She'd hate him for that last thought.

"Go to bed, Colton." She slapped a hand over her mouth. "I walk into it every time." She shook her head and yanked open the door, letting the cold air in.

He laughed and grabbed the first bag he could reach

and then slid past her onto the back porch. "Thanks for the food." She started to close the door.

"Hey, Harley, if I do go to bed, will you—" She slammed the door in his face.

He couldn't resist. She was too much fun.

Chapter Ten

Harley walked into the high school alone. She had arrived early, wanting to get out of the house before there was any chance Colton could come knocking on her door again. She'd spent half the night thinking about the innuendos between them. He was joking, but those suggestions aroused feelings in her better left undisturbed.

Most of the other teachers at Heritage River High weren't in the building yet. Her principal's car was front and center. Joann Humphreys ran a tight ship. She'd wanted to kick Knox out of the orchestra when he got into trouble, but Ben Myer had come to Knox's rescue. It didn't hurt that Knox was the best bassist in the band and Ben had wanted to impress the school board with the holiday concert performance. Too bad Ben wasn't going to make it to the show date, but his health was more important than a concert. The kids would bounce back from this one disappointment. Ben was a different story.

She swiped her ID card before opening the old wooden door. One of the best parts of working at the high school was walking up to the vintage stone building with its arched doorway and tall columns. Inside smelled like floor wax and sweat. But she didn't care. She loved it.

Her classroom was in the addition added several years back when housing boomed. Her section wasn't as ornate or charming as the front, but her classroom had large windows that let in a lot of light. With the extra time this morning, she wanted to get her hands on some clay to help settle her nerves.

She flipped the light switch and tried to drop her bags without spilling the coffee she'd picked up at May's on the way over. A knock at the door had her spinning around.

"Good morning, Joann." It was a good morning until about two seconds ago.

Joann Humphreys stood in the doorway, her gray hair pulled back into a tight bun at the nape. Her makeup had been applied with precision, and her navy-blue suit was crisply pressed. Harley hadn't bothered with much more than foundation and some lip gloss. Her hair was also pulled back, but strands had already escaped around her face. The loose strands were getting in her eyes and tickling her chin. She'd opted for classic leggings, knee-high black boots, and cardigan sweater with her favorite piece around her neck. She was second-guessing that decision at the moment.

"Good morning. I'm reminding everyone that class selection is happening earlier this year than last. Students will be choosing their classes by mid-January instead of early February. Class selection will influence changes in the curriculum."

In other words, prepared to be fired.

"I haven't decided yet who's ready for the honors art program. I need a few more weeks to allow them to finish some of their projects."

"You're going to have to find a way to decide. You aren't getting as much time this year."

As if she had any say. Why argue? "I'll see what I come up with. Are you finished with the reviews?" She might as well know what fate had in store for her.

"I'll be handing them out tomorrow."

Merry Christmas from your boss. "Has anyone decided to take Ben's place for the concert?"

"Not yet, and if someone doesn't by week's end, the show is off."

"You can't cancel the show, Joann. Those kids have worked too hard for it. They'll be crushed."

"There are far worse things in life than not performing at your high school band concert. In a few short years, most of those kids won't even remember if there was a concert. But I'll give it to week's end in fairness."

How could this woman have ever gone into education? It wasn't Harley's first choice, but she loved the kids and knew what art and music meant to the ones who didn't catch balls and run around turf to the cheers of fans. Joann would be singing a different song if the base-ball coach went on leave. In fact, she'd been turning a blind eye to the field hockey coach's encouragement of her players taunting those not on the team. What would Joann say if she knew Harley possessed that little tidbit of information?

"And next year? Are you planning on bringing the music program back?"

Joann let out a heavy sigh. "I don't want to get rid of any programs, but without the increase in budget, my hands are tied. The monies have to go to subjects on the standardized tests. Not to mention enrollment in the music classes are down as well. If no one wants to take music, what is the point in keeping the class?"

"No offense to Ben, but couldn't it be he hasn't been making the class interesting enough? Doesn't the attendance have something to do with him?" She could say the same thing about her classes. Wasn't she resistant to trying new things to get the kids to sign up? "Music can't come off the curriculum completely."

"I'm not sure the parents care that much. Music is a nice hobby, but it doesn't make money. Parents want to know their children won't struggle to make ends meet like they do. The math and science classes are what parents are looking for."

"Do I really have to tell you that students who take music and art do better in the academic classes? All art programs increase student motivation."

"You're preaching to the choir, but there isn't anything I can do."

Sure there was. She could fight for the programs, but Joann was part of the problem, not the solution. She wouldn't make waves and upset any of the parents or the board, and she'd never back her teachers.

"What if I raise the money to keep the programs afloat?" The words spilled out. She couldn't mop them up and put them back now.

"How do you plan on doing that?"

She had no clue. "An art show. The students could make pieces to exhibit, and we could sell them. I haven't worked all the details out yet, but I will." She could check into that empty store on Main Street she was looking at the other day. That would be a great space for the gallery. They'd need some kind of big attraction. She had no idea how she'd pull it off, but she could try.

"You'd need to have this money before winter break."

"Before winter break? That's impossible. I would need more time."

"You don't have the time. Class registration is coming up, and if you start this little project, you'd have to finish it regardless of your performance review." Joann pulled her phone out of her jacket pocket. "If you'll excuse me, I need to see a janitor about a mess." She turned on her heel and rushed from the room.

Harley flopped down in the chair behind her desk. The kids were outside, filing in and filling up parking spaces. So much for playing with a little clay this morning to work out the stress of having Colton living in her backyard. Now she had a much bigger stress on her hands. Her and her big mouth. How would she ever pull off an art show in three weeks?

Who was going to be the orchestra conductor by

Friday? What was going to happen to her art classes here? Not only had she failed as an artist, she was going to fail as a teacher too. Joann was going to see to that with the review and forcing the impossible task of raising money before Christmas. She'd been a fool to think she could make a career out of her dreams. That's why she didn't want Knox messing with music. Dreams were for other people. Not them.

Colton watched the taillights fade from view. His assistant, Paul, and his boyfriend, Steve, had dropped off his Audi, the 1969 Fender Stratocaster he purchased in auction from a private collection, his favorite music award, and a suitcase full of clothes. Paul also announced he and Steve were going away for the holidays and wouldn't be back until after the new year. If Colton needed something, he had to get it himself or he was shit out of luck.

He wiped a hand over his face. He'd hung onto Paul longer than he should have. He hadn't really needed an assistant in a while, and Paul reminded him of that often, but Colton paid well, so Paul stuck around. Besides, he wasn't exactly ready to admit he had space in his schedule. But that was about to change when he started touring again.

Colton jumped in the car and headed out of town to a big warehouse store far enough away he wouldn't run into anyone. He'd stock up on some food and whatever else he needed for his three weeks.

He pictured Harley last night in those screwy but adorable pajamas. His hand scratched at the spot on his chest where her hands rested when she shoved him out the door. He couldn't make the feeling go away, and he didn't want to if he were being honest. His skin would never forget how her touch burned and excited in a way no other's had, and he'd had plenty of women's hands on him. Probably best if he never mentioned that to her.

She had understood how music called out to him, but she never liked the girls who threw themselves at him. Even when they were only playing backyard parties and local bars, the women were everywhere, willing to do anything with the guys in the band. He used to think they were just some bums from Heritage River. Why had all these gorgeous women wanted them? After a while he came to expect it, and he liked the attention. What wasn't to like? He'd never cheated on Harley. Instead, he left her behind, thinking she wasn't enough for him.

She hadn't even argued with him about leaving. Not the first time they'd hit the road or after he returned for his father's funeral. She'd told him to go after what he wanted. She wasn't going to get in his way.

He parked the car at the back of the lot and meandered inside. The heat blasted on him as the glass doors slid open. A broad, smiling man with a white beard and a red vest greeted him. He offered an over-the-shoulder wave in return.

Christmas music piped in from speakers strategically

placed throughout the store for listening pleasure. He couldn't wait for the holidays to be over just so he'd stop hearing that music. The band had been invited once to play on a rock-and-roll Christmas album. He had turned down the offer without consulting the guys. They were pissed at him when they found out. There was a lot of money to be had in Christmas music.

He unzipped his coat and pushed a cart with an errant wheel as he tried to find his way around the store. He hadn't shopped for his meals in a while. During his stay at the rehab, he'd scored some kitchen duty to avoid having to clean the bathrooms. Cutting vegetables into small pieces and mixing chopped meat with his hands eased the noise in his head. If music hadn't been his first love, he could've been a chef. He might still have to be if this tour failed.

Did people really want to hear Savage songs if they weren't played by the entire band? Older bands, like Savage, toured and made money. The problem was those older bands only had one original member left. He'd seen Incomer a few years back. That night there wasn't one original member on stage. The fans didn't seem to care. Maybe it would be the same for him, though he'd rather play with Blaise, Troy, and Patrick.

He passed the artificial Christmas trees and turned into the produce section. The peppers were vibrant in their reds, oranges, and yellows. He squeezed a few and tossed them in the cart. The smells and textures of the fruits and vegetables lulled him into a trance.

"Colton, is that you?"

He spun around and dropped the lemon he held. It rolled under the pallet. *Shit.* He had nowhere to go. He stood facing the same gray eyes he'd looked into his whole life, because he couldn't remember a time when those piercing eyes weren't there. Today his kid sister's eyes were red, and her pupils were dilated even in the bright store. He was familiar with that look, but he doubted she was drunk. She'd lost some weight since the summer.

"What are you doing here?" He couldn't think of a more suitable question.

"I could ask the same of you. Why are you here?" She pulled her stretched-out and faded blue cardigan closed. Her hair had that windblown look, but as he really took her in, she looked more as if she'd lost touch with her brush.

"Are you all right?" It didn't matter that she refused to speak to him after what he did. Something was coming unhinged, and his instincts to protect her kicked in. He used to be able to make her laugh and keep her nightmares away. She had been so little when their mom died. It had been his room she ran to when she was scared.

She stood to her full height and tilted her chin up to challenge his gaze. "Of course, I'm all right. Why wouldn't I be? You didn't answer my question. I want to know why you're here." She didn't finish the rest, but he knew it would go something like "because I don't want you here."

"I'm helping out a friend." A lie was probably the wrong move. "How are the kids?" He didn't dare say his nephew's name. No telling what her reaction would be to the use of her firstborn's name.

"Does Blaise know you're here?" She spit the words at him.

"Blaise has been keeping close tabs on me recently. How's Adam?" Maybe asking about her husband would be safer ground, and maybe he could find out why Adam had looked so sick.

"Are you and Blaise speaking?"

"Define speaking." She was mad at him, and he was mad at Blaise. They were fighting as if they were still kids.

"I don't understand why you're in town, Colton. You don't belong here. No one wants you around... Well, Blaise probably does because you stuck up for his son and not mine, and he was always blinded by you because you made him rich." She didn't stop to breathe. "I don't want to bump into you while I'm out running my errands. When are you leaving?"

He held his hands up. "Look, Savannah, I'm not here to cause any trouble. I'm not going to be around long. I promise to keep my distance. I thought...it doesn't matter what I thought. I'm sorry. I really am."

Her eyes grew to size of a grapefruit. "You're sorry?" she hissed. "How can you stand there and look me in the eye and say you're sorry? You've never been sorry for a thing in your life. The great Colton Savage just leaves carnage everywhere he goes and thinks with a simple *sorry* or a check he can make everything right. Well, not anymore."

He took the hit. "I had to protect Cash." There was no point in defending himself further.

She leaned in and lowered her voice. "It's always about you and Blaise, isn't it? Did you ever think about what you were doing to Jud? Do my children ever factor in, or is it you only care about your brother's child?"

She was still mad at Blaise too. He knew she loved Cash and wouldn't want him hurt. She couldn't handle the fact the one who had hurt him was Jud. If it had been anyone else's child hurting Cash, she would have screamed for justice.

"Savannah, I did what was right."

Her laugh soured. "You do what's convenient." She ran a hand through her hair. "I hope I don't see you again."

"You were the one who came up to me. You could've just ditched me. I would never have seen you."

"I hate you. I hate that you're my brother. I hate that I'm a part of this family, and I'm glad Dad isn't alive to see what's happened to us." She turned her cart around and hurried away from him.

He sagged against the display of fruit. His heart played faster than his hands ever could. Did this place sell any whiskey? He squeezed his eyes shut and searched for the stupid rehab word. Instead, he found Haydn's Symphony no.104 in D Major tucked in the back of his mind. The rhythm of his heart began to return to normal.

Colton no longer wanted to make dinner or buy groceries. He shoved the cart away and bolted from the store. He lit a cigarette and reached for the Audi's door

121

handle. He didn't smoke in his car, and he remembered Harley's hatred for his bad habit.

If he couldn't drink, he would smoke. He'd always lived life his own way. No excuses. He'd never answered to anyone. He was Colton Savage, for Christ's sake.

He paced in the space beside the car until the cigarette burned down. Lately, it didn't seem to matter a whole hell of a lot who he was. Harley never cared about his fame. His sister had been crystal clear about his choices. Landing his ass in rehab hadn't added to his image, and he was about to go on tour with guys who weren't in his band. *His* band.

He put the cigarette out on the bottom of his boot. A red garbage can sat alongside the glass doors into the store. Did he toss the butt into the grass or march his sorry backside up to that can? What would Harley want him to do?

They had their first painting lesson tomorrow. Could she help him with that art stuff? Could he learn to handle the anger and the disappointment?

He took his burned-out cigarette and lumbered back to the front of the store. The glass doors slid open, offering another chance. The white-bearded man stared at him.

He tossed his trash in the can.

"Fuck." And he went inside.

Chapter Eleven

Harley pulled up to her house. Colton's sleek black car was parked out in front of the guest-house. She pushed out of her dirty Durango. His shiny vehicle, clearly expensive with its German emblem on the grill, probably had less than ten-thousand miles on its odometer. Her truck had over a hundred thousand, and it wasn't even ten years old yet.

Her performance review sat in the passenger seat, mocking her. She didn't need to look at it. The words *below expectations* were tattooed on her brain. This was her second bad review because she refused to follow the stupid rubric. Joann could have her tenure revoked now, which was exactly what that woman wanted. Joann hated her because Duke and Knox found trouble together. News flash—Knox didn't act alone. She was going to be out of a job by the end of the school year. Was there any point in saving the art program now? She should let the next teacher worry about it.

She had to get over to the community college for her art class and her lesson with Colton. Spending time with him was the last thing she wanted to do at the moment. Her head was always turned around when he was near. She needed her strength to keep up the façade she'd put in place. She was so tired of working hard to hold everything together all by herself she might actually spill the truth all over him. That would be bad for everyone. He'd made it very clear he didn't want to be a father.

Maybe a quick shower would perk her up or at least relax her tight muscles enough to keep away the headache threatening behind her eyes.

Her phone buzzed before she even had the front door open. "Hello."

"I can't believe you didn't tell me." Ella's voice boomed through the phone.

Harley dumped her keys on the table by the door and kicked off her shoes. In the kitchen, she flung her coat over a chair and deposited her bags on the floor. She grabbed a handful of pretzels. That was a healthy snack, wasn't it? Who cared? She was having a bad day.

"Tell you what?" She pulled a soda out of the fridge.

"That you're renting the guesthouse to Colton Savage."

"How did you know that?" It had barely been forty-eight hours.

"Billy Lewis told his brother who told his wife, and the rest is history, as they say."

All the hens in town would be clucking about her and Colton living together, even if they weren't really. Damn small town. "What's the word? Am I officially the town slut now?"

"Well, I was in the bookstore and the Busy Bees were meeting. The book talk turned from the monthly best seller to your old romance with Colton. Sorry. But that Shelby Baxter has the hots for Colton."

"She's like a hundred." Okay, she was more like sixty-nine and old enough to be Colton's mother, which just made the whole thing gross. "Of course the talk has begun. I shouldn't be surprised. No matter what, I'll always be Barbara Kenyon's daughter." Her mother's reputation would last like rusted metal.

"Why didn't you tell me?"

"I'm sorry. I wasn't trying to hide it." Or was she? Of course, she was. "I've been so busy with school, helping Andy Henson, and the art club. I just didn't have a chance to call." And she was afraid Ella would judge her choice. She'd been judging herself since the moment Colton took the key from her hands. Just that little touch had sent fire through her veins. She turned on the shower, yanked off her clothes, and tossed them on the floor.

"You're forgiven, but I want all the details."

"Details of what?" Was there something else Ella knew she wasn't telling?

"What it's like having your old stud only yards away."

"Oh my God, this is a business arrangement. Nothing is going to happen this time."

"Both of you should stop fighting it. I'll let you go. Call me later. Love you."

"There's nothing to fight." But her words fell on deaf ears. Ella had already hung up.

Steam filled the bathroom. If she could only go back in time and tell her younger self she was making the biggest mistake of her life. One mistake led to another and another until she was an avalanche of mistakes.

She'd better hurry with that shower if she was going to get to her class in time. The hot water eased the tension in her muscles. She let it run over her head and drown out the thoughts crashing around in her brain. She didn't want to think about Colton being in her guest-house, and her client. And she didn't want to think about losing her job or how she would pull off an art show or what she needed to do to finally get Andy to paint something and open up about his anger.

She missed her uncle. She needed him now to tell her what to do. Even with Knox and Ella, she felt all alone in the world.

"Harley?"

Someone banged on the bathroom door, and she jumped. She slipped on the wet tiled floor of the shower and windmilled her arms to keep from landing on her butt. "Oh my god, who's out there?"

"It's me."

"Colton, what are you doing here? Don't you dare come in this bathroom," she shouted over the sound of water. The glass door was steamed up. Should she stay in or try to grab her towel? She peeked out and froze. The metal of the empty towel rack twinkled in the light. The towel lay in a heap by the door, out of her reach. "Damn."

"Harley, I'm coming in, but I'll keep my eyes closed."

"Don't come in here." She turned in circles. There was nowhere to hide.

"Come on. It's not like I haven't seen you naked before." His laugh grew louder. He had pushed the door open and stood in her bathroom. She turned away from him and tried to cover what she could, hoping the water would stay hot and the steam would be her shield.

"My eyes are closed. I promise not to peek."

"What do you want, Colton?" Her stomach flipped. Now wasn't a good time to be sick.

"I saw your truck. Do you want to drive together over to the lesson?"

"No, absolutely not. I have a class before our lesson." Her tight voice made her sound like a goosed chicken. "Would you please get out of here?" She faced the wall, trying to hide the majority of her nakedness. She couldn't shrink any further into the corner of the shower, and the water was growing cold.

"I was just trying to be nice."

"Why?" Her voice shook.

"Why does everyone think I'm not a nice guy? I know I'm kind of full of myself. I don't try to hide that, but I have a heart."

She wanted him gone. The steam thinned out and shortened the time to debate his level of caring. "Okay, okay. You're a nice guy. Now go back down and leave me alone. I'll see you later."

"One more thing. You might want this." His voice sounded closer. She peered over her shoulder. He had propped open the shower door and held out her towel. His lips curled up into a bright smile. He winked.

She yanked the towel away from him and whipped it around her body. "Oh, you're impossible. I don't know what I ever saw in you." How much more embarrassing was the day going to get? First, Joann humiliated her with that review and now Colton.

He let the shower door slam shut, and she turned off the water. He opened the bathroom door but glanced back to her.

"And you still have a nice ass."

Okay, going into the bathroom was a bit too far.

Colton wrenched open his car door and slid in. The vision of her wet and naked had his low belly pulling tight. Her creamy skin and soft curves dried up his throat. He didn't need to count to ten or breathe deeply around her. He wanted to run his rough fingers across her soft skin. That was all he needed to stay calm and sober.

He smoothed his hands over the leather steering wheel. He really did want to know if she wanted to drive over with him. He wanted the company. After seeing Savannah, he needed to hear someone else's voice in his head. Harley's voice used to be his aria. Instead of spending time with her, he had paced the guesthouse until it was time to leave, making sure not to look over at his guitar at all.

128

He pointed the car toward the end of the driveway. His headlights lit up Knox center stage. He meandered up from the road. White earbuds hung from his ears; a backpack was slung over one shoulder. Colton eased the car up alongside him and rolled down the window. The cold air bit him on the face, and he hit the button for the seat heater.

"Hey, don't kids your age usually drive places?"

Knox yanked out the wires from his ears and let out a long sigh. "Yeah. Just not me anymore. Mom sold my car a few weeks ago. I got a ride home from my friend Duke." The kid's words fell flat.

Colton took a longer look at Knox. His clothes were wrinkled, and his hair looked as if it needed a good wash. He'd shown up at school in that same state many times just to aggravate his old man or to prove a point even when he didn't have a point to prove.

"Your mom's really messing with you."

"I guess I deserved it. She was pretty pissed off at me."

"What'd you do?" He thought back on a few of his antics as a teen. Tossing the principal's desk was a good one.

"It was stupid. I'm trying to forget about it."

"I did some dumb things, too, when I was your age. My father was in the principal's office a lot, which made him madder than a whore in church on Sunday since he was the music teacher back then. Said I was always embarrassing him."

The light returned to Knox's eyes. "My mom said the

129

same thing. Said she couldn't look the other teachers in the eye because of me."

"She probably didn't mean it." His father had meant it. He could still see the cold stare in the man's eyes when he spit the words out.

"Oh, she meant it. That's why the car is gone."

"She just wants you to be safe." The way he wanted Cash to be safe. That's why he stepped in to help him last summer. He knew the truth. He couldn't keep it to himself and let Cash get hurt. Tell the truth, no matter what.

"Whatever. I'm not going to do it again, so I wish she'd let up on all the stupid rules. Other than orchestra practice, I can't go anywhere. It sucks."

"What's it like being in the orchestra?" If he kept talking, he'd probably be late for his first art lesson, but he wanted to hear what this kid had to say. He could relate to the stupid mistakes and the music playing. And right now Knox Kenyon was the only person in Heritage River not judging him.

"I don't know. It's pretty good, I guess. The holiday show might not happen. Our teacher took a leave of absence, and no one else will step up to take his place. The computer teacher takes a nap while we practice."

"Your school will cancel the performance?" Well, his father would never have done that much, at least. "They can't hire a substitute or something?"

"Got me. We might be practicing for nothing. Kind of sucks since it's my senior year."

"I refused to be in the orchestra when I was your age."

"Why?" Knox scrunched up his face, as if not being in the orchestra was the dumbest idea he'd ever heard.

Staying out of the orchestra had been a dumb idea, and one he'd convinced Blaise to have as well. If he could go back, he'd make some different choices. "Good question." He had tried to make his dad mad. It worked too. Which didn't matter a whole hell of a lot now, did it? "Do you play in any bands?"

"I've tried but can't get anything off the ground. Can't find anyone as serious about it as I am. I heard your brother and his son once. They're good, but you know that. Don't know why I'm telling you that. Sorry."

He wasn't surprised Blaise and Cash could put down the chops. They were both talented. Cash had been sending him videos for years with him playing in bands with other kids. The back of his throat itched. He checked the clock. "Nothing to be sorry about. Hey, I have to get to my art lesson with your mom, and if I'm late—"

"She's going to be pissed at you too," Knox said.

She probably already was, after his antics in her bathroom. "Exactly. But if you ever want to talk music, let me know. And if you want to jam while I'm here."

Knox stared with wide eyes. "Are you kidding?"

"I never joke about music."

"Wow, thanks. That would be great." He ducked his head, but his smile peeked out. "I'll definitely stop by."

His face dropped. "Wait. My mom might not let me. She knows how much that would mean to me."

"Maybe she can give it to you as a Christmas gift."

"You don't know my mom very well, do you?"

Oh, he knew her, too well. But he wasn't going to tell her kid that. Colton had that much sense. "She might surprise you. I'd better hit the road."

He pulled out onto the street. He could talk to Harley about letting Knox play with him. She used to listen to him. Maybe she would again. Or maybe she'd throw his ass out on the street, and he'd deserve it after the bathroom stunt. Considering she hadn't done that yet, she might actually like having him around. That idea had him speeding over the bridge and on his way to his art lesson.

Chapter Twelve

He was late. Of course he was, because Colton Savage only cared about himself and her time was the last thing on his mind and certainly wasn't important to him. It never had been. Harley paced her classroom at the community college. The last student left ten minutes ago. The heat had been turned up, and she was sweating in her wool sweater and high boots. Or she was having a hot flash. Wonderful. Soon her face would bloom red, and her hair would be sticking to her skin. She swiped her hair up in a knot. She wanted to rip her clothes off to cool down. She gritted her teeth. Why was she thinking about ripping off her clothes and Colton Savage in the same breath?

Her face still burned when she thought about Colton standing in her bathroom. He wasn't respecting her boundaries either. The devil was teasing her, and she was rising to the bait. When he got there, she'd tell him the deal was off. He'd have to get out of her guesthouse too.

"I'm sorry." Colton skid into the classroom after his words. His hair was slightly windblown. His leather coat flapped open. His navy sweater fit snug to his muscular chest.

"I'm late, I know. I was talking to Knox. I passed him coming home."

He was talking to Knox? "About what?" Her words squeaked out. She braced herself.

His easy smile slid across his face. "Music." The smile faded, and he stared at her with clouded eyes.

Her stomach dropped. "What?"

"You sold his car? What'd you do that for?"

She let out a deep breath and plopped into the chair. They had stayed on safe ground. "He went to school drunk and ended up suspended."

"Harley, you got drunk at his age. I believe I helped you with that a few times. Do you remember when you fell in the lake?"

"Colton, I'm not in the mood for memory lane." She hated that he knew so much about her. Okay, *hate* was a strong word. *Unnerved* was a better one. Colton unnerved her. Still. "I never showed up at school like that, and I'm not about to share my teenage mistakes with him. So don't you dare tell him what you know about me."

"Not me. I'm done getting involved in family affairs. Can you get his car back?"

"I thought you weren't going to get involved?"

"Let him have his ride back. You're probably dampening his chances with the girls. A guy has to have his ride."

"I am not about to encourage my teenage son to have sex." *Let someone in her family make better choices than the rest of them.*

"Come on, babe. A kid his age, that good looking, who can bang out the chops on the guitar is getting laid. Trust me, I know."

She slapped her hands over her ears. "This is my child we're talking about." She didn't want to think about Knox doing it with anyone. She wanted to think about him as a little boy with chubby cheeks and chubby hands to match, wearing a bright orange fishing hat while he inspected every stone he passed.

Did Colton call her "babe"? She was sliding down the slope, and if she were going to be honest for once, she kind of liked it. This man was so much trouble with his charm.

"Have you ever painted before?" She needed to get on firmer ground and stick to topics she could control.

His lips curled into a full smile showing off his straight white teeth. "Other than painting a house, no." The lines around his eyes deepened when he smiled. His jaw was more pronounced in his older years. The silver in his hair gave him that grown-up sexy man look.

The anger about his being late cooled down, as her sweaty skin had.

"I'm sorry about barging in on you earlier. I can't seem to control myself. Wait. Forget I said that. I can control myself. I'll behave. I swear."

Her cheeks flushed again. "If we're going to be able to work together, I need you to respect my boundaries." And somehow they were off the safe topic and back to her being naked in his presence.

"I will. I saw Savannah earlier today. It didn't go well. I thought I could use some company." He told her about the incident. "Cash might be right about me needing your art lessons. Being with you feels good." He circled his hand between them.

Why couldn't things feel bad between them? That would be so much easier for her. But there he was, and every time he showed up in her life, she couldn't turn him away. That's how she got herself into trouble, and she couldn't forget that. Too much was at stake if she forgot.

"Painting can be a way to deal with your anger and stress. It's a vehicle for exploring the truth buried deep inside you."

"The truth about what?"

"About whatever makes you drink too much."

"Just for the record, that was the first time in a very long time I took a drink. I've been, well, I was sober for a long time. Until I fucked up."

"Something made you angry or upset enough to force you to make the choice to drink. Painting will help you deal with that." She pulled up a stool beside the table. She motioned for him to take a seat and pulled another stool up next to him.

His muscular thigh was only inches from hers. Her mind tugged at a memory of his bare leg against hers like a loose thread. *Focus. Your job is to help him, not screw his brains out.*

"It was Blaise's fault. If he hadn't left the tour, I wouldn't have gotten so mad."

"Do you think Blaise left to hurt you?" She grabbed some paper and opened a few paints.

Colton held a paintbrush in his hand like a miniature guitar. He absently strummed at it. The motion made warmth spread through her chest. She always loved to watch him play.

"Well, no. He didn't walk on stage that night planning to screw up the rest of the show. He had to get home to Cash, and that part I didn't mind. I love that kid too, but I don't understand how he threw it all away after that. We're a team. It's always been him and me."

They were getting to something, and she hadn't even dipped a brush into any paint. It might be better to slow him down. Too much too soon was liable to scare him. He wasn't one to admit his feelings willingly.

"Let's start with a small project for now. Use whatever colors you want, but when you put the brush to the paper, close your eyes. Don't worry about whether or not what you paint looks like a picture. This is an exercise to get you to feel the brush in your hand, quiet your mind a little. Ready?"

"Not really, but if you say so."

"I do." That warm feeling spread lower this time.

She stepped away from the table to give him some space and let him explore a little. She walked over to the windows. The parking lot lights spread a buttery gold

Stacey Wilk

into the inky night behind them. The rolling hills out in the distance were speckled in white. People at home were probably making dinner or wrapping Christmas presents, and she stood feet from the only man she ever loved. *Enough of that thinking.*

"Time's up."

Colton opened his eyes, and his mouth dropped. "I suck at this."

She walked around to see, but he folded the paper in half, smearing the paint.

"This is an exercise in no judgement. The idea wasn't to create a masterpiece. It's just to get to know the medium a little. How did you feel while you were painting?"

"I don't know. Stupid." He pushed off from the stool. "I'm a musician, not an artist."

"Are they really that different?"

"Hell, yes, they are. From the minute I picked up a guitar, I made that baby sing. I could hear any tune and replay it."

Like Knox.

He waved his hand toward his work. "That's just a big mess. You sure you know what you're doing?" A darkness passed over his gray eyes. He crumpled the paper. "Where's the garbage?"

She pointed to the wicker basket in the corner. "Sometimes it takes time to get good at something. Not everything in your life is going to be like guitar playing."

"You're right about that. And nothing is as important." He wiped a hand over his face. "I'm done here."

"You're quitting because you weren't good at it the first time?" She had a hard time hiding the disdain from her voice. He was acting like a child who couldn't have his way, and she wanted to tell him that. "You can't live your life hiding behind your image." Okay, too far.

"What do you know about how I live my life? You haven't seen me in, what, eighteen years?"

On the money.

"Now in ten minutes you're going to diagnose me?"

She took a deep breath. "I've done this a time or two, Colton. Painting takes time. It's about being truthful with your feelings. It's about learning to deal with your stress. The painting will help you."

"All I need is to get back on the road and play my music. My music." He pounded his chest with one finger. "Not new stuff someone else wrote, not the stuff Blaise is writing without me. My music. When I'm playing the music I created for Savage, I'm fine."

"You're not fine. You drove drunk into a fence. Your nephew and Billy brought you home because they love you and want what's best for you. Let's just paint together. Nothing more. We don't have to talk about anything. Just put the paint on the page. If you'd rather, slap it on the paper. I have banner-size paper we can tape to the walls. No rules. No technique. What do you say?"

He tossed the brush on the table and dropped onto the stool. "Why did my brother leave the band?"

Oh boy. She didn't have a good answer for that. "Have you ever asked him?"

"He says he doesn't want to play our music anymore."

"Blaise's decision to move on isn't about you." Which was a very hard thing for Colton to understand. "It's about his choices."

"If he still wanted to play with me, he would. He doesn't want to play with me anymore."

"Is that really true?" She stepped closer to him. His cedar-and-oak scent wafted toward her. She clasped her hands together to keep from touching him.

"I don't know."

That was a start. "Do you want to paint some more?"

"No. Do you want to grab some dinner? I'm starving."

His eyes pleaded with her. He'd just shared some deep truths. Could she really turn him away now? If she said no, what would he do to fill the time? He didn't have many people in Heritage River who cared about him for who he was. They were dazzled by who he'd become, or they were so mad at him they'd stopped talking to him.

"I'm not sure. I don't want to leave Knox out. Maybe another time."

"He can come. We'll grab him."

Knox and Colton having a meal together made her stomach clench. "I'm sure you have better things to do than hang with me and my son."

"That sounds like the best idea I've heard in a long time. What you do say? I promise to respect your boundaries. No teasing. I really don't want to eat alone tonight."

She pressed her lips together. One meal out in public

couldn't hurt, could it? Colton and Knox could talk music. That was safe, wasn't it? "Okay. I just need to stop in my office and grab my stuff."

He kept pace beside her as they made their way to her office. She flipped on the light, throwing her cluttered desk into the harsh brightness of fluorescence, and gathered her belongings.

"You kept your photo of the bridge." He ran a finger along the edge of the photo.

He stared at the shot she took a long time ago of the bridge at sunset. "You remember that?"

She'd often wondered if he ever thought about how they would walk to town from his parents' house and stop at the bridge. They'd watch the sun set over the dark water, and they'd dream together. He'd talk about making it big with his music, and she'd imagine what her life would be like as an artist in galleries. He'd wrap his fingers around hers, and she'd feel his calloused skin against hers. They were going to be big. Tears threatened to give her away. She choked them back.

"Why did you give up your art?"

She grabbed her coat and bag. "All set."

"You're avoiding my question." He followed her into the hall.

She locked the door behind them. Their footsteps echoed against the floor. "I didn't give up. I tried, things didn't work out the way I thought they would, so I had to adjust. At least I have health benefits. For now."

They pushed through the doors out into the cold night. The air smelled like snow. A white Christmas would be nice, but not likely. Harley pulled her coat closer. The wind fought its way through the wool, and she shivered. She still had presents to buy. There would be only lint in her wallet soon. She stole a glance at Colton. Who would be buying him gifts this year?

"What's this "for now" business?" Colton plucked his cigarettes from his jacket and lit up, and she tried not to make a face.

She didn't want to think about her future, but he watched her with those intense eyes. He'd always looked at her as if she were the only other person in the room. "My performance review came back today. I'm going to lose my tenure and probably my job. The administration is considering cutting the art and music programs. Well, art is definitely going. Music will be fast on its heels." Spilling the words lifted the weight off her chest.

They reached the Durango. She shifted her bag on her shoulder. He was so easy to talk to she forgot to guard her heart. When he soaked her in with those stormy eyes, she could see the chance of a life together because he had a way of making anything possible, but she needed to be strong. She was too old for plastering broken dreams back together.

"The school is willing to kill the music program? No one can stop them?" He sucked on the cigarette and blew the smoke away from her.

"If the students don't register for class, they can't justify keeping it. Same for art. Any chance you'll quit smoking?"

"Nope." He narrowed his eyes. "You're going to do something about keeping the programs, aren't you?"

"I told my boss I was planning an art show to raise money to offset the budget cuts."

"That's great."

"I lied."

His mouth dropped open. "Why did you lie? Lying isn't going to help anything."

No one would believe the man who left a trail of destroyed hotel rooms in his wake had such a strong moral compass. "I wanted her to think I was being proactive. And I want to save the programs because those students deserve to be exposed to the arts." She leaned against the truck and kicked the ground. "It burns me up that the arts always get cut first. Everyone thinks art and music are a waste of time because they aren't math or science. Or worse, the sports programs get all the attention."

"You're grandstanding to the wrong person over here."

She met his gaze and smiled. "I should keep my head down and stay out of it. Let the next teacher worry about the outcome of the art programs."

"Why would you allow music and art to be cut from the school? Would you really want to disappoint your son like that?" Colton put out his cigarette and cupped the butt in his hand. He kicked the ground with the toe of his boot. "Do you have a garbage in that truck of yours?"

She popped the hatch and handed him a plastic bag. Did she have something to do with his decision not to litter? She liked the idea of that. "Knox is leaving after this school year. He can play music anywhere. I'd be letting down the students still coming up, but is it worth it to stir the proverbial paint can?" She leaned back against the Durango.

"It's worth it if you believe in what you're going after. You used to believe in your talent." He leaned next to her and crossed his long legs. His arm pressed against hers. The friction sent heat through her veins.

She stole a side-glance at him. "That was when I was young and naive. Maybe I shouldn't encourage students to reach for an unattainable dream."

"Babe, you've become cynical." He took the bag off her shoulder and the key from her hand. He unlocked her door and shoved the bag inside. He turned and put his hands on her shoulders. "Dreams do come true."

"You don't understand how real life works. In your world, you snap your fingers and people jump to make you happy. They can't race fast enough to give you what you want. I don't have that kind of clout. Never did. Never will. No, in my world, I have to toe the line or get run over." She shifted under his hold. "Can we get some dinner? I'm starving."

He stepped back. "You're stalling. You don't have to take this on all by yourself, you know."

"I hate that you know me so well." She dropped her gaze to the ground. "There isn't anyone who can help me. I've lost my job all by myself. I couldn't pull off a career as an artist all by myself either. How can I save the art and the music programs?" She didn't have what it took.

He tilted her chin up with his strong finger. His silvery eyes, as lustrous as iron, held her gaze. Saving the art program and accomplishing her dreams seemed attainable in that moment. He was like a drug for her.

The air between them became charged. If he leaned in to kiss her, she'd kiss him back.

He dropped his hand. "If you had someone in your corner willing to fight with you, would you try and keep the music and art programs?"

She thought about it for a second. "It doesn't matter because there isn't anyone. We can't even get a teacher to step in and run the orchestra before the show in a couple of weeks. If they don't have one by Friday, the show is going to be canceled."

"How does someone become a teacher who runs an orchestra?"

"Have a teaching degree. But at this point, I think the school will settle for anyone with music experience. They don't want to disappoint the students this late in the game. They'll disappoint them in the fall. They'll have the summer break to deal with it."

"What if I did it?"

"Excuse me?"

He stared wide eyed at her. "Me, Harley. What if I directed the orchestra for the show? Would you fight for the programs then?"

She tried to hold back the laughter, but it bubbled out into white puffs all around her. "You shouldn't tease like that."

"I'm not teasing."

The words died on her tongue. He was serious? That was impossible. "Do you even like kids?"

"I like my niece and nephews. I like Knox. That's enough."

"You hardly know my son." She turned her gaze away from him.

"I can tell a good kid when I see one."

"Why do you want to do this?" She couldn't get her head around it. Colton Savage wanted to help out a bunch of high school kids? Impossible.

"I don't know. To keep you looking at me the way you just did. Maybe to prove to myself and my family I'm not such a bad guy."

She couldn't help herself. She reached up and cupped the side of his face. "You aren't a bad guy, Colton. Don't let anyone tell you that."

He took her hand and laced their fingers together. The connection charged every nerve ending. She should pull away, get in her truck, and not look back, but she wanted this moment to go on forever.

"You are the only person who sees behind my stage presence. When you look at me, I'm not the drunk who drives into fences."

"You are so much more than that. You always have been." She needed to go. She didn't trust herself. She wanted to pull him close and kiss him until the world stopped. She dropped her hand from his and stepped away. She jumped in the truck and kicked it over. "I think I'll take a rain check on that dinner." She needed space and time to think.

"What do you say? If I take on this orchestra in need of some help, will you have your art show?"

"I don't know. I have to think about it." Hadn't she already committed by opening her mouth to Joann? Was she seriously considering backing out so Joann had something else to hold over her head besides a bad review?

"I guess I can settle for that—for now."

"You can't swoop in and be the hero and then change your mind halfway through when it gets hard or those students get difficult. You'd have to stick it out to the end, and that's not exactly your strong suit."

"You feel like giving a guy a break? I thought we had made some progress here. You were feeling it the same as me, weren't you?"

Heat filled her cheeks. She couldn't deny how he made her feel, and it wasn't just physical. She loved his sense of humor, his integrity, and his compassion. He hid those softer qualities, but she'd always known where to look for them. To hear he was feeling the same things as she was sent images flashing through her mind of what could be between them. Her nerve endings were on high alert. They'd been down this dead end before.

"I'm sorry. You're right. It was wrong of me to say you don't stick around when things get tough."

"Did you say I was right?" His eyes shone with delight.

She couldn't help but smile at him. "Yes, I said you were right."

He cupped his hands around his mouth. "Did anyone else hear that? Harley Kenyon said I was right."

Laughter bubbled up inside her like a root beer float. "Okay, okay. Stop yelling. It's no big deal."

"It's a big deal to me, darling. That might be a first."

Even though she was sitting, her knees went weak. "Are you seriously thinking about helping us out?" The heater blasted warm, but her insides were heating up because of him.

"I never joke about music."

"Come by the school in the morning. I'll introduce you to the principal, but don't be surprised if she doesn't like you."

"They usually don't. Let me buy you dinner." He wagged his eyebrows and offered up his dimpled smile.

Her brain yelled at her to run away. She was playing with fire but couldn't seem to look away from the flames. "I'll pick up Knox and meet you at Jake's."

"Give that boy his car back."

"You didn't charm me that much."

"Not yet, babe. Not yet."

Chapter Thirteen

Colton's hands shook. He clenched them into fists and counted to twenty before he grabbed the metal handle of the front door into Heritage River High School. He hadn't been inside that school in more years than he wanted to count. The last time had probably been Savannah's graduation since he missed Jud's last year. He couldn't let his mind wander to his sister now. He had to meet the principal in five minutes.

Why had he opened his big mouth to Harley and made a suggestion like helping a bunch of kids with their school concert? The drinking must've drowned the last of his brain cells. He might be able to pound out the licks on the guitar, and in his day he could write a mean-ass song. He could hammer out the keys on any piano. He understood key signatures and tempo, but conduct an orchestra? And they probably played Christmas music.

The front door led to another set of glass doors

blocking his entrance. He tried them all, but they were locked. He searched for a button or something. Instead, he saw a small black box in the corner with a handwritten sign above it.

Please put your driver's license up to the camera. Thank you. Mrs. Humphreys and the staff at HRHS.

His driver's license? What the hell? He fished out his wallet from the front pocket of his jeans and plucked out his license. He held it up to the little black box. A buzz sounded. He jumped for the door and tugged it open.

A woman sat behind an open window. Red hair frizzed out around her head and matched the freckles spotting her face. She offered a welcoming smile.

"When did showing a driver's license to get into a school become a thing?" He shoved his wallet back in his jeans.

"I'm afraid it's been that way for a while now. Can't be too careful. How may I help you?" She checked her computer screen. "Mr. Savage? Savage? Are you related to Savannah?"

She didn't know who he was? That was happening more and more these days, but in Heritage River? Times really were changing. Yet if he were going to be honest, the school was Savannah's domain. She was the celebrity here.

"As a matter of fact"—he checked the name tag hanging around the woman's neck—"Tess, Savannah is my sister." *But don't tell her you spoke to me, because she will hate you for life.*

Her big smile spread across her face again and lit up

her eyes the same color as her freckles. She blended into herself. "How lovely. We adore Savannah here. She always volunteers."

"That's Savannah. Everyone's best friend." Except his.

"Greyson must be your nephew. Well, of course he is." She swatted the air and glanced at him through the corner of her eye. "Silly me. Are you here for him? I can call him down. Let me check his schedule."

"Not necessary. I'm here to see the principal." He patted his pockets. What did he do with that paper? "I can't remember her name. Harley Kenyon set it up."

Tess giggled. "Getting in trouble with the principal at your age?"

Was she flirting with him? Didn't matter. If he were to get involved with anyone, it would be his art teacher. He forced a laugh out.

"I'll let her know you're here. Can you sign in right here, please?"

He paced the waxed floor of the lobby. The smell of burnt food and sweaty socks rang familiar. Tess kept giving him glances. Where was this principal? Was it too late to make a run for it? He couldn't do this. If he wanted to kill time, he should have renovated Harley's kitchen. He liked that kind of work.

"Colton."

Too late to run.

Harley came toward him. Her hair was tied away from her face, but some wavy strands had come loose. He wanted to wrap her hair around his fingers. She wore tight

151

black pants tucked into high boots and a long flowery top. She smiled at him, and his shoulders dropped.

"It's good to see you." He leaned in and kissed her cheek. She smelled of honeysuckle and turpentine.

Her hand reached up to her cheek. "It's nice to see you too. Come with me."

Was she just saying that? She seemed okay with him last night. They even had a few laughs during dinner. He'd wanted to kiss her goodnight, but that would've been a mistake. He couldn't promise her a future. She deserved a man who would stick around.

"You look nice in those pants." There wasn't anything wrong with complimenting an old friend, was there?

She blushed. "Thanks. Right through here."

A tall woman waited as they entered. Her hair was pinned up in a tight bun that made the corners of her eyes lift toward her forehead. That or she had a bad run with plastic surgery. She wore the expected skirt suit and sensible shoes. Not his type at all. Though he heard those women were pretty good in bed. He was never interested in finding out. Not when a wild hair beauty with a fantastic smile was always an arm's length away. Like Harley. No, not like Harley. Harley was better than any wild woman he'd had before.

"Good morning. I'm Joann Humphreys." She had a solid grip. "I'm a big fan. When Harley mentioned your interest, I was thrilled."

He eased his hand free, afraid she might not give it back. "Harley explained the orchestra needed some help.

I'm in town for a few weeks. Figured I'd throw my hat in."

"Please sit down. Colton, may I call you 'Colton'?" She flashed a sugar-added smile.

"Everyone does." He tried not to look over at Harley and raise his eyebrows. He was never going to be comfortable in a principal's office.

"Harley, we have it from here. Thank you." The principal shuffled some papers on her desk, keeping her head down.

Harley tucked her hair behind her ear. The tip of her tongue shot out and back in.

Colton stopped halfway to his seat. "Joann—I can call you 'Joann,' can't I?"

"Of course."

"Harley stays."

Red blotches crept up Joann's neck. The smile was coated with less sugar this time. "Certainly."

"She's a bitch." Colton pulled out his smokes. Harley placed a hand on his arm. It was the first time she'd touched him since last night. His insides warmed in the cold air. They had walked outside after the meeting with the Ice Queen and leaned against his car.

"Please don't smoke here."

"Even this far from the building?" Damn these no smoking rules. Couldn't they go back to the way it was in the eighties when he could smoke right outside the door of the school?

"She might be watching. And you're right. She's a bitch." Harley ducked her head, but a smile crept up into the corners of her mouth. "Thank you for insisting I stay. She was looking for a way to get rid of me all morning."

"How'd you like the part where I insisted you help me through the practices and the night of the performance?" The principal's friendly mask had fallen off before she could catch it when she'd heard that idea.

"Harley must be terribly busy," Joann had said.

But Harley hadn't missed a beat and agreed to help him. He'd offered the suggestion so she could help him with the kids, because being a teacher was the last thing he ever thought he'd be and swore to hell and back he'd never be. Yet here he was hanging onto the folder of the music they were playing. The ink had barely dried on the substitute paperwork.

"I know you suggested it just to aggravate her. I don't have to help out. I doubt you'll need me." She wrapped her arms around her middle.

"You want my jacket?" He started to slip it off his shoulders.

"No, thanks. I have to get back inside."

"I do need your help. I have no idea how to corral a bunch of teens. Honestly, I can't believe I'm doing this." He might be in shock, actually. It must be the time spent in the rehab. Was he suffering from some kind of post-traumatic stress making him do crazy things like managing a high school orchestra?

"You're going to be fine. The kids will love you. It's not every day a celebrity walks into their high school and becomes their teacher. They'll talk about this when they're old like us. You're making a big difference. You should be proud."

"I'm not old."

She rolled her eyes. "Whatever."

"I'm not trying to save the world either. I just want to see you get off your butt and put a piece of art on display in an art gallery."

She squared her shoulders. "The art show isn't about me."

"Why not? You deserve to keep your job. People should buy your work. You're good."

"I'm not like you, Colton. I don't think the world waits for me to show up, and besides, my dreams are ancient history. The art show is about saving a program that allows students to belong to something when there isn't anything else for them. Art helps students feel competent."

He loved her feisty side. *Careful with the L word.*

She didn't need to hear that come out of his mouth. Even though he'd said it to her years ago, and he'd meant it back then, he wouldn't hurt her again by saying it now. *In other words, don't go thinking with your junk.*

"When are you going to stop selling yourself short? You don't have to worry. I'll be at that art show with you. All you'll have to do is look over at me."

She hugged herself tighter. "I need to get back inside. I'm telling all my students today about the show so they can pull something together if they want. I'm even going to give them extra credit for participating. That should aggravate Joann more. I can't wait. I'm going to give my relaxation students a chance to participate too. I hope Andy Henson paints something. You know, you could too." She turned on her heel with a smirk.

"Hell no. Not me." She'd ignored his offer for support. The rub wore at his insides like corrosion on guitar strings. "Harley, you can have it all. I'm living proof of that." He shouted at her retreating back. He didn't want her to go away frustrated. He didn't want her to go away at all. "Don't forget my art lessons tonight."

She ignored him, and he hated it. He watched until she had long disappeared behind the glass doors. "When will you start believing you're good enough?" he whispered.

And what had he done to prove to her she was?

Chapter Fourteen

"Knox, get up. You're going to be late." Harley banged on Knox's bedroom door for the second time that morning. It was only six fifteen, and her blood pounded in her ears. How many times would she have to yell at him before he heard her? Was it too much to ask for him to just get up on his own once? Didn't he realize she had to get ready for work? Of course not. He was a teenager.

He threw open the door. "I'm up," he growled.

"I can see that. Hurry up."

"Geez, Mom, I know."

His hair stuck up in the back. He needed a shave, but her breath still caught every time she saw her little boy looking more and more like a man. His shoulders were broadening, and his legs getting more muscular. His frame was all Colton.

Her heart split in two. What was she doing spending time with that man? She had no right to enjoy his company as much as she did. She'd have to tell him the truth if she continued to hang around him, and that wasn't going to happen. Not when his history had been to leave just when she believed they had a chance. What had her aunt Katherine always said? "Believe people when they show you who they are."

"I don't want you to be late." She hurried down the hall to her room.

"Who cares if I am? What else are you going to take away from me? The concert?"

She took a deep breath. "I don't want to talk about that now. Get ready for school. And pick up your dirty clothes off the floor."

"When are you going to realize I made a stupid mistake? Didn't you ever make a mistake at my age?" he yelled at her back.

She closed her bedroom door without answering. She had made plenty of mistakes in her younger years, and that was why she wanted her point to hit home. "Don't make my mistakes," she whispered to the empty room.

Having Knox wasn't a mistake. He was the best thing she'd ever done, the only right thing in her life. She couldn't make her dreams come true, she couldn't hold onto the one man she truly loved, and she failed at being a teacher.

Harley hurried to finish getting dressed. She swept some powder over her face. That was all she had time for this morning. Breakfast would have to be the sugary cereal again. One of these days she'd give herself enough time to make herself and Knox a real breakfast before school.

"You are like the only mother on the planet who allows her kid to eat cereals made from refined sugar." Knox ambled into the kitchen and shook the cereal box at her while she poured some coffee in her to-go mug.

"I don't like my cereal to taste like the box. All the healthy cereal does. Here, have a banana." She shoved the fruit at him.

He took the banana and peeled it, his eyes glued on his task. "Mom, can I ask you something?"

Uh-oh. "Sure." The coffee burned her mouth.

"The orchestra is going out after the practice tonight. I want to go."

"You know my answer."

"I'm sorry about what I did. I really am. It won't happen again. It never even happened before. Why can't you give me a break? I'm almost eighteen years old." He tossed the peel in the garbage.

"As long as I fund your life, it's my rules we live by."

"I hate your stupid rules. You're impossible since Uncle Hank died. I hate living here, and I wish I had another parent I could go live with. I want to try and find my father." His brown eyes were as cold as stone.

She clamped her lips down to keep from spitting out the coffee. *Tell him.* It was time to spill the proverbial beans. She couldn't keep it a secret any longer. The lies and the stories exhausted her. With the truth out in the open, maybe they'd have a chance to have a real family.

"Is this still about that stupid history project?"

Someone banged on the back door. "We'll talk about this later."

"I'm getting a ride to school from Duke." He yanked his coat off the hook, hoisted his backpack over one shoulder, and marched toward the front door before she could shout "anyone but Duke." When was he going to stop being that child's friend? The banging, or more like knocking without patience, continued.

"Just a second," she shouted, wanting to run after her son.

She jerked open the door and was glad she still wasn't drinking coffee.

"I brought you some breakfast." Colton held up a white bag and a drink carrier holding three paper cups with lids.

"That was very nice but not necessary. Knox has already left for school, and I'm about to head out too. I'm sorry you put yourself out for nothing."

"I forgot my ID." Knox's voice climbed over her shoulder and landed between her and Colton.

"Looks like he's still here." Colton brushed past her. "Knox, I have egg sandwiches with bacon. You want one?" He put the drinks down on the table. He scooped into the bag and handed Knox a sandwich covered in aluminum foil as if it were first prize at a talent show. He wore his rock-star smile, the one that made his eyes dusky and her knees weak.

"Thanks." Knox reached for the prize.

Harley stepped between them and deflected the gift

back to Colton. "We don't need breakfast. Knox, I thought your ride was waiting for you."

"He is."

Colton handed over the food. "Take it. Eat it on the way. I know your mother probably gave you Cheetos for breakfast."

They shared a laugh at her expense—a bonding moment. The whole scene was all wrong. They couldn't become friends. Please, anything but that.

"I do not feed him that."

Colton grabbed the cereal box. She shook her head.

"Gotta run. Thanks, Colton." Knox shook Colton's hand. "See ya, Mother." He gave her an eye roll before turning his back and returning to the front door.

She flopped into the chair.

"I have one for you too." He waved the sandwich under her nose.

The smell of pork, eggs, and butter made her stomach growl, but she didn't take the sandwich. "What are you doing up so early?"

"Couldn't sleep." He handed her the cup of coffee. She pointed to her to-go mug.

"Mine's probably better." His smile teased out his dimple.

That stupid dimple was what put her in all this trouble in the first place. They had been at the cherry festival. She stood at the corner of the makeshift stage with a group of her friends waiting for Savage to come out and play. The crowd had been growing, and they wanted to be able to see the boys up close.

Colton paraded on stage holding his guitar over his head. His hair had been long and wavy, falling past his shoulders. Troy, their lead singer, knew her from church. He waved to her, and she waved back. Colton leaned in and said something in Troy's ear. He'd turned to her then and smiled with that dimple. She had been hooked. There had never been any other man like Colton Savage in her life.

"Harley." His deep voice brought her out of her memory. "Where'd you go?"

She should just come clean and end all the suffering and unanswered questions. Maybe he would like being a father. She could hope, couldn't she?

"Colton?" She stopped. There would be no undoing this.

"Yeah?"

He hadn't shaved. Gray-and-brown scruff dusted his strong jaw. She wanted to touch it just one more time. His dark blue flannel shirt hung loose over his slim hips. His jeans were faded and well worn. Her belly twisted with desire and fear.

"I've got to get to school too. I'm going to be late. I'd rather not give Joann a reason to complain." She didn't care about work at the moment. Her whole life was her son. He was the only thing she'd done right in the world. She couldn't lose him, and telling would guarantee that.

She shrugged into her coat. The tears burned the back of her throat. She pressed both hands on the table and hung her head, taking deep breaths so she wouldn't break down in front of Colton.

"Hey, are you all right?"

The pressure of his strong hand was against her back. He leaned in close, smelling clean and male and caramelly. She stole a glance at him through the strands of her hair falling in her face. It was too much. She opened her mouth to speak, and the tears pooled in her eyes. She nodded.

"You don't look okay. Are you sick? Should I call an ambulance?"

"Knox told me he hates me right before you knocked." She straightened up and looked him in the eye. That was as much truth as she could offer.

"He doesn't hate you. Sure, he's pissed off that he's grounded. What kid doesn't get mad about that? Hell, I fought my old man's rules every chance I got."

"I don't know what to do with him."

"Are you going to get him his car back?" He handed her the coffee, and this time she took it.

"No." She couldn't afford to buy it back, even if she wanted to now.

"He got drunk. It happens. Kids his age do that kind of thing. I remember being his age and doing that stuff too." Colton unwrapped the sandwich and held it before her.

She shook her head. Her stomach tangled up like a kite in the branches of a tree. She couldn't eat. Shrugging, he tore a big chunk out of her sandwich with his teeth.

The heat from wearing her coat and from thinking about Knox wanting to find his father made sweat pop out over her skin. She tore the coat off and tossed it on the chair.

"It wasn't just that he got drunk. He went to school that way. The place I work. He embarrassed himself and me. He could've gotten in a lot more trouble than he did. I don't want him to keep making that mistake and become an alcoholic."

"Getting drunk once as a kid doesn't mean he'll end up with a drinking problem his whole life. It doesn't really work that way."

"Why did you start drinking? Your parents weren't big drinkers, were they? I didn't think your dad was anyway."

"Not Jedidiah Savage." He let out a small laugh. "The man absorbed in the rules. I never saw him drink. I drank because he didn't."

"How did it become a problem for you?" Had he felt let down by his dad somehow? Did he think drinking was a way to hide feeling inferior? But how could this man who had the world on a string for so long think he wasn't good enough? And yet even with all those musical skills, he still longed for his family to accept him. His deeply hidden vulnerabilities made her love him more. *Love.* Too strong a word.

"I thought it was cool to drink. It relaxed me, I guess. Then when we were writing our second album, the deadline was so tight and the record company was breathing down our necks I took drugs to keep me up and drank so I could sleep. Blaise tried to stop me from doing the drugs, but I was king of the world back then. I didn't think anything could stop me." He folded himself into the chair and stretched out his long legs.

She was going to be so late for work, but having Colton in her kitchen relaxed and sharing with her was worth it. And they weren't even painting.

He leaned forward. "Look, your kid made one stupid mistake. It happens. He didn't inherit some alcoholic disease. You're not that way. Is his father?"

The words froze in her mouth. She could only shake her head.

"Okay then. He's a kid, babe. Let it go. You grounded him, or whatever it is you did. It sounds like he learned his lesson. Don't torture him or yourself. He's going to turn out fine. You're his mom." His slow smile lit up his face and made his gray eyes glitter.

"Thank you for that." She was supposed to be helping him, and he was helping her. Maybe she could back off on some of the rules at least for now and see how things went. Maybe that would distract Knox's need to ask about his father. The tears brimmed again.

Colton stood and wiped away a single tear from her cheek with his thumb. His touch had her wanting to lean in a press her lips to his.

She pulled away, breaking the current. "I really have to get to work."

He handed over the last sandwich. She took it and shoved it in her bag.

"How come you don't have a Christmas tree yet?"

"I haven't felt like it since Hank was gone. I guess I should. Knox probably thinks I'm punishing him with that too. I really am a Scrooge."

"But a much prettier one."

His compliment was like a warm apple turnover straight from the oven. She wanted to eat the whole thing at once, licking her fingers as she devoured every crumb, but shouldn't even look twice at it.

"Orchestra practice starts at three. Don't be late." It was better to try to keep things businesslike. "We could have an art lesson in my studio tonight if you want." Helping him was what she was supposed to be doing. She needed to stay focused for the next few weeks; then he'd be gone for good again, and she and Knox could go back to their lives as they were.

"I guess I should let you teach me to paint. I have to hold up my promise to Cash, or he'll be the next relative mad at me. Anything else, captain?" He saluted her.

"Get out of my house." But the smile on her face matched the one in her voice.

His deep throaty laugh followed her out the door.

Harley raced down the hall toward the auditorium, the heels of her boots clacking against the linoleum. She was late. A student had stayed to finish up an art project due before the winter break, and right as she was about to shut the lights of her classroom, Joann stopped in to let her know the kids had heard Colton was coming in to save the day and wondered if he might be the new music teacher.

Did Harley think he'd be interested? She had laughed, then said no. It would be a cold day in hell before Colton Savage stepped off the stage to teach in Heritage River. Joann didn't appreciate her honesty.

Her students were on board with the art show. They had brainstormed ideas for pieces they could display and sell. Their faces lit up at the thought of someone buying the art they created. She envied their idealism. She was like them a long time ago, before the real world had shown her a rough and jagged side that cut deeply. The truth was she wasn't talented enough. Artists either had the gift or they didn't. She didn't.

But Colton had said he'd be there for her if she took the chance and displayed her own work. His belief in her might give her the strength to try again. Through his eyes, she saw herself bathed in strong light reserved for the finest sculptures.

She grabbed the auditorium door and opened it with a swoosh. The house lights were low. The stage lights burned like the afternoon sun. The kids sat on the stage in an arch formation. Someone hit a note much like the sound of a sick chicken. Colton paced the stage, running a hand over the back of his head. She made her way closer to the front and slid into a cushioned seat undetected.

"Okay, okay. Stop." He waved his arms in the air.

"Mr. Savage, that's not the conductor's signal to stop," Elizabeth Jones said as she flipped her long, curly hair off her shoulder. She elbowed Bella Perry, the flute player next to her, causing Bella's flute to hit her in the teeth.

Colton stopped and turned to Elizabeth. "What's your name again?"

She sat up straighter in her seat. "Bethy."

"Okay, Bethy, I'm new at this conductor sh—I mean stuff. How about you go easy on me for today?"

A few kids in the back chuckled.

"I thought you might want to know, is all. You can't stand up there the night of the concert waving your arms for us to stop."

Harley leaned back in the seat. How would Colton handle the persistent Miss Jones? Harley had Bethy her first year. Bethy never missed an opportunity to show off the information stored in her young brain.

"I promise you I have some experience playing music. In fact, I can play several instruments. Some people even think I'm good enough to charge for my performances. But I won't wave my arms during your concert if you let me do what I do best in the meantime."

"I was just trying to help."

"You are a big help, and I want you to keep giving me suggestions." His voice was smooth and pleasant. He flashed his wide stage smile to the group. All charm. As usual.

Harley wanted to applaud him for not saying "You are a big pain in the backside."

"Okay, kids, that basically sucked. Sorry. I'm probably not supposed to say that, but let's try it from the top. I need to get an idea of who's only pretending to play their instrument."

There was a soft gasp from somewhere in the middle.

"I told you I knew what I was doing. On my mark." He waved his hands, and the band fired up.

"Hey, Harley."

Harley swung her head up to the direction of the male voice. "Hey, Cash. Did you come to watch?"

Cash took the seat next to her. His long legs stretched out into the aisle. Did all the Savage men have long legs? The orchestra banged and blew their way through "The Christmas Song."

"I was hoping my uncle didn't crash and burn on his first day. I thought maybe I could help him if he hit trouble. Not everyone appreciates his honesty." He winked.

"That's very sweet of you to worry about him."

"He wants everyone to think he's too tough to break, but even the great Colton Savage has a breaking point. He's always been there for me, even when me and my dad were having some troubles. I trust Uncle C more than anyone, well, except for my dad." He turned his attention to the beeping from his phone.

She waited for him to finish. "Hey, Cash. I was thinking about taking the relaxation class on a trip to the museum. Would you be into something like that?" She had been trying to find a way to help Andy Henson believe in himself. If someone like Cash went along, Andy would be more likely to go too. She hadn't missed the way Andy hung on Cash's every word.

"Sure, I'd go. I think the class would like it."

"Great. I'll keep you posted." She'd have to send out permission slips for the students who were under eighteen, and she hoped the Impressionist exhibit she wanted Andy to see was still there.

By the end of practice, Colton had the kids laughing. They sat at the edge of their seats as he told some stories of being on the road and some of the famous people he'd worked with. He jumped on the piano and banged out a few tunes with them. A couple of the kids joined in, while the others either clapped or danced in their seats. At the end, they gave him a round of applause.

Colton puffed up his chest and sauntered off the stage. The glow was painted across his cheeks in reds. She loved to see him in his element.

Cash pushed up out of the seat and leaned in to half hug, half pat Colton on the back. "You're pretty good at this conductor stuff. Those kids were eating out of your hands."

Colton looked back at the students packing up. "I'm okay, not great—yet. Did you come by to see if your old uncle could handle the stress?"

"I was in the neighborhood."

Colton laughed. "Yeah. I'm surprised Billy didn't walk in here to take my blood pressure. There's a lot of work to do in a short time, but I think they can handle it. They won't be perfect, but I doubt the parents will care about that. Am I right, Harley?"

She stepped closer to them. "You are right. The

parents want to see their children on the stage playing. They don't care about anything else."

"I only asked if I was right so you'd say yes again." His fingers brushed her jaw.

Cash passed a glance between them. She hoped her cheeks weren't blushing too much.

Some of the students passed them on their way out. Colton gave them a high-five.

"Knox." She called as her son took the steps two at a time.

He dipped his chin at her but scooted out the side door. Her heart sank. She wanted to have a talk with him on the way home. Maybe give him back his phone as a peace offering.

"Maybe he's getting a ride home with his friend," Colton said.

"Yeah, that's probably it."

"Cash, do you want to grab some dinner? You want to come, Harley?"

"Uncle Colton, can we do that some other time? Dad and I needed to add a practice for Friday's gig. Tonight's the only time we could get into the space. Hey, do you want to come to the practice? Harley, you could come too."

The smile dipped off Colton's face before he righted it. "No, thanks, kid. I don't want to get in the way while you're working, but I'm glad you stopped by."

"You're going to come watch us play Friday, right?"

"I don't know. I'll text you."

"You should go." She wanted him to try to mend

some fences. It would be good for him to start taking steps to work things out with his brother. "It'll probably be fun."

"Okay."

"Really?" Cash's eyes went wide.

"Only if Harley goes with me."

"Oh, I don't... I might have something."

Colton crossed his arms over his chest and looked her square in the eye. "If you think it's a good idea and would be fun, then you should come along. Something tells me it's been a while since you had a night out."

Longer than he knew. When was there time to go out? She'd been preoccupied raising a boy. And men never held her interest for very long. She was too busy measuring them up to Colton.

"Come on, Harley." Cash put an arm around her shoulder. "I never had a teacher come to one of my shows before. I'll be the most popular guy in school."

Cash Savage was as charming as his uncle. She laughed. "Okay, I'll go." Having Colton creeping into the edges of her life made her forget the need to keep him away. She wanted him there.

"Cool. We'll drive over together, like a date." Colton flashed her his dimple and rocked on his heels.

"Not a date. Just as friends." She hoped she wouldn't regret taking so many chances.

"Uncle C, you better take what you can get." Cash laughed and headed out of the auditorium.

"You're not going to let my nephew think I struck out,

are you?" Colton leaned in and whispered in her ear. His warm breath sent shivers over her skin.

"You should set a better example for him. He's an impressionable young man."

He tossed his head back and laughed. "I do believe, ma'am, you and I were making some questionable decisions at that age."

Memories of their young lovemaking burned her neck and face. Time to change the subject. "You had a good practice, Colton. I knew the kids would like you. Sorry to rush off, but I have some Christmas errands to finish." She grabbed her coat and hurried from the auditorium before he could say anything else.

Harley shoved her way out the door and into the cold air. The sky was cloud covered, and the wind kicked around the bare trees. The sun had set while she was inside agreeing to a date with Colton. Okay, it wasn't a real date, and she shouldn't go thinking about his invitation that way. He would leave, like every other time before this. She needed him to leave and never look back. Better to remember that and not get caught up in nostalgia. She was too old for fantasies. The closer she got to Colton, the closer the truth would be to revealing itself. She had to protect her secret and her son. If Colton rejected Knox, what would her boy believe about himself?

But her insides sizzled at the idea of going out Friday night, and her insides had sizzled when he brushed against her jaw. She pressed cold fingers to her hot face.

She longed to touch him again and to feel his strong hands across her body.

"Harley," a male voice shouted.

She jumped out of her deep thought. A stout man hurried across the parking lot toward her, waving his arm. His trench coat blew behind him. It took a moment for her to realize it was Joe Henson, the father of her student Andy. She let her thoughts of Colton blow away in the wind and repositioned her expression into one more appropriate for a teacher.

"Hello, Joe. What brings you by?"

"I was hoping to catch you still here. My lucky day, I guess. I wanted to talk with you a minute about Andy's time in your art class."

"Sure." Was he waiting for her? What an unusual thing to do when the phone or email worked.

"How long do you think it will take for Andy to get on the straight and narrow?"

"Well, what do you mean by that? Andy is a good student with good grades."

"I'm talking about the bathroom incident. How long before we're guaranteed that won't happen again? Isn't that what your art class is supposed to do?"

She squared her shoulders. "My class is to help Andy deal with the stress in his life. That takes time."

"Are you planning on dragging out those lessons?"

"It's not my intention to take your money."

"He's been painting at home. Making a mess of my basement, in fact. Says he's creating. I think he's doing it just to upset me. But I don't see any difference in him.

He's still belligerent. He's not doing his homework. I don't know how to reach him. I've thought a good kick up side his head would do the trick."

She wasn't supposed to judge, but a father who couldn't understand his child was hurting was going to make her job and his son's job much harder. "Please don't do that. The kind of work we're doing takes time. If you acknowledge his feelings, that will go a long way to helping him relax. He only wants his parents' approval. I'm glad he's doing some extra painting at home." Maybe he would be agreeable to participating in the art show. She hadn't had a chance to ask him yet.

"You're aren't the one who has to clean it up. Never mind that. I'm not going to acknowledge his feelings. We've been tiptoeing around his feelings since he was a boy. I told his mother Andy needed to toughen up, but she coddled his every whim. Now look where that got us. I want to see results from this art class."

"I know this is frustrating and you might feel like you can't help your son, but I assure you—"

He shoved his palm inches from her face. "Don't go psychoanalyzing me. I expect you to fix my son as soon as possible. I need my house back in order." He turned and marched back toward his car. His overcoat still floated behind him, like the cape of a villain after his nemesis.

She shivered in her coat and then slid into her Durango and rested her head on the steering wheel. She'd never be able to reach Andy if his parents weren't supporting him, and his jerk of a father would blame her.

She sat up and slapped the wheel. What would

Colton do in a situation like this? He wouldn't sit around feeling sorry for himself. He'd tell her to prove the asshole wrong because that's what he would do. She'd help Andy, and she'd start with that trip to the museum.

Harley slipped the Durango into traffic with a newfound purpose, heat in her cheeks and quivering in her stomach. Joe Henson would eat his words.

And she had a date Friday night.

Chapter Fifteen

Colton moved around the tiny kitchen in Harley's guesthouse. He chopped up vegetables while a piece of chicken cooked on a tiny electric grill he found in the cabinet. That thing was pretty cool. Maybe he should cook up extra and take it next door. Harley was probably making peanut butter and marshmallows for dinner. He laughed. Her bad eating habits were part of her charm. He arranged two more chicken breasts on the grill. They just fit.

The orchestra practice earlier surprised him. The kids were better than he thought they'd be, and they liked him. They had some technical problems that might not get fixed in time, but he had some tricks up his sleeve that might be able to help them. He'd have to break them down and work with each section separately for that to happen, but he could probably swing it. It had been some time since he tried to straighten out the kinks in a band of any size.

He picked up the phone twice to call Blaise, so his little brother could bust his chops about teaching a group of kids, but he changed his mind each time. Those days were over. Blaise and his damn desire to write new music and become a stay-at-home dad.

His own father had been convinced Colton persuaded Blaise into the rock-and-roll life. What would his father say about Colton and Blaise now? Probably a big fat "I told you so." Their music career together was over, and their relationship was in ruins— and to Jedidiah Savage, it would've been all Colton's fault.

He tossed the vegetables into a skillet and let the sizzle play its tune. His phone sang out the lyrics from an old blues song. Well, it wasn't a family member. He wiped his hands and reached for the phone.

"Colton Savage."

"Hey, bro, what's going on?" His friend Michael shouted into the phone.

Colton jerked the phone from his ear. "Christ, man, why are you yelling?"

"Can't you hear it?"

Sounds of people screaming.

"Mick's doing his solo. They are loving us, bro." Michael was touring with some guys on a reunion tour. That seemed to be what every musician his age was doing these days. Reunion tours with half the original band missing because either they were out of the business or dead. That had never been Savage. They had stayed together until now, and in a few weeks Colton would be playing Savage songs on tour with Michael and two other guys.

"The guys in the band heard we're hitting the road right after Christmas and want to know if they could join us. Maybe get a third band and be a New Year's Beasts of Southern Rock tour. What do you think?"

"Three bands?" The ticket prices would be higher, the crowd bigger. But did he really want to be like those guys who had to tour with other bands because they couldn't sell enough tickets by themselves? That wasn't him, yet. Was it? "Let me think about it."

"It would be great to have a group of guys together. We can stay up and drink all night like the old days. Maybe bust up a few hotel rooms. Beasts of Rock, baby," Michael shouted again. He was probably drunk.

Colton's days of staying up all night drinking were behind him now. He couldn't make that mistake again. "Don't you need to get back on stage?" Mick's solo couldn't go on for that long. He usually lost his place halfway and gave up. He sucked.

"Yeah, yeah. Sounds like Mick is wrapping up. Three bands is the way to go, bro. Don't sit on this too long. We've got to get the billing all set up." Michael ended the call and silenced the screaming.

He looked at his phone and said to no one, "Stop calling me 'bro.'"

Blaise would tell him to ditch the tour. He glanced over at his Gibson leaning against the wall. "You shut up too."

Colton scooped out the vegetables and chicken. He plated his food, ready to sit down with a little Verdi playing on his phone. A knock at the door interrupted his first mouthful. Maybe Harley wanted to have an early date with him. Okay, not a real date. He wasn't going to take any chances with her feelings this time.

He opened the door to find Knox standing there. His hair hung in his face. His backpack was slung over his shoulder. A guitar in his hand.

"What's up?" He checked over Knox's shoulder for any sign of Harley.

"Hey. I was wondering if I could take you up on your offer to jam." Knox backed up. "But if it's a bad time, I can come back later."

"No, no. Come on in." Colton swung the door open wider. "Are you hungry? I have extra."

"Um, no thanks. I'll grab something later."

He pressed his lips together. What would that be? French fries? "I'm a pretty good cook, but if you want to pass." Colton sat back at the counter.

Knox stood by the door.

"Kid, you're making me nervous. Come in and eat, and then we'll jam. I'm starving. I haven't eaten since this morning." He pointed to the seat.

Knox dumped his belongings and grabbed a plate from the cabinet, making his way around the kitchen with ease. He slid onto the stool beside Colton.

"It's weird having you in my uncle's place, but it's cool at the same time."

Colton stabbed at his food. "It's decent of you to let me stay here."

"My mom wanted to rent it out for the extra money. I'm glad it was you and not some stranger. I don't think I could've handled having someone here she didn't know. I miss having Hank around. He was our only family."

"Where's your father?"

"Never met him." Knox shoveled in his food.

"His loss, kid."

"My mom never told him about me. Said they didn't mean anything to each other. He was an artist, like her, and he had some big break. She let him go without telling him."

Colton pushed the remains of his food around the plate. Harley let the guy off too easy—not that he would've wanted some woman knocking on his door with news like that. He'd always been smart when it came to making sure he didn't leave little Coltons in his wake.

"Your mom was smart and brave to raise you alone." She could've repeated history, but she stuck around and did the right thing by her boy. There was no way she would've made any other choice. She had hated being the girl whose mother had dumped her, but she'd never complained. She'd held her head up high. He'd always admired that about her.

"She's not smart enough to give me my privileges back."

Colton grabbed Knox's hand before he could shove more food in his mouth. "Hey, that's your ma. Don't talk about her like that."

Knox hung his head. "Sorry."

"Do you want me to say something to her? Maybe get your phone back at least?"

"Nah, but thanks. What did you think of the practice?"

He caught the shift in subject and went along with it. "The kids are pretty good."

"I thought we sounded bad."

Colton laughed. "Okay, if we're being honest, it was bad, but I think I can help that."

"Mr. Myer couldn't."

"Mr. Myer ain't me, kid." Colton grabbed their plates and strutted around the kitchen, cleaning up. Yeah, he could work with that motley crew. He laughed at his bad pun.

"What?" Knox helped load the dishwasher.

"Nothing. What pieces do you want to jam?" Colton hesitated but grabbed his Gibson leaning near the fireplace.

"Whatever you want. I won't be as good as you, but I'll try to keep up."

"You'll be fine. Follow my lead." Colton slid the round leather ottoman over and took a seat.

Knox sat opposite him on the couch.

He strapped on the guitar and tuned the strings. "Ready?" He grabbed a pick and placed it between his thumb and middle finger. Knox did the same. "You don't have to hold your pick that way just 'cause I am."

"What way?" Knox looked down at his hand. "I

The Bridge Between Love and Lies

always do this. Don't know why. My first guitar teacher always tried to get me to stop, but I kept going back to it. Feels more comfortable that way."

"Yeah, me too. Fuck the guitar teachers." Colton struck up the first notes from a Savage song that had been overplayed on the radio. Knox chimed right in.

They sat that way for a while. Colton moved from tune to tune, and Knox kept up, never missing a beat or hitting the wrong chord. He even took some of the solos off in a direction Colton hadn't thought about.

"You're good," Colton said when they came up for air.

"Really?" Knox's face lit up.

"You don't know that?" This kid played better than he did at that age. "You'll go pretty far if you want to with that much talent. When you're ready, give me a call. I can introduce you to a few people."

Knox's neck turned red. "Thanks, I will. My mom will be furious, but I don't care. This is all I ever dreamed about. Making music, that is. I want to stand on the stage under those hot lights, ripping through a solo I wrote, with everyone screaming. When the audience applauds at the orchestra concerts or the school musicals, I feel something like an electric charge across my skin. It's the best feeling in the world." He stopped short and dropped his head. "Sorry. I rambled there."

"Hey, no need to apologize to me. I got you. That's how I feel too. It's the greatest thing in the world and why I'm always on the road. As long as there are people chanting my name, I'm high, and that's a way better high than drugs or alcohol."

"There's still my mom to think about. She might stop speaking to me if I tell her you're going to help me become a musician."

"Let me handle your mother."

Chapter Sixteen

Harley dumped her purse on the kitchen counter and stacked her packages neatly beside it. Christmas shopping had been a success. She managed to find the top thing on Knox's list, and she found a CD and the romantic comedy Ella wanted. Her heart ached a little that she wouldn't be getting Uncle Hank a sweater he swore he loved and wore every day for a month. She'd bought him a new scarf every year so he could wrap it around his head in the brisk winters and shovel if snow decided to show up. She'd planned to buy him a pizza stone this year, but obviously not now.

She'd also spoken to the landlord of the empty store on Main Street. They could use it for the art show. She couldn't believe how easy it had been to get him to agree. His daughter had been in the musicals when she was in school, so he supported the arts.

She went around the house and turned on all the

lights. The bright light added to her better mood. She played some Christmas music too. She might be able to save the art program, even if she couldn't save her job.

"Knox, I'm home," she shouted up the steps. Sometimes she sent him a text to let him know she was there, but since she had his phone, that was pointless. She'd give it back to him during dinner. Colton had been right. Yes, again. She laughed. It felt good to laugh. She didn't do it enough these days.

What to make for dinner? The question of the century. She opened the fridge. Would boiled hot dogs work? She didn't have the energy for more. Maybe she'd crack open a can of beans. Beans were a vegetable, weren't they?

"Knox," she yelled again.

She marched up the steps. Maybe she'd order a pizza instead. How many times could you eat pizza in a week and still be healthy? She knocked on his closed door. No answer. She gently opened the door. The room was dark, with bedsheets twirled together like a serpent and pillows scattered on the floor. His dirty clothes were still a permanent decoration on the floor. The room smelled of sweat. She pulled her sweater up over her nose and opened the window to let in some fresh air. "Teenage boys smell."

Where was he? She checked the front room and the kitchen for a note. He had asked about going out after practice. Had he deliberately disobeyed her? His coat and backpack were missing. He had gone against her wishes.

Her head buzzed. How could he do this? Well, that was it. He'd be grounded for life now. But what if something happened to him? A car accident? Did he walk home in the dark? She didn't like him doing that. Anyone could come along and grab him. Okay, deep breath. He wasn't exactly the target serial killers were looking for. Yeah, well, there had been Jeffrey Dahmer.

She reached for her cell to call him, then stopped. "Damn it. Think, Harley. Think." She had Joann's number in her phone. She hit the button and waited. "Hi, Joann, it's Harley. Is Duke home?"

"Hello, Harley. Yes, we're just down to dinner. Is there something I can help you with?"

"Can you ask him if he knows where Knox is?"

"Hang on." There was a muffled sound on the other end. "He says he hasn't seen Knox since the end of the day. Sorry. Is everything okay? Do you need me to send Rich over?"

"No, it's fine. Thank you." She ended the call before Joann could ask any more questions.

She tried Ella. "I can't find Knox. Call me." She hated voice mail.

Her stomach twisted in braids. Should she call the sheriff? No, she was getting ahead of herself. She'd go look for him. That's what rational people did, didn't they?

She hurried out to the Durango and stopped. The lights were on in the guesthouse, and Colton's fancy car was parked off to the side. Maybe he'd come with her. She wouldn't mind the company. Someone to at least keep her from veering off the road into a ditch. Those braids in her stomach were getting tighter. Now wasn't the time to puke.

She banged on the front door. Music played on the other side. Not just music. Colton on his damn guitar. He'd never hear her. She banged harder.

"Hold on." His voice resonated from the other side before he swung open the door. His smile began to spread, then stopped. "Are you okay? You look like you saw a ghost."

"I don't know where Knox is. Will you help me look?"

He stepped aside and laughed. Knox stood at the kitchen counter, his hand halfway to his mouth holding something that resembled a carrot. He waved with his free hand.

Her knees buckled. Colton grabbed her elbow. She'd forgotten to take her coat, and the cold wind blew through the thin fabric of her clothes. Her hands shook. Relief and fear washed over her in alternating waves. Her son was fine. Her son was at Colton's. What had they been talking about? What secrets did they share?

Knox came around the counter. "Mom, are you all right?"

"I'm fine. I was just worried about you. I'm glad you're okay." She turned and hurried back to the house.

The cold wind slapped against her face.

"Harley, wait."

She didn't turn around but forced her legs forward. She tripped up the back steps. Her hands collided with the worn wood of the stoop, and a splinter pierced her palm. She forced herself up on shaking legs. Footfalls pounded the steps behind her. She ran into the kitchen and slammed the back door behind her.

He didn't knock but shoved his way into her kitchen. Colton rounded the table and headed her off at the faucet. "Hey, did you hurt yourself?"

He tried to reach for her hands, but she shoved them under the hot water. "I'm fine. A splinter." Her bottom lip shook. She clamped it down between her teeth, hoping to stop what was only seconds away from happening. *Please don't let me cry now. Not now.* She kept her eyes on the water. Her skin turned pink.

Colton reached into the water and took her hands in his strong ones. "Let me see. I'm pretty good with splinters." That damn dimple again. "You were worried about Knox."

She nodded. Too soon to start talking. She didn't trust the tears.

He rubbed his knuckle over the splinter. "I can push this out. I'm sorry. I didn't realize you didn't know where he was. I should've thought about that. See? I would've sucked as a parent." His smile was a thin line. "He's a great kid, Harley. We jammed together. Blew my mind. He's amazing. He just wants you to be proud of him."

"That's not true."

He lifted his gaze and met hers. "I'm telling you. He wants you to understand why he needs to play so much."

"No, no. You would've been a great parent." The tears leaked free. She used her free hand to swipe them away. What had she done? How could she have denied them both a chance to know each other? Why did she think she had to be alone all the time? Because when a mother abandoned a child and never returned, that child believed she was unlovable. And when that child grew into a woman and lost the only man she ever cared about, she didn't want him to believe he had been trapped.

She had lived with the lie every day, pretended it didn't exist. She went about her life doing all the mundane things everyone else did. She pretended for so long the lie became the truth. No one ever had to know if she kept on pretending.

But her son deserved a father, and she had lied. *Dear God.* Her whole life had been one lie.

"Colton." Her voice was just a whisper. She wanted to hide in the shadows so he couldn't see her face. It was time to tell.

He pinched the end of the splinter and pulled it free. The pain stung. She deserved that. A drop of blood formed. He took her hand and ran it back under the water before he brought it up to his lips. His soft lips met her sore skin. A current ran up her arm and straight to her heart.

"You don't have to worry. Knox is okay. He's going to turn out just fine. Like you." He held her hand, and she didn't pull away. His voice was deep and throaty. He reached over and turned off the water. He was so close she could see the tiny scar on his jaw made when a guitar neck caught him in the face.

Colton turned his head. They locked eyes. Heat filled her belly. She pulled her hand away and rested it against his face. His stubble was prickly on her fingers, just the way she thought it would be. The heat in her belly dropped lower.

He stood to his full height and took her hand from his cheek and kissed her palm. He took the other hand and kissed that one too. With one very skilled finger, he tilted her chin up toward him. His lips were soft and warm against hers. The heat in her belly spread throughout her body. He deepened the kiss, and she fell into it. His tongue pushed her lips apart, and she went to him.

He tasted sweet, and she forgot all reasonable thought, never wanted to be logical again. He tangled his fingers in her hair and brought her head closer so their kiss went even deeper. She sought his tongue with her own.

This was where she always wanted to be, on the edge of every electric feeling in her nerves. She could light the world on fire when she was with him.

Anything seemed possible when she was with Colton.

The door banged open. "Oh, wow. Sorry."

They broke apart. She nearly fell from the force. Her face burned. Busted by her son. How stupid. She adjusted her clothing. Not that her clothing—or the removal of it—had been involved in the kiss. She wanted her clothes to be taken off. She couldn't deny that. Damn it. She was supposed to keep this professional, and one stupid moment could've ruined everything.

"Um, I was just coming to make sure everything was okay. Y'all were gone a while." Knox ducked his head and looked up at them through his long eyelashes. A thin smile played across his face.

Colton leaned against the counter and crossed his legs. "Everything's fine. Next time leave her a note so she doesn't worry." And just like that, he had control of the situation. A warm flush spread across her. Her hormones were ridiculous.

"I promise."

She found her voice. "Your phone. Take your phone back." She scrambled through her purse and found it at the bottom, under a half-eaten cookie in its brown wrapper. She handed the phone over. "We'll start with this. So you can call me when you're going to be late or need a ride or something."

Knox stared at the cell as if he hadn't seen it before. "Thanks."

She wanted to hug him, to feel her son in her arms again, but she stayed planted and waited for his move. He nodded and left the room, as if he always walked in on his mother kissing at the kitchen sink. She sank against the counter.

"We can't do that again." Her face still burned.

"Why not?" Colton closed the space between them to inches. His body's magnetic force pulled hers toward him. "You seemed like you were enjoying yourself." His smile broadened, lighting up his eyes too.

That wasn't exactly the point. "We can't start something we're not going to finish. I won't do it again. I refuse to be some woman you mess around with while passing through. I'm done being that person." It was all or nothing for her, but she knew better than to expect it. He wasn't capable of a long-term commitment except to his guitar.

His lips caressed the side of her neck. "Oh, I can finish it." The side of her neck tingled everywhere his lips lingered.

She braced her palms against his hard chest. "Colton, I mean it. I'm not looking for another one-night stand." She pushed him away.

The current broke. He looked at her as if he just realized where he was. He scratched at the back of his neck. "You're right. I'm sorry. It's just, well, when I'm with you, I want to be with you more."

"And when you're not with me, you forget about me."

"That isn't true. It was never the right time for me to get too serious. I couldn't settle down and be on the road. You would've hated that life."

"You didn't even give me a chance to try." The fight was still there between them. It was as if no time at all had gone by.

He had just walked away from her that night. He'd brought her to the bridge and told her his good news. Savage had made it. They were flying out the very next day to record the first album. She was happy for him, but her heart had shattered into a million tiny red pieces. He hadn't asked her to come. He hadn't asked her to wait for him. He was gone as if he'd never been there. No phone calls, no letters. Seven years passed before she saw him again. And another eighteen after that.

"You know what? I don't want to have this argument again." He threw his hands up.

"What argument would that be, Colton? The one you never stick around for?" The footing of the conversation was quickly slipping, but she didn't think she could right it.

"You knew what I wanted. I never hid that from you. Ever. It was always going to be my music. Music has been my entire life. Why can't you understand that?"

"You wanted music. Well, you certainly have it. You have music instead of a relationship with your siblings. You got music instead of time with your father. The man who did his best to raise his three children by himself after his wife died. My father spit in my face. I would've killed for the family you have, and you don't care about them at all. All you care about is music. Go to it, then. Go back on the road where you belong, where no one needs you. Where everyone is busy shouting your name, but I'll tell you what. Someday there won't be anyone left to scream for you and then you'll be all alone. Can you stand that?"

"Never tell me I don't care about my family." He pushed the words out through gritted teeth. The vein on the side of his neck pulsed.

Before she could say another word, he turned on his heel and stormed out the back door. The glass pane shook. She sank against the counter again.

Her phone sang to life. Ella. If she hadn't left a frantic message earlier, she would let the call go to voice mail. "I'm sorry if I scared you with that call."

"Is Knox okay? I just got your message."

Harley pushed her hair away from her face. Her hand still throbbed, but she could feel the softness of Colton's lips against her palm. She shook her hand to make the feeling go away. "He's fine. I overreacted." Nothing new there.

"Thank goodness. I was getting ready to call the cavalry. Stephanie said she saw him at school today, but that was the last time she saw him."

Harley wished Knox would ask Stephanie out. Sometimes Harley and Ella would sit around over a glass of wine and imagine what it would be like to be related if on some far-off possibility, Stephanie and Knox got hitched. Harley just liked the idea of being related to someone. She would always search for that family she couldn't have.

"Where was he?"

She wasn't sure if she could keep the truth out of her voice. She needed to unload the burden she'd been carrying around and let someone else hold it for a little while. Telling Ella wouldn't be fair if she wasn't willing to tell the truth to the two people who needed to hear it most.

"Duke gave him a ride home. Took longer than he thought." More lies. They were everywhere. She bit her lip to keep from laughing, and it wasn't even funny. None of it was.

"Are you trying to tell me Duke got lost on the ride home?"

She probably should have edited her response. "No,

of course not. Duke made a stop first." There. That was a better lie.

"Are you sure you want Knox still hanging around with Duke?"

"Well, no. But it's complicated with him being my boss's son. I better run. Thanks for getting back to me."

Harley plugged the phone into the charger. She really needed to get something on for dinner, or they'd starve. She piled the Christmas packages in the mudroom and put up water for pasta. She could pop open a jar of sauce. Simple carbohydrates were better than nothing.

While she waited for the water to boil, she grabbed her laptop, drafted a flyer for the art show, and researched the exhibits at the museum. Her hand still hurt, and she could still feel Colton's lips on hers. If Knox hadn't come in, who knew how far they would've taken things. She couldn't control herself around him. He had a hold on her heart.

The time had passed to get rid of him. The problem was she wanted him. She could deny it, hide from it, try to disguise it. She loved him.

Still.

Chapter Seventeen

Colton turned off Winding Way and headed toward the school. He planned to tell Joann Humphreys he couldn't help out with the orchestra. His duffel was packed, and his Gibson lay across the backseat. He was headed home and as far away from Heritage River as possible.

He didn't need those art lessons. The rehab had been enough. He didn't even want a drink.

He did last night, but he opted for smoking behind the guesthouse until he nearly smoked the entire pack and spent fifteen minutes hacking up a lung. He thought he might've needed the emergency room, but he'd pulled himself together eventually.

He could still feel Harley's lips on his, and he couldn't stop thinking about the way she looked up at him when he leaned over to turn off the water running across her bruised hand. She had smelled like honeysuckle and vanilla. He had wanted to touch and kiss her skin in places he hadn't seen in a long time. He wanted to make her call out his name with those big brown eyes staring up into his. Those thoughts had him pacing most of the night.

But she had said he didn't care about his family and he only cared about the screaming crowds. Her words had stung like a broken guitar string snapping against his wrist. No, he wasn't going to stay here and put up with that from her. She didn't understand him. Never had. Never would.

That wasn't true. She understood him better than anyone except Blaise.

Colton parked his car at the back of the lot, away from the other cars. Practice started in ten minutes. He probably should have called earlier, but he wanted to quit in person and didn't want to interrupt their workday.

"Keep telling yourself that." He yanked open the glass doors.

The smell of waxed floors, fried food, and sweat hit him.

He turned right, toward Joann's office. Hopefully, Harley wasn't in there. He planned to call her from the car on his way out of town. He'd have to call Cash too and explain he wouldn't be at the gig Friday night. He didn't want to let his nephew down, and leaving would, but Cash would have to understand. He could fly Cash out to a show and get him up on stage to jam. If he had an ounce of Savage blood in his veins, he'd love being in front of a big crowd.

His steps faltered. *Don't think about disappointing*

him or Harley. He couldn't stay. He wasn't supposed to get involved. It was bad for his recovery. But last night he'd wanted her until she'd said those things. Hell, he still wanted her. He didn't want to hear what an ass he'd been, because he wasn't some fuck up who didn't care. Okay, maybe he had been, but not anymore.

"Hey, Colton."

He stopped in his tracks and turned around. Knox raised a bottle of soda at him.

"Hey." How was he going to explain his leaving to this kid?

"Are you ready for today's practice?"

"I, um, I need to speak to Mrs. Humphreys first. Is she in her office?"

"I don't know. I'm going over to the band room. You want to walk together? I downloaded an old interview with you back when your career was just starting. You had a lot of hair back then. Just joking. You were talking about playing in the high school battle of the bands and how y'all always won. It was cool."

Colton's hand went to his head. "The one where I'm sitting in front of my amp and Blaise came sliding on the stage behind me in his socks yelling like Tarzan." He smirked at the memory. That was one of his first interviews with a music magazine. He had been desperate to sound like a real rocker and not some dumb kid from Heritage River. He wanted to punch Blaise for the stunt too. Did Blaise remember that day? Christ, he didn't need to keep thinking about Blaise right now.

"Yeah, that's the one. Y'all were intense. Can you

show me that thing you did with your hands when the interviewer asked you to play? Are you coming? We're going to be late. Mom will mark it down. If I'm late three times, I get detention."

Colton glanced over his shoulder at Joann's office and back at Knox. The boy's eyes were wide with expectancy. For a moment, he saw himself with that same look, staring into the cold eyes of his father and feeling the icy dread of disappointment every time he spoke about rock and roll to his old man.

Those kids, especially Knox, were relying on him to get them to that show. He had two weeks left until the tour took off. What was he going to do during that time anyway? Walking into that practice would save him explaining to Cash he left. And Billy. Christ, he'd forgotten about Billy. That old coot would chase him down and make him come back. But sticking around would mean facing Harley and her truths about his family. He'd spent a lot of time avoiding ties, but somehow they managed to snake up around him and bind him close.

"Detention blows. Let's go and I will show you my move, but you can't share it with anyone else."

"Cool."

They fist-bumped.

Harley watched the door to the auditorium and checked the time on her phone for the third time in five minutes.

She picked at the paint stuck to her wrists. They were late. Okay, it was only two minutes, and most of the kids hadn't even taken their seats yet. Where were they? What were they talking about now? Her phone vibrated in her pocket, and she pulled it out. Andy had sent a text. *I can go to the museum. no to the art show. Ty.*

Her heart sank. He had some talent buried deep if he'd only give himself a chance. He might even realize painting allowed him to do better in his classes and would offer a tool to handle his stress. At least he said yes to the trip. She'd have to figure out a way to convince him to be in the show.

The door swung open, throwing the hallway light into the aisle. Joann Humphreys headed down toward her with a purpose to her step. *Great. What next?*

"The practice hasn't started yet?" Joann wore her signature suit with perfect creases and starched blouse. Why couldn't this woman dress like other principals in leggings and an oversized sweater? Harley glanced at her own clothing. Jeans that could use a date with the iron, but who ironed jeans? And her black cardigan with thumbholes that had gold paint speckled across the front from class earlier. It might even look as if she'd meant to do that. Yeah, okay.

"Just waiting for Colton and Knox to arrive. Kids, take your seats and warm up." Better to look like she knew what she was doing. The students ignored her.

Joann whistled through her fingers. All the kids turned. "Take your seats. This isn't public speaking class. I should hear instruments and not mouths yapping."

"Sorry we're late." Colton's voice boomed as he paraded into the auditorium. Knox was right behind him. Colton took off his coat and threw it on the back of one of the seats. "We have a lot of work to do." He moved past them. "Joann. Harley." He marched right up on the stage.

"Rob, can I see that violin?" Colton took the instrument and made it come to life. He moved around the stage, a smile on his face, turning that one violin into a full-blown rock concert. The kids stared on in amazement.

They burst into applause and shouts of praise when he finished with a big ending complete with standing on one of the chairs. "That's the way I like to start a practice. If you aren't having any fun playing music, what the hell is the point?"

"Mr. Savage, we don't use language like that in school." Joann raised her voice above the student's laughter.

Colton gave her a quick salute but turned back to his task. He probably heard the old grouch yelling at the kids and didn't want her taking over his practice. She could suck the fun out of rainbows and unicorns.

"I see he likes to ham it up." Joann crossed her arms over her chest, her brows creased together.

"That he does. How's Duke doing these days?"

"I don't see any progress. Rich and I are very concerned. He stopped handing in his homework again. He says he and Knox have a bet who can skip homework the longest."

Colton queued up the band, and they played "Sleigh Ride."

Knox was doing his homework. She wanted to stick out her tongue and tell old cranky pants just that. "What are the consequences at home for not handing in his homework?" She turned back to watch Colton direct the band. His arms kept time. He seemed to be almost dancing as he moved side to side and pointed at different sections. He called out a few commands.

"What else can I take away from him? Nothing we do works. I've told him not to spend any further time with Knox."

Harley snapped her head around, yanking her gaze away from Colton's well-fitting jeans. "You don't want him to spend time with Knox?" She must've misheard. It was Joann's son who had convinced Knox to drink before school. It was Joann's son who was always in trouble. Duke was the one who brought alcohol to the junior prom and got sent home from a trip because he was caught drinking.

Duke's misdemeanors added up to letting kids who had forgotten their IDs into the building. He didn't care about incomplete assignments, which forced teachers to give the principal's son bad grades. He vaped in the bathroom and who knew what else.

Knox had never been in trouble before this year. She'd been so afraid to see him act out she'd been the worst kind of helicopter parent. She always checked on him. She insisted on knowing his friends. She'd let her rules go when he started hanging with Duke. She didn't know how to tell him to stop when her job was on the line. She should have. If she'd been a better mother, she would've seen the drinking incident coming a mile away.

"Knox isn't the problem."

"Harley, I know it's hard to see our children's short-comings. No one knows this better than I, but Knox is headed for trouble, and I don't want Duke mixed up with him."

He'd made one stupid mistake, just as Colton had said. She unclenched her fists and straightened her shoulders. "I agree, Joann. The boys should find other friends. Best idea I've heard in a long time."

"One more thing—I heard you're renting your guest-house out to Colton."

Was there a threatening tone in her voice?

The orchestra had moved on to "O Tanenbaum." Colton moved around the students, correcting form and cracking jokes. The cello player lost his place because he laughed out loud.

"I am renting the place to Colton." Harley wasn't going to back down, not after Joann basically said she was a bad mother. Most days she might agree, but not when Miss Neat Creases said it.

"I know you dated him once. How long ago was it?"

"Why does that matter?" She wasn't about to share her personal life with this woman.

"It doesn't look good for a teacher to be shacking up with another teacher."

"What is this? The nineteen fifties?" She laughed at the absurdity of Joann's comment. After what she said to him last night, she was surprised he hadn't moved out. The art lessons would certainly come to a stop.

She turned back to the band. They'd segued into a medley of songs that had Colton's face scrunched up and his head shaking. She wasn't going to let her libido get her into any more trouble. The kiss at the sink was a mistake, a mistake she wouldn't make again.

"Just be certain I have nothing to concern myself with. There's one more thing," Joann said.

She pushed out a long breath. "What's that?"

"Now that the reviews are in, the decision has been made to bring in the artists-in-residence program next year."

"But I'm planning that art show to raise the funds to keep the program intact." Not to mention she was trying to keep her job.

"The funds you raise can still help to pay for whomever the school decides to bring in to teach."

"But it won't be me. You're firing me."

"You have your job until May, but you only have yourself to blame, Harley. You refuse to follow protocol. You've had multiple chances to change. I see where your son gets his behavior choices." Joann turned and marched back up the aisle.

Harley sank into the nearest seat. Joann had won. She'd successfully removed her from her job all because she refused to stifle creativity. Losing her job would mean she'd never have to worry about Joann again. That would be a huge relief. How would she support herself and Knox? Who would hire a teacher with bad performance reviews? Would there be any point in holding the art show? Maybe it was time to clean off her paintbrushes for good and start a whole new career, like balloon artist or prima ballerina.

"Everyone make sure to practice at home. We don't want to suck in front of your parents," Colton yelled above the clatter and clanks of the students packing up instruments.

He really didn't need her here. Even with his colorful language, he was great with those kids. All the kids stared up at him with eyes of wonder. He made them laugh and encouraged them to keep trying. Her heart squeezed for his success. He'd deserved everything he had. No one had worked harder than Colton.

"You have no idea how good you are as a teacher, do you?" she said to him as he retrieved his jacket.

"Paying me compliments now?" He shrugged into his coat.

"When you deserve them." She straightened her shoulders.

He leaned in. He smelled clean and slightly sweet. "What you said last night, it isn't true." he whispered.

"Why is that?"

"I never traded my family for music. My father traded me." He leaned in even closer. His breath was hot against her ear. "And I never forgot about you." He straightened and took the heat with him. He turned, sauntered up the aisle and out the door. She wanted to run after him.

"Mom, did Colton leave? I was hoping he'd give me a ride back. Duke said he can't drive me."

Knox's words forced her to look away from the path Colton took. "He already left. I'll take you, but I want to stop at May's first. I need something sweet."

"I hope that's not dinner."

"Smart-ass."

Chapter Eighteen

Colton left Harley behind and pushed through the glass doors into the parking lot at the high school. He hadn't forgotten about her, even though she'd accused him of that last night. She'd wanted more than to only be tangled in his thoughts. She'd wanted all of him, and he'd kept himself from her. He'd had a plan, and a committed relationship hadn't been part of it.

He chased away thoughts of his hands on her skin and tried to focus on the practice tonight. He had to admit he liked those kids. Harley said he was a good teacher. He was good with them. Stupid. He was Colton Savage, not a music teacher.

He couldn't deny what he needed to do. Stay. He'd finish out the two weeks here. He'd have to sneak his belongings back into the house when he was certain Harley and Knox were asleep. He didn't want to explain what he'd been thinking. She'd never let him live it down. She'd already accused him of running. And what if he did once in a while? Did he have to stick around every time someone didn't like him? Who wanted to put up with that much punishment?

He hit the button to start the car and made his way through the empty lot. Only Harley's truck and one other vehicle were there. He knew that car too. What was she doing here?

He got in the Audi, veered over, and parked. No point in avoiding her. He knocked on the driver's side window. "What do you want, Savannah?"

She jumped out of the car before he finished his sentence. She looked better than the last time he'd seen her. "So it's true. Greyson came home the other day and said kids were talking about the new orchestra teacher— his uncle. I didn't believe him. I laughed, in fact."

"I'm stepping in for the guy who's sick." His support of a music program wasn't that far of a stretch. She didn't need to laugh at him.

"You have no business being here. I'm going to put a stop to this charade by morning. I know everyone on the board. I've had those people in my home. I've been to their parties, funerals, and fundraisers. You will not be a teacher at this school. Do you hear me?"

"Me and the whole goddamn town. It's temporary. Why do you care?"

"Because you're a bad influence. Do they know you have a drinking problem?"

He clenched his fists and tried to count to ten. Where were his smokes? He had his drinking under control. He wouldn't do anything to jeopardize the kids in any way. What kind of a monster did she think he was? "There must be a teacher in that school at home boozing it up right now."

"Of course, you'd make a joke. When will you ever take responsibility for your actions?"

"I keep telling you I'm not sticking around. They needed someone to help out with the orchestra concert. The end. After that I'm leaving. Don't go getting your panties all scrunched up. I'll keep away from you."

"I want you to stay away from Grey too. If you see him in the hallway, walk the other way."

"Christ, Savannah, can we please get past this? I'm sorry. For fuck's sake, I'm so damn sorry. I never meant to hurt you, but your son was being an ass. Don't you get it? And he was being an ass to Blaise's son. Blaise, your brother. The brother who read to you at night before you went to bed. The brother who followed you home from a party and kept those guys from trying to get you in their car."

"Don't remind me of those times. I don't want to think about it." Her shoulders sagged.

"You can't stay mad at me forever."

"I can, and I will."

"Is everything okay here?"

Colton spun around. Harley stood only feet away. He hadn't heard her walk up. She dangled her keys in her hand. Knox waited back at her truck. "We're fine." His belly tightened at the thought of her walking over and interrupting his fight.

"Really? Because I could hear yelling back at the building."

"Colton could never keep his anger in check." Savannah kicked the dirt.

"I was referring to you, Savannah."

Savannah took a step back. He bit his cheek not to laugh.

"I beg your pardon?"

"I know this isn't any of my business and I should let you two work out whatever it is that's going on between you. I'm breaking every social etiquette rule in the book, but when I heard you yelling at him, I just couldn't sit back mute. Your brother might be a gigantic pain in the ass—no one knows this better than I do—but he loves you, and if you're too blind to see that, you're not as smart as you think you are."

Savannah opened her mouth to say something.

"Wait." Harley stopped her. "You Savages don't know how lucky you are to have each other. I've wanted a family like yours my whole life. When Colton used to bring me over and you'd all sit around and swap stories or joke around or play games together, I had to stop myself from crying because no matter how much my aunt and uncle loved me, I'd never have what you all had. Families like yours are hard to come by. Colton has been fighting to make you forgive him. You should think about it. He's a good guy. And you." She turned on him. "Forgive your brother. He loves you and so does Cash. They need you. You all need each other." She took a deep breath. "Well then, okay. I've said my peace and overstayed my welcome. Good night." She turned on her heel and walked away.

Colton watched her slide into her truck and drive into the night.

"She still loves you." Savannah's voice had come down out of the rafters into her normal octave.

"I doubt that." But he did have to pick his mouth up off the asphalt.

"Are you really that dense? Of course, you are. You've had so many women throwing themselves at you, you don't know the real thing when it's staring you in the face. I've spent enough time on you. I have to go."

"Can you forgive me, Savannah?"

She swatted at her face. "I don't know. I can't think about it now."

"Does that mean you won't try and get me thrown out of the school? I like the kids. They're talented. You should see them when they play. It reminds me of when we were kids." He hoped his face showed her what he was having a hard time saying.

"Don't go being nice. I hate it when you're you. That damn charm of yours." She yanked open the car door. "I won't say anything to anyone about you. Are you really going to be gone soon?"

"Yes."

"I guess that's enough."

Savannah started the car and drove away without another look at him.

She'd went a whole five minutes without yelling at him. It was a start. Now, what was he going to do about Harley?

Chapter Nineteen

Harley struggled to find a place to park on Main Street. She eased into a spot opposite Jake's. A Christmas-tree lot had shoved its way in between Jake's and Toy's Galore. The empty store on the other side sat dark. She'd need to find a way to display the artwork. Some of her art-relaxation students wanted to showcase photos they'd taken, but not Andy. How was she going to convince him to paint something?

"Do you want to wait in the car or come in to May's?"

Knox had his face in his phone. His fingers flew over the screen. He barely looked up. "I'll wait. But can you get me something?"

"See? Dessert is pretty good as a meal choice."

"Mother, how many times do I have to tell you dessert isn't on the food pyramid?" His lip curled into a smile.

She ruffled his hair. They might actually be okay. Colton had been right about that too. She pushed out of the truck before she could think on that any further because if she kept thinking about how Colton understood what Knox needed from her and how to handle those kids at school, she'd have to admit she'd ruined all their lives by safeguarding her secret.

Would it count that she had been young and afraid when she'd made the decision? Would she lose points for becoming exactly like her own mother? Would it matter that she wanted to go back and do it all over? Her head ached from all the bouncing thoughts.

The wind blew her hair back, and the air smelled like snow. Gray clouds filled the sky like wet cotton. Main Street bustled with Christmas shoppers weaving up and down the street. Some were buried in their coats while others were in deep conversation. Harley hurried into May's, where Christmas music soothed her nerves.

The store smelled like cinnamon and baked bread. Harley found her place at the end of a long line. She'd wanted something to help her get to the end of the day. Losing out to an artists-in-residence program more than stung, though walking over and standing up for Colton had helped her mood.

She should have minded her business, but Savannah was being too harsh on him. She hadn't seen him with those kids or the way he was with Knox. Harley owed him enough to come to his defense. She'd denied him so much she could never make up for it all. She wouldn't get the chance either. It was best that he went on the road.

Colton used to like coffee cake. She could pick up some of that for him. Payment for breakfast the other day and for what she said about him substituting his family for music.

"If it isn't Harley Kenyon."

She spun around, her smile ready to meet whoever had called out to her. "Rowan."

Rowan McGee was a member of the board of education and a local developer. His family had been part of Heritage River's roots. His great-grandfather had been one of the men whose sweat was all over the buildings of Main Street. Rowan had parlayed the family business into a multimillion-dollar empire complete with an entire development of cookie-cutter tiny mansions right outside of town named McGee Estates. His salt-and-pepper hair was slicked back to match that slick smile on his face. He carried a brown shopping bag in one hand.

"How is that boy of yours?" His voice carried across the room.

After Knox got suspended, Rowan had called her at home to tell her he'd personally spoken with Joann, saying boys will be boys and asking her to go easy on them. He'd also asked Harley out for coffee sometime. She'd quietly refused him.

"He's doing well, thank you. Practicing for the winter concert."

"Ah, yes. Colton Savage is acting as substitute. Can't believe Joann allowed that, but I was the only one on the board against it. Wasn't worth the argument since it's only temporary. He's not messing up too badly, is he?"

Her insides heated up with anger. Rowan never liked

Colton. She unzipped her coat. "The kids love him. You should come out to the show and see it."

"I'll do that. See what my old rival is up to. Hopefully, he won't be falling on his face. Does someone like him even know how to conduct an orchestra full of teenagers?"

The line moved forward. She clenched her fist around her wallet. "He's doing a fantastic job. In fact, Joann asked me if he'd be interested in teaching the music class full-time." She raised her chin.

"I'll make sure that doesn't happen."

"You'd deny the students of the school you sit on the board for a chance to have a real professional teach them? I didn't think you would be that narrow minded, Rowan. You aren't jealous, are you?"

They'd been high school rivals a long time ago. Rowan had been the jock, the high school hero. Colton had been the troublemaker who smoked out by the bleachers and played his loud music on the weekends. On the surface, it appeared Rowan was the star, but she knew even then who the star was.

Rowan laughed. "Jealous of Savage? His money, maybe, but nothing more." He leaned in. "Well, maybe the fact he'd won you over back in the day."

She ignored him. "What would you say about me saving the art program as it is instead of the residency program?"

"You need the parents to get involved, darlin'. The board listens best when the parents shout the loudest. Do you have yourself the money? Is Savage planning on donating to the cause? He's not already donating, is he?" He raised an eyebrow.

She gave her order to the pregnant woman behind the counter and continued to ignore his innuendo. "Thanks for the input." She handed over her a twenty-dollar bill.

"You know, Harley." Rowan stood behind her. His presence pressed down on her. Locked between him and the counter, she had to turn to look up at him. "We could discuss it more over dinner on Friday night. I might be able to help you with the parents. I know a lot of people."

She wanted to back up and put space between them, but there was nowhere to go. The mommy-to-be handed her the bag of goodies over the counter. Rowan snagged it and held it near Harley's chin. He didn't release his grip when she tried to take it.

"What do you say? Two old friends having dinner together and trying to find a way to save her job. Who else could help you with that? Not Savage. His clout can't handle keeping you employed."

They weren't old friends. When they were Knox's age, Rowan had the idea if her mother was the town's cliché, she would be too. He'd propositioned her in the hallways at school and behind the bleachers at football games. He even followed her into the bathroom once, hoping to sit her on the sink and have a feel up her skirt.

She avoided him, shoved at him, even scratched his face once to keep him from taking what wasn't his. Then she started dating Colton, and her world shifted. She wasn't that pathetic girl anymore. She had become someone special. But Rowan wasn't quick to give up what he wanted. He was accustomed to getting his way.

He cornered her in the high school hallway when no one was around and forced his stale breath on her face. He asked if he could kiss her, and when she said no, he tried to shove his tongue in her mouth. She stomped his foot and shoved his nose with the palm of her hand. He wasn't expecting it, so he stumbled back and hit his head on the fire extinguisher. Harley ran, not waiting to see if she'd knocked him out or if he was fast on her heels. When she told Colton, he and Blaise managed to turn Rowan's new car over on its side right out in front of Rowan's house. After that Rowan had avoided her because he had to explain to his father, who was quick with a switch, why his expensive vehicle was scraping the asphalt.

She yanked the bag from his grip. "Thanks for the offer, but I have plans Friday night." She shoved her way around him and sucked in the fresh air as she made her way to the door.

"Some other time, then," he called after her.

After dinner Harley made her way to her art studio out in the garage. Rowan's proposition sat like lead in her belly, and the doughnut she so desperately wanted had tasted like dust instead. She brewed up some chamomile tea, turned on Christmas music, and decided what she needed was to hear the scraping of pencil against drawing paper. Sometimes the answers came when she stopped focusing.

Go after the parents. It was so obvious, she'd missed it. She could solicit their help for the art show, but she'd have to do it soon. Time was running out.

She sat back on the small sofa she'd dragged into the space once upon a time ago, tucked her legs under her, and leaned into the soft, worn cushions while she worked. Her hand moved across the white paper. She didn't want to think about what she was doing. Instead, she willed her mind to empty of the nagging thoughts, and the creativity began to flow. Thoughts always steered to the place she tried to avoid, and up until Colton had walked into her classroom, she'd done a damn good job of avoiding them. It was her and Knox against the world. Most times he was okay with that. Until that history project made him ask questions.

A knock stopped her drawing. She swiped at her face and untangled herself. She pulled the door open.

"It wasn't locked," she said.

"I didn't know what the rules were." Colton leaned against the doorframe, his hands shoved under his arms. He'd come outside without a coat. His black sweater pressed against his broad shoulders. His hips narrowed into his faded jeans. His boots were untied.

The magnetic pull in her belly perked up. "I don't have any rules for this space. Come in. You must be cold out there."

He glanced up at the sky. "Think it will snow?"

"A white Christmas would be nice." She shut the door, leaving the cold behind them.

He took in her small space. "Christmas music?"

"You know I love it. You might too if you gave it a try."

"Not happening."

What did he think of the unfinished canvases leaning against the wall? Or the half-completed drawings? Or the photographs piled up on her table doing nothing but collecting dust? Or the paintbrushes that sat dry and unused?

He went straight to where she had been sitting and grabbed her notebook. She'd forgotten to close it.

"That's just a rough draft. Don't look at it." She tried to grab it, but he turned away from her.

"You drew the bridge."

She tugged her cardigan closed. "I guess. I wasn't really paying attention to what I was doing."

"You guess? Looks like the bridge to me." He held the page toward her.

She laughed. "Okay, it's the bridge. Better?"

"Don't doubt your talent so much. You're better than you think, and I'm not saying that because you're cute in tight jeans. I'm saying it because even this pencil drawing is better than the real thing."

She looked away and rolled her bottom lip between her teeth. "I'm not that good, Colton. You know that."

"Can I keep it?" He tore it from the notebook without waiting for an answer.

"Why?"

He raised his eyebrows. "Because, stubborn woman, I like it. All your work is good." He swung his arm to take in the room. "Why aren't you doing anything with this stuff? You're letting the world miss out on you."

The compliment spread over her like warm caramel. She dropped onto the stool. "I tried a long time ago. I couldn't make it work, but thank you for the compliment."

"So can I keep the drawing?" He waved the paper at her.

"If you want it that badly." She laughed. As if he would take no for an answer.

"I also like when you laugh. You should do it more often." He placed the drawing on the table. "I don't want to fold it. Do you still go to the bridge at sunset?"

He'd remembered. Did he ever think about their time standing on the bridge, watching the sun dip behind the horizon and burn the world in pinks and golds? They'd hold hands, and she'd imagine the whole world was waiting for her to light it on fire. She'd had big dreams once. A woman her age could only daydream.

"I haven't walked over there in years. No time." That wasn't entirely true. She'd drive over when she could to watch the sun set. Sometimes she needed to wrap herself in the comfort of the memories.

"I still have the drawing you made for me." He lowered himself onto the couch and rested his elbows on his knees. His long legs looked great touching the ottoman that doubled as a small table.

He still had the drawing? Had she heard him right?

She didn't know that scribble meant so much to him. She figured he'd thrown it out and long since forgotten about it. Wasn't she the only one hanging onto moments from the past as if they were long-forgotten pieces of art? All those years on the road and he still had it. That magnetic pull was back.

"The one I drew for you, what, twenty-five years ago? It must be faded by now."

"It's not. I keep it wrapped in a plastic sleeve."

"You do?"

"Don't be surprised, Harley. Our time together meant something to me too, you know." He clasped his hands together and glanced at the ground before looking back at her. "I wanted to thank you for what you said to Savannah earlier. She actually stopped biting my head off for a second."

She picked up a pencil and gnawed on its end. Her ears still rang with the admission she had meant something to him all this time. "I should've minded my own business. I have no right getting involved in your family affairs."

His face lit up. "Are you kidding? That was cool. No one's done something like that for me, ever. I'm always out in the front taking care of myself. I'm used to it, and I prefer it that way, but tonight..." He leaned back. "Thanks. You were unexpected."

Desire intoxicated her. "I was only saying the truth. You and your family should work things out. Especially whatever you have going on with you and Blaise."

"I know. He only wanted to be good father to Cash. I

223

get that part, really. I love that kid like he's mine. That's funny, isn't it? A kid of my own. That would've been a bad idea. What kind of father would I have been getting drunk all the time?"

She dropped the pencil and sat on her hands.

"Blaise left the band because I won't write new music. He wanted to move forward. He says I'm stuck in the past."

"Are you?" It was easier to shift into teacher mode and lock up her emotions for this man.

Colton looked off into the distance at something only he could see. "I don't know. Maybe. We were so great once. Selling out arenas show after show. Traveling the world where everyone wanted to see us, be us, touch us. The world was ours. But then things started to change. I couldn't write anymore, and I didn't want anyone else writing without me. It pissed me off." He leaned forward again and clasped his hands together. He sneered. "I'm a bastard, aren't I?"

She left the stool and sat beside him. She tucked her legs under her and faced him. He was close enough to see the scar on his jaw under his scruffy beard. He smelled like cedar and oak and all male. "You wanted the dream to keep going. No one wants to be left behind."

"I didn't think I'd ever be the one left behind."

She never thought she was going to be left behind either. "It's not too late. You could start writing again."

"Like you could start showing again?"

She sat back. "That's over. I'm done begging people

to like me. I'm too old to start again. If I were still twenty, but I have to take care of Knox."

"How come it's not too late for me to start writing, but you're all washed up? What happened when you tried?" He tapped his finger on her knee, and his touch sent fire through her veins.

"I went to New York like every other starving artist thinking that big city was going to be the answer to my prayers. I figured I'd get there and someone would see how amazing I was and want me immediately." She smirked. "Only it was the exact opposite. I was one in a million. I didn't know a soul and couldn't get anyone to give me a chance. It got harder with Knox. I had him to think about, and babysitters cost a fortune. I gave up, and Uncle Hank was all too happy to have us back. That's when I got my teaching degree."

"Was Knox's father an artist too?"

She jumped up and went back to the stool. "I don't want to talk about him."

"Sure. Got it. Topic off limits."

Damn the ease in his voice. She kept her back to him and took a deep breath. "Colton, I need to talk to you." If she kept her eyes anywhere but on him, she might get through what she was about to say.

His warm breath was on her neck. The heat from his body so close to hers ran up her back. His hands rested on her shoulders. "Can we talk later? You owe me an art lesson."

"We need to talk." Her voice was a whisper.

His lips placed small, gentle kisses on her neck. Her

skin tingled as his lips moved lower to her shoulder. "I've been wanting to do this since Knox walked in on us." His voice was deeper and his southern accent more pronounced.

"Colton." Her thoughts floated away from her. She needed to wrap her hands around them and pull them in, but she couldn't grab onto them. She had to tell him.

"I love my name on your lips. Tonight at the school, my God, woman, when you came over with fire in your voice, I wanted you that second. Right there."

She felt his erection against her low back. Flashes of heat pushed the last of her reason away. He was here. His hands on her like before. The past didn't matter. This man always had the key to her heart. No one else had ever measured up. She was alive when she was with him, and all things seemed possible with Colton.

He turned her to face him. "Tell me no, and I'll go away."

"You're going to go away anyway." That should stop her. She didn't want to be his one-night stand. She wanted it all, but he'd never promised that. She wanted to believe she'd be enough for him to stick around. She wanted to believe his feelings for her would be enough to ground him, but nothing could ground this man in one place. His free spirit was part of his charm.

"Is that a yes?" He took her ear between his teeth and lightly bit down. His hands pushed her cardigan aside and found the bottom of her T-shirt. His calloused fingers rubbed against her low back, sending fire across her flesh.

Her hands went up to his neck. She tangled her fingers in his hair the way she'd wanted for days and pulled him closer. He pressed his lips to hers, and she opened her mouth to him. Their tongues danced to their familiar song. *Always him* chanted in her head. Their kiss deepened. For years she'd longed to be surrounded by his desire. She had thought about it over and over when she was alone late at night.

She pulled away but kept her hands on his shoulders. "I want you. I've always wanted you." Her voice was dry. She licked her lips. "But I don't want to be something you do while you pass through. Not this time."

He released her. The cold air swirled around her and set her off balance.

"Okay, I get it." He scratched the back of his neck. "You deserve more than a fling. I'm sorry. I didn't mean to hurt you again." He stepped around her.

"Wait." She wanted to run to him and stop him from leaving.

"It's okay, Harley. I can't promise you what you want. I have the tour in a couple of weeks. I'll be on the road for months, and I don't know where I'm going to land after that. I won't make the same mistakes with you. I'm not that kid anymore. Look, rehab taught me something." The smile flickered across his face. He opened the door but stopped. "Thanks for saying all that stuff before. If you want, I'd still like to take you to see Cash play tomorrow night. Just as friends."

"I'd like that." She choked on the words.

"Cool. Night, babe." He shut the door, leaving her alone.

Again.

Chapter Twenty

Colton threw open every window in the guesthouse and lit up his smokes. The cold, damp air rushed in and bit at his skin, but he didn't care. He needed the cigarette. He paced the place in two steps before turning around and pacing back. He shoved the sofa out of the way just to have more room to move.

What the hell was he thinking? Oh, he knew what he was thinking all right, but was he out of his mind? That woman drove him mad. She didn't know her own worth, and he wanted to show her in the best way he could—and plenty of other ways too. When Harley had stood up to Savannah, his insides swelled like a crescendo. And what she'd said to him just moments before he kissed her about trying to produce another song. Was it too late for him to try writing music again? Why did she think it was too late for her? Why was it too late for them?

He yanked his phone out of his pocket, ready to hit

the saved number, and stopped. He kicked the table leg. "Fuck." He couldn't call the person he went to first for everything, the person who'd been by his side his entire life, keeping up with his guitar licks and his antics.

He could try Billy, but it was late.

The phone vibrated in his hand. Harley? When he saw the number, he wanted to kick the table again. "Mike, what's up? I'm in the middle of something," he growled.

"Bro, pull the stick out of your ass. I'm calling about the show. I spoke to Mick. They're definitely in. Said we can headline, of course." Mike laughed. "That's three bands. We're definitely calling it the Beasts of Rock. The promo material's being made up right now. I'd send you the artwork, but we don't have time to waste."

They were making decisions without him? This was his tour. "I'm the lead on this, Mike. Why didn't anyone call me?"

"I can't reach you. You never answer your stupid phone."

He was talking about those calls during the orchestra practice Colton had ignored. "Tell Mick to go fuck himself. He's not touring with me."

"Colton, man, you're making a mistake."

"I'm Colton Savage. I don't make mistakes where music is concerned."

"Look, man, you know I'm on your side, but you've got to face some serious facts. You haven't put out anything new in something like fifteen years. The fans, even the critics, want to hear what you've got. You aren't selling out shows anymore either. Rock ain't what it used to be. We need the extra bands if we're going to sell enough tickets so everyone can get paid."

His head hurt. "I can't talk about this now. I'll call you tomorrow." He hung up before Mike said another thing.

Colton grabbed his keys and hurried into the night. His hands ached from the cold. The lights were out in the studio. Had she gone to bed?

He made his way across the drive. Was he too old to climb up to her window? Probably. And she didn't want him anyway. She'd made it clear, and he would respect that.

He jumped into the car and drove away, careful not to kick up dirt.

He turned on Dogwood Drive and killed the lights. Making a call would've been easier, but he never did easy in his life. He slowed his speed and parked on the opposite side of the street.

Blaise's truck was in the driveway, and the house was dark. He should go home. Home. Where was that exactly? Blaise's house had been his home once when they were kids. That was the place he'd taken Harley when she witnessed the Savage family laughing, joking, playing games. But Blaise bought the house from him and Savannah after their father died. Colton couldn't understand why Blaise wanted it. Now Colton couldn't imagine it belonging to anyone else.

"You really do suck." Colton pushed his way out of the car and marched across the lawn before he thought anymore. He needed his brother. He banged on the door. A light went on inside. He tried to steady his breath. He patted his pockets and realized he'd forgotten his smokes. "Shit."

Blaise opened the door. His hair stuck up in different directions. His eyes were swollen from sleep. He wore a long-sleeved T-shirt and flannel pants. "Is everything all right?" His voice croaked.

"You sleep in that stupid outfit? You've got a beautiful woman in your bed. You should be sleeping with your ass out."

"I didn't want to make whatever idiot was at the door jealous. Come in. It's cold." Blaise swung the door open wider, and Colton stepped inside. "Have you been drinking?"

"What? No. What the fuck, Blaise?"

"You show up at my house late at night when you won't even speak to me. It's not like you haven't shown up drunk before. What do you expect me to think?"

Colton wiped a hand over his face. "I'm not drinking. I haven't had a drink in forty-five days. I'm never going to drink again. I'm through. Okay?"

"Good enough. You want some coffee?"

"Sure. Thanks." It would give him something warm to wrap his hands around.

Blaise turned on the light above the stove and moved around the kitchen. It was small, but Blaise had the entire house renovated once he took ownership. Now the kitchen was white with stainless steel appliances and hardwood floors.

He handed Colton the mug. "Why are you here?"

"Do you have to whisper?"

"Grace and Cash are asleep. I'd like to not wake them if possible. Unless you need me to call an ambulance or something like that."

"Funny. Jerk." Now that he sat opposite his kid brother, he didn't know what to say or where to begin even. What did he really expect Blaise to do? "I probably shouldn't have come."

"Yeah, probably not, but you did, so spill it." Blaise leaned back and sipped his coffee.

"It's Mike and Harley. Mike's making plans for the tour without me. He wants Mick and some other band to tour with us. Calling it some stupid name I can't remember. Says ticket sales are low. We have to do this. He said it's been too long since I wrote something."

"Sounds familiar."

"Shut up. There's no way I'm going to tour with that idiot Mick. I tried to get Patrick and Troy to come back on the road with me, but they're in the studio with that young guy burning up the charts. What's his name?"

"No clue, bro. Patrick and Troy are done with Savage."

"I'm not."

"Whether you like it or not, Mike's right. You need those other bands if you're going to make any money. He can play pretty well. He's not me on the drums, but he won't screw up too badly." Blaise's lip curled into a smile.

No one was Blaise on the drums. Colton took a deep breath. He wasn't ready to walk off the stage, but to have become the guy that can't sell tickets without other bands? Worse, to become the guy whose entire band left and he was stuck still playing their old tunes with guys who weren't even born when they were on the road? Had his career really become that bad? Had his father been right about Colton's kind of music all along?

"I don't know if I can go on tour with them." If he stayed behind, what would Harley say? He'd say he wanted to try with her for the first time in ages. She'd say she was the consolation prize because he couldn't tour the way he wanted with his brother, Troy, and Patrick. Would Harley give him another chance?

"Tell me what happened with Harley."

Had Blaise read his mind? "Did I mention Harley?"

"You did."

"Savannah showed up at the school tonight after practice and threatened to have me removed from the orchestra. Harley came out of nowhere and blasted her for the way she was talking to me. It was cool, bro. You should've seen it. No one ever talks to Savannah like that."

"Especially not us."

"Exactly. I went looking for Harley and found her in her art studio. She's amazing, but she doesn't know it. Her paintings and drawings are filled with the pain and emotion she sees the world through. I just wanted to thank her for standing up to Savannah. No one has ever done that for me before. She had drawn our bridge tonight and when I saw it...I knew I should've stopped, but—"

"You slept with her?" Blaise sat forward.

"No, Christ. Let me tell the story."

Blaise leaned back in his chair. Colton went on to tell him what had happened and what had happened at her kitchen sink. "She rejected me."

Blaise laughed. "You're not used to women telling you no."

"Are you going to be any help, or are you going to sit there in your old-man pajamas and look like an idiot?"

"Hey, Grace bought these for me."

"You're whipped. It's pathetic."

Blaise crossed his arms and smiled. "I prefer to think of it as getting wise. I'm one lucky SOB to have a woman like Grace."

"You're making my head hurt." Colton pinched the bridge of his nose.

"Look, Colton, it doesn't sound like Harley rejected you. She just wants to know that this time you're for real. Sounds like she wants the whole picture. Like what Grace and I have. Why Harley wants your sorry ass is beyond me, but she's not completely pushing you away. What do you want from her?"

Colton raised an eyebrow.

"Besides that."

Colton leaned back in his chair and crossed his ankles. "I don't know." He wanted her to look up at him with those big brown eyes and call out his name. He wanted her standing beside him and coming to his defense. He wanted to make her laugh. He wanted to play his guitar for her.

"It sounds like you love her, bro. You always have. I don't know why you keep fighting it."

"But the tour." He'd never bagged on a gig before. His name was all over the promo. People would be expecting to see him. Savage might be done, but he still had fans who wanted to watch him play. Did he throw away another chance to stand under the lights and rip up an amazing riff? They'd worked so hard to be the best rock band. Was it really time to let someone else take center stage? The idea made Colton's skin squirm. No, he wasn't ready to go yet. Maybe someday, but not yet.

"Screw the tour. You don't need the money. You can play somewhere else on your terms. You could stick around and be the orchestra teacher."

"Hell no. Not me."

Blaise threw up his hands. "Okay. Okay. No teaching music. You'll figure it out, but I wouldn't give up on Harley because of some tour. If you want her, go to her. Ask her to wait for you. Tell her how you feel."

He didn't know how he felt. "It would be easier to keep my distance until I hit the road."

"But would that make you happy? Wouldn't being in the arms of a beautiful woman be better?"

"You're sounding like a greeting card. You really are whipped." Colton stood. "Thanks, though. Thanks for, you know"—he swung his hand in a circle—"for this."

"The coffee?"

"Yeah, that."

Blaise stood too. "Does this mean you forgive me for leaving the tour?"

"I guess." He stared at his brother. Blaise had been telling him for a long time to give up the road and write new music. He didn't want to listen. And he wasn't sure he was ready to start anything new. But Harley had said it too. Blaise had done it for himself. Could he? "Are you happy playing in small places? Making music on your own?"

"You'll see tomorrow night. You're coming, right? Cash is going to blow you away. He's way better than either of us ever were. We wrote a bunch of new songs. You'll like them." Blaise's face lit up.

He hadn't seen his brother this excited in a while. Their old life had been weighing Blaise down, and Colton hadn't noticed. "I'll be there. I'm bringing Harley." He put up a hand. "As friends. That's it. I'm not going anywhere near her unless she says it's okay, which she won't because she can't get over the fact I left her twice."

"Give her some time."

Colton turned toward the door. "I should go. You know, I think I'll bring her son, Knox. You know him?"

"I've met him a couple of times. He's a big fan of yours."

"Of course, he is."

"Spoken just like my dumb-ass older brother." Blaise patted him on the shoulder.

"Knox is pretty good on the guitar. I was impressed when I heard him. He might enjoy your show too."

They stood at the door. "Colton, you didn't really answer my question. Are you ready to let this fight between us go? Can I have my brother back, please?"

He grabbed his kid brother in a hug, then pushed him away just as fast. "Prick."

"Idiot."

Colton slapped Blaise upside his head. "I'll see you tomorrow night. Don't fuck it all up and repeat what happened that time in Atlanta," he called over his shoulder as he drifted down the steps.

"That wasn't me. That was you."

"That was me? Oh yeah, right. It had something to do with a girl and a guitar. If I remember it correctly."

"When you're involved, big brother, it usually does."

They both laughed.

Chapter Twenty-One

"What do you think of this?" Harley held out her red wraparound blouse for Ella to see. They'd been in her bedroom for an hour. Ella tried to help her find something to wear on her date that wasn't really a date at all. Colton would arrive any second. She broke a sweat trying to find the perfect thing to wear. If she didn't hurry up, she'd need another shower.

"Too much boob. Unless you want to show him some boob, which you should." Ella leaned back against Harley's headboard, chomping on carrot sticks. "But then I'd change that bra and borrow the one I brought over."

Harley shoved the blouse back in the closet. "You're not helping. I don't want to lead him on. I'm not going to wear that see-through thing you call a bra."

"It isn't meant to hold them up. It's meant to be taken off."

"At my age, I need something with strength."

"Forget practical. Think sensual. When was the last time you got laid? Eighteen years ago?"

Harley's hand slipped off the hanger. "No, thank you very much. It was— Never mind that. How about this?" She pulled out a simple black, fitted long-sleeved top with a high neck. It accented her shoulders and her figure, which might not be the best thing to do since she'd stopped going to the gym.

"Mom, Colton's here," Knox yelled up the steps.

"Looks like that's the winner." Ella jumped off the bed and helped her straighten the shirt. She grabbed a red lipstick. "Pout."

"Not the red. Too suggestive. Give me the brown."

"Harley, he wants you. Why are you fighting it?"

Harley lowered her voice. "Because he isn't going to stick around and I don't want to be his one-night stand again. I want the whole picture this time." And there was that little sticky point of the big fat secret she held that was bound to implode on all of them if she couldn't keep her legs together.

"Why does it have to be all or nothing? You deserve a little fun, and he's pretty hot." Ella swung her hips and swatted Harley's bottom.

Laughing, she brushed her friend away.

"Am I interrupting something?" Colton filled out her bedroom doorway.

He hadn't been up there since that night, but he seemed to fit right in. His hair was slicked back as if he'd just come from the shower. She could smell his woodsy cologne. She took a deep breath. His muscular chest filled out the light blue button-down he wore over a pair of slim dark jeans. His smile turned his eyes silver.

"She looks great, doesn't she, Colton?" Ella wagged a carrot at him. Harley wanted to swat her again.

"She always does."

Harley smoothed her wavy hair down in back. "We should get going. I've made us late."

Ella shrugged into her coat. "Okay, kids, don't stay out too late." She kissed Knox on the cheek and leaned in to give Harley a hug. "Have some fun tonight, please. Do you need any condoms?" she

whispered.

Harley groaned.

"What was all that about?" Colton opened the passenger's car door for her.

She slid in, hoping to avoid his question. Had he heard? Knox climbed into the backseat on the driver's side, head planted in his phone.

"You know Ella. Always cracking jokes."

She gripped the door as they drove over the bridge. Colton had taken that picture she drew the other night. When she went into the studio after work today, the drawing was gone. She'd even taken the garbage apart, but it wasn't there.

"This is a nice car." The silence made her squirm. She needed the sound of voices to keep her from thinking about him sitting so close.

He glanced in her direction. "Thanks. I bought it on a dare."

"Who buys a car on a dare?" She couldn't do that

with her teacher's salary or with a kid who was about to go to college. She'd be driving that Durango until she was old enough to have her license taken away.

"I needed a practical car to drive around. My Maserati doesn't come out much."

Knox leaned between the seats. "You have a Maserati too? Cool. I want one of those."

Of course, he heard that. She didn't want to tell him how hard it would be to buy a car like a Maserati and how Colton seemed to forget what it was like to live a regular life. All his talk about fancy cars would put unattainable ideas in a young boy's mind.

"I'll let you drive her. She's got a sweet ride."

"Oh no, you're not letting my son drive in a fast car like that. He's too inexperienced."

"He'll be fine. I didn't get into my first car crash until a few months ago." His dimple showed.

"Your last car accident isn't the best example." Considering he was drunk at the time, she didn't want him romanticizing his choices to Knox.

"Knox, don't drink and drive." He turned back to her and smiled. "Better?"

"Thank you." She turned toward the window again. "Who dared you to buy the car?" She couldn't remember the last time she took a dare. Maybe the age of twelve?

"Blaise. He really dared me to ask the saleswoman at the car dealership out because she wanted no part of the rock band in her showroom. The only way she'd go was if I bought the car." He laughed. "She had a sweet ride too."

"Colton, my son is in the car." Her voice squealed. Why had she asked?

"Relax, Mom. I've heard worse from guys my age."

She groaned and turned to look out the window again. She needed strength to get through the night.

Colton turned the car into a small gravel parking lot. He slowed down to look for a parking spot in the already-full lot. A low-lying restaurant sat alongside a bay. The place had a deck in the back lit up with white lights, but no one was outside. A wreath hung on the front door. As they walked across the lot, music blasting from inside made the restaurant vibrate.

"At least it's not Christmas music." Colton held the door open for her.

"What's wrong with Christmas music?" She really didn't understand his disdain for the festive tunes. She loved that music. She hadn't baked her aunt's cookies at all this year and still hadn't bought a tree. She turned to Knox. "Let's get a tree this weekend."

He shrugged. *Teens.* If she'd said "Let's buy a Maserati," he'd been all ears.

"Christmas music isn't real music, babe." Colton leaned in and said into her ear. It was the only way she'd be able to hear him over the band playing. His warm breath sent waves of tingles across her skin. She tried to shake them off. Instead, she smelled his cologne again and wanted to keep sniffing him, but that might look bad, especially in front of her son.

A four-piece band played classic rock tunes on a small stage toward the back of the restaurant. The place was dark, and the walls paneled in wood. A large bar formed a circle in the center. Tables sat around it. Most of the patrons, all way younger than she was by fifteen years at least, stood around the bar, holding bottles and glasses filled with different colored drinks. Christmas lights hung from the ceiling.

They found a table off to the side with a decent view of the stage and the windows behind it. On a summer night, you could probably see the sun setting back there. She thought of the bridge and of Colton holding her hand while they stood and watched the sun spin its magic over them. She shook her head and tried to think of something else, like what day she had to take out the recycling.

The band finished up to a pallid round of applause. A young man with the sides of his head shaved and the hair in the middle scooped back took the mic. "Let's hear it for Africa." A few more claps spread around the room. "Our next band will be up in about ten minutes after the set change. Sit tight. You don't want to miss the styling sounds of Limited Daylight. Don't forget to take care of your bartenders."

"Did he just say Limited Daylight? Is that the name my brother came up with?" Colton shook his head and laughed.

"I think it's cute."

"*Cute?* The most bad-ass drummer of all times is now *cute.* I didn't think I'd live to see the day." He signaled for a waitress, but she turned and ignored him.

"Guess she doesn't know who I am."

"Guess not." Harley pressed her lips together and shook her head. "I bet Cash and Blaise will be great."

"I don't doubt that. They need a new name."

"What are they going to play?" Knox came up out of his phone.

"Beats me." Colton tried to get the waitress again. This time she gave him the one-minute sign. "She just lost her tip."

"It's tough not having everyone jump at your whim, isn't it?" She laughed because he scrunched up his face as the waitress kept passing by to get other people's orders.

He leaned in. "I'd like to see if I could make you jump," he whispered.

Before she could react or touch her face to see if it was really on fire, Cash appeared at their table. "Uncle Colton, you made it."

Colton gave him a big hug. Cash shook hands with Knox, which put a huge smile on her son's face. Colton gave Knox a chance to be a part of something bigger than he was. He was accepted by and taken into the fold of people he admired. What kid didn't want that? Wasn't that exactly what she'd wanted her whole life?

"Can you come backstage? Dad's having a problem with his guitar."

Colton was up in a flash. "I'll be right back. Knox, why don't you come with me?"

Harley opened her mouth to protest, but Knox followed Colton and Cash before she could say anything. She needed to stop fighting the fact Colton was Knox's musical hero. She'd set this whole escapade in motion by dumping coffee over his head and then agreeing to painting lessons.

Knox should have had the chance to grow up as a Savage. Her son had deserved his real last name, and she took it away from him. Was it better to know who your father was even if he couldn't commit to raising you, or was it better not knowing the heartache being abandoned caused? She had put her own hang-ups caused by her parents discarding her on Knox's shoulders.

Tears stung the back of her eyes. Where was the ladies' room? She craned her neck to see.

"Excuse me. Are you Harley?" A pretty woman with long blonde hair and wide eyes placed a hand on her arm. "I'm Grace Starr. Blaise's"—she giggled— "Blaise's girl-friend. I'm sorry. I still get a little giddy when I say that. I'm far too old to be anyone's girlfriend."

If Grace thought she was too old to be someone's girl-friend, what the heck did that make Harley? Ready for the grave? Harley stuck out her hand. "It's nice to meet you."

"I was backstage and realized you'd been ditched out here all alone. If you don't mind, could I join you? The guys are talking about instruments, chords, and other musical things I don't understand. When Blaise hit Colton in the back of the head for something he said about Blaise's playing, I thought it was better if I left. Would you prefer to sit alone?"

"Please. Sit." What would she say to Blaise's girlfriend?

The waitress finally came over to the table. Harley

ordered a soda for herself, Knox, and Colton. Grace ordered a seltzer. The waitress whisked away as fast as she came.

"I wanted to meet the woman who stole Colton's heart."

Harley coughed. "That's not me." The one thing she'd never been able to do was capture his heart, or any other part of him.

Grace waved a hand at her. "Don't be modest."

"No, seriously, Colton and I aren't a thing. He's just passing through town like he always does. After the school concert, he's hitting the road again."

"That's not the way Blaise tells it. The other night when Colton stopped by, he was pretty upset about a fight you two had or something."

The waitress came with their drinks. Harley gulped hers. "Colton went to your house?" He hadn't mentioned it to her, not that he would. She'd practically thrown him out the other night in her studio. His demeanor was cool at best at the practice earlier in the day.

"He showed up the other night pretty late, but when Blaise came back to bed, he woke me to tell me there was a woman who had Colton all turned around. Only a woman who had hooked him could do that. No one can ruffle Colton's feathers, but I don't have to tell you that, I'm sure."

Words failed her. She sat there and stared at Grace.

"Can I say something honestly?" Grace played with the straw in her seltzer.

"Sure." Harley couldn't get her head around the idea

that Colton thought of her as anything more than a fling. She gulped more of the soda, wishing it were stronger.

"Last summer when I met Colton, I thought he was arrogant, self-absorbed, and a big windbag. No offense." Grace held up her hand. "But then I got to know him while he worked on my house. He's fiercely protective of the people he loves. Blaise loves him enormously. That alone was enough proof for me that Colton is a great guy underneath all that bravado. Whatever he's done, and I'm sure he's done something, I hope you can work it out. He deserves some real happiness. Having their music business struggle, and everything that's happened with Blaise and Savannah has been hard on him."

Harley continued to stare at Grace. What could she say? Colton deserved a relationship built on honesty. She couldn't give him that.

"I'm sorry if I've overstepped." Grace's face blossomed red.

"Oh no, it's fine. Colton and I aren't together, really. Whatever he told Blaise couldn't have been about me."

Grace swirled the straw around in her drink, as if she searched for a treasure in the glass. "I'm pretty sure Blaise said your name. I wouldn't be out here if he hadn't. Neither would you, I think. Colton doesn't exactly hang out with people he doesn't want to be with." She patted Harley's arm.

"We just aren't a thing anymore. That was a long time ago. We're friends now."

A round of applause cut off whatever Grace was about to say. Cash and Blaise walked onstage and took their places. Grace turned her chair to get a better view of the stage. She waved to Blaise, and he blew her a kiss. Harley wished she were as lucky as Grace. She grabbed her soda to keep herself from looking for Colton.

Knox hadn't returned either. She sat on the edge of her seat and searched the crowd.

Cash and Blaise blew her away. They had so much talent. Knox could play almost as well as they did, and with time and practice he'd be the kind of musician all the Savages were.

They finished the final song. Blaise stood at the mic. "If y'all don't mind, we have one more song to play and a bit of a surprise. Let's hear it for the greatest guitar of all times. My brother, Colton Savage."

Cash led the applause. The electricity in the crowd tingled around the room. Colton paraded out on stage, his chest and shoulders back. He held a guitar up over his head. The room cheered. These were Savage fans. They knew exactly who had walked on stage, and they ate it up. So did Colton.

Her heart nearly stopped when Knox followed Colton onto the stage. He had a guitar strapped around his neck. He grabbed a long black cord off the floor and plugged in his guitar. He kept his eyes down. Cash whispered something in his ear, and he nodded. Her beautiful boy was on stage with his father. The tears threatened to spill, and she choked on her soda.

"Are you okay?' Grace patted her back.

She nodded, but she was anything other than fine. She blinked away the tears. She didn't want to miss a second of Knox performing. Colton had just given Knox a gift she never could. She should have, but she hadn't. *Dear Lord, she hadn't.*

Colton went to the mic and raised his arm to quiet the crowd. "Thanks, everyone. It's good to be on stage with my brother and nephew again. I also have the pleasure of bringing on some new talent. Keep your eyes open for this one. Let's give it up for my friend Knox Kenyon."

She wiped her eyes with the wet napkin under her drink. Her lungs swelled, unable to take in anymore air.

Colton made the guitar come to life. Cash and Blaise joined in. Knox strummed right along. His foot tapped on the stage to the beat. His smile was the size of Tennessee and bright enough to power the solar system. Her smile stretched until her cheeks hurt.

Colton's face lit up as his playing took off like lightning. His hands sailed along the neck of the guitar in a blur. His music took on a life of its own. He made magic right before their eyes. No one really knew how he performed the way he did. She never tired of watching him.

He walked over to Knox, faced him, and together they hit the same notes as if they'd practice together for years. Colton's mouth opened wide, and he laughed. He took a split second to pat Knox on the shoulder and then stood beside Cash, their opposite shoulders touching. Uncle and nephew shared a piece of Colton's most famous solo. She might faint.

"They're unbelievable." Grace had to yell into Harley's ear to be heard.

Too stunned to speak, she nodded.

The guys finished the song with a drum solo from Blaise. The crowd went crazy. Grace clapped with her arms over her head and whistled through her teeth.

Harley excused herself to go to the ladies' room as Colton and Knox walked off backstage. She needed to get her breathing under control before they returned to the table. She splashed cold water on her face to make the tears stop. She didn't want to look as if she'd been crying the whole time.

She returned to the table. Grace had left, and Colton stood looking around. Knox bounced on his toes.

Colton grabbed her hand and pulled her close. "Did you see us? Tell me you weren't in the bathroom the entire time, babe."

She liked it when he called her "babe"—and wished she didn't. "No, no. I saw the entire thing. You both were fantastic. Knox, you were amazing, buddy."

"Thanks." He nodded his head. His smile never faltered. "But I could've been better."

"You rocked it, kid." Colton gripped Knox's shoulder. "You knew every note and nailed them."

"When you asked me to come on stage with you, my chest was so tight I thought I'd have a heart attack, but when you walked over to me and we played together, I thought I could take over the world." Knox's eyes gleamed.

If Knox wasn't hooked on music before, he surely was now.

The air in the room became thick and sticky. The

crowd seemed to swell and sway, almost as if it wanted to suck her in. "I'm so proud of you." She gave Knox a high-five. Trying to hug him would be out of the question in such a public place. "I need some air. If you two don't mind, I'll meet you outside by the car."

"We'll be out in a few minutes." Colton handed her the keys. "Start the car so you'll be warm. We won't be long."

She pushed her way through the crowd before anyone could stop her. Outside she gulped in the cold night air. It froze up her lungs and stopped the swirling thoughts in her head. He'd offered her son the sweetest, most generous gesture he ever could have. She loved him even more, as if that were even possible. He would hate her when he found out. That would be her punishment. She deserved it.

Colton and Knox sauntered out into the parking lot, laughing over something. Colton patted Knox on the shoulder. "Good one."

"Mom, would it be okay if I went out to grab something to eat with Cash and his friends? Can you believe he invited me along? I know I'm still grounded, but could you make an exception? They're inside waiting."

"I don't know." What if there was drinking? She had to think about the consequences of Cash and Knox hanging out. Was it wise to allow that friendship to bloom?

Knox's face dropped before she could get all her thoughts straight. "Mom. Come on. You know Cash. He's cool."

252

Colton squeezed her hand. She turned her head to face him, and he gave her the tiniest of nods. She wasn't even sure she saw it. He was telling her to let him go. Knox's shoulders hung. He looked at her through his hair. What was right and what wasn't?

Colton squeezed her hand again.

"Okay. I guess it's okay. Will he drive you home? Don't be late." *Don't drink. Don't get too attached.* All things she wouldn't say.

"Cash will take him home. He's a great kid. They'll be fine." Colton pointed a finger at Knox. "But if anything comes up, you want to leave early, or someone is doing something stupid, just call me and I'll come get you."

"Deal. Thanks, Mom." Knox threw his arms around her.

She grabbed onto his shoulders to stop herself from toppling back. She squeezed her eyes shut. "Have fun." She pressed her fingers against her lips.

Knox hustled back inside.

"Can we go?" She struggled to form the words.

"He's going to be fine. I promise."

That was a promise he couldn't make, but his trying to soothe her about her boy out on the town turned her insides warm and fuzzy. Colton held the car door open for her, and she hopped in. "Thank you for suggesting I let him go. I realize I have to start letting up on some of the reins. Sometimes it's hard to be the only one making decisions."

He ran around the front of the car and slid in beside

her. He pulled out into traffic and headed toward Heritage River.

"Where are we going?" She wanted to go home. The night had taken its toll on her.

"Let's take a ride." His dimple showed again.

She wrung her hands in her lap. "Thank you for what you did for Knox. You were more than generous."

He stole a glance at her. "He's talented, babe. I could help him get a career going if you'd allow it."

"Would it be okay if we talked about that some other time? I'm just not ready."

"You can't put off the inevitable. He's going after his dreams. I see it in his eyes. I had that same look, and nothing was going to stop me. At least I could keep my eye on him for you."

Please stop being so sweet. I can't take it. Her brain kept short-circuiting because her heart wanted to tell her what to do.

He crossed the bridge back into town and pulled the car over on the side. "Want to take a walk?"

"Now? In the cold? I don't think so."

"Cold air is good for you." He jumped out of the car and ran around to her side. He opened the door and held out his hand for her. She slid hers into his calloused one, and a warmth ran through her belly. Damn her attraction to him.

With her hand still in his, they took the walking path. He stopped at the center of the bridge, as he always had, and pulled her close. "This should keep some of the cold away."

"You were great tonight. Performing agrees with you."

"I was, wasn't I?" He winked, but his smile spread across his face and lit up his eyes. "Blaise and Cash are doing a bang-up job. I didn't think they could pull it off, but it's working. I'm proud of them."

"What they did tonight, playing in small places, was that something you'd want to do?" She edged near the topic as if she were approaching a cliff. Could she possibly dream he would want to stay behind for her?

He looked down at her. "I don't know. Maybe. My tour isn't working out the way I'd hoped. I don't like all the bands and people making decisions for me."

She laughed. "Sorry to laugh, but boy, is that a true statement."

He tickled her side. She tried to pull away, but he held her tighter. Their eyes met and held. "I don't know what I'd do if I don't tour. I've been on the road most of my life. Settling down wasn't anything I've considered."

"Blaise did it." Was she actually trying to encourage him to stay in one place? And what place did she have in mind for him? Her bedroom? Could there be any possibility everything would work out the way she wanted? *Stop it. Dreams aren't for you anymore.*

"My brother has a much softer side than I do." Also true.

"You could become the music teacher."

"Not me, babe. The kids are great, but being shoved into a classroom all day following rules I didn't set doesn't suit me. How's your art show coming? Any progress?"

"I can't get Andy Henson to put a piece in, and I think it would be good for him."

"You enjoy rescuing people, don't you?" He wrapped his arms tighter around her waist and held her against him.

"I don't know about that, but I'm taking him and a few other students to the museum to see an exhibit. I'm hoping that inspires him."

"Yeah, we're all your stray cats, and you gather us up and fix us."

"I can't fix anyone. That's all up to you." She didn't want to change anyone. She only wanted to shelter them from life's hurts.

The wind picked up over the water, and she shivered. Without thinking, she snuggled in closer to him. She didn't want to talk about her job. For just a little while, she wanted to pretend he was hers and it had all worked out. "It's cold out here."

"Do you want to go?" He started to ease away.

She gripped his arm. "Let's stay. I haven't been here like this in ages. It's beautiful at night with the moon on the water."

"The view from here is pretty good."

He looked down at her. She tilted her chin up to him. He took her face between his fingers and brushed his soft lips against hers. The heat inside her warmed her against the cold.

"Did you get your review back?" He stayed close. His breath brushed against her skin, and more heat warmed her from the belly out.

She told him about her evaluations and the school's plans to take away the teaching position.

"That sucks. You don't deserve to be fired. You can teach somewhere else. Screw Joann Humphreys. You don't need her."

When he said she didn't need anyone or anything, she believed him. "I haven't figured out what to do. Do I stay and fight for my job? Do I fight for the art program? Or do I move on? Maybe move out of Heritage River and start over somewhere brand new where no one knows me."

"Heritage River is in your blood. I don't see you living anywhere else." He twirled the ends of her hair around his fingers.

"I bumped into Rowan McGee. He's on the board. He suggested I get the parents involved. I don't know why I didn't think of it sooner." She wanted to stick her hands in his back pockets the way she did when they were young, but she kept her hands on his back. The hugging would have to be enough.

"McGee's on the board? Figures. Is he still the same giant pain in the ass he was back in school?"

"Pretty much."

"Still, it's not a bad idea. Did he have any other suggestions?"

"He said if I went out with him, he'd make sure the program stayed."

Colton stepped back and let her go. The cold air swooped in between them and chilled her bones. "What? That fucker came on to you like that? He never learned. I'll beat him senseless for trying to proposition you."

She bit her lip and grabbed his arm. "It's okay. You don't have to fight for my honor. We're not in high school anymore. Though I appreciate it."

He pulled her close, and the warmth returned. "Just say the word. Blaise and I will flip his car again."

"You do remember." She suspected he might. Who forgets turning a car on its side? But hearing him bring up the old memory heated her up more.

"I told you I've never forgotten. I remember everything we did."

Chapter Twenty-Two

The wind had wanted them off the bridge. Harley's toes were frozen, and as much as she hated to let go of the moment and of Colton, they had to get back in the car and blast the heat. On the way home, he had held her hand the entire time. He played soft music and explained beats and counts to her. She didn't know what he was talking about, but she didn't care. She sat back and let the cadence of his words wash over her.

They'd said goodnight in the driveway. Knox had texted that he was fine and would be home in an hour. She had let herself in and made a cup of tea. They still needed a Christmas tree. She'd buy one tomorrow. The house was too empty for her. The ghosts of Christmas past floated around her and reminded her of all that hadn't happened in her life.

She grabbed her coat and headed for the art studio. If she stayed busy, she wouldn't think about Colton's soft kisses on her lips or the fact she wanted more from him. So much more. If she could paint for a while, she wouldn't think about her bad choices or about her son. Every mistake she'd made with him was out of love. That much she knew for sure.

She squeezed paint onto the board and grabbed a brush. A soft knock at the door interrupted her. She opened it. Colton leaned against the frame, his legs crossed.

"Guess you couldn't sleep either?" he said.

"Just wanted some unwind time." She stepped back to let him in.

"Were you painting? I could go back to the guesthouse."

"No, I hadn't started." She walked around to the blank canvas she'd pulled out. She had no idea what she was going to paint. Her muse had abandoned her, but with Colton in her studio, her desire to paint paled in comparison to her desire for him.

"You haven't given me any more lessons." He picked up her brush and swished it across his palm.

"I think you're doing fine without them. You really aren't going to drink anymore, are you?"

"I don't think so. I don't even want to. Well, that's not totally true, but being here with you makes me strong."

"Me? I didn't do anything."

"You believe in me no matter how much I screw up. Besides Billy, you're the only person who's ever been really glad to see me. You made me see it was time to forgive my brother."

Grace's words played in her head. "Grace said you stopped by there."

He stepped closer, took her hand in his, and ran the paintbrush along her wrist. "I needed to talk some things out. I'm learning to do that too, it seems."

"I'm glad you've worked things out with Blaise. He was excited to have you on stage with him tonight." The bristles sent shivers over her skin.

"He's my best friend. Stupid, right?" He continued to caress her wrist with the paintbrush.

"Not at all. I wish I had a brother or a sister." She tried to keep her mind focused on the conversation and not the sensual stroke of the brush.

"But you have Ella." Colton moved over to the paints. "Isn't she like a sister? You two were giggling it up pretty good earlier tonight." He flipped the top of a red and squirted some onto her paint board.

"Do you want me to show you how to do some painting?" She wanted something to do with her hands, something that didn't involve them on his thin hips.

"Not tonight." He dipped his finger in the paint and drew a line across her collarbone. "There's something else I want to do with this paint."

The cold paint and his calloused touch made her impatient for more. He held her gaze with his. She saw forever in his gray eyes.

"Colton, I need to say something." Her fingers went to the paint on her skin. Its surface stuck to her fingertips.

He took her fingers and wiped them clean, then

kissed each one. "If I could paint, I'd paint you. Every beautiful inch of you."

She broke their stare and looked down at her hands. Blue veins pushed against her dry skin. "I'm not beautiful."

He pushed up the sleeve of her shirt and turned the inside of her arm over. "That's where you're wrong." He drew another paint line down her skin. His finger circled at her wrist.

She craved his touch, wanting to burn from the inside out because of it. "Maybe once, when I was younger." And her breasts didn't sag, or she didn't find wiry gray hairs in her head.

He took her other arm and left a trail along her skin, with his lips this time. "Wrong again. You're the most beautiful, special woman I've ever met." He dipped his finger into the paint and drew a line from the base of her neck to the top of her breasts.

"You're getting paint all over me." She couldn't help but laugh. She'd spent a good portion of her life covered in paint, but never this way.

"That's the idea. Then I can clean you up." His voice was low and thick.

The heat in her belly dropped lower to her core. His fingers traced her collarbone again and up the side of her neck. Her skin was on fire everywhere he touched.

"There's something I should tell you." She took his hand in his.

"Can we talk later? I need to do this first." He

brought his lips to hers, parting them with his tongue. He tasted minty and sweet.

He groaned low in his throat, and she was lost in the wave of emotions she'd fought all night. She wanted him inside her, to feel alive and desired again.

He tangled his fingers in her hair and pulled her closer to deepen the kiss. Her hands ran over the back of his shirt, making his muscles flex against her touch. She needed to feel his skin and searched out the lines and planes of his chest under his soft button-down.

He pressed his hands against her lower back, his need hard against her belly. She needed him too and fumbled with the buttons of his shirt.

His rough hands slid under her top, claiming what was once his and igniting the heat between her legs. He broke the kiss, and her head spun. His breath was short, but he held her close. "You're the most beautiful woman in the world."

"I don't look like I did the last time we were together. My skin is older, my body."

He pressed his finger to her lips. "Stop doubting yourself. You've invaded my thoughts for years. I couldn't shake you ever. It's why I kept that first drawing of the bridge you did and why I wanted the one from the other night. It's the only thing I had to stay connected to you."

His mouth was on hers again, and she swallowed the words she needed to say. He didn't give her another chance to think when he unhooked her bra. She wrestled with the buttons on his shirt again, wanting his skin against hers.

He pulled away only long enough to help her. "I like this shirt, babe," he said with a laugh, but he had the shirt off in seconds.

She tugged at his belt while his hands reached inside her jeans. She helped him until a pile of clothes littered the floor. He scooped her up and brought her to the couch.

"Unless you want to do it standing." He winked.

Her hands hunted every inch of him, memorizing him because she knew this would be the last time for them. She replayed his words. He'd thought of her for years. He'd said everything she wanted to hear, but he'd said things like that before. He'd leave her again, and that was best this time. No matter how much she wanted him to stay.

He lay on top of her, their gazes locked. She traced the tiny scar on his jaw. His stubble tickled against the pads of her fingers. She burned this night into her memory.

"There's never been anyone but you." She kissed him, this time trying to tell him how much he'd meant to her. How when she was with him she saw herself through his eyes and not through the eyes of her mother. When she was with him, her self-doubt wasn't as loud.

His hands were across her belly, going lower until he found what he was looking for and what she'd wanted from the second he'd drawn paint on her. A low groan was in her throat. His fingers curled inside her, and she called his name.

"Say my name again." He kissed her neck.

"Colton. Now. Colton." Her breath quickened, and her heart swelled.

He entered her and took her soaring. They rocked together in perfect rhythm. Their bodies remembered the pace they liked best. They didn't have to say it or wonder. Making love had always been this brilliant between them.

He waited for her sweet explosion, then joined her with his own flight. They collapsed in satiated warmth. Colton wrapped his arms around her and tucked her against him. She snuggled closer. Her body ached for more already.

"We've still got it." He smiled into her hair.

She giggled. "I guess so."

"You guess? Are you kidding?" He tickled her side, and she squirmed to get away. But he held her close, not that there was far to go on the couch. "Woman, admit we were great, or I'll tickle you again until you beg me to stop." His hand poised at her side.

"Okay, okay. We were great." Being with him was more than great.

"Good. I'd rather you beg me for something else anyway." He turned on his side to face her. He cupped her face and brought her in for a lingering kiss.

"I've missed being with you like this, and not just the sex. Just being with you. Tonight when I was playing, I kept trying to see if you were out there watching. I only wanted to play for you."

She laced her fingers through his. "I loved watching

you play. I always have. I'm glad I had a chance to see you on stage before you left."

His hands strumming her belly heated her insides again. "What if I didn't leave?" His words were a whisper.

She rested her head under his chin. She couldn't meet his gaze. "Don't tease me."

"I would never tease about something like that, babe. Playing with Blaise, Cash, and even Knox tonight was as right as I've felt in a long time. Until right now." He kissed the top of her head. His fingers played out a tune on her skin.

She ached to feel him inside her again. "You'd hate staying in Heritage River."

His hand stopped. "Are you telling me you don't want me to stick around?"

She turned to look at him, then pushed up on an elbow. "Are you serious? You're thinking about not going on tour? Why?"

He scratched the back of his head. "I don't know. It's all I've ever wanted, but with Mike making all these decisions I don't like...and after tonight. It doesn't feel right to play without my brother. Maybe I could create a whole new band—me, Blaise, Cash, and Knox. If that was okay with you. Maybe I could try to write something new." He turned his gaze away.

He was making huge steps to move forward from the past. "Whatever you decide will be great. I don't know about Knox, though. Could we save that idea for later?"

His hand brushed against her breast and set her skin

on fire again. His lips tasted hers. "Okay, let's shelve all the talking. There's other things I'd rather do with you."

He took his time exploring her body, making her tremble under his touch. He made her want him more. Nothing but him inside her would do. "Now, Colton."

He whispered in her ear. "Not yet, babe. This is the best way I can show you how I feel, if I make love to you like I'm playing a song."

He wanted to stay with her. He was ready to give up the road for her. The words she needed to say fought their way forward, but the fire in her soul burned them to ashes. She'd tell him tomorrow. First thing. But for now, he was with her, in her, loving her and calling her name.

Chapter Twenty-Three

Colton woke with a kink in his neck, a smile on his face, and the smell of Harley on him. He reached for her, but her spot on the couch was empty. A blanket covered his naked body. "Babe?" He pushed up to sit. Every joint complained about the early hour. Even his fingers ached. He opened and closed his fists. "Damn cold air."

Harley wasn't there. He scooped his jeans off the floor and shoved his legs in. She'd left without saying anything? Was she second-guessing what had happened between them? He'd meant what he'd said. He was thinking about staying, but only if she wanted him to. Without her, there wasn't any point in staying in Heritage River after the holiday concert. He'd go back to his home in Bayton and figure out his next move.

His next move? Was he really thinking about ditching the tour? Talk about never say never. Blaise would rub him about this for the rest of his life. Colton shook his head. He hadn't decided yet. Two weeks didn't seem long enough. The memory of Harley under him sent heat through his groin. He wanted more of her. Every damn day if she'd let him.

He reached for his shirt. A piece of paper floated to the ground. He fumbled for it.

Colton,

I had a wonderful night. Thank you, but it wouldn't look good if Knox found us out in the studio together. H.

He turned the paper over. What was he expecting? Hearts drawn all over it? He grabbed his phone and sent her a text.

Missed you this morning. Breakfast?

Nothing came back. A shower would get rid of the aches and pains. All worth it, of course. He shut the studio door behind him. Her Durango was in the driveway. He checked his phone again. Nothing.

He let himself into the guesthouse. His phone vibrated, and he yanked it out, hoping to see Harley's name. He tried not to notice the disappointment stuck in his chest when he answered. "Hey, it's the musical genius."

"Hey, Uncle Colton, last night rocked, right?"

"It sure did, kid. Haven't had that much fun in a while. Thanks for letting me jam at your session."

"We'd let you play with us all the time if you wanted."

Maybe he did want that. Savage 2.0. Badder and

better than before. "Did you need something this morning?"

"Dad and I are going to May's for breakfast, and then I'm going to the museum with Harley's class. I wanted to know if you wanted to come along."

His phone buzzed. A text had come in. He licked his lips with cautious hope the text was from Harley. "Hang on, Cash."

He muted the call and jumped over to his messages. *Class trip today. Rain check?*

He sent her a thumbs-up and pushed away the ache that she didn't ask him to join her on the trip. He jumped back to the call. "I'll be there in twenty."

Colton opened the door to May's and the smell of coffee and hot bread wafted around him. His stomach growled. People packed the place. Lost in deep conversation, they sipped from white ceramic mugs. Shopping bags took up too much floor space. The piped-in Christmas music gave him a headache. He'd get Harley and Knox presents. He knew exactly what Knox would like. Harley would be harder. He'd call Paul for an idea, make his assistant earn some of that money.

Blaise and Cash sat at a table in the corner. They waved him over. It was good to have part of his family back. This might be all he'd ever get. Savannah wasn't going to give in too easily.

He pulled up a chair.

"My social media is burning up." Cash held up his phone for Colton to see. "They loved us last night. The place booked us for five more gigs. Will Knox play again? He killed it."

"Harley doesn't want him playing, but I'll talk her into it. I need some coffee." He looked over his shoulder, but the line at the register wrapped around the store.

"Didn't get much sleep after your hot date, brother?" Blaise's face had a shit-eating grin on it.

"I slept fine." He would've felt better if Harley had still been in his arms when he woke. "What are you smiling about?"

"I'm happy to have had a night on stage with my son and my brother. Felt like old times, but better with the addition of Knox, right?"

"Last night rocked. I'd forgotten what it was like to play in a smaller place with the crowd right there. I had a good time. Happy now?"

"I'd be happier if you said you'd jam with us again." Blaise stood up and went behind the counter, placed a kiss on May's cheek, and helped himself to some coffee. May laughed and swatted at him.

Blaise placed the coffee on the table in front of Colton. "I ordered you some eggs. What's going on with you and Harley?"

"Yeah, tell us." Cash looked at his father, and they laughed.

"You two are huge pains in the ass. Did you ask me

out here so I could tell you if I got laid last night?" The coffee warmed his throat and his hands.

"That's gross, Uncle Colton. TMI. We want to know about the art lessons."

"Shut up."

Blaise and Cash laughed harder. Colton shook his head. The volume in the shop grew. More people had arrived. The line grew longer, and every table was full.

"Hey, Blaise, great job last night," a tall guy with wavy silver hair and sunglasses propped up on his head said. He and the woman with him grabbed a place in line, not far from their table.

Silver Hair leaned into the woman. "Too bad the brother showed up. He's a thing of the past. Someone needs to tell him."

"Shh, lower you voice, Fred." The woman pushed him away.

"Yeah, Fred, lower your big trap," Blaise said loud enough for good old Fred to turn around and turn red. Blaise turned back to Colton. "Sorry, bro."

"Can't please them all." But the words stung more than Colton expected. Twice in two days he'd heard he was past tense. Hell, that wasn't anything new. Blaise had been trying to tell him that for years, but until these past few weeks, it didn't seem true. But the truth nipped at his heels now.

He saw the future when he looked at his brother and nephew. Kids like Knox were the future, and man, that kid was as gifted as Cash. Their talent pushed players like Colton aside. *You can't move forward if you keep looking back.* Wasn't that something he'd heard in rehab? Did he want to be a part of something better or be forgotten? His fingers tapped on his leg. Could he write something after all this time? He wanted to talk to Harley about it all. He'd be cashing that rain check in sooner rather than later.

May brought over their food. "Good morning, Colton. Are you treating our Harley like a lady?"

This damn town. Nothing was a secret here. It hadn't even been twenty-four hours, and the rumors were going crazy. "Geez, May. What the hell makes you think anything has happened between me and Harley?"

She smacked the back of his head. "Don't talk like that. Just remember—if you go doing something inappropriate with her, Billy will chase you down. You need to make an honest woman out of her once and for all." Blaise laughed, and she pointed a finger at him. "That's enough out of you."

"Yes, ma'am."

Cash ducked into his phone. Smart boy.

"We're grown-ups now. Harley and I don't have to explain what we're doing."

"Not Harley. Just you." May turned and poured coffee for another patron.

"What time is that class trip?" He was ready to blow this place.

Cash checked his phone. "Now."

"Let's beat it."

Harley waited in the two-story lobby of the Heritage River Museum of Art as her relaxation students wandered in. The sun streamed in through the glass front and painted prism streaks on the black tile floor. She handed out the tickets for entrance. "Has anyone seen Andy or Cash?"

Andrea Kapner, a college student who took the class as a way to handle her parents' divorce, grabbed the ticket. "I think I saw Cash parking. I don't know who Andy is. Sorry."

Not a surprise. Andy mostly kept to himself. "You might as well get started. Everyone is on their own. The American Impressionism exhibit is upstairs. We'll meet in the café for lunch. Have fun."

The students meandered in different directions. The day would be a bust if Andy didn't show.

"Harley."

She turned at the voice echoing off the high walls. Andy trotted toward her. He scooped the front of his hair to the side. His smile was wide. "Sorry I'm late. My mom just dropped me off. We had to wait for my dad to leave before we could go. We didn't tell him about the trip. He thinks art is kind of dumb. Sorry." He ducked his head.

"No problem. Not everyone appreciates art. I'm glad you're here." She handed him his ticket. "Some of the other students are already walking around if you want to catch up to them."

"Is Cash here yet?"

"Right here." Cash saddled up alongside Andy and patted him on the back. Cash had a few inches on Andy, making him look up at the older boy. "Let's go see this exhibit Harley wants us to look at. I hear there's a John Henry Twachtman on display. We'll meet you upstairs?" They headed for the escalators.

"Hey."

Her head snapped around before she could follow Cash. "What are you doing here?"

Colton stood with his hands in his jacket pockets and rocked on his feet. "Cash invited me along, and since you were gone when I woke up this morning, I wanted to see why this place was more interesting than having breakfast with me."

"I'm trying to get Andy to trust himself. I thought he might see a little of himself in the artists on display. I wasn't trying to ditch you." Well, a little, but no need to bring that up. She had to worry about Andy now. "Let's catch up to Cash and Andy. The museum also has a music exhibit on display you might enjoy."

He laced his fingers through hers, and they climbed the escalator to the Impressionism exhibit. Cash leaned into the paintings to read the descriptions under them. Andy stood with his head tilted up and his mouth hanging open as he took in the Twachtman.

"Babe, I'm going to wander around. Go help your student." He leaned in and placed a soft kiss on her cheek. He was always full of surprises. One minute he wanted her attention and then gave her the space she needed the next. Another reason she loved him so much.

She approached Andy. "That's his *White Bridge*. Twachtman's paintings are here on loan for the exhibit. His bridge reminds me of Monet's *The Japanese Footbridge*. That's the painting I really wanted you to see, but we'd have to take a trip to Washington, DC, for that. It's in The National Gallery of Art. You can Google it, but seeing a painting in person makes a bigger impact." Like seeing a favorite rock star on stage performing. She checked over her shoulder. No sign of Colton. He must've found the music exhibit.

"I like *The Waterfall, Blue Brook*. All those blues. I feel like I could swim in it and let the water just wash over and relax me. I needed that painting the day I took the SATs." Red splashes covered his neck and face.

"Andy, everyone makes mistakes. It's what we take away from those mistakes that's important." "I guess."

She needed to start following her own advice. Maybe she shouldn't settle for a career she didn't love any longer. Maybe losing her job was a second chance to start over. How many people got one of those? Maybe Colton and Knox would be able to forgive her when they found out the truth. "Have you seen the *Hemlock Pool?* It's on loan from a private collection."

They spent the rest of the morning investigating the other artists in the exhibit. Colton bought everyone lunch, and by the end of the day her students had seen the possibilities of creativity. She hoped they were as inspired as she was.

"Andy, do you think you might put a piece in our art

show?" They waited outside for his mother to pick him up. Cash and Colton waited by Cash's car.

"I don't know. Maybe. If I could paint like that John Henry guy, definitely."

"He had to start somewhere."

Andy's mom pulled up and honked. With a wave, he jumped into the car and they sped away.

Had she saved that young man at all today? Or had he helped save her just a little?

Harley had avoided Colton after the trip to the museum. She'd begged off his offers with the excuse of working on saving the art program. She had been too. She'd sent emails to the parents of her high school and studio students. She'd even included her adult students on the list. She was surprised by the overwhelming acceptance to come to her house Tuesday, the night before the holiday concert, to discuss options.

She needed to tell Colton the truth. Tonight. No more stalling. Her phone rang to life. A text.

I know you're home. Why are you avoiding me?

Her fingers hovered over the screen. Damn. Sexy and smart. *Not avoiding you.* "Come over and make love to me all night long." *The back door is open,* she typed instead.

In seconds, banging commenced on the back door. She pushed herself off the chair by the fireplace and trudged into the kitchen. The banging continued with a sense of urgency.

"Colton, it's open. Just come in." She made it all the way to the door, and the banging grew louder and faster. "You're going to break the glass." She pulled hard on the door and froze.

Colton wasn't standing at the back door. She was met with a large Douglas fir and the smell of cedar. Branches shook as if they were waving at her. A laugh escaped from her lips.

"Woman, I never thought you'd come to the door. Can you let us in? It's freezing out here."

She pushed some of the branches to the side. Colton smiled at her. A blue knit cap was pulled low on his head. "Nice hat," she said.

"You can have it if you'll get out of the way so I can come in."

She laughed again. "Can I help you with the tree?"

"I've got it." Colton pushed and wedged the tree through the door. Needles spilled across the floor. Inside, he pulled off the hat and shook his head. "It was the biggest one on the lot." His smile spread across his face.

Her cheeks hurt from smiling back. Of course, he'd bought the biggest one. Only the biggest and best for him. "You didn't have to do that. I was planning on taking Knox."

His smile crashed. "Did I screw up? I didn't mean to interrupt a tradition or something. I can take it back."

"No." She reached to stop him. She wanted that

smile back. "No, it's great. Thank you. He can help put up the ornaments, if he even wants to. I'll get the stand."

Colton dragged the tree into the front room. He held it while she tried to secure the trunk. Pine needles rained down on her.

She climbed out from under the tree, and he was inches from her. "It looks great. Thank you again. I appreciate it." Heat filled her cheeks. He smelled all male, wintery, and a little smoky.

He wiped his hands together and looked down at her with a sheepish smile. "Can I make you some dinner?"

"I think I only have some stale bread and potatoes."

"I went to the store after the museum." He slid his hand into hers, and she curled her fingers around his. "Come with me."

"I shouldn't. We need to talk about something."

"Are you sorry about the other night?" He didn't let go of her. "Tell me to go away, babe. I'll walk out and never come back."

Her throat tightened. "Are you seriously saying you'd stay this time? Why now?"

"Because I know what I want. I had my time in the lights. Someone else should take over now. I want to spend time with my family while I still have them. I'm good with doing something else. If I want, I can visit the big stage once in a while. And you. I want to stay with you if you'll have me. I watched you today with that kid. You're strong, smart. Your face lights up when you talk about art. Watching you makes me high. That's the kind of high I need in my life."

The words she'd wanted to hear her entire life were too late. Why couldn't he have said them eighteen years ago? Because back then he wanted his career. He wanted to be famous.

"Dinner would be nice." *Coward.* She shrugged into her coat and held his hand as they made their way across the yard.

A car sped down her driveway and skid to a stop inches from her Durango.

"Who the fuck is that tearing up the dirt?" He dropped her hand.

"You've got to be kidding me." She couldn't believe what was happening.

Joe Henson jumped from his car and barreled over to them. "Why did you take my son to an art museum today? He came home talking about majoring in art instead of science. What kind of a career is he going to have with an art degree? A teacher?" He sneered.

Colton stepped forward. "Hey, pal—"

"I've got this." She gripped his arm. She met Joe's wild gaze. "People like you are the reason art, creativity, and innovation are dying in this country. Have you ever watched a movie all the way to the end? All those people's names scrolling across the screen are in the arts. All the characters drawn for film, TV, or print are in the arts. The makeup artists and the set designers for musicals and plays are in the arts.

"I'd rather see kids like Andy and my son take a chance at their dreams than end up like me wondering *what if* all the time. This man"—she pointed to Colton—

"wasn't afraid to go after his artistic dreams when his father told him it was a waste of time. The world would've missed out on his music if he'd listened to his father. But Andy will crumble under your rules if you hold him back. Don't come back here, or I will call the sheriff and have you arrested, Mr. Henson. Go home and tell your son you love him and believe in him before it's too late and Andy does something far worse than kick in a bathroom stall."

Joe Henson flinched as if he'd been hit. "You haven't heard the last of me." He turned on his wing-tipped heel and returned to his car.

They watched him drive away.

Colton turned her to him. "Thank you for saying those things about me. You were amazing and hot getting feisty like that, standing up for what you believe in. Do you realize you said you wanted Knox to go after his dreams too?"

"I did not say that." Had she?

"You did." He smiled down at her showing off his dimple.

"Well, I still want Knox to have a backup plan. It's different for us."

"No, it isn't. You just have to believe, babe."

"Colton, the only thing I believe in is a paycheck and chocolate ice cream."

"You believe in me."

"Okay, you too. Does your dinner offer still stand? I'm starving." Even though she didn't want to think about it, the argument with Joe Henson had her fired up.

Colton let her into the guesthouse. "Sit here. I'll take care of everything."

Her gaze never left him as he moved around the small kitchen and shredded lettuce and carrots. He diced up peppers and threw some mushrooms in a skillet. He put up a pot of water to boil.

"You're pretty good in the kitchen."

"I'm pretty good in every room."

"Remind me what it is I like about you." The banter between them eased the tension in her shoulders. The adrenaline rush was over. She wanted to forget about Joe Henson.

"A little of this." He air-guitared a solo for her.

She threw slices of avocado at him. "You're impossible."

He pulled her close and wrapped his arms around her, pinning her to his chest. "Is this too impossible for you?" His voice was low and hoarse. His eyes were dark and smoky.

Her heart beat in rhythm with his. "You're bearable." She ran her finger under the collar of his shirt.

"Just bearable? I usually hear I'm extreme." His hands slid down her backside.

"Insufferable." She pressed against him and wrapped her arms around his neck.

His mouth was on hers. She laced her fingers through his hair. His need pressed against her, and she leaned closer into him, wanting him to know how much she needed him too.

They became a tangle of hands and arms reaching for

each other. He pulled her shirt over her head, unhooked her bra and pushed the straps from her shoulders. His fingers traced lines across her skin. She shivered.

"Are you cold?"

"Not possible." She stepped out of her pants and kicked them aside.

He took her in with a slow gaze. "Much better." His mouth was on hers again. He trailed kisses down her neck and over her shoulders.

He brought her to the bedroom this time, but she would've been fine on the floor. She was good anywhere he was. "You're still wearing your clothes."

He pulled his shirt up over his muscular chest. He was still so beautiful, even all these years later.

He stepped out of his jeans and lay beside her. His hands stroked her skin again, making her crave his touch everywhere. "I've wanted to do this since I woke up alone this morning."

"I'm sorry about that." She traced a finger around his chest.

He took her finger in his mouth and sucked. "Never be sorry."

Their lovemaking was just as it was when they were young. His hands sought the heat between her legs, and she wrapped hers around the full width of him, bringing him pleasure in slow strokes, until she wasn't sure she could take anymore.

He threw his head back. "Damn, woman, you will be the end of me."

He kissed her again, and she forgot everything else.

When he entered her, she soared. Her hips went up to meet his, taking him in and filling her up. Her heart was going to burst with the love she had for this man. He took care of her, holding back until she finished, and then he joined her, breathing hard in her ear. He left kisses on her cheeks, jaw, and neck. He repeated her name like a song. She would always love him, no matter how badly this all ended.

His fingers traced the edge of her jaw. "Harley—"

"Don't say anything." She put a finger to his lips. "I don't want to talk. I only want to feel you against me." She snuggled closer, never wanting to let him go.

He kissed her finger. "I'm sorry I left you all those years ago."

"No, Colton. Don't ever be sorry. You wanted a career, a big career, and you went for it, just like I told Joe Henson. I don't blame you. Please stop talking and kiss me again." He couldn't be sorry now. The only excuse she ever had for keeping such a big secret from him was not wanting to hold him back from his dreams.

He couldn't change that now.

"But I need you to hear this."

"No, I don't need anything except you and this moment."

"Why won't you let me talk?" He sat up on an elbow and looked down at her.

"I thought guys didn't like to talk after sex. Don't you need to take a nap or something?"

"I'll show you a nap." He tickled her side, and she squealed. "How's that?"

She tried to get away from him, but he kept her in place with his strong leg. He continued to tickle her. "Colton, stop." Tears streamed down her face. Her cheeks hurt from laughing so much.

"No way." His fingers gave no reprieve. She tried to tickle him back, but he rolled on top of her. He took her hand in one swift move and held it over her head. Their gazes locked. "I love you."

Her body went limp under him. The words he hadn't said in twenty-five years. The words she'd wondered if he ever really meant. "Colton, I, I, have something to tell you."

His phone rattled against the side table. "It's Savannah." He released her and sat up. He grabbed the phone. "Should I get it? I can wait if you want me to."

But she knew how much he wanted a call from his sister. "No, it's fine." She pulled the sheet up over her.

"Hey." He reached for his clothes on the floor. "No, it's fine. Shit, really? I'll be right there."

"Is everything okay?"

"It's Adam. He's in the hospital. I knew he looked sick." He ran a hand over his face and shoved his legs into his jeans. "Savannah wants me to come. It doesn't look good, babe. Will you come with me?"

"This is your family. I shouldn't intrude." She hurried to get dressed. She had no place with the Savages. "I'll pray for him. Call me when you know something. I'll wait up for you."

He kissed the top of her head. "I'm sorry to run off

after we just made love. You know this isn't on purpose, right?"

"My God, of course. Go. Savannah needs you."

He wrenched opened the door and then ran back to kiss her one more time. "I love you. I shouldn't have wasted so much time fighting it."

She shivered as she watched his car speed down the driveway. A low moan escaped her lips. "I'm sorry," she said into the wind that swallowed her words and tossed them away, worthless as they were.

Chapter Twenty-Four

On the way to the hospital, Colton took every turn on two wheels. Savannah needed him, and he was going to get there if it killed him. He wished Harley had come, but he didn't know what he was going to find at the hospital. It was better she stayed behind. Knowing she would wait for him was enough for now. She'd been waiting for him a long time. Too long. Well, he'd spend the rest of his life making up for those lost years. If she'd let him.

He ran through the bright lobby of the Heritage River Hospital and tried not to bite the head off the man behind the desk.

"I need some identification, please." The man had wisps of white hair and cloudy blue eyes. His gnarled hands reached out for Colton's license.

He wanted to yell "Don't you know who I am?" but losing his shit wasn't going to help this time.

He ran out of the elevator onto the fifth floor. The

bright lights made it seem as if it were the middle of the day instead of sometime at night. The waiting room sat right off the elevator, and it was filled. Blaise, Grace, Cash, Savannah, and her three kids: Caroline, Greyson, and Jud. *Jud.* What would he say to Jud after all that had happened between them?

Savannah looked up and met his gaze. He stopped in his tracks, not sure how to approach her, but she ran to him and threw her arms around his neck. Her tears wet his shirt. She was his little sister again, scared of the thunder after a bad dream when only sleeping next to him holding a flashlight would settle her down.

"You came."

He set her right and looked into her face. He wiped some of the tears. "Of course, I'd come."

She wiped her nose with the back of her hand. "I've been such a bitch to you. Adam kept telling me to let it go, that I was at fault. We were even fighting about that right before..." She started crying again. Her shoulders shuddered in his hands.

"Forget it."

She shook her head. "He was right, and I might not get to tell him. What if I can't tell him? He's not conscious."

Grace came over and put an arm around Savannah. She smiled up at Colton. "Let's sit. I can get you a cup of tea."

She led Savannah away like a willing child. The distraught woman allowing someone else to take charge wasn't his sister, and his heart hollowed out for what was happening.

He signaled for Blaise to come over. "What's going on?"

Blaise shoved his hands in his pockets. "He's got pancreatic cancer. It's aggressive and pretty far along. He had a heart attack or stroke or something at home today. They were having lunch. She's been here the whole time with the kids. She called me only an hour ago. The doctor came out after Grace, Cash, and I got here. He said Adam had hours left. That's when she called you. She was afraid you wouldn't take her call."

"Shit."

"Well said." Blaise patted him on the shoulder. "All we can do now is wait. You want to sit?"

"What do I say to Jud?"

"Same thing you'd say to Caroline and Grey. Does anything that happened last summer between us even matter now?"

Colton went over to Caroline and scooped his young niece into a fierce hug. She clung to him and cried like her mother. He kissed the top of her head and dried her tears. Grey pushed his head into Colton's chest. When Grey was done crying, Colton turned to Jud. He'd grown even more since last summer. He looked more like Savannah every day.

"I'm sorry." Colton held out his hand.

Jud stared down at his outstretched hand, then back up at him. Jud's face was as unreadable as blank sheet music. Colton was about to pull his hand away when Jud gripped it with force.

"Me too." Jud let go quickly and went to sit with his mother. Colton found a spot between Blaise and Cash.

Savannah left them to go sit with Adam. A while later she called in the kids. Sometime after that Blaise shook him awake. "It's over."

He stayed around until Savannah was ready to leave the hospital. The sun peeked over the bare trees by the time they made their way outside. He drove her and the kids home.

"It's been a long night, and it's a drive back to Harley's. Do you want to catch a few winks here?" Savannah tossed her bag on the table covered in plates, cups, a bottle of mustard, a bottle of soda, used napkins.

A chair was turned on its side. He righted it.

"I'll get out of your hair. You need to get some rest, but if you need anything at all, call me. I'll come right back."

"Will you stick around for the funeral?" She ran her finger over the rim of a half-empty glass.

"I'm sticking around for good, sis."

She looked up at him. "Ah, another Savage man in love." Her smile was thin, and tears brimmed her eyes. "What's going to happen to me?"

He folded his arms around her and let her cry. He had no idea how to answer that question, but his sister was the toughest of the Savage clan. She'd bounce back eventually and take the world by storm.

The sun hung high in the blue sky by the time Colton let himself into the guesthouse. He kicked off his boots, searching for a sign of Harley. He knew she wouldn't be there, not after he ran out last night. A note from her covered in her honeysuckle scent would be nice, though.

She had made the bed. A smile slipped across his lips. He climbed under the covers with all his clothes on. His body ached from the long night. He hoped to get a whiff of her on his sheets. He'd sleep for a while and then call her and take her to dinner, a proper dinner with good food and dim lighting so he could press his lips against her neck.

Harley had wanted to tell him something before Savannah had called. Was she going to tell him to take a hike for good? He deserved that. Her feelings hadn't been his top concern when he was young and full of himself. If she said she wanted him to stay, he would spend the rest of his life making it all up to her. He'd be the man she deserved.

He thought of the darkness that had passed over her face when he said he loved her. Maybe saying the *L* word was too much too soon. He'd worry about his big mouth later, after he got some sleep.

Chapter Twenty-Five

Harley rearranged the snacks on her coffee table again. The parents were due at her house in a few minutes. Maybe she should have bought more vegetables instead of three variety of chips. That's what Colton would've done. She stared at her newly decorated Christmas tree. He was everywhere she looked.

She flopped onto the couch and held her head in her hands. Colton. He'd been so busy helping his sister the past two days she barely saw him, which was a good thing and a not-so-good thing. She had to tell him, or maybe she should tell Knox first. Either way, telling the truth was going to end badly for her, and she deserved whatever consequence was dealt.

What if something happened to Colton and she never got the chance to tell him? Who was expecting Adam Montgomery to die? Was she really going to let everyone's lives end with her secret tucked away? Fear certainly had had its way with her. Well, no more.

She checked out the back window. Her breath hitched in her throat. His car was parked in its usual spot. She could go to the guesthouse right now before the parents arrived. She needed to spill before she poisoned herself with the lie.

The doorbell interrupted her runaway thoughts. Her wobbly legs led her to the door. She wiped her hands on her pants and pulled open the door to Colton's wide smile.

"Boy, are you a sight for sore eyes." He stepped through the doorway and took her face in his hands. His lips were on hers, devouring them with desperation. His tongue pushed her lips apart and made the kiss deeper. She leaned into him with relief and wound her hands into his hair. He was here, and he was hers.

She pulled away from the kiss. "Hello to you too." Heat flushed her cheeks. Now wasn't the time for lovemaking. "I have the parents coming." She stepped away from him, and the heat raced from her body, chilling her skin. She wanted to press up against him again. To hell with the parents.

"That's why I'm here. I didn't want to miss your important meeting."

"Doesn't Savannah need you?" His support might just choke her to death. She didn't deserve his kindness. She could justify her choices when he was acting like an ass.

He hung his jacket on the hook by the door. He wore

his black sweater that accented his broad shoulders. "Blaise is with her."

"How are she and the kids doing?"

"She's being Savannah. She cleaned the whole house top to bottom before anyone could come over and pay their respects. I never saw so many pans of lasagna, vegetable platters, or boxes of cookies."

She understood. When Hank died, the town had rallied around her too. She still had pans of food in the freezer. Nothing compared to a small town. "Making food helps people feel useful when they don't know what else to do."

"She made me fix all the little projects that had been neglected while Adam was sick. I've been up and down a ladder and under all her sinks for the past two days." He rolled his head on his neck. "Sleeping on her couch hasn't helped my neck. She's organized the memorial service by herself. Blaise tried to help her, and I believe her response was 'Blaise William Savage, if I want your help I will request it. In the meantime, shut the hell up.'" He raised his voice to try to meet Savannah's octave and shoved his hands on his hips as his sister would.

She bit her lip to stop from laughing and not to encourage him. "She's hurting."

He came over and wrapped his arms around her. "Oh, I know it, and Blaise knows it. Savannah is so used to being our mother hen and being in charge. We let her go until she settles her feathers down. I stood in the corner hoping she'd forget I was there because she would have yelled at me for being present. About ten minutes after she handed Blaise his head, she asked him what he thought of some of her decisions."

"What did Blaise do?" She curled up against him.

"He was Blaise. He kissed the top of her head and told her she was doing a great job."

Harley's heart ached. She'd wanted so much to be welcomed into the folds of the Savage clan. They fought with each other, but they loved each other fiercely, always watching each other's backs. She fought the tears threatening to split her world in two.

He kissed the top of her head again and released her. "What can I do to help?" He eyed the snacks on the coffee table. "You're serving that?"

"I didn't know what to have. They might not even want to eat. What if no one shows up anyway?"

He reached over and settled her waving hands in his own. "Babe, chill. You'll be fine. You're tougher than you think."

"Why do you think I'm capable of so much?"

"Because I'm me, and I'm never wrong." He winked.

That damn wink.

"Do you have any coffee?" He didn't wait for an answer but went into the kitchen. She followed. "You wanted to tell me something the other night when I had you swooning in my bed. What was it? You want any?"

Her face flushed again. She shook her head and tucked a hair behind her ear. She found something very interesting to look at on the floor before she raised her gaze to meet his. "It can wait. You have a lot going on with Savannah."

She'd lost her earlier bravado. The last thing she needed to do was dump her news on him while he dealt with his family's loss and the upcoming holiday concert. Right after the funeral and the concert, she'd tell him.

The doorbell made its unwanted presence known again. She hurried to the door. Ella held two brown bags in her arms. "Reinforcements." She planted a kiss on Harley's cheek and plowed her way into the house. "Nice to see you again, Colton." She wagged her eyebrows at him and deposited the bags and her coat at the kitchen table.

"Ella." He saluted her with his mug.

"You didn't have to bring anything. I had it under control." She didn't really, but it was time she started pretending she did.

"The best way to win people over is to feed them, right?" Ella pulled out a pink box from one of the bags. "I stopped at May's for cookies and Jake's for some finger sandwiches. Have you seen his son JT? He's a cutie. Go get those greasy chips before anyone sees them. I also brought veggies."

"See, babe." He leaned against the doorframe with his ankles crossed, his tight jeans molded to his strong legs. Her lower belly ached with the knowledge of those legs entwined with hers.

"Okay, you two, no ganging up on me and my eating habits. I did get veggies," she yelled over her shoulder on the way into the living room.

The doorbell rang again. Harley jumped. "Here goes."

Her living room filled up with the parents of her high school students and a few students from the art classes at Community. May walked in with Jake. "Howdy, Harley. Thought we'd stop by to give our two cents."

She was about to close the door, but something stopped her.

"Hi." Rowan McGee stood on her porch in his shearling coat and cowboy boots. "I heard there was a meeting going on that could use my help."

Colton whisked over and occupied the space beside her. "Well, if it isn't Rowan McGee. What are you driving these days, old man?"

Rowan stuck out his hand. "Colton Savage. The rumor mill is churning with stories about your return. Something along the lines of a drunk-driving accident. Is that true?"

Colton shook his hand, but his eyes were as cold as steel. "Don't believe everything you read."

"Why don't we get this meeting started?" Harley led the men into her living room. They settled in opposite corners. "Thank you all for coming tonight. As you know, I'm hoping to save the art program at the high school."

The crowd burst out with support and suggestions. She tried to wrangle them in, hoping they'd speak one at a time, but it was May who finally got them all to quiet down.

Colton never left her side. She was acutely aware of his presence, even though the only time he spoke was to whisper in her ear, "I'm right here. You've got this."

"Let's add something to the art show," May said.

"Let's give the people who come to buy the kids' work something extra. The more money we raise, the better chance of saving Harley's job."

"It's not just about my job." Which would end in May. She didn't know how much longer she wanted to work for Joann Humphreys, even if she wasn't going to be replaced. "The arts are being taken away from schools everywhere. It's been proven that kids do better in all subjects when they have a chance to paint or play music. Anyone can pick up a paintbrush or an instrument. Not everyone can throw a ball with enough power to make the team."

"Colton, are you going to stay on as the music teacher?" Rowan smirked.

"This meeting is about to how to save the art program. It's not about me."

"Are you going to chip in to the pot?" Rowan was like a dog with a bone. He didn't want to let Colton off the hook.

Colton's body stiffened beside hers. "I can match whatever you're giving."

May clapped her hands. "Wonderful. We have a starting point. What can we do to get the people more involved?"

Jake cleared his throat and scratched his chin. "Thank you all for letting me come to this meeting. The music and art programs helped my boy JT when he was in high school. That awful guitar gave him something to focus on instead of getting in trouble. It didn't always work, but it helped. No offense, Colton.

You're pretty good at playing. JT was better at other things."

"None taken. JT was always better at dragging my gear around than playing it. Haven't seen him in ages. I'll stop by the deli and bust his ass a little." Colton laughed, and the tension left Jake's shoulders.

"Anyway, I'd like to offer up Eat at Jake's. Have people come in for a meal. I'll donate all the profits to the program. What do you think?"

The crowd took to Jake's idea. Ella jotted notes on the specifics. In no time at all, they had a plan. Harley couldn't believe what she heard. They'd all come to help because she'd asked them to help her.

Her guests filed out. Ella hugged her. "Great night. It's all going to be okay."

"I hope so."

"Have faith. Good night, Colton." Ella waved over her head on the way out the door.

Harley handed Rowan his big, heavy coat. "Thanks for coming, Rowan."

"I'll donate whatever he does."

Colton placed a hand on her shoulder. "Name your price."

"I'd say a date with Harley, but I don't want you tipping my car over again. This one costs a hell of a lot more than that old one did." Rowan stuck out his hand.

Colton hesitated, and she held her breath.

"Do you want to go on a date with him?" Colton stared down at her.

"What? No." Heat filled her cheeks and neck. Why

would he ask her such a thing? "Sorry, Rowan. It's nothing personal." Even though in a way it was.

Colton shook his hand. "Looks like she chose me."

"Lucky man, but you always were where Harley was concerned. Night, y'all."

She turned on Colton the second the door was closed. "Do you think I want to date Rowan?" She didn't know if she should be mad at him for suggesting it or glad that he let her speak for herself.

"I don't usually ask questions I don't know the answer to, but I was hoping you wouldn't make me look like an ass in front of Rowan." He closed the gap between them. "You did great tonight."

"This fundraiser might not be enough." Her hands traced the muscles in his arms. His sweater was soft under her touch. "We have to pull this off before the kids register for classes next month. If the class doesn't get enough attendance, the school won't bring the program back at all. But if you stay on as the music teacher, you can save the music program." If he stayed, then she would go and give up her small town.

"I'm not going to stay on and teach a bunch of kids if you don't have your job too. Honestly, babe, I don't even know if I want to teach." His fingers played with the ends of her hair.

"I won't have my job in August no matter what happens." She lifted her chin. "If you become the music teacher, it doesn't mean you became your father."

Colton laughed. "It doesn't? Teaching music at my

old high school sure feels like I turned into my dad. I'd rather just write a check. I'm good at that."

"Colton, I don't want you to save the programs with a check." She touched the soft spot at the bottom of his neck. "Give those kids the gift of you."

"I'm more like a last resort." He leaned in and kissed her below her ear. Her skin tingled.

The kids would love having him as a teacher, and they'd be lucky to get him. She wished she could convince him to take on the challenge even if his time at the school was short.

She tilted her head back as his lips left a hot trail down her neck. His hands ran up and down her back. She slid her hands under his sweater. His muscles flexed under her touch. She was quickly becoming liquid heat.

"Knox will be home soon."

"Then I guess we better hurry."

She tasted sweet. The way she had tasted all those years ago. She kissed him back with an intensity that made him want her more. His hands sought her skin.

"This sweater is in my way." He teased her.

She surprised him by stepping back and yanking the thing over her head. She had on a tight tank top that outlined her breasts. His insides ached for her like a country love song. "You know how to drive me crazy." He pulled her close and wrapped his fingers in her hair, but it was Harley who pulled him in for the kiss. His hands slid across her middle and up her sides, strumming on her ribs. He unhooked her bra, and she responded with a low moan.

He pulled away. "Hang on a second."

"Colton, it's cold. Hurry back."

He turned off all the lights except for the colored lights on the Christmas tree. They cast the room in soft hues of blues, reds, and greens.

"I thought you didn't like Christmas lights." She wrapped her arms around his neck as he pulled her close again. Their body heat mixed together and warmed them up.

"I don't like Christmas *music*. Besides, you like the lights."

"They're pretty."

"Not as pretty as you are." He traced his finger around her nipple.

"We could go upstairs." She took his hand and pressed it against her breast.

"Here's fine." He grabbed her backside and lifted her. She wrapped her legs around him and kept her arms wound tightly around his neck.

"Are we going to do it standing?" A smile played across her lips. "Do you remember that time we tried to do it standing in your basement?"

"I had to walk us over to the pool table." He tilted his head back and laughed. "I couldn't look at that thing the same after. Every time Blaise played pool, I burst out laughing."

Okay, maybe standing sex at their ages was a bad

idea. He tried to be romantic or some shit and now she was wrapped around him and they were both still wearing their pants. "Not sure I can walk us into the other room like this."

"What? Are you getting old or something?" She nibbled his ear, and he growled.

"I could take you right here, you know."

"Not with your pants on."

He dumped them both on the couch. She let out a full laugh, which made the yearning low in his belly stronger. He tugged at her jeans while she fought to get his belt off. They were a tangle of arms. Her hands slid over his waist and found what she wanted. She wrapped her hand around him and stroked.

"Harley."

She pushed him back on the couch and straddled him. "I want you to feel the way you make me feel."

Her mouth burned a trail down his chest. He closed his eyes. If he could feel this high all the time, he'd never think about a drink again. She laced her fingers through his while her other hand cupped him. Her tongue wet the tip of him. Bright stage lights exploded behind his eyes. He gripped her arms and pulled her up to him.

He kissed her again, searching for more and needing her like never before. His fingers found her heat and stroked her like a slow melody. She pressed into his grip. He turned her around so she was beneath him.

"Do you remember the first time we did it? At the lake? You hid under the blanket when you thought someone was coming." He traced circles around her tight nipple.

She sucked in a breath. "I remember, but we can we talk about it later? I need you inside me right now."

He took her then on the sofa painted in the lights from the tree. Their bodies rocked to their familiar rhythm. He waited for her to call out his name again and felt the pounding in his chest speed up as she said it over and over. He wanted his name on her lips like that every night. When she cried out for him the final time, he met her with his own declaration. They held each other with chests heaving. The cold air settled on his sweaty skin.

"We'd better get dressed. I don't want your son to find my naked ass staring at him when he comes through that door." He handed her the sweater she'd tossed away earlier.

"Always the practical one." But she was smiling.

"If I were practical, we'd be behind a closed door with a lock, but practical isn't my style. You know that."

"You just couldn't control yourself." She bit his shoulder.

He tilted her face to his. "I believe that was you, babe." He pulled her mouth to his. Heat was still in her tongue.

"We still have a little time." She raised an eyebrow at him. Her laugh was full and sexy.

"Christ, woman." She was going to be the death of him.

Chapter Twenty-Six

Colton couldn't sleep. He wanted Harley wrapped in his arms, but she shooed him out of her house before Knox came back. "He can't find you in my bed," she'd said. "It's not a good example." To hell with an example. He loved her, and Knox might as well find out about it.

He threw the covers back and shoved open a window. He lit a cigarette and blew the smoke out into the night. His fingers itched for something to do.

When he was a kid, he used to sit alongside his father and watch his dad's hands glide across the piano. The notes and chords his father played cried out or whispered to him or called to him to play along. He had wanted to make music the way his father did. Then he found the guitar and knew he could make music in his own way. His dad always said the guitar wasn't a real instrument if you were going to play music. Orchestral music was the only real music. Everything else was inferior, but Colton disagreed.

He'd brought Blaise to hear the high school battle of the bands. Blaise had only been about ten, but his eyes lit up when that drummer took his own solo. "I want to do that," he'd said. Savage was born, even though they hadn't realized it yet.

He went to the closet and yanked out his Gibson.

He rested it on his knee and let his fingers travel across the strings. He tuned the guitar until he liked what he heard. He played some of his favorites, Dickey Betts and T-Bone Walker. He fingerpicked the steel strings without thinking. When he played, his mind shut down. He could be everywhere and nowhere at the same time. Playing was the only freeing thing in the world. Foolishly, he'd let his demons get in the way of that. He'd forgotten who he was. He'd been broken, and Harley had started to heal him. *Harley.* Why had he been fighting what was between them? With her by his side, he could've been sober his entire life.

He messed with the strings some more, but his fingers returned to the sounds he was familiar with. He played Savage tunes front-ways and backward. There was nothing new in his head. There may never be again.

He pounded his fist on the table, shaking the dented centerpiece. He couldn't jam with Blaise any more than he could be the orchestra teacher. The only thing he'd ever been any good at was being the lead man in Savage. He couldn't toss all that away. But there was Harley, and he didn't want to throw away his last chance with her.

He grabbed his phone and hit Blaise's number.

"What's up?" Blaise growled.

"Bro, sorry to wake you. I can't do it."

"Do what?"

"Is everything all right?" Grace's voice was in the background.

"Just my stupid brother."

"Tell Grace I'm sorry I woke her."

"You're sorry? That's a first. Hang on. I'll go into the other room."

Colton lit another cigarette and waited.

"Okay, what can't you do?"

"There's no more music in me. I can play our stuff and the classics with no problem, but there isn't anything new. I'm done. Dad was right. I'm no good at this. Never was. I've been fooling everyone for so long I believed my own shit."

"Whoa. Hang on. Where is this coming from?"

"You've been telling me the same thing for years." He packed up his Gibson and shoved it in the closet, out of sight.

"I never said you sucked. You're the best musician I know. You just want to live in the glory days, and we can't do that anymore. I always thought if you cleaned up and stopped drinking you'd write again."

"But I never did." He took a deep breath. "I want our old career back."

"You can't have it. We have to reinvent ourselves if we're going to stay current. You can do it."

"I can't, and I don't know if I can stay here. I can't teach those kids. I can't become Dad."

"Man, look, you've had a lot on your plate recently, and now with Adam dying, don't try to figure it all out. Have you talked to Harley about any of this?"

"I don't want to hurt her." And he would if he stuck around. She deserved better than an old, washed-up guitar player.

"Then don't. Just tell her what you're thinking."

He didn't know what he was thinking. "I'm sorry I woke you. Get some sleep before the funeral."

"You're not going to do anything stupid, are you?"

He was long past stupid.

Chapter Twenty-Seven

Harley had thirty minutes to get ready, and she was covered in paint. Colton had insisted she and Knox come with him to the funeral. She wanted to be there to support him and his family, but she didn't belong. She had tried to calm her nerves by painting. Sleep had evaded her hours ago. All she'd managed to do was spill the bold colors down her legs and on the floor of her art studio.

"Mom, can you help me tie this?" Knox stepped through the doorway. He held a silver tie in one hand. His dress shirt was a little wrinkled.

Her breath caught. Her little boy had become a man while she was busy trying to be his only parent. How didn't anyone else see what she saw? If you stared long enough, Knox's eyes were the shape of Colton's. He had the tiniest of dimples in his right cheek that hollowed out when his smile spread wide. His hair was lighter, like hers, and the shape of his face was the same as hers, but he was tall like all the Savage men, with their broad shoulders and strong arms. He was all music all the time. Even now, his earbuds were around his neck and trailing to the phone stuffed into the pocket of his suit pants.

"I need to change first." She held up her hands to reveal the red streaks across her palms. "Give me fifteen minutes, and I'll help you."

"I can do it." Colton filled out the doorway behind Knox. Her breath caught again.

"You look very nice." Her words were winded. She was proud, in love, and ashamed all at once.

He wore a black suit with a subtle herringbone design. His dress shirt was crisp, and the jacket's two buttons were undone and revealed the flat-front trousers that narrowed down his toned legs. She thought about what was underneath those trousers and had to look away.

"I think you'd better go change. Knox and I have it from here." He winked and took the tie from her son.

"I'll hurry." She turned to run into the house but stopped, out of sight, to watch them.

Colton stood before Knox and hooked the tie around Knox's neck. "I hate wearing ties."

Knox laughed. "Me too. I can never remember how to tie it the right way. Mom's not very good at doing it either, but don't tell her I said that."

Colton flipped the wide end of the tie over the smaller one. "Your secret is safe with me. My dad taught me and Blaise how to do this when we were kids. 'My boys will look respectable, and the first way to do that is wearing a crisp tie.' " He imitated his father. "If it had been up to him, we'd have worn suits to play in the dirt. Pull the wide end from under here. See?" He pulled the wide end and created a knot.

"When did your dad die?"

"About eighteen years ago. He was one tough SOB, but I miss him."

"I wish I knew who my dad was."

Harley's legs shook. *Tell them.* But she stayed put.

Later. Let them have this moment. It's going to be the only one you'll ever watch. Was it wrong to steal this moment too?

"It's none of my business, kid. Your mom is all the parent you need."

"She's great and all, but I'm the kid in town without a dad, just like her. That label makes you stand out in a bad way."

"Screw what other people think. That's how I lived my life, and it worked out for me. Trust me. Your friend Duke accepts you for who you are."

"Duke's all right."

"You sure about that?" He tucked the tie through the knot and adjusted it against Knox's neck. "There." Colton stepped back. "Not bad for an old rock and roller." He patted Knox on the shoulder. "Any time you need help tying that tie or anything else, you ask, okay?"

"Cool. Thanks." Knox ducked his head.

Harley ran for the house. Her tears mixed with the spilled paint.

Colton stole a glance at Harley. She patted her eyes with a tissue, and he slipped his hand into her cold one. The sun burned high in the sky but did little to warm the frigid day. A walnut coffin circled by poinsettia plants perched above the open ground. The minister spoke words he wasn't listening to. Adam was a good guy, and he died too soon. What else was there to say?

Savannah wore a wide-brimmed black hat and sunglasses. She sat in the front row with her children, her head high and her shoulders back. She'd never cry here, not in front of most of the town that had come out in support.

Blaise kept his arm around Grace. She leaned her head against his shoulder. Cash sat on his other side. Blaise leaned over and kissed Cash on the head. Cash wiped the kiss away, but Blaise only smiled.

Maybe Blaise had had this family thing right all along. Blaise had tried to marry and have a family. He ended up with Grace, whom he loved more than anything, and a brand-new relationship with his son.

Colton wasn't getting any younger. Had he really accomplished everything he wanted? How much longer did he have on this planet? He didn't want the end of his life to pop up with any regrets. He squeezed Harley's hand. She gave him a thin smile back.

She had barely said two words since they'd left. It was a terrible day for everyone, but something else was going on with her. He sensed it.

Savannah stood and placed a single white rose on the coffin. She kissed her hand and laid it on the coffin. Jud, Grey, and Caroline followed her. Adam's sister sobbed as her husband guided her out through the chairs.

The attendees headed toward their cars. He wanted to get Harley alone before they got in his car. He needed to talk to her and find out what was bothering her.

He found himself walking alongside Jud. "How are you holding up?"

Jud glanced at him from the corner of his eye. "I don't know. You're not going to give me the man-of-the-house speech, are you?"

He shoved his hands in his coat pockets. "Not me. Leave the corny speeches to Blaise."

Jud smirked. "I need to catch up to Mom."

"Sure." He'd try to work on his relationship with Jud for Savannah's sake, but he doubted they'd get far. He and Jud had never been close, not even before last summer.

Someone patted him on the back. "How are you doing?"

He turned to find Billy wrapped in a fur-lined coat and battling with his tie. "I'm fine. Thanks for coming."

"All this." Billy turned his finger in the air. "Is it upsetting you at all?"

"What if I said it wasn't? Wouldn't you be more worried? I'm fine, old man, really."

"You come find me if you need me. I don't want to hear about any more trouble for you. You've had enough."

"You can stop worrying. I'm coming to my senses."

"Good. That's what I want to hear. I'm glad you patched things up with your siblings. That Harley is good for you. She keeps your feet planted and helps you remember where you belong."

"I suppose she does."

"You're finally sounding like the man I know. Now, I'll see you back at Savannah's. Don't be late. You hear?"

Colton laughed, grateful for Billy in his life. "Yes, sir."

Billy trudged off to join Hoke Carter and his wife. Family formed in unexpected places. That was for certain.

Harley and Knox waited for him by the car. They could talk later while he made love to her all night. She wasn't going to get him out of her bed as easily tonight. His phone vibrated in his jacket pocket. Colton reached in and grabbed it. "Mike, man, what's up?"

"You never answer your phone. When are you flying out? We need to rehearse."

Colton clenched his fist. He looked over at Harley. Her face was scrunched up, wondering what he was doing. She banged her feet against the pavement, probably trying to keep warm in those silly heels. He caught a glimpse of Savannah as she slid into the back of the long black town car. Life was too short, and he'd made enough mistakes.

"Mike, I'm out."

"What the fuck, man? You can't back out. What the hell is wrong with you and your brother? You both lost your minds this past year. The show producers are going to sue you, and I'm going to sue you too."

"So sue me." Colton ended the call and jogged over to the car. "Can I talk to you a minute?"

"I'm freezing. Can we talk in the car on the way to Savannah's?" Harley blew into her hands.

He pushed the key fob. The car kicked over. "Knox, turn up the heat. I need your mom for just a second."

He took her hands and rubbed them between his. "I don't know if this is the right time to say what I'm about to say, but I can't wait any longer. I've wasted enough time." The muscles in his belly pulled like tightened guitar strings. "I thought the road was all I ever wanted, and it was for a very long time. When I hit that fence and woke up with a bloody nose and a fat lip, I knew I needed to change. I just didn't know how or when or if I'd ever do it. Until I saw you in that classroom. I've been running from the very thing I've always wanted, and I see that now. Maybe it's because Adam died. I don't know." He closed his eyes. The words floated out of reach. Lyrics were never his thing. If he could play for her how he felt, she might understand what he was trying to say.

"We don't have to talk about this now. Your sister needs you." She pulled her hands away.

"Is there something bothering you?"

"Why do you ask that?" She looked over her shoulder at the car.

"You've been avoiding me, for one. I can tell there's something up because you won't even look me in the eye." He wanted to turn her face to meet his gaze, but he kept his hands in his pockets.

"After how we were together last night, you think I'm avoiding you? I don't want to interfere where your family is concerned. This is a private time for you all."

"I want you to interfere. I want you with me all the time. When I'm not with you, all I do is think about being with you."

"Colton, you deserve better than me." She stared off into the distance. The last of the cars had pulled away. They were the only ones left. The wind picked up and pushed her hair from her face.

He turned her face to look at him. He couldn't stand having her look anywhere else. "You're wrong. You deserve better than *me*. I'm the one with the drinking problem. Five minutes ago I tanked what's left of my career. I've made a lot of empty promises to you over the years. I put you second. I let too much time go by between us, but if you'll give me a chance to make it up to you, I'll spend the rest of my sorry life doing just that."

Her brown eyes brimmed with tears. She placed a hand on his cheek. "I've waited my whole life to hear you say that. All the nights I sat alone thinking about you and wondering where you were or how you were doing. I'd hear one of your songs on the radio and hoped you were somewhere thinking about me. I know that was foolish since you had plenty of women around to fill my shoes."

He placed a finger over her soft lips. "Let me make it up to you. Let me love you. I know we're too old to start a family of our own, but maybe you'll let me share yours."

A single tear slid down her cheek. He wiped it away. She wasn't saying anything. He didn't know what to do. Should he say more or shut up and wait for her to say something? "Harley."

"Colton, I would love to share Knox with you. He needs you. I'm not enough for him. A boy deserves to have a father, don't you think?" Her tears fell faster. Her lip quivered. She swiped at her face.

He wanted to kiss her hurt away. "Hey, I didn't mean to make you cry. I went about this all wrong. Let's get to Savannah's. They're probably wondering where we are anyway. We can talk more later."

"We should finish this now."

His mouth went dry. Did she want to end things between them when he was just getting his act together? He couldn't let her do that. He'd prove to her he was worth another chance. He'd kill himself trying. "Let's talk about this later. It's been a hard day for everyone, okay?"

"Okay." She kissed his cheek.

Yeah, they'd talk later. The cemetery had been the wrong place. He should have waited to be at home with her by her Christmas tree or something like that. Maybe he should have taken her to the bridge. He'd thrown too much at her, come on too strong. He'd start over and say it slowly. He'd find the right words. He could find a song and use those lyrics.

Everything would be okay. He knew it.

Chapter Twenty-Eight

Harley's hands shook. Her last art relaxation class had gone badly. She'd held it in the high school because the holiday concert was only moments away.

Andy Henson had stormed out of the room, convinced his father hated him. He'd thrown the sketch pad and pencils all over the place. She squatted down to pick up the supplies.

She couldn't focus on any of her students, and that poor, hurting young man had deserved her attention. Instead, her mind wandered to the mess of her own life. How could she help anyone else if she couldn't help herself? All that would change in a few hours. She wiped her nose with the back of her hand. She couldn't break down now.

She needed to get to the auditorium, where the orchestra students were setting up, but her legs wouldn't cooperate. She hadn't wanted to be late, and now she couldn't bring herself to leave the room. She certainly couldn't stay there all night, but her body felt too broken to move.

She flopped down on the stool and tossed the pencils on the art table. They scattered, rolled, and fell back on the floor.

Someone knocked on the classroom door. She swung her head around. "Rowan. What are you doing here?" She sniffed and wiped her nose again. God, she was a mess. She smoothed down her hair.

Rowan moved into the classroom. He wore a white dress shirt tucked into faded jeans and boots. His black hair was slicked back. He smiled, but that smile never seemed to reach his black eyes. "I'm here for the show. I saw your light on. Are you okay? You look a little upset. Do you have a student skipping class?"

The joke might have made her laugh another time, but not tonight. She opened her mouth, and her face crumbled. The tears spilled like a paint can tipped over. She covered her face with her hands.

"Whoa. Okay. Okay. It's okay. Here." Rowan handed her a wad of tissues.

She grabbed them and stuffed them under her nose. She bit her lip to stop the flood of tears, but she couldn't. He slid his arm around her shoulder. She wanted to push him away because he offered her no comfort, but if she moved at all, she'd keep crying. She focused on her breath. Maybe the tears would retreat soon, and he'd leave her alone.

"Do you want to tell me what's wrong?"

She shook her head.

He stroked her hair. A sour taste filled her mouth, but she lacked the ability to push him away. In a few minutes, she'd be able to pull herself together and get to the auditorium. She was supposed to be helping the orchestra, not falling to pieces in her classroom with Rowan McGee so close she could smell his tacky cologne.

"Someone want to tell me what the hell is going on here?" Colton's deep voice washed over her.

She wanted to run into his arms and run away from him at the same time. The tears surfaced again. Rowan slid away from her.

"I know you aren't stupid enough to try and come on to my woman with me only feet away. You must've learned something since high school." He barreled further into the room and stood by her side.

Rowan threw his hands in the air. "Easy. She was upset. I was just offering a shoulder."

"She doesn't need your shoulder. I've got it from here." The muscle in his jaw twitched.

"No problem. Harley, if you need any help with the Eat-In project to save the art program, just let me know."

"Rowan, beat it." Colton gritted his teeth again. He waited for Rowan to leave before he came to her and gathered her in his arms.

She breathed in his woodsy scent. "You're wearing a tuxedo." She smiled. The fancy suit accented his toned body.

He looked down at her. "I borrowed it from Blaise. The kids told me I'm supposed to dress up, and I didn't have time to go back to my house in Bayton and get mine. Does it look okay?"

She unraveled her arms from around his waist.

"You'd look great in anything."

"I know." He wagged his eyebrows.

She couldn't help but laugh, and that set more tears in motion.

"Do you want to tell me what's going on? Are you sick or something? I know it's not Knox. He's warming up in the auditorium."

She shook her head and wiped her nose with the tissue wad. She couldn't tell him before the concert. The kids needed him. "After the show. You need to be focused on the performance."

"Babe, I've played before crowds a hundred times the size of this one. I was high and drunk and still played my best. I can handle whatever you're going to say." He chuckled. "Just tell me what's going on. I want to help you."

She smoothed down his lapel. He gripped her hand and held it against his chest. She pressed her lips together and let out a slow breath. "Meet me at the bridge when you're done tonight."

He searched her face. "Are you breaking it off between us?"

"Mr. Savage, we've been looking all over for you. We have a problem." Elizabeth Jones stood in the doorway with her flute in hand.

Colton let out a soft growl before turning to Elizabeth. "What's up?"

"Jean broke her violin string."

"My soloist? Now? Shit. Sorry. I know, no language." He turned to her. "I've got to go. We don't have enough time to restring it. I need to figure something else out. Don't leave tonight without me, okay? You'll wait for me?"

"Sure."

He kissed her, and Elizabeth giggled. He ran from the room. Elizabeth ran after Colton.

Harley gathered the pencils from the floor for the second time and shoved them in a glass jar. She grabbed her things and turned out the lights. Her heart splintered as she made her way toward the auditorium.

The kids moved around the stage. Some tuned instruments. Others gathered in small groups and talked. A few parents searched for the best seats.

"Kyle, give your violin to Jean," Colton shouted above the noise on the stage.

"Me? Why me? That means I won't be able to play." Kyle looked around for someone to come to his rescue. Jean stood there with her hand out.

Harley hurried on stage and grabbed Colton by the elbow. "Can't we find another violin for Jean?" she whispered in his ear.

"Sorry. There aren't any extras. He's going to have to sit this one out. Jean's the best violinist I've got. We need her."

"Can he play another instrument?"

"Kyle, can you play anything besides the violin?"

Kyle shook his head. Red blotches deepened on his

face, and his shoulders sagged. Harley's heart ached for him.

"Christ," Colton muttered. He went over to the boy and slid an arm around his shoulder. "What grade are you in?"

"Sophomore."

"Great. You'll be able to play next year."

"There isn't going to be a music program next year, remember?" Kyle said.

"Yeah, right. Listen, man. I'm sorry. I really am." Colton raised his eyebrows to her in question and then turned back to Kyle. "Crappy things happen in life all the time, but the show must go on. As artists, we have to adapt to whatever punches us in the jaw. You know what I mean? Jean has to do the solo. Sometimes good players get rolled. I know that sucks to hear, but it doesn't mean you suck. Do you get me?"

Kyle nodded and handed his violin to Jean.

Colton stood beside her. He wiped a hand over his face. "I'm not cut out for this teacher crap."

She placed a hand on his strong arm. "You were great with him. You told it to him straight. He might not like hearing it, but you were honest. You're better at this teacher thing than you think."

"If you say so."

"I do. Trust me."

"Are his parents going to yell at me?"

"Probably."

"Will you shield me?" He pulled her in front of him and leaned over to kiss her.

"Colton, we're at school." She tried to pull away, but he held her tighter. Thankfully, the students weren't paying them any attention.

He leaned in and whispered, "You're way hotter than any teacher I ever had as a kid."

Her insides burned, but this wasn't the time. There wasn't going to be any more time for that. She put space between them. "Break a leg tonight. I'll see you at the bridge later."

"You're going to watch the show, right?"

"Wouldn't miss it."

"Mr. Savage..." Tracy Young called to him from the saxophone section.

He gave Harley a nod and went in the direction of his student. He really didn't need her tonight. The show would be a success because of him. He never needed her. She had needed him because without him she hadn't felt whole.

"Mom, hang on a second." Knox made his way through the chairs. "Some of the kids are going out after the show. Can I go?"

"Who's going?"

"Stephanie. Kyle." He hesitated. "Duke maybe."

Duke. She should say no. Tonight was a school night and nothing would warm her to Duke, but she was tired and didn't have the energy to argue. Allowing Knox to go out with his friends might be the last thing she could do to make him happy for a very long time. After she told Colton, she'd have to tell Knox. By tomorrow morning, her beautiful son would look at her with eyes filled with hate.

"Sure, Knox. Don't be out too late, okay?"

"Thanks." He surprised her and leaned in for a hug. She held on for a second longer than she should, imprinting this moment on her memory. When she let him go, his face beamed. He turned to be swallowed up by the crowd.

She found her seat. Blaise and Cash sat a few rows in front of her. Had Colton seen them? He'd be pleased to know his family was there for support.

The house lights dimmed. Colton took the stage to a loud round of applause. He waved to the crowd, and they clapped louder. Cash offered an extra shout. Colton tapped his chest in response.

The festive music did little to lighten her mood. Only when Knox stood for a solo during "The Holly and the Ivy" did she perk up. Her heart filled with pride instead of hurt. He hadn't told her about the solo.

The final piece was "Sleigh Ride." As much as she loved this song and wanted to hear the kids, she had to leave.

She hurried out of the school. The cold air smacked her, and she pulled her coat closer. In the Durango, she turned up the heat and made her way to the bridge. All she could do now was wait.

Chapter Twenty-Nine

Colton tried to get away. He'd searched the auditorium, but Harley wasn't there. Keith Mulligan, the maintenance director, saw her leave during the last song while he created the light-show finale. The parents intercepted him every few feet. He shook hands and signed a couple of autographs. He dodged the questions about his return to the music program.

He wouldn't stay unless Harley had her job too. The school would have to take both of them. Before he gave the music program another thought, he needed to find her. She couldn't end it between them. He wouldn't let her, not after he'd finally come to his senses.

"Bro, great job." Blaise caught him coming out from backstage. "Dad would be proud."

"Dad would've said I told you so." He checked the thinning crowd in the hallway. No sign of Harley.

Blaise laughed. "Yeah, he might've. Still, the kids

sounded great. The orchestra was impressive for a high school ensemble."

He pulled out his phone. She'd left a text. *I'm at the bridge.*

"Thanks. Listen, I've got to get out of here. I'm going to duck out the back. I'll call you tomorrow."

"Everything okay?"

"I don't know."

"Do you need me to come with you?"

His kid brother always had his back. He'd been a dick to him for years. He'd bossed him around and told him he was nothing without their band. He'd even stolen a couple of his girlfriends. No matter what stupid shit he did, he could count on Blaise like no one else.

"I've got this one."

"Call me before you do anything stupid."

He patted Blaise's shoulder. "I'm done being stupid."

He hurried from the building and raced to his car. He took turns faster than he should and was glad Sheriff Jones wasn't patrolling the roads.

Harley's SUV came into view. She'd parked in the grass. He pulled alongside her vehicle and got out. Halfway down the bridge, she stood wrapped in her coat, and looking up at the sky from between the crisscross posts. The moon cast its glow on the rippling water. One tall black lantern lit up the walking path and his way to her.

She turned and smiled as he approached. "Hey."

"Hey, yourself." His insides ached for her. He pulled her close and gave her a soft kiss on her lips. "It's freezing out here. How about we take this party someplace warmer? If you're lucky, I'll let you undress me."

She smiled up at him. "I love this bridge. I always thought it would be beautiful all lit up for Christmas. Maybe a wreath that hung from the roof would be nice." She snuggled closer to him. She smelled like Harley—honeysuckle and home.

"You do like your Christmas."

"I like what it stands for—peace, love, kindness, family. The music is fun."

He groaned, but she laughed. Her laugh was music to him. "You know, you can have all those things other times of the year too. Except the music. Promise me you won't play Christmas music all year."

"Scrooge," she said against his chest. "The orchestra sounded wonderful even playing that music you hate so much."

"The kids were great. I'll admit it. I had a good time too. I didn't think I would, but you were right."

"I told you so."

He laughed, thinking of what Blaise had said about their dad.

They stood for a while in silence. The cold seeped through his dress shoes and froze off his toes. "So do you want to tell me why Rowan McGee had his arm around you? I didn't like that. I know how that sounds, but I don't care." He pulled back to look at her.

"It was sweet of you to go all macho on me, but you don't have to worry about Rowan." Pain etched her face. Tears filled her eyes.

He leaned his forehead against hers. "Just say it, babe. I can take it. Whatever it is, I promise I won't go drinking."

"It can hold a few more minutes. Would you mind just watching the sky with me?"

He'd hold her and look at whatever she wanted for as long she wanted. If this was going to be the end of them, he wanted the end to last.

Harley was going to be sick. The cold air did nothing to ease the queasiness in her stomach. Colton's arms around her couldn't quell the shivers racking her body. Coming to the bridge to tell the truth seemed like a good idea, but all she wanted to do was throw herself off it.

"Our time together has been amazing." She had to tell him how she felt. "I've wanted to be with you for so long. I dreamed about it for years. These past weeks with you has made me happier than I could've imagined."

"It doesn't have to end." He took her face in his hands.

She reached up and laced her fingers through his and held them against her chest. She kissed his knuckles. "I used to think we would be perfect together. When I was with you, I wasn't the girl whose mother dumped her. I wasn't the girl who didn't know her own father. You made me feel special because you are special. You never looked at me and felt sorry for me. I thought when you looked at me you really saw me."

"I did. I do. I know I fucked things up royally. I let my big fat ego get in the way of what could've been a great life together. Please give me a chance to make it up to you."

"Colton, I'm not breaking up with you."

He let out a breath. "You're not? I thought for sure you were dumping my ass. You've been so distant at times. I thought you were mad at me. I couldn't figure it out."

"I'm not breaking up with you, but what I'm about to tell you is going to change how you feel about me."

He stepped back. His face was a mask of confusion. "I'm not following."

Her head spun. She wasn't sure if her legs could keep doing their job. "Can we sit on the bench?"

"We could sit in my warm car and talk."

She was afraid to be stuck in the car when he heard what she was going to say. "I'd rather stay out here." They made their way to the end of the bridge where a small fenced-off cement area jutted out over the rocks.

They sat on the bench, and she took his hands.

"Have you ever done something you regret?"

"You're asking me that?"

She'd miss the way he could make her smile.

"Babe, this is killing me. Just say it. What did you do? Rob a bank? Cheat on your taxes?" His face crumbled. "Did you fuck Rowan? Please tell me you didn't have sex with him."

If only it were that easy. "No. This has nothing to do with Rowan, though I don't appreciate you thinking I'd jump into bed with him." Did she really have any cause to be righteous?

"I'm sorry. The idea of you with another man makes me crazy."

He said all the things she'd longed to hear. Why had she been so stupid? Why hadn't she trusted him? Because she had been afraid. She was fairly certain the Colton Savage of eighteen years ago would've still hopped on the next plane out of town. He would've sent her money for Knox. He took care of his responsibilities, but she wanted to be more than that. Her fear allowed history to repeat itself. She could've broken her family cycle, but she hadn't.

"So what is it?"

"I lied to you." Her eyes filled with tears.

He pulled his hands away and sat back. "What about?"

The tears threatened to choke her. She had to hold it together. She blinked and bit her lip. "Do you remember when you came home for your father's funeral?"

"Yeah."

"When you knocked on my door, I thought that time was going to be for good. I thought you'd come back to me. The pain was on your face when I wrapped my arms around you. The tears you cried while I held you made me think I was the only person you'd share your pain with. I misunderstood what that all meant. I thought you loved me and needed me. I thought that of all the people in the world, you'd come to me for comfort. That had to mean something, but I was wrong."

331

"You weren't wrong. I was screwed up back then. I didn't know how to handle losing my father."

"But you left again. You'd only come back for a, what, a week maybe? You were gone as quickly as you'd come. You never promised me anything. I just assumed, and I was wrong."

"I'm sorry. I didn't mean to use you. I knew you'd let me fall apart. I trusted you'd be there for me, but we had to get back on the road. I always let the road get in the way. I know. I hurt all my relationships with my need to be the rock star. I'm sorry."

"There's nothing to be sorry about. You'd always made it very clear what came first. I knew how much being a musician and being successful meant to you. I wanted you to have your dreams. I loved you too much to get in the way of that. I didn't want you to feel obligated to me."

A car passed by and honked.

"I cried for days after you left. My uncle came to me and said it was time to get my life back on track. I had to leave you in the past, or I'd never move forward. He said you were traveling the world, playing your junky music with a woman in every city. I shouldn't be pining over you."

"Your uncle never liked me."

The laughing helped to keep the tears away. "No, he never did. So I left for New York right after you went back on the road. I had to try and make a go of my art, only I started to feel sick. I thought it was a bug at first."

"Why didn't you tell me? I would've sent you money for the best doctors."

She put up her hand. "Colton, please let me finish. I've never told another soul what I'm about to say. I've hid this secret very well. Getting it out is harder than I thought it would be."

"You're starting to scare me," he whispered.

"I'm scared too." She took a deep breath. She wanted to hold his hands or feel his arms around her, but she had to stay strong and tell this story alone. "I wasn't sick. It was something worse and wonderful at the same time."

His face showed no sign he understood what she was trying to say.

"Colton, I was pregnant."

Chapter Thirty

The feedback in Colton's head messed up his hearing. Did Harley just say she was pregnant? His insides boiled. He forgot about being cold. "Pregnant?"

She nodded.

He jumped up from the bench and paced. He clenched his fists, afraid he might swing at something. He tried to count to ten and repeat that stupid word rehab wanted him to memorize. The feedback in his head had cranked up louder. He couldn't get past the number one. He patted his pockets. Where were his smokes? He'd left them at home because he couldn't smoke at the school. Fuck.

"Colton, say something, please. Yell, curse, anything."

Why hadn't he seen it? *You arrogant, asshole.* He believed he hadn't left a string of kids around the world. Joke was on him. He had made a baby with the only woman he ever loved, and she forgot to tell him.

Thoughts crashed into him—that night in Harley's room after his father's funeral. He'd made love to her as if he were holding on to life. Knox was the right age. Knox played music better than he did. How was it he hadn't connected the way Knox held his pic when he played? *The way he did.* Or Harley's overreaction to Knox's drinking? He flopped back on the bench.

"Say it," he said through gritted teeth.

"Say what?"

He banged the bench with his fists. She jumped. "Tell me, damn it."

Big fat tears rolled down her cheeks. "Knox is your son."

He dropped his head into his hands. "That's what you've been trying to tell me. How could you do this to me?" He sat back up. "He doesn't know either. How could you lie to him, you of all people? You know better than anyone what it's like to grow up without a father." He couldn't suck air into his lungs.

"I'm so sorry. I know those words aren't enough."

"Why, Harley? Why would you keep this from me? Why would you deny me and Knox a life together? Was it revenge for the way I treated you?"

"Oh no. It was never that."

"You had so many chances to tell me. God, every day we'd been together. You could have said something while we were in bed." The recent nights she wrapped herself around him and allowed him to love her—were they lies too? "You slept with me knowing my son was yards away. How could you?" He wanted to understand.

"I was wrong. I let my feelings for you cloud my decisions. It's no excuse, but I was afraid to tell you."

He looked at her. "Afraid I'd do what? Yell, scream, kick over a chair? That's my boy. Mine. And you let him grow up thinking his father was better off not knowing about him. Would I have been so bad to have as a dad?" His voice broke. Christ, he hadn't cried since his father died, and he was about to do it again.

He wiped a hand over his face.

She swiped at the tears on her face. "I don't know what kind of a father you would've been. You were never around. You didn't want the kind of life your father had, raising kids. Were you really going to give up the touring and the music to raise a child with me?"

"I could've done both." Would he have? He never once told Blaise to take time off to be with Cash. Blaise had almost ruined his relationship with his son because the band had been on the road so much.

"I wanted to tell you. I tried at first. I wrote you letters, but a note didn't seem the right way to explain myself. The more time that went by, the harder it was to tell. The lies got so deep I was buried under them with no way out. Only this time you told me how you felt, and you want to stay because of me. I couldn't keep it any longer. I should've told you the truth. I'm so completely sorry. I know you can't forgive me, though I hope someday you will." She chewed on her lip. "I love you."

"You have a funny way of loving me." He shook his head. How was this happening? He was ready to give up the road and settle down with this woman. He'd even spent a minute thinking about taking over that stupid music program. He thought he could have what Blaise and Savannah had—a family. He'd been so stupid asking Harley if he could share Knox.

"When are you going to tell Knox?"

"He's out with friends right now. When he gets home. I'll wait up for him."

"Make sure he knows I had no idea until right now."

"Of course. I'm the one to blame. I will be the one he hates." The tears ran down her cheeks again.

He wanted to reach out and make her stop crying, but his hands stayed put. He didn't want Knox to hate her. She was a good mother. She'd raised him right, and she'd done it all alone when she didn't have to. What kind of a beast was he that she was too afraid to tell him about their child? He'd given her every reason to believe he didn't want a child or a family. Every choice he'd made screamed leave him alone. He'd led her to believe he cared about her, but not enough to stick around for more than five minutes.

"I want to talk to him after you do."

"I understand."

He wished she'd call him names or tell him it was all his fault. Instead, she sat there with tears rolling down her face and asked for his forgiveness.

"You swear no one else knows?" What was everyone going to say when they found out?

"Hank figured it out eventually."

"That man hated me so much he encouraged you to keep your secret?" And the hits kept on coming.

She grabbed his arm, but he flinched, and she pulled back. "That's not it at all. Hank told me to find you."

"But you didn't."

"I did come looking for you. Once. You were on tour in New Jersey. I was eight months pregnant. The arena you were playing at wasn't far from New York City. I rented a car and drove to the hotel you stayed at."

"I had given you the list of hotels we were booked at in case you wanted to fly out and meet us." He'd known she'd never do it. That's why he gave it to her.

She offered him a thin smile. "Yeah. Anyway, I went to the hotel. When I came off the elevator, the whole floor was one giant party. The hallway was packed with people. Loud music was playing. I saw you through the crowd, and I thought everything would be okay. I could make you understand, and my big belly would've explained everything. The crowd shifted a little. I had a better view of you. Your back was to me. A woman danced on a table in her underwear. She threw herself into your arms, and you started kissing her. Some people cheered you on. You scooped her up and carried her down the hall into a room. When the door shut, I turned and ran for the elevator."

He ran his hands through his hair. Christ, he was a dick. "You should've tried again."

"You never wanted to be tied down. You'd made that clear. I didn't know what to do or what to think. Somehow the years kept adding up. Every year that went by made it harder and harder. You were living the life you'd dreamed about. Knox and I were managing okay.

We had Hank. I was wrong, Colton. I was so wrong. If I could go back, I'd do it differently. Please understand once I'd kept the secret I didn't know how to tell."

He stood, unable to listen to her apologies. He needed time to think. "I don't want to see you anymore. I'll get my things out of the guesthouse in the morning."

She chewed on her lip and nodded.

He left her without another word. If she called out to him, he might stay, but she didn't. She hadn't even moved when he checked his rearview mirror as he drove away from the bridge.

His hands shook while he tugged his phone out of his jacket pocket. What was he going to do now? He'd fucked up the tour. His reputation was going to be worse than it had already been. Who was going to play with him?

She turned his heart into a broken six string. He loved her, but he'd told her too late. If he had said it the night his father had died, he would've known his son. A son. What would Knox say when he found out? He punched the phone screen for his brother's number.

"What's up?" Blaise answered right away.

"I'm about to do something stupid."

Chapter Thirty-One

Harley struggled to inhale. She had cried hard and long. Her nose had plugged up. She didn't have a tissue. She had to use the sleeve of her coat to stop the snot from running into her mouth.

She wasn't sure how long she'd been sitting there. She didn't want to go home, and she didn't want to keep sitting on the bench out in the cold, dark night. But she stayed.

She had no excuses for what she'd done. She had been hiding behind a veil her entire life. She had never deserved to succeed, and that's why she never had. She'd failed at everything: mother, artist, teacher, and lover. All because she'd been too damn afraid to tell him. She had been afraid he'd reject her, and he had anyway. She had been afraid to tell Knox his father preferred beer and cheap women to a family. The irony was she'd been wrong about that. She figured out he wanted a family eighteen years too late.

She would hand in her resignation at the school. She wouldn't wait until May for her job to end. She couldn't stay now that everyone would know Colton was Knox's father. Everyone thought there were no secrets in a small town. Those people didn't know how to keep a secret.

Would Knox want to come with her? He might choose to live with Colton. She'd have to accept that. Colton would be good to her son. He'd take good care of Knox.

The moon sat pregnant in the sky. Time to go. She needed to get home and tell her son the truth. Her phone vibrated in her pocket. *Knox.*

She took a deep breath, afraid she'd break down when she heard his voice. "Hey, kiddo."

"Ms. Kenyon, it's Stephanie Knicks. There's been an accident."

Chapter Thirty-Two

Colton dragged the nicotine into his lungs, then let out a long stream of smoke. His hands trembled less. He turned the car onto Dogwood Drive and parked across the street from Blaise's. The lights were on next door at Grace's house. Blaise came out of Grace's front door and waited for him on the lawn.

He struggled out of the car and tossed his cigarette on the road. He waited for Blaise to say something about littering, but he didn't.

"Why do you two still have both houses?" He shoved his hands into his coat pockets and crossed the street.

"She won't move in with me yet, no matter how many times I've asked her." Blaise searched his face. "I know you didn't come here to talk about the houses. What's going on with you? Is there someone I should call?"

"I'm not drinking, asshole." He smirked and shook his head. "Not that I don't want to, because right now that's about all I want to do."

"Let's go inside, and you can tell me what's up."

"Let's sit on the porch. I need to smoke." He yanked out another cigarette.

"The porch, it is." Blaise dropped down on the swing and zipped his fleece up to his neck.

Colton leaned against the railing. He held out his trembling hand for Blaise to see. "I haven't had the shakes this badly since the first time I detoxed."

"Is it the tour?"

He couldn't look his brother in the eye. "Nope. I quit."

"You did what?"

He dragged his gaze back to Blaise. "I told Mike to shove it."

"Why did you do that?"

"Would you believe me if I told you I was in love?" He lit up and took a drag. Just admitting to Blaise that he could love someone made his whole body shake.

"Finally. You've come to your senses. I don't understand what the problem is. Harley is crazy about you. She always has been, not that I could ever figure out why."

He took another drag and let the tar burn his lungs. "I'm a total fuckup, aren't I?"

Blaise leaned forward. His eyes narrowed. "I was joking. What's going on, Colton?"

He opened his mouth to say the words, but he clamped it shut. Once he said Knox was his son, it would be real. "She's been keeping a secret from me for years. Eighteen years, in fact. Knox is mine." He ran a hand through his hair. Each time he thought about having a kid, it was a punch to the throat.

Blaise's mouth fell open. "Get the fuck out of here."

"Yeah, I'm making it up, asshole. Christ, Blaise, what do I do?"

Blaise fell back against the swing and shook his head. "Holy shit. When did this happen?"

"The week of Dad's funeral." He pushed the images of Harley waiting for him each night that week away. She'd been there for him, no questions asked.

"You never told me you went to see her."

"I went a few times that week."

"Bro, are you sure he's yours?"

"She only told me because I offered to stay here and build a life with her. If I hit the road, she wasn't going to say a word, so yeah, he's mine. What do I do?" Because he didn't have the first idea of how to handle this new piece of information that would forever turn his life on its head.

"Does Knox know?"

"Harley's probably telling him now." What was he going to say to this kid? *Hi, I'm your fucked-up, drunk father who can tie a pretty good Windsor knot?*

Blaise stood. "I'm freezing out here. Can we go inside?"

He held up the cigarette. He couldn't go inside and face Cash just yet.

Blaise leaned near him and blew on his hands. "Do you want to get to know your son better?"

"What if he doesn't like the fact I'm his father?"

Would Knox resent how he'd treated his mother all these years? Would he wonder why Colton had been too stupid to figure out Knox belonged to him, and hate him for it?

"I don't normally say this to you because your ego is big enough as it is, but you're cool. Cash loves you. I love you. The whole family loves you. We look to you to guide us around. Well, except for Savannah. She fights pretty hard for the family-leader spot." Blaise chuckled. "Knox is going to love you too, if he doesn't already."

He thought about the few times he jammed with Knox. Knox had listened to his instructions with wide eyes, but that was when Knox believed he was just a famous musician hanging around his mother. How would Knox look at him knowing he was his father?

"Can I stay on your couch tonight? I can't go back to Harley's, and I'm not about to go to Billy's tonight." Christ, he'd have to tell Billy too. He ran his hand through his hair again. He was going to end up yanking it all by the end of this mess.

"You can even sleep in the guest room."

"I don't understand how she kept this from me. She let all those years go by and lied to us all."

"She messed up, but I wouldn't have told you about a baby either." Blaise held his gaze.

Colton tossed the cigarette in the front yard. His insides boiled.

Blaise shoved him. "Jesus, you're disgusting." He stomped down the steps, retrieved the butt, and tossed it in the garbage can. "I'm only giving you a pass on that one because of the night you're having, but don't do that again. My yard isn't an ashtray, asswipe."

"Sorry." It was his turn to flop onto the swing. He hung his head. "Why do you think she was right to keep this from me? She kept my child from me. I can't forgive her for that."

"Listen, you'll have to decide yourself if you want to forgive her. I get why she didn't tell you, though. There was no room in your life for a child or a family outside of me and Savannah."

He looked up at Blaise. "What are you saying?"

"I have to spell it out for you? When we went on the road the very first time, did you ask Harley to wait for you? Did you ask her to come with us?"

"No."

"Of course not, and you didn't act like you had a girl back home. That's for sure. The week of Dad's funeral, did you even take her out to dinner or, and I'm going out on a limb here, possibly promise her a future?"

"No."

"Typical Colton Savage. Last summer when you were in town, did you go see her?"

He had hoped to make up for all those bad decisions, but she'd changed the song in the middle of the verse. He didn't want to be with her, and he didn't know what he was going to do without her now. "Okay, okay, I get it. I'm a dick."

"Most of us try to overlook that. You made it very clear to her and everyone around you that your whole life belonged to your music career. You're the reason we were famous. Nothing stopped you. She knew what you wanted, and she loved you enough to let you have it. She didn't want to trap you in anything."

"How do you know this?"

"Because I'm the smart brother." Blaise curled his lips into a smile. "You're an open book, bro. It wasn't hard to figure out where your priorities were. They might be different now, and believe me, I'm glad. Back then and until you drove your car into a fence a few weeks ago, you were nothing but Savage. The rest of the world be damned."

Blaise was right. He'd ruined every important relationship he had because of his self-centered point of view. He had never given Harley a reason to believe he'd welcome her news of a child. Back then, he would've demanded a paternity test. He knew she'd always be waiting for him, and he'd taken advantage of that while he was hurting from losing his dad. He really was a dick.

"I've got a lot to think about, and I need to get some sleep." The weight of the day crushed him. He pushed off the swing.

"You're not going to sleep in my tuxedo, are you?"

"Hell no. I sleep butt naked."

"Gross. Now I have the image of your hairy ass in my head."

Colton punched his arm. Blaise tried to turn sideways to block him, and Colton connected with his shoulder. They both laughed.

"Thanks, Blaise. Thanks for putting up with me."

"Ah, I just feel sorry for you 'cause you're such a lousy guitar player."

Colton smacked him in the head, and Blaise smacked him back. He was starting to feel a little better.

His phone buzzed in his pocket. He thought about ignoring it, but Harley may have told Knox. That was something he wanted to know. She sent a text.

Knox. Accident. Hospital.

Chapter Thirty-Three

The smell of antiseptic made Harley's eyes water—that or she was crying again. Strangers moved in and around her. Some sat in plastic chairs, heads in their hands. Others stared at the television secured to the wall, while others held hands wrapped in makeshift bandages covered in blood. Three police officers whispered in the corner near a Christmas tree decorated in bandage boxes, gauze, and colored lights. She threw herself at the reception desk in the emergency room.

A thin woman with wavy, red hair and candy-cane pins on her shirt jumped back in her chair. "Can I help you?"

"My son was brought here in an ambulance. He was in a car accident." Didn't this woman know where Knox was? Or that Harley had to get to him right this very minute. Her baby needed her.

She typed on her computer. "What's his name?"

They didn't have time for this. "Knox Kenyon." *Savage.* If his last name had been Savage, would this woman at reception make her wait to find her child?

"Harley." Ella shouted down a long hallway filled with people dressed in scrubs and moving at top speed in and out of curtained rooms.

She ran to Ella and gripped her arm. "What happened? Where are the kids?"

Ella brushed the hair from her face. Shadows circled her eyes. She had on a sweatshirt, pajama pants, and slippers. "Stephanie called me. They were in Duke's car." She took a deep breath and leaned in. "Duke was drinking."

Harley's breath caught in her throat. Why had she let Knox go out after the concert? She should have told him to stay away from Duke, but she had wanted him to have a little fun before she blew his world wide open. For once in her life, she should have listened to the little voice scratching at her brain. "Where are Knox and Stephanie?"

"Ma'am?" One of the police officers approached her. "I'm Officer Hoffman. I overheard you say your son was brought in by ambulance from an accident. I was at the scene. Is your son"—he checked his notes—

"Duke Humphreys?"

"No. Knox Kenyon."

He nodded. "It appears Mr. Humphrey's blood alcohol content was point one. Over the legal limit. We tested the other passengers too." He checked his notes again. "Your son came up clean. He gave us his statement at the scene. Mr. Humphrey's ran a red light. The other car didn't have a chance to stop. Your son is very lucky."

"What happens to Duke Humphreys? Did you write him a ticket? Will he have his license taken away? Does he get in trouble for hurting my child?" Her voice rose with each question. People started to stare, but she didn't care. Duke had been the troublemaker, and now he'd gone too far. She couldn't lose Knox like this.

"Harley." Ella placed a hand on her arm. "Let's go see the kids."

"In a second. Officer Hoffman, does Duke get into trouble?" Because he had damn well better.

Office Hoffman flipped his notebook closed. "A citation was issued for reckless driving and driving while intoxicated. He'll very likely lose his license temporarily." He handed her his card. "If you want a copy of the report, it will be ready in a few days. I hope your son recovers quickly." He turned and went back to the other officers.

She grabbed Ella's hands. "That boy could've killed our kids. Thank God Knox wasn't drinking." He'd done the right thing. "Is Stephanie okay? I'm sorry I haven't even asked."

"Stephanie is down the hall. She's fine. She has some cuts from her glasses, and her knees are bruised from hitting the seat in front of her. More scared than anything. Duke wasn't wearing his seat belt. He's banged up pretty badly."

She wasn't mentioning Knox. The room spun.

Harley's legs trembled. "Where is Knox?" Her strangled voice had heads turning in her direction.

Ella squeezed her hands. "He's okay. He's a little banged up, Harley. They took him in for tests for internal bleeding."

"Internal bleeding?" She willed her legs to move. "I need to see him." Was he wearing his seat belt? How many times had she told him to? Why did he get in a car with Duke if he'd been drinking? She'd told him again and again she'd come for him no matter what, and no matter where, but he should never get in a car with a drunk driver.

"Harley." A voice yelled from behind her.

She spun around to find Joann running toward her. Joann grabbed the collar of her coat and yanked her forward.

"What did you do with my son?" Joann screamed.

"Whoa." Ella tried to push Joann back, but she didn't release the death grip on her coat.

"Where is he, Harley? This is your fault. You did this." Joann shook her.

Harley shoved her, and she stumbled back. "Are you crazy, Joann? Your son was drinking and driving. He could've killed everyone."

"My son has an illness. He can't help himself. Drinking isn't his fault. Your son encourages him to behave badly because you have that rock star living in your house like the slut you are."

She raised her hand ready to smack the bitch in the head.

The redhead from behind the counter ran over. "Ladies, you need to pull yourselves together, or I'm going to have to ask you to leave."

Joann shoved a finger in her face. "I'm going to get you for this. I'll see to it you never teach another class as long as you live. When I'm done with you, there won't be a parent in three counties willing to trust their child with you. Just wait." She turned and hurried to the reception desk. Officer Hoffman intercepted Joann.

Harley's head spun, and black spots danced before her eyes. She tried to suck more air into her lungs. "Get me to Knox," she said to Ella.

The glass doors to the emergency room slid open. Colton bolted in, with Blaise fast on his heels. Colton's long black coat flapped behind him, and his bow tie hung undone around his neck. Her lungs started to work again. He was here.

His gaze searched the waiting area and landed on her. He rushed over. "What happened? Where is he?"

"He's at the end of the hall, near Stephanie so I could keep an eye on him." Ella motioned for them to follow her.

Ella pulled back the curtain, and the blood left Harley's head. Her body broke out in sweat. The room spun again.

Her boy lay in the small bed with his eyes closed. Was he unconscious? Machines surrounded him. They were lit up and beeping. Wires snaked from each one and into his arms and under the hospital gown hanging on his thin frame. His hair stuck to his head. He had a bandage over his left ear. His skin was the color of parchment paper. A neck brace was coiled around his neck.

"Do you need to sit down?" Ella said.

She shook her head. If she spoke, she'd faint.

"Where's the doctor?" Colton pushed back into the hallway. "I want to talk to a doctor right now, or I'm going to beat the shit out of someone."

Blaise punched his shoulder. "No one is going to talk to you if you don't stop acting like an asshole. Stop yelling."

"Why isn't someone taking care of him?" Colton ran a hand through his hair. "I need a cigarette."

A short, balding man wearing glasses and dark blue scrubs entered the small area. "I'm Dr. Baker. Are you the parents?"

Colton turned to her. She grabbed his hand. He didn't pull away. "Yes," she said.

Ella gasped. Blaise looked at the ground. She would explain to her friend later. If Ella hated her for keeping that kind of secret, she'd deal with the consequences.

The doctor checked his notes. "Your son was in a car accident."

"Yeah, we know that already. How is he?"

"Colton, shut up and let the man talk," Blaise said.

"Your son suffered bruising to his abdomen due to the seat belt, but no internal bleeding. We ran a CT scan that came back clean. He has a concussion and damage to his eardrum from the impact of the driver."

"Hold on." Colton put up a hand. "The driver hit him in the head? With what?"

"As far as we can tell, from his head. The driver wasn't wearing his seatbelt. Anything in a car that is not secured can become dangerous in an accident. Even a cell phone. There may be some hearing loss. We'll test when the eardrum has a chance to heal."

"Why is he unconscious?" She glanced back at her baby. She wanted to crawl into the bed with him and hold him.

When he was three, he'd ask her to sleep with him at night. She always told him no. Why didn't she just lie with him when he looked up at her with those big brown eyes? What had she been so worried would happen if she indulged his innocent requests? Why hadn't she told him about Colton one of those nights so long ago?

"He's asleep. He was pretty agitated before the CT scan. We gave him something to relax in the tube. The neck brace is a precaution. Whiplash is pretty common in a car accident. We want to observe him overnight just as a safety measure. If you have any questions, let me know. We're just waiting for a bed to be ready for him. Then we'll admit him. The nurse will be in with some papers for you to sign. If you'll excuse me..."

Colton dropped her hand, and she instantly missed the comfort holding his hand brought. She unbuttoned her coat. The small space was hot and stuffy.

"I'm going to check on Steph." Ella slipped out.

"I need some coffee. You two want any?" Blaise pointed to her and Colton.

"No, thank you," she said.

"Yeah, bro. I need something to do with my hands. Make sure it's black and hot."

They were alone, standing at the foot of their son's bed. Her legs buckled. She dropped into the plastic chair and hung her head between her legs.

"I'll pay for whatever he needs. If this Baker guy doesn't know what he's talking about, I'll fly the best doctors in."

She looked up at him. "That's not necessary. I can take care of it." Only if she still had a teaching job, which she didn't.

"It is necessary, Harley." He punctuated each word. "You stole all my other chances to be his father. You can't take away my chance to help here." A darkness passed over his eyes. "Are you going to keep him from me now? Are you going to push me away so I can't be involved at all?"

"No, of course not. Can we just get him better first, and then we'll tell him you're his father? You can even be there when I do, if you want." She didn't know how to make her mistake right. All she wanted was to get Knox well and home. After that she'd figure out a way to make him understand.

"No more secrets. I want to get to know my son and be with him, if he wants me. You owe me that much." Colton ran a hand through his hair.

"Mom?"

Her head snapped around. She jumped up and went to the side of the bed. "Hey, bud. How do you feel?"

Knox's gaze jumped from her to Colton and back like

a trapped cat. "Did you just say Colton is my father?" His voice was low and hoarse.

She squeezed her eyes shut and bit down on her lip to keep the low moan in her throat. When she forced them open, they both stared at her. *Oh God. Not here. Not now.*

She placed a hand on his arm. "Knox..." The words dried up in her throat. She swallowed and tried again. "Knox, I've wanted to tell you for a long time, but there never seemed to be the right way or the right time."

Colton waited on the other side of the bed. His gray eyes were stone cold. He shoved his hands in his pockets, then yanked them out again.

Knox's gaze continued to jump between her and Colton. The heart rate monitor beeped over and over.

"Colton is your dad." She folded into the plastic chair.

"Is this some kind of a joke?" Knox's lips pressed into a thin line. "Because it isn't funny."

"It's no joke, kid." Colton's face softened as he looked at Knox. "I know I'm not exactly a prize, but it's me. I'm your dad."

Her heart ached. Colton was wrong. He was a good man with so much love to offer. His mistakes didn't matter.

"You are really my father? But I don't understand. Mom, how is Colton my dad? You said it happened in New York. Were you in New York with her?"

"I wasn't in New York when she was there. I came back to Heritage River when my dad died. It happened then." He bounced on his feet, and sweat beaded on his upper lip. He shoved his hands in and out of his jacket pockets.

"Are you okay?" Had he been drinking? Did her confession make him fall off the wagon tonight? And now the accident. Would he be able to get through the stress of the situation?

"I'm fine, Harley. I can handle this."

"You never told him?" Knox searched her face.

"I tried, but I didn't do a very good job of it. You have to understand, Knox. This is all my fault. Colton didn't know until tonight. I was too afraid to tell him and you. I kept you from your dad, and I shouldn't have. Don't be mad at Colton, okay? He would've been a great dad, and I didn't let him have the chance. Please give him a chance."

Knox stared at her. "All this time you knew, and you kept it from me?"

"It was a mistake. I'm so sorry. I hurt you, and I had no right. I hope someday you'll be able to forgive me."

He continued to stare at her for a long time, his face made of stone.

"Knox, if you have something to say, it's okay to say it. I won't be mad no matter what it is." She'd take whatever he said to her because she'd deserve it. "I'll answer any questions."

He turned his back to her. "Get out."

"What?"

"Get out of here." He turned back and shot his fiery gaze on her. "You lied to me and to him. I wanted to find my dad my whole life. You knew where he was when you said you didn't even know his last name. You know how awful it is to grow up without a father, and you let me be that kid. It never mattered that people accepted me or that I had you and Uncle Hank. I was still the loser without a father. I thought maybe someone had raped you in New York and you were too embarrassed to tell me. I could understand that. But this? Colton Savage is my dad, and you kept that from me? I hate you. Leave."

Her heart pummeled her chest. She didn't know what to do. She wanted to plead with Colton to help her make Knox understand, but how could he? He didn't understand her choice either.

"Knox, man, I know this is a lot to swallow, but you need your mom right now. She's going to help you get better. After that, we can all talk and figure out what to do next."

He threw her a bone. She bit her lip to keep from sobbing.

"I don't want her to help me anymore. I can take care of myself. I'll be eighteen soon."

Colton ran a hand over his face. "It's not entirely her fault, okay? I wasn't the most upstanding guy back then. I'm not proud of that. I made it clear I didn't want her in my life. It's because of me she didn't tell."

Tears choked her. She wasn't expecting him to come to her defense at all.

Knox tried to sit up. She jumped up to help him, but he put up a hand to stop her. He locked his gaze on her. "I wish you weren't my mother."

The room spun again. She raced from the curtained

area to get air and collided into Blaise holding two cups of hot coffee. The coffee spilled over both of them and splashed on the floor. Her skin burned, but she deserved that.

"Holy shit, that's hot!" Blaise jumped back.

"I'm sorry." She pushed past him and ran for the sliding glass doors.

"Harley, wait," Colton called after her.

She kept going until she was in the middle of the parking lot. She bent over with her hands on her knees and gulped in cold air. What was she going to do? She needed to be inside tending to her son, but she wanted to give him space. He couldn't have meant what he said, could he? Did he really wish she wasn't his mother? Hadn't she wished the same thing of her own mother? Her greatest fear had come true. What had she expected by keeping a secret like the identity of Knox's father?

"Harley," Ella shouted. "Where are you?"

She wanted to duck down behind a car. "I'm over here."

Ella made her way between parked cars to her side. "You smell like coffee."

"Not my best look." She pointed to the large coffee stain soaking through to her skin, then sagged against a car.

Ella leaned next to her. "Are you okay?"

"Yes. No. You didn't have to come out here. I'll pull myself together and go back inside in a minute." As much as Knox didn't want her, she had to be there to sign papers and talk to doctors, get him settled into the hospital room. He would need his belongings from home too.

"Things were getting pretty rough in there. I thought you could use a friend."

"So you heard everything?"

"The curtains aren't soundproof. Plus, I had a suspicion when you grabbed Colton's hand and answered yes to the parent question. Kind of a giveaway." Ella pressed her lips together.

Most of the emergency room had probably heard her too. The news would be on the front page of the *Heritage River Herald* by morning.

"I'm a complete screwup." The coffee on her clothes started to cool down. "I need to get back to Knox. What if the doctor comes back?"

"He's okay for now. Colton and Blaise are with him. You can take the minute you need." Ella wrapped her arms around her middle. "Why didn't you tell me?"

"Because I couldn't imagine what kind of terrible person you'd think I was."

"You've been my friend forever. I would never judge you. I can't imagine what you must've been going through back then. You didn't exactly get pregnant with the local accountant, if you know what I mean."

Oh, she knew exactly what Ella meant. "I'm so sorry I never said anything. I know I'm a terrible friend. I thought if you knew, then you'd have to keep the secret too, and I didn't want to burden you with my crap. I'll understand if you hate me. I hate me right about now."

Ella grabbed her hand. "Hey, I don't hate you. Are

you kidding? The secret was yours to keep. I can't believe you carried it alone for eighteen years. All that time probably needing someone to talk to about it. I can't imagine what you've been thinking or feeling about Colton being Knox's dad."

"I was afraid, Ella. Just stupid fear stopped me, and as the years went by, I didn't know how to dig myself out of the trouble I caused. Until now." She hadn't liked her choices—tell and lose him or keep the secret and hold onto him.

"You did the right thing by telling him, even if it's later instead of sooner. He and Knox will have a chance to get to know each other now. He was actually worried I was going to break up with him. He probably wishes that was what I was going to say instead of the bomb I dropped. I couldn't go on lying to him while he was promising me the life I always wanted with him."

"I'm proud of you, Harley."

She squinted at Ella. "Proud? I'm pathetic. God, I'm so in love with him. He's everything to me and always has been, even though his actions always said he never wanted me. I still pine after him like a lovesick teenager." She started to laugh, but none of it was funny. "Now he comes back to town after all these years and wants to build a life with me. He offered me the very thing I dreamt about my entire life, but I had to do the right thing this time and speak the truth."

"Timing is a bitch."

"Isn't that supposed to be karma?"

"She's a bitch too." Ella nudged her. "I wish you felt

like you could've come to me. I want to be there to help you through this. Don't try to figure it all out alone."

"I really thought I was going to lose you too if you knew, and I wouldn't have blamed you."

"You're stuck with me, kid." Ella wrapped an arm around her shoulder and hugged her close.

She smiled for the first time since Colton showed up at the bridge. "Thank you for understanding. I'm lucky to have you in my corner." Ella might be the very last person standing beside her.

"What happens next?"

"I have no idea. Get Knox better and home, I guess. If he'll let me anywhere near him. He inherited Colton's temper and uses it quite well." She pushed away the image of his face when he told her to get out of his hospital room. "After that, it's all up to the universe."

"How mad was Colton?"

She raised an eyebrow. "He has a right to be furious. He'll never forgive me. I just hope he and Knox can make up for lost time." She hoped Knox would forgive her someday too.

"He loves you. He might forgive you."

"It would be a Christmas miracle."

Chapter Thirty-Four

Colton stared at his son. *Son.* The word knocked him over. How could someone like him be a father? He'd been as crazy as they'd come. He'd trashed hotel rooms, been arrested for public drunkenness, and even managed to jump out of a moving Ferris wheel carriage at a county fair in Georgia.

"When can I get out of here?" Knox broke into his thoughts.

"They want to keep you overnight for observations. Make sure your hearing is okay and the concussion."

Blaise came back into the curtained area. Someone found him a clean scrub top to wear. He carried a plastic bag filled with his shirt covered in the spilled coffee. Colton's hands shook from wanting a drink so badly. He'd told Harley he could handle what was happening. He wasn't so sure.

Blaise flopped into the chair and closed his eyes. It had been a long night for everyone.

"Bro, call Grace and go home." He'd be okay without Blaise. Well, probably. "Thanks for sticking around. I appreciate it."

"I can stay. I don't mind."

"No, go. I'll be by after Knox is settled, if the offer for the extra room still stands."

Blaise kept his eyes closed and his head back. "Savages stick together. If you two don't mind, I'm just going to catch a few winks. Wake me when we go upstairs." He stretched out his legs.

Leave it to Blaise to accept Knox into their fold, no questions asked. He said Knox was his son, and Blaise immediately wrapped his protective cloak around him too. Colton shook his head. He was one lucky son of a bitch, and he didn't deserve to be.

He kicked Blaise's foot. "Go home. If I need you, I'll call. I promise."

Blaise peeled himself off the chair and patted him on the shoulder. "I'll leave the door unlocked. Knox, I don't know what to say. You must have a lot of stuff running around in your head. If you need someone to talk about it, I'm all ears, but I'll tell you this much. My brother is the best man I've ever known. Flaws and all." He offered Knox a fist bump. Knox returned it.

Colton pulled the chair up to the bed. "Can we talk for a minute?"

"You aren't going to stay in the guesthouse anymore?" Knox pressed on the bandage over his ear.

"I'll probably head back to my place in Bayton in the next day or two. You can visit me there if you want." He'd like Knox to spend some time with him. Would he be willing to come over a school break or before he went off to college? He wanted a chance to know his son. Maybe build a relationship of some kind.

"My mom really fucked everything up." Knox turned his head and swatted at his eyes.

"Hey, don't be mad at her. I was in a bad place back then. My dad had died, and that really threw me. I was drinking pretty much all the time. I did plenty of things I would never tell you about, things I'm not proud of doing. If your mom had found me back then, and she tried, I wouldn't have been man enough to handle my responsibilities."

"Are you mad at her?"

"I'm trying not to be." He wasn't mad. He was hurt. She didn't trust him with something so important. She hadn't given him a chance to prove himself. He was ashamed of his bad choices that kept him from knowing his son. He'd had a chance to have what Blaise and Savannah had, and he missed it, with no one to blame but himself.

He'd finally seen himself through everyone else's eyes. He hadn't cared about anyone but himself for years. He'd nearly wrecked every relationship he'd ever had. How his siblings could stand behind him was beyond his understanding.

He'd used Harley for comfort when he was broken, and that made him sick. He'd really loved her, but he couldn't say it back then. He still loved her. He hadn't been man enough to show her that either, because he was too busy being the big bad rock star. He wasn't that anymore. Why hadn't he seen what Blaise had been trying to tell him?

"I don't want to go home with her. Can I come home with you?"

He didn't want to take Knox from Harley. "How about when school lets out next week you come back to Bayton?"

Knox shook his head, then squeezed his eyes shut.

"Are you okay? Should I get a doctor?"

"My head hurts a lot. My ear is ringing too. I can't go home with her. She lied to me. She's such a hypocrite, always telling me to tell the truth and grounding me for drinking when the whole time she was lying." He leaned back against the pillow. "Can you get me something to drink? Maybe a Coke."

"Sure. I'll be right back." He stopped. "No. I think we should talk about what happened in that car tonight. I'm in no position to judge, but I know what's right and wrong."

"Are you going to go all parent on me now?" Knox rolled his eyes.

"If asking you what the fuck happened that landed you in the hospital with a concussion and a bruised abdomen is going all parent, then yeah, I guess I am." He'd ask the same question of Cash or any of Savannah's kids if they were lying in that bed.

"I don't want to talk about it."

"You told the police at the scene. You might as well tell me. I can get a copy of the police report."

"Fine. A bunch of us went to the lake after the concert. Duke pulled out some whiskey. He drank half of it by himself. I wasn't planning on getting in the car with him. I was going to call Mom to come and get me, but Duke wanted to drive himself home. We tried to stop him. I thought if I could keep him focused he'd be okay, but he wouldn't listen to me. He was driving on the wrong side of the road, weaving back and forth. The light had turned yellow, and he floored it. By the time we got to the intersection, the other side had started to go."

"You're all lucky to be alive." He remembered being just like Duke. No one could stop him when he wanted to drink. He thought he was invincible. He pretty much thought that until he hit the fence. He'd been sober for years, and in one night he'd undone all his hard work. "Do you know what it would have done to your mom if you got hurt or worse?"

"I'm sorry. I thought I could handle the situation. I didn't think anyone would get hurt."

"Yeah, that's what we all think when we're doing something stupid. I'll get that Coke for you now."

He pushed back the curtain to find Harley standing there. Her makeup had run under her red, swollen eyes. The coffee stain covered most of her shirt. She was a mess and beautiful at the same time. "Were you eavesdropping?"

"I didn't hear anything. Did the doctor come back?" She tucked a hair behind her ear. Her gaze searched for somewhere to land.

"Not yet. I'm going to get Knox something to drink.

I'll be back, if that's okay with you. If you don't want me here, just say it and I'll go, but I'd like to be here."

"You should stay. You have every right to be here."

He wanted her to fight with him so he wouldn't feel like such a jerk for the way he'd treated her all those times. "I'm going to be staying with Blaise for a few days. Then I'm heading back to Bayton. I'll be out of your hair."

"Whatever you think is best, but I hope you'll let Knox come visit you."

As if he knew what the hell was best for any of them. "He's welcome anytime." He had no plans at the moment. He didn't know what he was going to do about his music career.

She placed a hand on his arm but quickly drew it away. "Colton, please try to make plans with him. Don't let my mistakes stop you from being with him. He's a great kid. He deserves the chance to get to know you as well as I know you." She chewed on her bottom lip. Her brown eyes filled with tears.

How could he want to pull her into his arms and want to push her away at the same time? She knew him as well as anyone, and she'd always been there for him in spite of how he acted. That didn't change the confusion running through his head like a lousy guitar solo. "Knox and I will figure it out. I'd better get that drink."

"Yeah." She stepped around him and inside the cubicle area.

He wanted to follow her, but he turned and searched for that soda. For his son.

Chapter Thirty-Five

Harley didn't know what to do. Should she go? Should she stay? Colton was about to arrive with Knox from the hospital. He'd spent the night, and Dr. Baker cleared him this morning to come home. Knox hadn't said a word to her the entire night while she sat curled up and cramped in the chair in his room. He only spoke to Colton. She had tried to keep her breaking heart to herself.

Colton had stayed all night as well, in another chair shoved as far away from her as the private room would allow. He wanted Knox to have his own room. He'd pulled out his wallet and shoved a credit card at the woman in admissions until she took it and Knox was wheeled into a private room.

The front door swung open and sent in a blast of cold air followed by Knox and Colton. She took a step forward, ready to run to them, but stopped. They didn't want her arms around their waists. She prayed Knox would come around soon. That was the most she could ask for. Her time with Colton was over. Forever.

Knox moved slowly. His hand rested against his bruised middle. The bandage on his ear was smaller. He still had the ringing, but in time, that might go away too. Colton stepped in behind him, carrying Knox's bag. He hadn't shaved. The whiskers only managed to make him better looking.

She swallowed the lump in her throat. "You're home."

Knox rolled his eyes.

"Of course, you're home. Stupid of me to say. Your room is clean and ready for you. Or you can rest in the den. Wherever you think you'll be most comfortable. Are you hungry?" Her mouth ran like wet paint.

"I'm not hungry. I'm going to my room." He turned to take the bag from Colton.

"I'll carry it upstairs." Colton pulled the bag out of Knox's reach.

They walked past her without another word. She busied herself with fixing throw pillows that didn't need fixing.

Colton bounded back down the steps. "He's resting. His stomach still hurts, and so does his arm. He says he doesn't want you to fuss over him, but you should. The ibuprofen isn't doing much for his aches and pains."

Colton had insisted no prescription painkillers for Knox. She agreed. "Thank you for bringing him home."

He shrugged.

"You're good with him."

"Harley, I'm wiped out. I don't have the energy for any kind of conversation right now. Especially one where you pay me compliments about my parenting skills. If you think I'm such a goddamn good father, why didn't you let be one from the beginning?" he growled between pressed lips. "I'm sorry. I swore I wouldn't do this."

She bit back the tears constantly on the verge of spilling down her cheeks. Crying was her new normal. "You're right. I should've let you decide whether you wanted to be a father. I had no right to make that choice for you. I'm sorry. I will always be sorry because I can never make that right."

"I'm going to pack up my stuff and head to Blaise's. If Knox needs anything from me, he can call me. I'll come right back."

"Will you be at the dine-in art show tomorrow night?"

"I don't think so." He turned for the door.

The bright light he'd once shone on her burned out, but she still didn't want him to leave. "Stay in town and be the music teacher. The kids need you. The school needs you too. I won't be in your way. I'm resigning now. There's no point in me finishing out the school year. You won't have to worry about me getting in your way there." She was considering leaving town too, but she hadn't figured out where yet.

He turned back. "I can't stay here. Every time I turn the corner, I'll see you. I'll smell your scent. I won't be able to shake you, and if I'm going to survive this and stay sober, I can't keep loving you."

He closed the door behind him. She couldn't hold the tears back any longer. Her shoulders shook with sobs. She covered her face with her hands and cried without sound so Knox wouldn't hear.

Colton threw the last of his things into his duffel. He took one last look around the small guesthouse. He'd left it the way he found it; that was the least he could do for her. His body ached from sleeping in that chair at the hospital, and his head hurt from too much thinking.

He'd stayed all night because Knox asked him to and because secretly he wanted to be near Harley. He wanted one final chance to wake up with her, but seeing her across the room with pain etched on her face even while she dozed broke him up inside. He'd wanted to go to her, but no matter how many times he told himself it was his fault she didn't tell him about Knox, he couldn't get out of that damn chair.

He flopped down on the sofa and grabbed his Gibson. He should go straight to Bayton, but being alone now was a bad idea. He wanted his support system around him. The last thing he needed was to start drinking. He had to stay sober for himself and for Knox. He couldn't fuck up the only chance he'd get to be a father.

He strummed on the guitar without much thought. A *father*. What would his own dad say about that? Probably have himself a good laugh over it. His son, the screwup, trying to be a responsible parent would be a joke.

Jedidiah Savage never thought he would amount to much besides being a drunk rock star. "You were right, Dad. That's all I ever was."

His fingers played chords. A melody whispered in his head, but he couldn't reach it. He strummed an old sad tune instead.

When he was with Harley, he didn't want to drink. She kept him strong. Her love flowed over him smooth and sweet. Like whiskey.

His hand ran up the neck of the guitar while he picked at the strings with the other. He let the ache over losing her grow with each chord he played. Until he let Harley in, the only love he ever needed was music.

Now he'd lost her, and the bottom of a bottle looked good.

His guitar sang the blues, and he pictured Harley pressed against him swaying to the tune in his head. He closed his eyes and let his hands stroke the guitar. He captured the low notes and wrapped the song in a slow melody, as if the sound could wrap around him the way Harley wrapped around him when they made love.

His fingers coaxed a solo out of the guitar and finished up with the bluesy drawl he'd started with. He opened his eyes. The thrill of what he'd done ran across his clammy skin. He grabbed paper and jotted it all down before he had a chance to forget it. He'd been in the business long enough to know when a piece was good. He'd just written the first decent thing of his life.

And no one would ever hear it.

Chapter Thirty-Six

For the first time in a very long time, Harley didn't need to hide. The art show and dine-in were tomorrow, and she still had the artwork to display. She'd called the students who'd volunteered to help and told them she had the setup under control. She had nothing under control at the moment, but she wanted to be alone.

Knox still hadn't spoken to her. He'd slept most of the night, which made her breathe with ease. She'd never been so scared as she was trying to get to the hospital, knowing he was hurt. She'd checked on him every hour through the night. Now her eyes burned from the lack of sleep.

The empty store on Main Street had been transformed into a small art gallery. She'd hung white Christmas lights around the windows and around the metal poles throughout the space. The cocktail tables were covered in shimmery gold tablecloths with clusters of tiny white candles on top. The flicker of the flames caught the sparkle in the cloths, making the tables look as if gold had melted over them.

A portable bar had been set up in the corner for patrons to purchase drinks while they took in the exhibits. She had secretly promised no Christmas music, and only a few days ago had hoped Colton would notice her attention to detail, but he wouldn't be there. She didn't have him to look over at and know everything would be okay.

She pulled out her students' artwork from cardboard boxes. She'd wrapped everything in tissue paper to keep the pieces safe. Some students had painted, while others had taken photographs. A few had created small sculptures.

The last piece she unwrapped was her own. She'd painted a landscape in her signature pastel colors with muted edges. She'd chosen a cherry blossom tree for the foreground. White feathers dusted the earth beneath the tree. The feathers represented new beginnings because she had nowhere to go but up.

She'd included the Heritage River Covered Bridge, her bridge, as part of the backdrop of the painting. Well, it wasn't her bridge any longer. She'd have to let go of the past if she were going to move forward. This new bridge led to the unknown. Her future was one big unknown now, and it scared the hell out of her. At her age, she was starting over. She'd decided to hang the piece in the back of the room, out of the way but still visible. She wasn't ready to shine a spotlight on herself just yet. Small steps first.

She banged the nail into the wall. The door swung in. Andy Henson brought the blistering cold air and a smile on his face with him.

"Andy, what brings you by?"

He held up a rectangle wrapped in brown paper. "Hi, Harley. If it's not too late, I have something for the show." He eased the canvas out of the paper and held it up for her to view.

Her heart swelled right into her throat. "You painted the Heritage River Bridge and the water behind it." He'd used the picture he brought to class. "It's lovely. You're very talented." She wasn't just saying that. He had so much potential.

"I kept thinking about the paintings we saw at the museum and how much I like the bridge right here in town. Bridges mean connections, journeys, taking chances. I wanted to take a chance for once. I don't care if it sells. I wanted to be in the show to help you because you've helped me so much. Thanks." He ducked his head.

His words echoed in her head. No longer hiding behind her secret could take her from her fears to what seemed possible. She could build a future on faith and hope. The way a bridge was built. "I'm glad the class has been helpful for you. Promise me you'll keep painting."

"I will. I'm going to give art a try at school in the fall. Who knows? Maybe I'll be as good as Twachtman someday."

"You're already better. Do you want to help me hang it?"

"Sure."

Together they hung his painting, and then he helped her hang hers. She was proud of Andy. She had taught him something, but she had learned from him too. There still may be space in her life to teach.

"Will you be at the show?" She pounded the last nail into the wall.

"I think so."

"How about your dad?" Would Joe Henson be able to change the way he viewed his son and let go of the expectations he put on him?

He shrugged and hung a photo on the wall.

"Give him time."

Was she saying that to Andy or herself?

Chapter Thirty-Seven

Harley searched for a parking spot on Main Street. She was late—again. She'd sat in the Durango in her driveway and debated on coming. The event was a go. Plenty of parents had stepped in to help. Ella had slid in as head coordinator, somehow knowing Harley needed her to take the lead so she could slide into the background. She wasn't prepared to answer the questions about Knox and Colton that were bound to come. The whole town must know by now. A secret that big would run like a mudslide.

She was forced to park in the library lot and walk up to the little art gallery she'd created. Harley's Art Gallery. It had a nice ring to it. Maybe, but it had to be a space where kids like Andy could come to create.

Knox wanted to stay home and rest. That's what he said, but he wanted to avoid her and the event. She hadn't argued. He probably didn't want the stares either, and she wanted to give him the space he needed to find a way to forgive her. He wasn't going back to school until after the winter break. Maybe by then the gossip would die down some and he'd be talking to her.

She straightened her shoulders. Tonight was about the kids. Her shady past would have to wait. She smiled and slipped into the storefront all set up for the art gallery. The candles on the tables had been lit. She smelled vanilla and moist air. Someone piped soft music in throughout the space. No Christmas music, just as she'd asked.

Her heart swelled as she took in the work her students had created. The talent that decorated the walls was amazing. These kids had far more talent than she'd ever possessed, and certainly never at their age.

People milled around admiring the work, pointing, and commenting. A few people stood at the tables, holding glasses of wine. Many of the faces she didn't recognize. The advertisements had paid off. She hadn't wanted to depend on only the locals for this event. Many of them wouldn't have the money to purchase the artwork.

Ella waved to her from across the room, and she hurried over. "You won't believe it. We've sold ten paintings so far. Isn't that great?"

"It's fantastic." She really was happy for them all.

They'd priced the paintings and the photos at the prices of a professional's first show. The kids were thrilled to be considered professionals. She never doubted they'd sell.

"You don't sound pleased. Are you okay?" Ella asked.

"I'm fine." Or she would be. Her new focus had to be her future and not what she'd lost. Colton's car had still been at the guesthouse when she'd left. By the time she returned, he'd be gone.

"How's Knox?"

"Ignoring me every chance he gets."

"Give him time." Ella squeezed her arm.

Those were the words she'd said to Andy. Time was the one thing she had now.

"Excuse me." A woman with wavy hair streaked gray and wearing a burgundy suit with gold buttons grasped Harley's elbow. "We'd like to place a bid. Can we bid on just one guitar, or do we have to bid on both of them?"

"Which guitars are those?" She hadn't unpacked any guitars.

"Colton and Blaise donated guitars to be auctioned off." Ella turned back to the woman. "Come with me. I'll show you." She whisked the lady away, who left a trail of flowery perfume in her wake.

Even while he hated her, he'd done the right thing by the kids. How could she ever have doubted him?

Harley weaved her way through the tables to some of the photos in the back. She had hung a collection of black-and-white portraits under the soft lighting.

A presence slid up alongside her. "These are good. They really capture the emotion of each person," the female said.

Harley turned. "Savannah. Thank you for coming." Standing next to Colton's sister might be too much to handle. Did she know? What was she thinking?

"I want to help save the art program. If you can work hard for a job you're losing, I certainly can buy a picture. Plus, I need something to do besides packing up my husband's belongings."

Savannah stood there, poised, wearing a long black cardigan and black turtleneck underneath. A silver chain hung low and shimmered against the dark clothes. She'd carefully applied makeup. Her hair was tied back neatly. No one would know by looking at her that she'd suffered such a tragedy. She was an inspiration.

Harley pointed to the black-and-white portraits. "Cash really has an eye, don't you think? My favorite is of Caroline running through the tall grass with the flowers in her hair. She doesn't even realize the camera is on her. Cash told an entire story by capturing her dazzling smile. She's beautiful."

"Thank you. Caroline can be a handful, though."

Her other favorite was the one Cash took of Colton playing guitar on Blaise's front porch. The sun set behind him. He had a cigarette hanging out of his mouth. His head was turned toward the guitar. His eyes were closed, keeping out everyone and everything as he played. The lines between his brows and around his mouth had deepened with concentration. He was truly in love with his music, and Cash had captured the moment.

"Harley, I hope you don't mind me saying."

Savannah's words dragged her attention back. *Oh boy, here it comes.*

"You should've told him."

"I know. I'm sorry, Savannah—"

"Hang on." She put up a hand to stop her. "You should've told him, but I can't imagine what you were going through. My brother is hardly the easiest of people to understand, and his choices, well, we know what his choices are like. The one thing I can always say about Colton is he loves his family. Whether I agree with the way he goes about caring for his family is something else altogether, but he would've loved Knox. He loves him now. I wish you would've given him the chance to love his own child all these years. He might've grown up a lot faster than he did. That would've been good for everyone."

"I wish I had told him too."

"Losing Adam unexpectedly has taught me one thing. Life is too short. Don't hold on to regret. If you love my brother—and if yelling at me in the parking lot of the school tells me anything, it tells me you do— fight for him. Don't miss another chance to tell him how you feel."

"Why are you being so nice to me? I thought you'd hate me for what I did to him."

"I'm the last person to judge you, but I know sometimes the wrong choices take us to the right places. Don't let him leave town again." Savannah took in the open space. "This store would make a cute tea shop." She shrugged. "Well, I have to buy that picture of Caroline. She and Blaise will never let me hear the end of it if I don't. Good luck tonight. With everything."

"Thanks." But Savannah had turned away before Harley spoke.

Fight for Colton. How could she fight for something so lost to her?

She snaked her way toward the back of the gallery. Two guitars stood on a table. She didn't know much about guitars, but their paint gleamed in the light directed on them. Each one was signed by both brothers. Several people had bid on them. She resisted the urge to run her fingers over Colton's name.

"Harley."

She turned to find Andy and his father coming toward her. "Hey, Andy. Joe."

"I wanted to come by and apologize for the way I've been acting lately. Andy and I had a long talk. I realized I'd rather be connected to my son than lose him. We only get one go around here on earth, right?"

His one-eighty made her head spin, but she wasn't going to argue. Change was always possible. Savannah was right about wrong choices and right places.

"Excuse me. I'm Marin Smith. I'm the curator at the Heritage River Museum. Who painted the bridge with all the blues?"

"That was me." Andy beamed.

"You're a very talented painter. Where do you study?"

"With Harley." Andy laughed as if the question were absurd.

"You're some teacher." Marin had warm brown skin and a dazzling smile.

"Thank you, but Andy is the one with the talent."

"I was wondering if we could get your students to do an exhibit for us? I like to feature students from around the state. We could also help to raise some funds to save your art program."

"That's wonderful. My students would love the opportunity, but I have to ask you. How did you hear about our little show?"

"Colton Savage found me and told me about you. He also said I'd be foolish to miss out on you. He's very persuasive. I'll be in touch." Marin touched her arm and slipped into the crowd.

Her heart stuttered.

"Harley, we're going to take a look around," Joe said. "Good luck tonight." They followed in Marin's footsteps.

She stood staring after them. Colton had steered success her way that day at the museum. That was why he'd been missing for so long, and she thought he'd been looking at the art. For all his mistakes in the past, he could always be counted on. She hadn't known that when she was young. If she could only go back, but she couldn't. She could only move forward.

She waved goodbye to Ella and went to Jake's, and nearly fell over. The place was packed. Jake waved from behind the counter, and she weaved her way through the crowd.

"What a group, huh?" He handed an order ticket to someone behind him, a tall, well-built man wearing a baseball hat backward. "JT, take this order, will ya?"

She hadn't recognized Jake's son. She wasn't

expecting to see him since he'd moved away and hadn't been back to Heritage River in some time.

Jake shook his head. "We're making a fortune. I've never made this many sandwiches and salads. Everyone came out to help support the art programs. You'll keep your job for sure now." Jake's face beamed.

She didn't have the heart to tell him the job would go to someone else. "I'm just glad the kids can keep art and music for at least another year." They could keep the music program if Colton would take the job.

"You might've saved the programs for longer than a year." Jake shook a stack of order forms. "How's it going at the gallery?"

"Great." Andy had a painting on the wall, the museum wanted to help the kids, and the guitars would bring a lot of money.

"Jake," Donna yelled from back in the kitchen. "We've got a problem."

"Excuse me, Harley." He turned and hurried off.

"Harley." Maybelline sauntered through the crowd and pulled her into a hug. "Sugar, you pulled this off right. You should be proud of yourself."

"It wasn't all me, May. I couldn't have done this without everyone else."

May waved a hand at her. "You don't give yourself enough credit. Everyone's here because of you and Knox. We love you. You're our family. When are you going to learn that?"

"That's sweet of you to say."

"Speaking of sweet, I want to help the cause. With every pecan pie I sell through Christmas, I'm donating the profits to the program." She leaned in and whispered, "You know how well my pecan pie sells. That pie is how I've kept my Pete all these years coming back for more of his May." She threw her head back and laughed.

Harley couldn't help but laugh too. "Thanks, May. You're the best."

May folded her in a warm hug. "It's all going to be okay, sugar. Now go and enjoy your night."

Somehow, she'd put the pieces of her life back together. No matter how long it took.

She pushed back out onto the sidewalk. The night air cooled her heated cheeks. She fought all the thoughts in her head until she pulled into her driveway. Was there some way she could fight for Colton? How would he ever forgive her when she wasn't sure she could forgive herself?

Colton's car was still parked by the guesthouse. Why was he still there? He was supposed to be long gone.

Here was her chance to prove herself. She knew what she needed to do and ran inside and upstairs to the attic pull down in the hallway. Yanking on the door, she lowered the wooden steps. Her coat offered protection from the cold attic.

She tugged on the string attached to the single light-bulb and pushed plastic boxes to the side. She'd kept everything of Knox's from birth, unable to part with a single piece of clothing or one art project. She dropped to her knees and shoved the cardboard box labeled "Toys" to the side, revealing a small filing cabinet.

The metal cabinet had been her uncle's idea. He wanted something that would protect from water and fire. He'd kept important papers in there and gave Harley the top drawer for anything she wanted safeguarded.

She pushed past some insurance documents and her will. Knox's birth certificate was in there with the line for the father's name blank. They'd have to change that. She reached into the very back of the drawer and pulled out an envelope.

The corners of the envelope had yellowed over the years. She hadn't thought about preserving it back then. Her bubbly script in blue ink across the front was unmistakable. She ran a finger over the address: Colton Savage, 2564 Lakeview Court, Bayton, TN 37053

She hurried out of the attic. Knox stood in the hallway. He held his phone in one hand and his earbuds in the other.

"What are you doing up there? You were making a lot of noise."

"Did I wake you? I'm sorry. I was looking for something."

"I wasn't sleeping. What's that?" He pointed to the envelope.

She pressed her lips together. This letter was proof for him too. "I had written a letter to Colton after you were born."

"But you didn't send it."

"No. I was afraid to. That's no excuse, but it's the

truth. I'm sorry I'm not the perfect mother. I wanted so desperately to be, and I thought I was enough for you. I hoped you wouldn't ever need a father in your life if you had me, but that was selfish. I let my fears affect you, and I shouldn't have done that."

"Are you going to give it to him now?"

"If he'll take it." She bit back the tears. There was no time for crying now.

"Good luck, I guess." He swung his earbuds around his fingers.

"Thanks."

He went back into his room and closed the door. The good luck wish wasn't much, but it was a start.

She hurried from the house and knocked on Colton's door. She tried a second time, and when he didn't come to the door, shame heated her cheeks. She went to his car and lifted the windshield wiper while the tears slipped down her face.

"Hey, I don't let people touch my car." He leaned against the doorframe with his ankles crossed and a smile on his face. The smile was going to undo her. The light from the living room washed him in a golden glow. "What do you want, Harley?" He straightened and met her halfway.

Except for the spot where his scar was, the scruff on his jaw was thick from not shaving. The stubble gave him that sexy ruggedness he wore so well. Her body responded to his nearness. Her hands shook. "I wanted you to have this."

He took the envelope. "What is it?"

"I wrote that right after Knox was born. I've kept it in the attic all these years. I don't want you to leave without having it." That letter was her last attempt to fight for him. If he read it and still couldn't forgive her, then at least she tried. She didn't expect him to love her anymore; that was too much to ask for.

"You said you could never put the words together to tell me in a letter."

"I said the words didn't come out right. I'm not sure they did. You'll have to decide. At least you can see I tried to tell you. I know trying isn't enough, but it's all I have."

He looked at the envelope and back at her. "I don't know what to say."

"You don't have to say anything. I'm not trying to change anything between us. We're through, and that's my fault." She wanted one last time to touch him, but she didn't. "Merry Christmas, Colton."

She hurried toward the house, not waiting for him to say something. On the porch, she fought the urge to turn back around to look at him. She might crumble into a million tiny jagged pieces if she saw the continued disappointment in his eyes. *How do you love someone your whole life and still manage to hurt him?*

Colton watched her until she'd walked onto the porch and went inside. He'd wanted to cup her face in his hands and kiss her furrowed brows until she smiled up at him. Instead, he'd let her stand there with trembling hands. Would he ever be able to forgive her? Would she ever forgive him for being so mad when he knew he was partially to blame?

He shoved the letter in his back pocket. What could she possibly have said that would make any difference now?

He threw his duffel and his guitars into the trunk and drove away. He didn't look back.

He had one place to stop before he went to Blaise's. Bayton was too far to drive to through the night, and the idea of being alone in a hotel room was more than he could handle. No more mistakes where his sobriety was concerned.

He turned off the main road to the dirt road leading to the lake. Billy's house was dark, but that didn't stop him from climbing the front steps and banging on the door.

The porch light flipped on. The front door swung open. "Whoever's at my door better have a good reason for being there. I've got a shotgun," Billy said.

Colton shook his head. Billy's white hair stuck up in all the wrong places. He wore a long-sleeved under-shirt tucked into his trousers. He hiked up his suspenders.

"It's just me, old man. Put your shotgun away before you shoot your foot off."

"I've never missed a target, and you know that, boy. Besides, my gun's in the other room. I forgot to grab it. What brings you by so late? Knox feeling okay?" He held the screen door open, and Colton stepped past him. Billy patted his shoulder as he went by. "You want some coffee?"

"No, thanks. Knox is getting better. Still has the ringing in his ear, but his head doesn't hurt as much." He followed Billy into the kitchen. Billy grabbed milk from the refrigerator and offered him some.

"I haven't had milk since I was a kid." He dropped into a chair.

"That might be part of your problem." Billy dragged out the chair next to him and flopped down. "So what brings you by?"

"I'm heading home in a day or two."

"Is Harley coming with you?" Billy eyed him over the glass.

"Just me." He lowered his gaze to the thin red-and-white tablecloth.

"You two can't make a go of it, then?"

"We tried, but it doesn't look like things will work out. I didn't want to leave without saying goodbye." He stood and stuck out his hand. Billy pointed to the chair, and Colton returned to the seat. "There's nothing more to discuss, Billy. It's over. I helped out at the school, and I donated to her cause. That's that. Time to move on."

"What about the boy?"

"Knox? What about him?"

Billy raised an eyebrow and stared at him.

"Did Blaise call you?" He gritted his teeth.

"Who do you think feeds me information about you? You think I would've had the right date you left rehab if it weren't for your brother? Who do you think told me about the stunts you've pulled in your life?"

"I'm going to kill him. He's worse than that Milly Franks who worked with my dad. She couldn't wait to run through the halls of the school sharing gossip."

"Don't go getting all riled up about your brother now. He's looking out for you is all, the way family should. You going to take care of Knox?"

He wiped his hands over his face. "Why do you think I wouldn't?"

"Colton, finding out you have a boy long after he's been born is bound to wallop anyone. You have a habit of running when things get tough. I'm not saying I'd blame you this time, but that boy needs you. In case you didn't know that."

"Yeah, I know. I told him whatever he needs, I'm there for him." He meant that.

"You can't care for him all the way in Bayton."

"I'm not staying here. No way. Besides, he's going to go off to college next fall. It doesn't matter where I live."

"Your sister needs you too."

"She's got Blaise and Grace and the kids. She doesn't need me, and she can call me. The phones still work, you know." He and Savannah were still finding their way back. She didn't want him hanging around.

"Ain't the same thing, and you know it. Your roots are here, and your family needs you to be strong for them. Your whole family. Even Harley."

"Harley is not my family. She sealed that fate a long time ago." He pushed out of the chair. The legs scraped against the wood floor. He stuck his hand out again. His heart picked up speed waiting for Billy to take it.

Billy stood and gripped him in a tight hug. "You're like one of my own." He pushed Colton back and held his gaze. His eyes were red rimmed. "Don't make another mistake you can't undo is all I'm saying. That girl has always had you in her heart. She's the one who can keep you straight. Better than me or Blaise ever could, and the good Lord knows you don't listen to no one but yourself, and her."

He didn't want to think about how Harley made him better or how he didn't want to drink when she was around. He didn't want to think about building a relationship with Knox and trying to avoid her at the same time. He wanted his heart and his brain to get on the same damn page so he could go back to his life. He missed the life he had before he drove his car into a fence.

"You want to sleep here tonight?"

"Nah. Thanks." Even though he wanted to ring Blaise's neck for telling his secret, that was where he wanted to be—with his kid brother.

"I'm going to Tulsa for Christmas. You want to come with me?"

Colton laughed and shook his head. The last thing he wanted was to spend Christmas with Billy's daughter and her uptight pencil-pushing husband. "No, thank you. I'll leave that visit to you."

"Then call me when you get home, and if you don't, I'm coming up to find you. Blaise will drive me." Billy pointed a finger at him, but warmth filled his eyes.

He laughed because it wasn't an idle threat. "Thanks."

"For what?" Billy held the door open for him.

"For putting up with me." Colton patted him on the shoulder.

"Family are the people who love you when you need them. Don't forget it."

Chapter Thirty-Eight

"Why did you tell Billy?" Colton pushed past Blaise into his living room. He dumped his duffel on the floor.

"Because you weren't going to." Blaise shut the door and leaned against it.

"It was my place to tell. Not yours. I don't need you in my business, and I don't want the whole town knowing." Everyone probably knew. Who was he kidding?

Blaise pushed off the door and stood toe to toe with him. "Knowing what? That Knox is your son or that Harley made you look like an ass? You'll be the headline for a few days, but nobody is going to care by the new year because the whole town loves her, and you, well, if it wasn't for your celebrity status around here, most of the town would think you're just an egocentric prick."

He flopped down on the couch and held his head in his hands. "I need a cigarette. Blaise, man, how fucked up am I that she couldn't tell me? I missed his whole life. We could've been playing together like you and Cash." He pressed his lips together. "Or all four us. That would've been cool."

Blaise sat next to him. "We still can, bro. Cash and I didn't always get along. You're forgetting it was you he was sharing his music with, not me. That about killed me, but I was glad it was you he went to and not someone else. You are a big pain in the ass, but I meant what I said to Knox the other night. You're the best man I know. You still have time with him, but maybe you should stay in town."

"Why does everyone keep saying that?" He leaned his head against the back of the couch and stared up at the ceiling. How could he stay when she'd be around every corner? How was he going to stay sober without her?

"We keep telling you to come home because we're right. It's up to you, but I'd like having my big brother living nearby again. I'm going next door to Grace's. If she's still up, I might even get lucky." Blaise winked and pushed off the couch. "You and Cash have the house to yourselves. Don't break anything."

Colton dragged himself down the hall and closed the door to the guest room. *The best man I know.* But Harley didn't think so—not really, not if she could lie next to him and keep the truth from him.

He didn't believe his worth either. Blaise was a better man than he was, and their father had been a better man too. Jedidiah had put his entire life on hold to raise his children. He wouldn't have done that, not back when he was still young, overstrung, and reckless.

He pulled the envelope, now bent and creased, from his pocket and ripped it open. His hands shook, but he managed to unfold the old and worn paper. A photo dropped out. A baby boy—he wasn't sure how old—smiled for the camera. The boy didn't have much hair, but what was there was blond. His brown eyes sparkled with laughter, as if he knew a great big secret.

He held a plastic guitar in one hand and fisted the other in the air. He was dressed in blue shorts and a bright orange Hawaiian shirt covered in large green flowers flanked by smaller white ones.

"Geez, Harley. That shirt is terrible." Laughter bubbled up in his chest and spilled out. He scratched the back of his neck as the smile on his face grew wider. He stared at the photo a long time, trying to memorize every detail of that untroubled little boy. Would he have made Knox happy, or would Knox have grown to resent him for picking the stage over fatherhood?

He propped the picture against the lamp on the nightstand and turned to the letter.

Dear Colton,

This letter probably comes as a big surprise. I've tried to write to you a hundred times, but I didn't know what to say. I'm opting for the truth this time. We have a son. Finally, I've said it. That's him in the picture. He's eight months old. His name is Knox. I hope you don't mind what I chose. I wanted his name to be strong so he'd grow into a man like his father. He's amazing. He laughs all the time. He loves music too. All I have to do is turn on the radio, and he claps and squeals as if he's joining in. I play your songs for him.

I'm so sorry I didn't tell you until now. I was afraid you wouldn't want him, but I hope you do. I know how awful it is to grow up without knowing your father. I don't want the same thing for our son. Love just him, Colton. I know there's no place for me in your world. I've accepted that, but please give Knox a chance. He's so sweet and loving. He deserves the best the world has to offer. That includes you.

I'm in New York now, but I'm heading back to Heritage River. You can find us at my uncle's place. I hope you'll come.

Love, Harley and Knox.

The moisture in his eyes took him off guard. He counted to ten and tried to get his heart to return to a normal rhythm. He reread the letter several times, all the while pacing the small room.

He shoved the letter and the photo into his duffel, grabbed the bag, and headed out. He was going back to Bayton tonight.

His car knew the way. He didn't have to think, which was exactly what he wanted. He blasted the stereo to push out any thoughts that might try to creep through. Heritage River needed to stay in the rearview mirror. He'd make a relationship of some kind with Knox, but he needed space from the pain in his chest. He couldn't think about Harley.

He hit the gas when he came to the bridge. He needed to get out of Heritage River before he drowned in regret or, worse, whiskey.

Chapter Thirty-Nine

Harley grabbed the cardboard box full of her stuff from her class and followed the hallway to the front of the school. She waited for all of the students and most of the staff to leave and start their winter break before she decided it was safe to turn out the lights and lock up her classroom for the very last time. Joann had accepted her resignation without so much as a blink or a comment. They hadn't spoken since the night in the hospital. What could she say, anyway? Duke wasn't going to get better until he and his parents were ready to accept there was a problem in the first place. Selfishly, she was glad her son wasn't the one drinking on the night of the car accident.

With no job except her private classes, she didn't know what the future held. She had a little money saved up. She'd live on that and credit cards until she figured out her next move. She had the whole winter break to think it through. Knox was going to Colton's for break.

She'd be all alone after Christmas, but that was fine. She kept thinking about her art gallery idea that offered a haven for kids to paint and explore. Could she help up-and-coming artists find a place to display their work and kids find the self-esteem they needed to cross into adulthood? She'd need a space outside of Heritage River with more foot traffic. All seeds of an idea that felt a little prickly to touch, but she wanted to run her fingers over them again.

Knox seemed to accept she'd kept his father from him. His sarcastic jabs were coming farther and farther apart. Maybe after a week with his dad, he would see fit to forgive her. Forgetting what she did was something else altogether. She wasn't expecting any Christmas gifts of that size.

Harley dumped the box of her things into the back of her Durango. The sky was cloud filled, blocking any warmth from the dwindling sunlight. The air smelled like snow. She pulled out into traffic and took the long route to Winding Way.

Ella had invited them to spend Christmas Eve with her family, but Harley wanted to stay home in her pajamas and watch cheesy Christmas movies with happy endings guaranteed to bring on the tears. Happy endings only happened on television. She needed to live through make-believe characters for a little while.

She'd send Knox over to Ella's. He didn't need to miss out on the fun because of her, and in the morning she'd make him breakfast—well, cereal—and they'd open presents before he would head out to Colton's. Blaise was picking him up at noon.

She turned into her drive. The empty guesthouse was too much of a reminder of all she'd lost. Maybe it was time to move on and leave the past behind.

She hadn't seen Knox as happy as he was after he spoke to Colton. The past few nights the sound of his guitar blasted through the house. The two of them were Facetiming and jamming together. It was a dream come true for him. She hadn't the heart to tell him to turn down the volume to save his ear, which was still ringing. She'd go back to being the bad guy after winter break. Colton deserved to be the hero right now.

She unlocked the front door. Knox's bags were by the door. She nearly tripped over them before depositing her box on the dining room table.

The shadows in the house were long. The day was almost a washout at this hour. She turned on a few lights and let their warm glow fill the room. She forced herself to turn on the Christmas tree lights too. The minute Knox went out the door she was going to drag that tree to the road. She needed to wipe the place clean of any memories of Colton loving her. Maybe she'd burn that couch while she was at it. She didn't want to think about him making love to her every time she walked past it. Her chest hurt. How was she ever going to get over him?

"Knox, I'm home," she shouted up the steps. "Get ready to go to Ella's. I'll drop you."

He came in from the back door, bringing the cold, damp air with him.

"Where were you?" She grabbed a bag of Cheetos out of the cabinet.

He hung up his coat and shook out his hair. "I was out with Stephanie. She needed to get a few presents."

"Go change, and I'll drop you off at Ella's. She said dinner at five."

"You should come with me."

She nearly dropped her snack. "You want me to come?"

"Sure, why not? It's Christmas Eve." He looked down at the ground. "And I'm going to be away all week."

That he was. "I'm not sure I'm up for a big party."

"Come on, Mom. It's Christmas. The time for peace and love and all that stuff." His lip curled up. Her breath caught. She could see the man he'd become, and he was all Colton in that minute.

"Okay, I'll get ready." She shoved the Cheetos back in the cabinet and wiped her fingers on her pants. She wouldn't argue any further if her son wanted to spend some time with her.

"Can I drive us over?"

They'd have to think about a car for him soon. He needed his independence. She should probably ask Colton what he thought. She wanted him to be involved in any decisions concerning Knox since there weren't as many any longer.

"Sure. Give me a few minutes to change out of my work clothes."

"You look nice," he said when she returned wearing wide black pants and a red fitted top. She opted for the high heels she saved for special occasions. Knox's talking to her as if nothing had happened between them was as special an occasion as she could get.

"Thank you."

Harley followed him out to the truck. He held the door open for her, and she patted his cheek. Her heart swelled with pride.

He turned out of the drive and headed down Winding Way.

"Are you okay with driving since the accident?"

"I think so." When he got to Bridge Street, he turned right instead of left.

"Hey, rock star, you're going the wrong way. Turn around in that driveway." She pointed up on the left.

He went past the driveway.

She looked out the back window. "Knox, you sure you don't want me to drive? Is it too dark for you to see?" Even with the gray clouds overhead, the night was inky. Was he nervous after all?

He glanced at her. "Mom, trust me, will you? I know where I'm going, and I know what you're thinking. I'm fine. "

"But Ella and Stephanie don't live this way."

"We're taking the long way."

The long way? "We're going to be late."

"Ella won't care."

Which was true, but it was rude to be late, even though she always was. "I don't understand. Why do you want to go this way? We're headed out of town."

"I need to make a stop first."

Tiny white lights sparkled in the distance. She squinted to get a better look. The bridge was up ahead and usually dark except for the one lantern.

Knox stopped the Durango and threw the truck in park. "Here we are."

"Um, we're in the middle of the road." The bridge was fifty yards away and lit up with white lights.

"This is where you get out." He smiled at her as if he'd handed her a gift.

"What? Turn the car around, Knox. This is silly." She wasn't getting out of the car. "Take us to Ella's."

He unlocked the doors with that smile on his face. "Look."

"I see the bridge. It's lit up with white lights. Why is it lit up?"

The covered bridge was wrapped up like a present in twinkling lights. Whoever went to the trouble covered the crisscross posts all along its sides with hundreds of tiny white lights. Lights dangled from the roof like icicles. A wreath was lit up in the center of the clapboard over-hang. More lights swirled around the beams underneath the roof like candy canes. The glow blurred before her. Someone had turned her bridge into a Christmas card.

Knox hopped out of the truck and ran around the front to her door. He pulled it open. "This is where I leave. I'm going to Ella's, but you need to walk to the bridge. Merry Christmas, Mom." He took her hand and helped her slide out. He leaned down and kissed her cheek.

Her fingers touched her face. Her beautiful grown son was smiling down at her as if the last week had never happened. "I don't understand. What is going on? How will I get to Ella's? You can't leave me here."

Knox laughed. "Sure, I can."

"Knox, knock it off. This isn't funny. Tell me what's going on."

"You'll see." He hopped back in the truck and backed up before turning around and heading the way they came.

"Knox," she yelled after the taillights.

Snowflakes began to float down around her and glisten against the glow from the bridge. "And I'm wearing my heels."

She didn't mind a practical joke, but she was cold and didn't understand the point of all this. She'd reached for her phone to call him back, but it was still in the truck. She hung her head. Now what was she going to do? She'd have to walk home or at least into town hoping she could find a phone.

Walk to the bridge. She hadn't really wanted to go to Ella's anyway, and maybe Knox didn't either, but he seemed glad to have her around. Okay, she'd play along. What other choice did she have at the moment? Sitting at the bridge in the snow wasn't cozy pajamas and cheesy movies, but the fresh air might clear her head. She took a tentative step toward the bridge.

Movement on the other side stopped her. A tall figure with broad shoulders stepped under the roof of the bridge. Something was slung against his back. He walked toward her until he was under the lights strung around the beams.

Even from the distance, she'd know that stance anywhere. He stood tall and strong. His hands were shoved deep in his coat pockets, and his legs were covered in those tight jeans she loved so much. She hurried forward. He'd cut his hair. His smile was as bright as the lights. He'd brought his guitar.

"Hey," he said when she was before him.

He smelled like Colton—woodsy, all male, and a little tobaccoy. It was the best smell.

"Hey, yourself." She wanted to touch him, but she kept her hands at her sides. "What's going on?" Her gaze went up toward the lights.

"Do you like it?"

"The lights? They're beautiful."

"I hoped you would."

"You put the lights up? I don't understand. How? Why?" She couldn't quite believe she was standing with him under their bridge with the snow falling around them. Knox had been in on this little surprise. Her insides warmed up. Things started to make sense.

He took her hands in his cold ones. "You wanted to see our bridge lit up for Christmas. Knox, Blaise, and Cash helped me. We didn't get permission, so don't be surprised if the lights are down by tomorrow." He winked.

Only he would act first and ask later. "The bridge

looks dreamy. But I don't understand why you'd do that for me. You've made it pretty clear how you feel." The tiniest sliver of hope cracked in the protective covering around her heart.

He took a deep breath and let it out slowly. "I've made a million mistakes in my life, and every time I hurt someone in the process, including you. I'm so sorry for that."

"You have nothing to apologize for. You've always been very up front about who you are." She loved him because he was able to say exactly what was on his mind all the time.

"It wasn't until I came home this time that I finally saw what I was doing wrong. You showed me that. You've always been trying to show me, by loving me at my worst times. I repaid you by pushing you away at your worst time. I'm sorry for that too."

Her breath caught in her throat. "Colton, you had every right to be mad. I wouldn't blame you for being mad at me forever. I would be if the tables were turned."

"Since there's no way I'm pushing a baby out of my junk, you'll never have to worry about the tables being turned." He squeezed her hands.

"Only you." She shook her head.

"To know me is to love me, babe."

And how she did. She'd loved him her entire life. "What changed your mind?"

"My brother. Billy. Your letter. Our bridge. After I read your letter, I hightailed it out of town. I was mad at myself for what I'd done to us, and I thought I couldn't stay another second in the same town as you. I came across this bridge doing a hundred, and then it hit me. There wasn't anywhere I wanted to be except with you and Knox. When I saw that picture of Knox, I realized how hard having a baby alone must've been for you, and there you were only asking me to love our son. You wanted nothing for yourself."

The tears filled her eyes. She blinked to keep his face in her sights. "I kept waiting for you to love me. That wasn't fair. I needed to love myself first. I'm sorry."

He squeezed her hands again. "I have always loved you."

"Colton, I needed to be stronger by myself. If I had been, I would've told you no matter the consequences. I thought I was doing you a favor by keeping Knox from you, but I was too afraid. I don't want to live my life in fear any longer. I want to be someone you could be proud of."

He narrowed his eyes. "Babe, I am proud of you. You raised our son by yourself, and you did a great job of it too. You made a life for yourself teaching and helping kids who need it. I'm the one who was too afraid to show my feelings. I kept all my feelings to myself. I let you think I didn't want you, and that wasn't the truth. The truth was I wasn't worthy of you. I'm still not, but I'm getting better. If you can ever forgive me, I'll keep getting better."

"You have nothing to ask for forgiveness for. It's me. I

was wrong. I kept Knox from you. How can you forgive *me*?"

"Stop doubting yourself, babe. You're amazing. You're smart and funny, and you have a huge heart. You stood by me, and you love Knox with a crazy fierceness. I'm only sorry I waited so long to tell you. We could've had our entire lives together. We could've raised our son together, but I let my affair with music get in my way. That old affair is over. I'll still play, but I'll do it differently now."

A car came up the road and honked its horn when the headlights shined on them blocking the way.

He pulled her to the side of the bridge, onto the walking path. "I should probably take you somewhere warm and out of the way of moving vehicles."

"No, this is perfect." He was telling her he loved her in spite of what she'd done. She may never want to leave this bridge again, and definitely not before the lights came down.

"If you don't mind being out in the snow, then come with me." He took her hand and led her to the bench. "Have a seat, ma'am." He swung his guitar off his back and hooked the strap around his neck. He dug a pick out of his pocket and placed it between his thumb and middle finger. Just like Knox. He propped his strong leg on the bench.

"I haven't been able to write a decent song in over a decade. That's why I wouldn't let the band play anything new. My ego couldn't take it, and when Blaise dropped out because I refused to listen to him, I broke inside. You healed me. I hope you like this. You're the first one to hear it." His smile sent shivers across her skin. "My fingers are killing me in this cold. I hope I don't fuck this all up, and my singing sucks. Sorry about that."

His guitar came to life under his skilled hands. He played a slow, bluesy melody filled with soul. The tune broke wide open that sliver of hope in her heart. His music caressed her skin. His voice was raspy and rugged, just as he was, and her lower belly ached with longing for him. He looked from the guitar to her. He sang about how his life was nothing more than a liquor bottle until his woman saved him. Being in her arms was the reason he could stay sober, and even though he was nothing more than a lost drunk, she loved him always.

Big fat tears ran down her cheeks.

He leaned the guitar against the bench. "That bad, huh? I can fix it."

She stood. "No, no. That song...that was fantastic. That's not even the right word. Colton, that was the most beautiful thing I've ever heard." She laughed and cried at the same time.

He closed the space between them. His stare swallowed her up before he wrapped a strong calloused hand around her neck and pulled her in for a kiss. His lips touched hers like the snow from the sky. He kept his eyes open, and so did she. Then his urgency grew, and his tongue sought after hers. He tasted sweet, and wonderful, and like Colton. She tangled her fingers in his freshly cut hair to bring him in closer. She didn't want the kiss or the moment to end.

The tears kept flowing. Their kiss turned salty, but she didn't care. She wanted him and needed him. He eased away slightly, but he still held her close.

"Woman, you keep crying like that while we're making out, I'm going to start doubting my moves."

She leaned her forehead against his chest. The tears turned to laughter. "Am I dreaming this?"

"Christ, I hope not. I about killed myself hanging those lights from the roof." His chest shook with laughter.

"Thank you for lighting up our bridge. Are you going to stay on as the music teacher? You'd be so great for the kids, and you could still play out at night."

"I haven't decided. Maybe you could help me figure out my next move?"

"I would love to."

He held her at arm's length, then let her go. She missed his warmth instantly. "There's one more thing I need to ask you."

She could handle any question now. She squared her shoulders. "Go for it."

He dug back in his pocket and pulled out a small black velvet box. He popped open the top. Her heart froze at the sight of the brilliant ring inside.

"Would you and Knox share my name?"

Share his name. Knox would finally have his father out in the open, and she would finally have her man by her side. She traced her finger along the edge of the soft velvet. She held his gaze. "It's enough that you lit up our bridge."

His eyes clouded, and he snapped the box closed,

missing her finger. "Are you saying you don't want to marry me?"

"You only like asking questions you know the answer to." Her lips curled up to smile.

"Damn straight. I was pretty sure I knew the answer to this one." He shook the box.

She placed a hand on his face. "You and Knox, our family, are all I ever wanted. You've given me the best Christmas present ever. I'd gladly share your name."

He scratched the back of his neck. "Christ, I really thought you were going to tell me no." He removed the brilliant ring from the box and slipped it on her finger.

Their laughter mingled with the snow. She took his hand, laced her fingers through his, and together, they crossed the bridge home.

But wait, there's more. Have a sneak peek at the next book in the Heritage River series:

The Essence of Whiskey and Tea

Chapter One

JT Davies made his own luck.

He'd spent the better part of his adult life making opportunities happen. He relied only on himself. Except for his dad, no one had given him a single thing. His dad had given him a ton of love, even when JT didn't deserve it, and now the deli, Eat At Jake's.

He didn't want the deli. He did want his father back, but God had him now. Lucky bastard. Jake Davies was the best man he'd ever known.

He didn't plan on a permanent return to Heritage River, but there he stood in the house he'd grown up in, with his fifteen-year-old daughter glaring at him.

"Do you want to come with me to the deli?" He patted his pockets, looking for his keys. Every room in the house was filled with cardboard boxes labeled with room names. The oversize furniture from their last house didn't seem to fit against any of the walls in the modest Queen Anne-style home. The beds needed clean sheets. The fridge was empty, but he had to take some measurements at the deli. After that he'd begin the settling-in process.

Maddy scooped up his keys from the top of a box that read *Office,* even though they were in the living room, and swung them back and forth. "Is there food at the deli? Because I'm starving. You promised after the movers left we'd get something to eat."

How did teenage girls perfect that scowl? What had happened to the little girl who thought her daddy was pretty cool? He was still cool, wasn't he? He was older, had less hair and more aches and pains, but he could still pull off some cool. Not according to Madeline Elizabeth Davies. His beautiful, tall daughter had become a snarly, still beautiful, still tall, and smart—too smart for her own good—teenager who would rather live with an alligator than him. Good thing alligators didn't rent rooms.

"You know the deli isn't operational." In fact, it was gutted. "But we can try to find something else."

Maybelline's Bakery had closed hours ago, before the sun had a chance to set. Except for the ice cream shop, no other dining establishments existed on Main Street, which was part of the reason he wanted a Whiskey Bar to go in the place of Eat At Jake's. He planned to open his fifth Whiskey Bar, this time right in Heritage River. Once the bar started making money and Maddy graduated from high school in two years, they'd hit the road.

Heritage River had done nothing for him, but he was glad to take their money, and he was very good at making money in exchange for good food and great whiskey.

"Does this town have a vegan place?" She flipped her head upside down and tied her hair into a knot on the top of her head.

He also didn't understand why anyone would be a vegan. He was convinced Maddy claimed to be a plant eater just to piss him off. "I doubt it."

"You were here like nine months ago. Didn't you notice?" The scowl returned. She flopped down on the couch and pulled out her phone.

"You were with me the last time I was here. Did you see one?" He hadn't noticed much of anything when he was in town the last two times.

His dad had called and told him about some tests the doctor wanted him to take. JT flew in to be there with him because his stepmother was good for just about nothing. He got lassoed in to helping out one night at the deli for some fundraiser to save the music and art programs at the high school. He flew out the next day. He had come back for the funeral, but that was it.

"How about a pizza?"

"Yeah, Dad, like cheese isn't dairy. Thanks a lot for respecting my choices. Forget it. I just won't eat." She returned to her phone. Her fingers flew across the screen.

He seemed to have lost another battle.

"Why do you have to go to the deli tonight anyway? You promised you'd spend less time at work if we were here. That's the only reason why I agreed to come to Heritage River and get dragged away from my friends and my school."

"Giving up those friends is no loss. Trust me." He grabbed his wallet and shoved it in his pocket. "I am going to work less once the Whiskey is up and running. I need to make a quick stop before the contractor comes over in the morning. I want to do that now so I can drive you to school in the morning." He was going to try to work less, but if he was going to get the Whiskey Bar operational quickly, he'd have to put in more hours than his child would want. "Are you coming with me, or should I bring you back a salad?"

"Bring me a salad but make sure it doesn't have any cheese or eggs on it. Can't I skip school tomorrow? What's the big deal if I start a day late?"

He needed to be at the store tomorrow and didn't want her sitting around the house all alone. At least at school, someone would be able to keep an eye on her. "Tomorrow. Drop it." He was working on the tough love thing.

"This school isn't going to be any different, you know. You can't fix me by moving me around from county to county. I hate school, and I'll hate this one too."

He had hated school too, when he was her age, but he was smart enough to know not to tell her that. He couldn't be the one to tell her about the things he used to do because then he'd lose all his parental leverage. But the truth was, he'd been a real pain in the ass as a kid, and so was his daughter. "You might not hate it so much if you tried a little to like it."

"Oh, so I don't try? Is that what you're saying? I'm just a big loser who doesn't give a shit about anything, right, Dad?"

"I didn't say that. You're not a loser. Why would you think I'd say something like that about you? And stop cursing." The whole situation spun out of control.

"You curse all the time, and you did say I didn't try, which is the same thing as saying I'm a loser. I'm going to set up my room." She pushed off the couch and unfolded her thin body cloaked in black, tight pants and a top that showed off her stomach. He shook his head. He'd have to buy a gun to keep the boys away, especially after the last time.

"I could help you when I get back."

"No, thanks." She marched up the steps, giving him her back and probably the finger.

Yeah, that went well. He snagged his keys and headed out. First, he'd stop at the deli, and then he'd try to find his vegan daughter an acceptable salad. He'd also buy himself a pint of whiskey. He needed it.

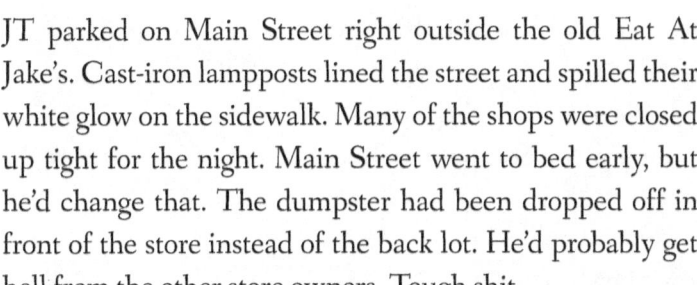

JT parked on Main Street right outside the old Eat At Jake's. Cast-iron lampposts lined the street and spilled their white glow on the sidewalk. Many of the shops were closed up tight for the night. Main Street went to bed early, but he'd change that. The dumpster had been dropped off in front of the store instead of the back lot. He'd probably get hell from the other store owners. Tough shit.

Of all the Whiskey Bars he owned, this location meant the most to him. Here he would prove to himself and everyone who said otherwise that he had made it.

He shoved his way out of the truck and stopped. When had that popped up? A sign hung above the last shop on the street. Savannah's Tea Room. *Savannah?* He stood under it and looked up.

"Nice, isn't it?" A man with white hair and a big gut appeared next to him, licking a melting ice cream cone.

"What's nice?"

"The sign. The flowers and teapot are nice, aren't they?"

"I guess." He didn't care what the sign looked like. A tea shop two doors down wouldn't hurt his business any. May's bakery had more to worry about than he did. "Who owns this place?" He'd known a Savannah a long time ago.

The man licked his cone. "Savannah Savage. Well, she's Montgomery now, or maybe she went back to Savage. I don't know which."

His Savannah owned that store? Well, she wasn't *his* Savannah. They had lasted all of five-minutes, but she had stuck her claws in him all the same. Savannah always liked to run things, to call the shots. Tell him what to do.

He'd shut her down.

He owed her that much.

READ MORE

Also by Stacey Wilk

Seduced by Denial

Chill in the Air

Fighting for Tessa

Nash's Promise

Cruz's Watch

Harlan Unleashed

Big Sky Country Series

Time Won't Erase

Stay Awhile

Love Never Ends

Dare to Tell (coming 2025)

A word about the author...

From an early age, best-selling and award-winning author, Stacey Wilk, told tales as a way to escape. At six she wrote short stories in composition notebooks, at twelve she wrote a novel on a typewriter, in high school biology she wrote rock star romances in her binder instead of paying attention.

But it wasn't until many years later, inspired by her children and a looming birthday, that she finally took her story-telling seriously. And published her first novel in 2013. Since then, she's gone on to publish twenty-seven more so women everywhere can indulge in books that hook them heart and soul.

She isn't done telling stories. Not by a long shot. If you want to read her emotional and honest books about family, romance, and second chances, visit her at www.s-taceywilk.com

To see what she writes next, follow her Facebook

group for her amazing readers – Stacey's Novel Family
https://bit.ly/2FK8Lae

Or join her newsletter - https://bit.ly/2AojEFk

www.ingramcontent.com/pod-product-compliance
Lightning Source LLC
Chambersburg PA
CBHW030759260626
47169CB00001B/117